GODS OF THE NOWHERE
A NOVEL OF HALLOWEEN

GODS OF THE
NOWHERE

A NOVEL OF HALLOWEEN

JAMES TIPPER

Cover art by JOHN PELICO

A Waxlight Press Book

LOS ANGELES

Library of Congress Registration # TXu 1-806-574
ISBN-13: 978-0-9882433-1-6 ISBN-10: 0988243318

Text set in Immortal and Constantia

Visit www.killerpumpkins.com for more of John Pelico's artwork.

To my angel, Peter, for reasons that could fill these pages.

'Tis now the very witching time of night,
When churchyards yawn and hell itself breathes out
Contagion to this world.

-William Shakespeare

Legends are but truths whispered.

- Tlachtga, Druid priestess

-CONTENTS-

Prologue
Ireland
239 AD

Part One
The City of the Dead
Colma, California
Present Day

Part Two
The Nowhere

Part Three
The Tomb of the False Prophet

Epitaph

Prologue
Samhain, Eve of the New Year
Ireland, 239 AD

-1-

A soldier, his face smeared with dirt and his eyes wild, stood before the King of Munster, "My liege, they have us surrounded. They command the highlands now and their magic is strong. They have dried up the wells and the river. There is no water for our men, no water for our horses. There is no water anywhere."

King Broadcrown of Munster was stone-faced. "And what did King Cormac's herald say?"

"King Cormac still maintains that Munster is two provinces," the soldier replied, "The North and The South. He says that your Highness must pay taxes to Tara for both."

"The treacherous bastard!" roared the King, slamming a fist onto the oaken table. The empty goblets jumped. The King rose, crossed to the window and scanned the fields, the colors of his clan spotting the land below. It was too quiet, unnervingly quiet. From his perch, the good King could hear only his army's leather creaking as they waited for the attack.

Turning from the window, King Broadcrown of Munster, his jaw clenched, continued addressing the young soldier, "Perhaps, if the King of Tara was more responsible with his coin, with his herds, with his crops – if he knew a thing at all about economy – then maybe he would have more than he finds himself with. Tara is indeed great, but I will see it fall before we are its slave."

Two noblemen sitting at the table in the King's chamber now eyed each other nervously. Both knew that Munster was not likely to beat Tara – not without a miracle – and as good councilors of the court, one of them had to remind the King of this. One of the noblemen nodded and widened his eyes at the other, but the other only frowned, shaking his head briskly.

Reluctantly, the first swallowed and spoke: "Sire, we cannot beat the druids of Tara by force alone."

The King of Munster turned to face them. They winced, bracing for further wrath, but the King only took a deep, solemn breath before squaring again with the young soldier. "Brennan, you are a brave warrior and your men will not thirst while I breathe. This battle can, and will, be won. Your men will be reinforced by the gods."

The two noblemen chanced an anxious glance at each other as the King continued: "Tell the herald that I will pay no such ransom to his King. The taxes I have paid to the Kingdom of Tara are sufficient and if his King will be gluttonous and deficient in discipline then he must learn now to look elsewhere for charity. He will no longer drink at Munster's trough. Now go."

The soldier bowed, turned and began to leave.

"Wait," implored one of the noblemen, his voice spiked with hope. The soldier stopped and turned. The nobleman stroked his beard in thought. "If this is true that the land has been drained of water, then how is their army at any advantage?"

"My lord," the soldier replied, shoving his helmet back onto his head, "it's Bairen, the one known as the Red Druid. He is the one leading King Cormac's army. His powers are great. He has halted the river only where it leaves the highlands of Knocklong and has summoned the rest of the water from our wells to their side with sorcery. They have all they need. The sons of whores are bathing in it."

His eyes ablaze and his heart a heavy stone in his chest, the soldier Brennan quit the King's chamber to return to the front line. He would never be seen again, but tales would be told of his bravery for generations to come, for what was about to happen on the rocky field below would become legend.

-2-

As night thickened, King Broadcrown of Munster summoned a scout to his chamber. The two were not in conference long before members of court witnessed the scout flying down the stone steps, taking them two at a time, and calling for his horse. Questions were fired at him, but the scout was not talking. The mission was secret.

But the two noblemen knew where the scout was headed. They had been in the meeting with the King, sitting in the shadows not daring to object, and they were not happy with the plan. It was a fool's

errand, but all they could do now was to wait until the scout returned –
if he ever did.

Until then, the two were left to pace the keep, the village, and
the outlying fields. They walked among the lines where soldiers stood,
peering towards the highlands for a glimpse of the enemy. The horizon
was glowing in all directions, lit only by bonfires as the peasants
celebrated the feast of Samhain – the last light before winter's darkness.
Just beneath the black plumes of smoke that curled towards the moon,
and just above the glowing orange band that lit the ridges of the rolling
hills, colonies of bats fluttered in silhouette against the sky, feeding on
swarms of mosquitoes that had been drawn to the light.

The two noblemen crossed to the river that ran past the North of
the village and stopped atop its bank. A woman crouched before them
in the dark with a little girl lying beside her. The woman's pail was
overturned and she stared helplessly at the dry riverbed, sobbing. One
arm held her daughter close. The woman slowly turned her head to look
at the approaching men, her tears glittering with moonlight.

"Dead," she moaned, stroking her daughter's hair. "My little girl
is dead. There is no water. They have killed her."

The woman kissed the forehead of the little body beside her and
turned her head back to the white scar in the earth that used to be a
river, the river that gave life to her village.

The two noblemen turned away from the riverbank, sickened.
Trudging back towards the castle, one spoke to the other, his voice
shaking with anger and frustration: "This is madness! They will kill our
children first, and then we will *all* shrivel up and blow away on the
wind. Why does the King place so much faith in summoning this old
druid?"

"Because," replied the other, "his majesty believes that Mog
Ruith is the greatest druid who has ever lived and nothing short of his
power is going to save us. He thinks he can find this Mog Ruith and he
thinks he can strike a deal with him. I hope he's right. What other
chance do we have?"

The first man clenched his teeth, and grabbed the other by the
arm: "We will all die before that happens. That scout will never find
Mog Ruith because it is only a name he seeks, a legend! He will walk the
island of Valentia in circles as our clan turns to dust. Time is not on our
side. Even the nobles have nothing but memories of their last drops of
water! I have heard that those who try to flee the area in search of it are
slaughtered on the road.

"Why doesn't the King just pay Tara what it wants? King Cormac has real sorcerers, ones of flesh, ones that breathe, and their magic is strong. You have heard of Bairen, the one they call the Red Druid? You know of the ballads written about his heartlessness and how he has Tara's King under his spell? THAT is who we face. You have seen for yourself what Bairen has done. We cannot beat them with tales!"

From behind them, a woman spoke. Frightened, the two spun in the direction of the voice, for they were far from the castle and sure that they had been alone. Their eyes flicked amongst the trees, their hands flying to the hilts of their swords.

A woman stared back at them, only she did not stand on the ground, but floated just above the rocky soil, her robes fluttering. She glowed from within.

"Be still," she whispered.

The words were an icy wind that blew through the men's veins. Shock numbed their hands, and they let their swords slip back into their scabbards. Their faces went ashen as the blood drained to their feet, rooting them to the ground.

The apparition spoke again, "My father sends tidings of hope to your clan."

"Who are you?" croaked one of the men. His mouth, already dry from lack of water, was now pasted over with the mineral taste of fear. He swallowed hard. "Who is your father?"

"I am Tlachtga, known as Clara to my clan." The woman drifted slowly through the forest like a feather lifted by a gentle breeze, the silver birch trees rippling through her. The men stared in terror and wonder as she rose to the bare canopy of branches above and looked down on them placidly, her form billowing and pulsing with blue light. "My father is Mog Ruith."

For a long time, the two men could not move, could not speak.

"Clack-ta?" managed one of them. Then, his eyes widened with recognition. "Tlachtga! Is it really you? You are well known, the mother of the druid clan! The hill that bears your name roars with fires on this night. We all pray for your light to remain, to guide us through winter. Forgive me! Please! We revere you. But..." The man trailed off, a shudder wracking his body. He was unsure of how to continue. Steeling himself, he whispered: "But...you died long ago."

"It is the feast night, Fergus" she replied. "The Veil is thin."

"So it is," said Lord Fergus, his voice shaking. She had known his name, somehow she had known it. His eyes flicked to the bonfires on the hills. "So it is..."

Tlachtga, known as Clara to her clan, drifted closer to the two men until they could feel the strange prickle of electricity cast from her glowing skin. She leaned towards them and spoke again, her voice soft and strong, her breath smelling of ozone: "Do you doubt the source of my power – my father, Mog Ruith?"

"No," said Fergus, who had indeed doubted only minutes before. "No more shall I doubt." His head fell in supplication. He reached out with a trembling hand to touch Clara's garments, but his hands fell through them, engulfed by their azure light.

She glided upwards, and producing a sickle of gold from within her robes, flew to a nearby oak tree among the birch and slashed at a clump of mistletoe which fell to earth with a thump. Clara's blade flashed again in the moonlight and then it was gone, hidden within the folds of her robes.

"Keep that plant close to your body until the yule," Clara said. "War is always dangerous, but war during the Thinning is a danger to your souls. The dead will not be stayed this night."

Gratefully, Fergus and his companion – known as Lord Ernin, Knight of Knocklong, and scribe of the King's Sept – stooped to pick up the mistletoe. Still on his knees and glancing upward at the vision above, Lord Ernin spoke: "We are under siege. The King of Tara has Bairen by his side and the Red Druid's powers are great."

Clara's feet touched earth, and she walked slowly towards the two men, her aura sizzling and popping, her eyes glowing like stars. "Fear not. My father has acquired wisdom over seven centuries. There are no further enchantments that he cannot accomplish, whether on this side of the Veil or the other, because none other of all the inhabitants of Ireland has ever been encased in flesh and bone so long, learning magic, save he."

She approached the two trembling men and looked from one to the other, as if peering straight into their souls. "You seek him."

Lords Fergus and Ernin, their eyes wide and their faces white, could only nod dumbly.

Clara suddenly rose again into the barren treetops, buoyant on a thermal of air, her arms wide, and closed her eyes. Her aura of silvery blue began to stretch from her form to the farthest branches, wrapping them in sizzling lace, like spider's webs of crackling light.

Wind began to skitter the dead leaves at the two men's feet.

Clara opened her eyes.

"Then, it is done," said the ghost. "My father approaches."

-3-

Bairen was a tall, thin man, elegant and compact, his features sharp and pale, and as he stood on a bluff overlooking Munster he might have been mistaken for a column of marble draped with a crimson robe, a robe speckled with black. His bony hand stroked his beard; a dark beard shocked with veins of white at its sides. The Red Druid stared at the village below with wolfish eyes.

Across the plain, the fires on the hill of Tlachtga were still bright. Bats, as if born from the plumes of black smoke, still fluttered there, feeding in their crests of orange light. Below, Munster was silent.

Perfect, thought Bairen. The feast night was perfect: the fires, the unsuspecting revelers, the sacrifices as far as the eye could see, they would all serve as welcomed distractions when his clan's King rode down on Munster, putting an end to their insolence.

"The time is now," he whispered at the night.

A bitter wind had kicked up. Bundling his robes, Bairen turned back to look at his grove of druids who stood solemnly in a circle by a fire, murmuring incantations. Beyond, warriors, fearsome in their bright paint and bone-white hair were waiting for their chance to kill.

As Bairen walked through the camp, he felt something was wrong. It was the wind. It had come from nowhere and had gotten stronger much too quickly. It was...

(unnatural)

What had started as nothing but a breeze from the North had increased to a gale in only a matter of minutes. Now, the wind was gusting hard. Soon, it began to howl like a pack of wolves. Soldiers began to squat or grab nearby trees for fear of falling over.

"What is this?" Bairen muttered, his robes flapping and cracking like sails.

On the rise above, a tree limb snapped. A large branch plummeted down toward a group of soldiers. With cat-like reflexes, a warrior batted the branch to the ground with his shield.

Bairen trudged across the camp against the rising wind, a brutal gust doubling him over and knocking the breath from his body. No, this was...

(all wrong)

Then sudden understanding widened his eyes.

(the Fifth Wind)

It was the Fifth Wind and it was coming for them.

Fear, a rare sensation for the Red Druid began to stroke his nerves with its cold hand. There was only one man he knew of who could summon the Fifth Wind.

(only one)

Another blast of air pushed Bairen in the small of his back, rocking him forward. Drawing a breath while he still could, he screamed in the direction of his clan, "It is Munster! They have magic!"

Dead leaves skittered from all corners of the camp and flew towards Bairen's druids, plastering briefly to their robes before peeling off and racing for the center of their circle, smothering the fire.

"What spells do you bring?" a Commander called over the howling wind.

"It is not us!!" cried a druid from the circle, backing away from the ring, "This is not our magic!"

The druids all began to step back, the circle widening. Bairen arrived and watched along with his priests as the crackling leaves gathered in a pile in the middle of the circle.

King Cormac, High King of Tara, appeared on a ledge above the clearing. He was flanked by his personal guards, his long robes whipping the air. "Bairen! Tame this! This is my moment of victory! I command you!"

But Bairen was lost in disbelief. The pile of dead leaves in the circle where the campfire had once been was beginning to rise in a funnel. High into the air the tornado of leaves soared. It expanded and thickened like the clay on a potter's wheel until the form of a human head towered above the camp, a face forming in the cyclonic foliage.

A booming laugh cleaved the air.

At once, the torches around the camp extinguished.

The head made of dead leaves turned to face Bairen, holes for eyes flashing moonlight.

"Bairen..." cooed the leaf man, its voice a hollow moan of wind. "Killer of children...you are too far from home. I have come to send you back."

Bairen's lips, blue from the wind, could only offer the darkness a single word:

"Mog..."

-4-

The wind died as quickly as it had come. All was still.

Bairen's eyes fluttered open to behold the moon above him, full and striped with smoke. His head throbbed. He felt stickiness as he patted his scalp. He flinched with pain. He got to his knees. His eyes focused and then widened with amazement and dread. The hill his clan had commanded only moments ago was now a field of rubble, littered with the tangle of splintered chariots and oxen on their sides. In all directions piles of agony moaned. Twisted limbs writhed and groped at nothing. Many had simply blown away to Waterford, or beyond into the sea. Many were dead, or wished for such mercy.

Bairen managed to get to his shaky feet and blinked hard. The destruction was vast, but the King and his guard were still alive. Bairen watched them emerge from their shelter in the ground, in the catacombs that were once caves, but now only pocks in the blighted face of the earth.

Bairen searched the rubble for his priests. A torch sputtered into life nearby. In its light he saw them, his grove of druids. Save for three of the nine, they were safe, but among the missing was Colphrea, the youngest, who had been Bairen's promising apprentice.

Bairen's cry of frustration was cut short by the King's voice, "How is this possible?"

"My liege," Bairen replied, humiliation flushing his face, "I...know not..."

Suddenly, a soldier shouted, his voice spiked with alarm, "Look!"

All snapped their gaze to where the soldier's finger stabbed the air. Struggling to their feet, the surviving warriors, pages and druids all kept their eyes on the sky as they gathered spears, shields, and hefted the grumbling oxen where they lay overturned in their yokes.

The horizon was dark, the feast night nearing its end. The gauze of smoke from the dying fires of Samhain humbled the moon's light. Still, the soldier pointed at the heavens, his outstretched arm trembling. "There!" he cried again.

Across the moon streaked an apparition, a chariot. It was drawn by horned beasts, dark and hulking in silhouette. The chariot turned sharply and with alarming speed began descending towards the tattered camp.

King Cormac cried out: "What is this, Bairen?" His voice was firm, but in spite of his efforts it shook with fear.

"It can't be..." Bairen said numbly. "He commands Roth Rámach?" He wheeled to face the King and shouted, "It is coming for us!"

"Who?" demanded the King. "Who is at its reins?"

"The slave of the wheel..." Bairen replied. "Mog Ruith! Take cover! For the sake of Tara! Take cover!!"

The stunned King, his once grey beard now black with earth, peeled his gaze away from the sky with difficulty, led away by his guards to a berm of tossed soil and felled trees.

The remaining soldiers, pale and trembling, watched the approaching chariot. It was bronze, a huge conveyance, its edges shimmering gold in the moon's light. Paralyzed by disbelief, they watched the flying machine take shape: it was pulled by black oxen, their hooves pawed the air, their nostrils flared. Their horns were as long as broadswords.

Stretched across the chariot's front was a bull hide. A man commanded the reins, flanked by two enormous, black Irish Wolfhounds. The hounds raised their muzzles into the air, black gums sneering, and breathed a pair of roaring pillars of fire into the sky.

The man at the reins was lit briefly by the fire at his sides. He had the head of a bird. Wild plumes of colored feathers circled his face. His eyes were dark holes. The man switched the reins to one hand, and with the other heavily muscled arm drew an ivory-hilted sword from his side and leveled it at the gathered below.

Staring in horror, one of Tara's remaining commanders managed to move, taking a step back, and then another. He turned to his army and screamed: "To arms! To arms for Tara!"

-5-

Back in Munster, King Broadcrown, flanked by Lords Fergus and Ernin, descended from the castle to the field. The waiting army parted, spears planting in salute, as the men made their way to the front line to view the horizon where once could be seen the highlands of Knocklong, but it was no longer there. Now, the moon revealed only misshapen tumors of earth behind a roiling wall of grey dust.

"My lords," said the King, his eyes wide, "we have unleashed Hell."

-6-

The chariot in the sky headed straight for the ruined camp. Bairen muttered incantations with trembling lips. Behind him, the remaining army was silent, frozen by the terrible sight.

The chariot descended as it raced towards them across the plain. It was now close enough to see the gleam of its bronze and the eyes of the black beasts that towed it. It touched down. The dark oxen's hooves struck the earth and the ground rumbled with their thunder. The chariot's wheels glanced against the rocky soil, sending sparks into the night sky. Then the great beasts, with chariot in tow, left the earth again, but only mere feet from the ground. They flew directly at the encampment, coming fast.

"Down!" cried the Commander.

At once, the army hit the dirt, arms splayed, swords clanging to earth. With a ferocious rush of wind the chariot was upon them, the black hooves passing only inches over their heads.

Too slow to duck to the ground, one soldier lost his head as one of the black beasts kicked it from his shoulders. The skull flew apart like a rotten melon. Another soldier, prone on the dirt, his shield raised in a final desperate reflex of protection, was sent flying as one of the chariot's wheels caught the shield's edge. Spinning like buzz saws and buoyant on freezing wind, the chariot's wheels passed overhead as the man's body tumbled over the prone infantry. His shield, with his arm still slipped through the bands, rolled to a stop yards away from his body, the arm spraying blood like a fizzling firework.

The chariot did not pass again. Instead, it rose, banked, and headed towards the nearby river that had been bridled by Bairen's magic.

Bairen got to his feet cautiously and looked towards the dammed river, towards his handiwork. His fellow druids did the same and joined him at his side.

"Is it really him?" a female druid whispered, her robe fouled with blood and soil.

"It is," Bairen told the gathered with quiet rage, "and he will wait for us in Munster. He will command the vengeance of their dead, the souls that are one with its soil. Tonight they stir, for The Veil that holds back the dead is thin. Let us pray that their miserable ancestors were stayed by the peasant's offerings. War during Samhain may have been a mistake."

Their eyes still on the horizon, they watched in silence as the chariot flew towards the river, the river that tossed violently against its unseen barrier. The black oxen reared briefly in mid-air, then the great druid raised a trident to the sky, and with a flash of his arm, Mog Ruith cast the trident at the river. It flew true, burying itself to the hilt in the dry, white scar of riverbed beyond the dam. At once, the water began to run once again, frothing white in the moonlight as it roared across the dark plain.

The chariot swooped down to the river, and with its wheels glancing across the rushing water, Mog yanked the trident free of the silt. The chariot rose, turned a tight circle in the air and hovered for a moment before Mog Ruith produced a whip made of light, as bright as a bolt of lightning. The light whip streaked the night sky and cracked on the hides of the black beasts, and as quick as it had come the chariot and its rider disappeared into the night.

-7-

Mog Ruith removed the bird mask and hung it on one of his oxen's horns as it grazed; its wild plumes bright against the animal's dark hide.

Mog Ruith was beardless. His hair was long, dark red and slicked back with sweat, falling over his broad shoulders. His nose was sharp, his eyes light and translucent as ice. His leather creaked as he bowed before the King of Munster. "Your Highness, I am at your service."

Stunned by the presence of a legend, a fairy tale that had just become real, Lords Fergus and Ernin stood by their King agape. For a moment, no one spoke and only the torches of the King's guard sputtered into the night. Mog glanced up from his crouch, a bemused smile playing at his rosy lips.

"Rise," said King Broadcrown, his voice only steadied by effort, "Munster is grateful. I have agreed to your price. Your ancestors will forever be lords in my kingdom, a kingdom whose future is now in your hands. My army is yours to command."

Mog rose and met the King's gaze, and in the light from the torches, the King caught sight of a twinkle passing through the druid's eyes, a perfect rainbow. Words failed the King and so did his breath.

"My liege," Mog said, "I am much obliged. But now the army of Tara is at your door, and they seek recompense for their dead." Mog turned and surveyed the gathered troops. "Believe in me now, for I stand before you! I commit myself to Munster before you all! I will fight until your land is safe for your clan and enriched with pride and vengeance for your dead! Now, drink! You will need your strength this night!"

A roar in the distance snapped all eyes across the field. The river returned, spraying foam up the far away bank and into the moonlight. A cheer erupted from the army. They stabbed the sky with their spears.

Mog continued: "The army of Tara will be upon you within the hour! The gods are with you, Munster!"

With this, Mog marched into the field, shouting orders to the men, to the King's guard, and to the people of the kingdom. With a final battle cry, the army ran into the fields to take their place in history.

The King and the Lords Fergus and Ernin turned to make their way back to the castle.

"Wait," said Fergus. "Look..."

A lamb was coming towards them from across the field.

"Strange..." Ernin wondered aloud, narrowing his eyes. These rocky fields have little to graze. That animal is surely far from home."

"True," Fergus agreed, "I know of no flocks in that direction. The shepherds all keep to the west. It must have come from the highlands of Knocklong...or where the highlands used to be."

Mog Ruith noticed the animal too, turned back, and approached the King's group, keeping an eye on the stray lamb that still lumbered towards them. "Take shelter, my Lords. I know what this is about."

The lamb slowed and approached Mog Ruith, stopping ten yards away. It stood watching, its wooly face impassive and its eyes glittering in the dark.

"Spy!" Mog spat.

Alarmed, the sheep began to back away.

Mog turned to his two black wolfhounds resting beside the chariot and nodded at them. The dogs nodded back and got to their feet. Slowly, the two huge dogs padded forward and faced the lamb. The lamb's eyes widened and just as it began to turn and flee, the hounds reared back. Twin pillars of fire shot from their mouths. The lamb screamed, its wool bursting into flames. It ran away trailing smoke, back across the field, back to the army of Tara.

-8-

"What is this?" whispered a young soldier of Tara who had been made to march on point, alone, and more than a hundred yards ahead of the rest of the army. "Shite!"

There was a ball of fire heading towards their position, and not just any fireball. As improbable as it was, the fire ball had crossed the clearing below and was now snaking up the hill on the old shepherd's trail. As if...

(it knows where it's going)

The soldier turned and ran towards the line marching down from the crumbling highlands, cupping his hands to his mouth to sound the alarm.

"Fire..." he began, and then lowered his hands.

Fire what, he thought, his mind reeling, searching for the right words. Fire is...

(running towards them)

He filled his lungs and tried again: "Fire is coming for us!"

Acrid smoke filled his nose. Whipping his head around, he saw the fireball rounding a bend and barreling down the center of the trail, heading straight for him, the flaming ball lighting the earth like daylight, black smoke trailing behind it. The fireball was screaming.

No, not screaming, it was bleating. It was bleating like a sheep.

Before the soldier could comprehend that the thing bearing down on him was a flaming animal, running at full speed, he had already launched himself head first into the tall grass beside the trail.

The wailing animal streaked by like a comet just as the army rounded the corner above. Soldiers scattered to arms. Druids fled into the brush. The animal slowed and all watched as the flaming sheep began to change back into human form, lengthening and rising up on two legs. The flames calmed as the blackened figure came to a stop. All stared in horror as the charred man sank to one knee, smoldering like a dying campfire.

"Bairen..." croaked the figure, puffing smoke through his blistered lips with each word, "I have failed you." With that, the blackened man collapsed and moved no more.

Bairen shoved aside two stunned soldiers and knelt on the trail beside the charred thing that was once a fellow druid.

"Your shape-shifters are no match for him," King Cormac chided from upslope. "Perhaps your pride is getting the better of you. It is time to call on your Master! Call on the one who guides you from Otherworld!"

"Never!" Bairen seethed. "This fight is mine!" He looked at the gathered, but the faces lacked faith. Even Bairen's own druids would not hold his gaze. "We are not beaten yet!" Bairen shouted, incensed by the silence that greeted him. "You question my power?"

Still, no one spoke.

The Red Druid turned back to the valley, narrowing his eyes. "Then, if I no longer have your faith, I will destroy them without it."

-9-

"Rise!" cried Mog Ruith as he plunged his trident into the cold, rocky soil. Throughout Munster a low and hollow moan began to shake the ground.

From their window in the castle, the two noblemen watched.

"Who does he summon?" whispered Fergus.

"I think..." began Ernin, swallowing hard. "...our fathers."

"Rise!" Mog Ruith commanded again, pulling the trident from the quaking ground.

Dirt in all directions began to dance where it lay, as if the core of the earth were boiling below, and under the watchful eye of the moon, white shoots began to sprout from the fields, reaching for the sky.

From the castle window, their faces flickering with candlelight, Fergus and Ernin watched, their eyes growing wider by the second. But the white things erupting from the ground were not shoots from some strange crop. They could see that now. No, they were arms – skeleton arms – and they were sprouting from their ancient graves, thousands of them. They stretched briefly for the sky, and then with a sound like pattering hail, they slapped the earth, clawing the dirt for purchase. The ground rumbled again, and all at once, the army of skeletons lifted themselves from their graves, dark soil raining from their bones. They stood, flexing their jaws at the moon and facing the river where the army of Tara now approached.

Stunned and pale, the living army of Munster that now stood alongside the army of the dead watched their new ranks with eyes that shook in their sockets.

Mog Ruith addressed the troops with a single voice that came from somewhere above, as if from the very night. "FIGHT WITH YOUR FATHERS, MUNSTER!"

The skeletons began to march towards the river, their bones rattling, advancing in a crouch, their arms forward and their bony hands clenching as if searching for a neck to throttle. With a gnashing of teeth, they began to run towards the river, towards the approaching army of Tara.

-10-

Bairen's face was bloodless at the sight.

"War during the Thinning was foolish," mumbled a nearby soldier.

Bairen shot the soldier a withering glance and turned his attention back to the other side of the river where the clatter of marching bones approached. He raised his eyes to the inky heavens, starlit and brittle with cold. He spoke within his head: "Master, he is better than me. He always was. His magic is from the Gods, and mine is only from will, but I will not go down without bringing him pain. This I can promise you."

Bairen whipped around to face his clan: "SHOW THEM THE POWER OF TARA!"

From behind him, Bairen's druids fanned out and flicked their robed arms towards Munster. Ravens flew from their sleeves and took to the night sky, shrieking and beating their dark wings.

Bairen turned and nodded at the army's commander: "Cross the river now! They have emptied their graves for us. We shall oblige to fill them again."

-11-

There was chaos in all directions. Screams and clashing iron filled the night sky. Troops splashed through the river and crossed swords in neck-deep water. Black ravens spiraled upward and blocked out the moon's light before catching fire and hammering the earth as a shower of blazing meteors.

Mog Ruith, flanked by his black hounds, stood motionless in the center of the field, his eyes locked on the river before him. The army of Tara had already crossed leaving only Bairen, with his druids in tow, to pull up the rear. The Red Druid was slogging through the shallows under the forward protection from the infantry.

On every side of Mog Ruith the re-animated dead bit into the flesh of the invading army. The skeletons climbed their backs and chewed their necks until the soldiers were forced to claw them away by dropping either shield or sword, affording the Munster soldiers opportunity to slay them where they stood.

Beside Mog, one of Munster's fighters had just run through a soldier of Tara. As the warrior was planting a foot on the fallen man's chest to pull his sword free of the ribcage, one of the flaming ravens dived for his head and landed on his white, spiked hair. The blue ball of flame consumed the man's head so quickly that he had no time to scream.

Mog Ruith's face was lit by the spectacle. He could feel the intense heat as the fireball melted the soldier's skull only feet away, but he kept his eyes on Bairen who had just cleared the river and was trudging up its bank in soaked robes. Bairen's druids were still behind, however, still in mid-stream.

Acting quickly, Mog Ruith lifted his trident and with one muscled arm, launched it towards the river. It flew straight and true.

Nearby, a commander of the Munster army had just dispatched a pair of Tara's infantry when he noticed the flying trident. Lowering his sword, he stopped to watch the weapon's flight in wonder. First, the trident shimmered with blue light. Then, the three points of the trident melded into a head, a flash of teeth at its tip. The commander blinked hard, but could not deny what he was seeing. The trident was turning into a serpent as it flew.

Bairen saw it coming too. He turned and shouted at his druids who were almost at the river's bank, "HURRY!"

One druid priestess made it onto the bank, but the man behind her lost his balance in the mud and splashed forward on his palms. The five remaining druids behind him halted briefly. That is when the trident, which had now become a flying black eel, soared over them all and slammed into the center of the river, electrifying the water.

The druids sizzled and popped, dancing in place, frying within their sodden robes. Then they fell, disappearing beneath the frothing water, leaving only tendrils of smoke where they had stood.

The eel slithered up the bank, darting around the fallen bodies of the battlefield, back to Mog Ruith, solidifying into a bronze trident at his feet. Mog Ruith stooped to pick up the weapon, never taking his eyes from Bairen.

Bairen peeled his gaze away from the sizzling river, his druids' grave. He turned to face Mog Ruith. He screamed with rage and raised his hand and tugged at his throat revealing an amulet hidden beneath his robes. It was a pendant, a scarab, and it began to move on his neck. The bug's jeweled legs kicked the air and clicked together as it writhed, as if longing to be freed of its golden chain.

Bairen spoke to it: "Hurt him," he whispered.

-12-

Behind Mog Ruith, the army of Munster had prevailed. The army of Tara, weakened by the storm they had faced at their camp, had been no match for the provincial fighters who had vowed to defend their land. They stood awaiting command. So too did the skeleton fighters, their bones smeared with dirt and blood, swaying in place and slowly gnashing their jaws.

Mog locked eyes with Bairen and with one hand, pushed his hand slowly downwards on the air behind him. "Sleep" he whispered.

The legion of skeletons began to claw headfirst into the earth. Within seconds, their kicking legs disappeared into the earth in a shower of dirt.

A Munster commander shouted: "To our dead!" and raised his sword. A cheer filled the night.

A soldier was about to embrace Mog Ruith when he noticed that the great druid was staring at something, a lone figure at the edge of the field, a man dressed in blood red robes.

"Mog Ruith," the soldier asked, "who is that druid? He is of Tara. He is not of our clan. Shall I take him prisoner?"

"You could not," Mog Ruith replied.

"Then I will kill him," the soldier said, narrowing his eyes at the figure who was now walking slowly towards them. He unsheathed his sword, but Mog's heavy hand stayed him, falling on the warrior's shoulder.

"You could not do that either," Mog Ruith warned. "Leave him to me."

The soldier looked stung and was about to protest when he was interrupted.

"Where is King Cormac Mac Airt?" asked an approaching commander. "Has he been killed? He has not been seen. Surely, his ransom will be great."

"The King of Tara is safe," Mog Ruith replied. "He and his guard never crossed the river. Tell your King that I wish him to live. He and his guard will live as proof of Munster's great mercy."

Both soldiers' jaws tightened, disappointed with the loss of the spoil.

"Go," Mog Ruith commanded, "or the Red Druid will destroy you both."

The men flushed, but then nodded tersely and turned back to face the troops. The commander pointed at the sky where a thin band of light striped the horizon. "Hark! The New Year approaches! Victory is ours!"

Another cheer and the army began to make their way home.

Mog returned his attention to Bairen who had now stopped advancing and was clutching the scarab amulet at his chest.

"The Master gave it to you?" Mog shouted at Bairen. "And why would he do a thing like that??"

There was no answer, only a flash of green as the beetle at Bairen's neck reared and spit. The amulet's front legs kicked. Its green carapace flared, and a pulsing stream of acid shot from between its mandibles, trained on Mog Ruith's face. Mog Ruith was fast, but he was not fast enough. He screamed and dropped to his knees, clapping a hand over his smoking eye.

"Mog," Bairen said approaching, the acid streaming relentlessly from the yawning mouth of the beetle at his neck, "it's been a while. Too bad you had to go hide on your island like an old maid. You could have ruled all of Ireland with us. Now, you will be nothing but a worthless fairy tale. And I will see to it that the scribes never write down your name. The mere mention of you will be punishable by death."

The stream of acid ceased and the scarab around Bairen's neck stopped moving. Mog's face was wet with the corrosive liquid, the rocks beneath him sizzling like frying fat as it ran from his face.

Mog Ruith's eye was now a smoking socket. He got to one knee and glared at Bairen with the other, his breathing rattling through his chest as he wiped his face furiously with the hem of his tunic. The pain was unbearable and Mog screamed again. Unable to get to his feet, he watched his world begin to fade at the edges, darkness reaching for him.

"Now," said Bairen, pulling a jeweled dagger from his cloak, "the peasants have sacrificed more than enough blood to your whore of a daughter this night. The fools think she can shorten their winter – the great Earth Spear."

Bairen laughed contemptuously, raising the dagger.

"But winter will never leave this land. I will see to that. Yet, I think a final sacrifice is in order just for good measure. But this one...oh...this one is just for me. Your blood for my glory. Maybe you will see our master again. Though, I think Hell may want you more."

Slowly, Mog's hand glanced across the soil and lit on his trident.

"Fool," Mog Ruith whispered, his remaining eye now fixed on the Red Druid. "Go back to school. What made you think you were ready for me?"

With a flick of his wrist, Mog Ruith sent his trident hurling at Bairen. The weapon hissed upwards, became a serpent, and buried its teeth into Bairen's left eye, wrapping its body around the druid's face in three coils with the speed of a bullwhip. Then, the snake's head reared back, its mouth stretching open, fangs dripping venom, and it plunged its teeth deep into the arteries of Bairen's neck.

Bairen's howl was muffled as he clawed at the fat tubes of serpent wrapped around his head. The Red Druid sank to his knees. The snake uncoiled itself and fled back to Mog Ruith's feet, revealing Bairen's purple and surprised face, a bubble of blood inflating and popping at the Druid's mouth.

Bairen fell face-first onto the soil of Munster, dead.

PART ONE
THE CITY OF THE DEAD

Colma, California
Present Day

I.
Sam and Lucia Have Company

-1-

Just south of San Francisco, California lies the small town of Colma. There are only about 1,500 people living in Colma, enough to fill a small municipal auditorium, but what really makes this town interesting, above all other towns, is that the majority of the city's residents are dead.

Aside from the 1,500 who are still breathing in Colma, there are 1.5 million who are not. Currently, this would set the ratio at one thousand dead people per every living resident. This fact becomes even more startling when you consider that Colma takes up only two square miles of land.

Colma has more dead bodies per square inch than any other town in the world with seventeen cemeteries within its modest borders, which include memorial parks specific to Catholics, Jews, Italians, Greek Orthodox, Serbs, Japanese and even two set aside for pets. As a result of this distinction, most of the residents of Colma are not likely to cause any problems.

Some of them used to, of course. In fact, some of them were very controversial people in their time, but unfortunately, if you were to come to the town to rub elbows with its most famous residents – William Randolph Hearst, Levi Strauss, Joe DiMaggio, Lefty O'Doul and Wyatt Earp – you would find them to be very dull company indeed.

How the town of Colma came to exist is a combination of hysteria and good sense. In 1900, San Francisco was getting crowded. The families of the gold rush had grown roots and now the prospectors were seeing their children have grandchildren. The railroads were built and the Chinese who built them were sticking around. So did the many Italians, filling the waterfront with fishing trawlers. In short, word had gotten out that there was something for everyone in the City by the Bay. Its streets and hills were beginning to bustle without much space for bustling.

It is unclear who started the outcry for more space, but among the loudest voices were real estate developers, city planners, and of course the politicians who were very eager to please whomever seemed to be successfully convincing the public. Talks began about moving San Francisco's cemeteries to somewhere else – somewhere kind of nice and sort of close by, but somewhere else nonetheless.

"Crime!" cried some residents. "Cemeteries attract drunks, grave robbers and ne'er-do-wells!"

"Take care of the living!" cried the real estate developers, investors and city planners. "Cemeteries breed disease!"

This got people's attention. After all, the land occupied by cemeteries was very valuable and often located in some very desirable locations. So the campaign to instill fear in the public went on, and it seemed to be working – at least at first. But it wasn't long before all of this talk of moving their forefathers out of town started making the public more nervous than they were afraid.

A compromise began to take shape: simply prohibit any more people from being buried in the City. Of course, there was a problem with this. There were already countless bodies in the ground, at rest, and occupying the land.

"Dig them up and move them!" cried the real estate developers.

"Dig them up and move them," echoed the politicians.

"Dig them up and move them," the public agreed.

But not all of the public, especially those whose loved ones were already underground, their plots paid for, and their souls ostensibly at rest. To disturb the dead was not only prohibited by virtually every religious law on the books – not to mention traumatic to the families of the deceased – it was, at the very least, in incredibly bad taste.

So the great tug-of-war for public opinion went on and on, neither side seeming to achieve enough traction to stop the fight. Then one day in 1914, the San Francisco City Council finally caved under the pressure by the planners and developers and passed an ordinance that there would be no more cemeteries within the city limits. Eviction notices went out to the graveyards. The non-rent-paying dead needed to get out of town.

So, thousands of bodies were dug up. Monuments, tombstones, mausoleums and everything else within the iron gates of all of the city's cemeteries were loaded onto a procession of wagons.

The public was outraged.

Father Patrick Riordan, a Catholic priest and respected figure in the City, urged calm. Years earlier he had blessed a potato field south of the City and had already established Holy Cross cemetery for his Catholic followers.

"There is plenty of room for all of the displaced in Colma," wrote Father Patrick to the office of one of the doomed graveyards. "All children of God are welcomed. Here they will find peace. Bring your dead to Colma and we will look after them as God looks after us all."

So they did. The dead came to Colma, and they came by the tens of thousands.

-2-

Colma's strange distinction is apparent as soon as you drive into town on its main thoroughfare, El Camino Real. Visitors begin to see the preoccupation with death almost immediately. Lining the streets are casket dealers, funeral homes and florists. Little chapels and big churches of all kinds are everywhere. Along the roads, and among the listing tombstones and stark white crosses, solemn, stone faces of innumerable saints and winged angels gaze contemplatively towards oncoming traffic. Some are displayed right on the curb – the monument dealers setting them out before rush hour to tempt passersby to plan early for their respective dirt naps.

Lately, Colma has made an attempt to steer away from being known as a simple necropolis, a city that caters to only the silent. Big box stores, a large shopping mall and a string of car dealerships have all moved in over the last twenty years. Now, there is something for everyone with most of the typical modern distractions and conveniences within spitting distance of the bone yards. Many families have even been enticed in the past decade to move to Colma, lured by its low home prices and proximity to San Francisco, but it is not for everyone.

For those who don't mind, Colma is safe, quiet and certainly not lacking in green space. Gardens of stone slope gently among sheltering oaks dotted with plenty of marble benches and gurgling fountains.

For others though, the expanse of cemeteries is foreboding, the tombstones like jagged teeth against the night sky. This imagery, coupled with the thought of being very, very outnumbered by the dead is still too much to bear, and the majority of the millions of residents living in the San Francisco Bay Area simply drive by Colma, and as quickly as possible.

-3-

Samuel McGrath is not bothered by the graveyards. He has lived here his entire life: seventeen years, soon to be eighteen in a matter of days. To him, the cemeteries are almost invisible, the way noise can become of increasingly less concern the longer one lives beneath a flight path or in proximity to a freeway. He notices them, but he gives no extra thought to what may lie beneath the spongy grass.

Sam glides on his skateboard down one of the serpentine hills, along one of the wide and almost always deserted visitors' roads that wends its way through Cypress Lawn. He grinds the painted, white curb with his skateboard, pops it up, and grabs the front of the board with his hand. He crosses a short island of grass, dodging a tombstone and gains another road that will lead him further downhill towards the cemetery gates.

To Sam, the graveyards are a godsend. They have always meant freedom to him. Blind in one eye and with questionable use of the right side of his body from being hit by a car as a child, the wide-open spaces of the City's memorial parks are the only place where he feels safe enough to skateboard, where he has the confidence to try some of the tricks his friends can do. The caretakers usually frown on such activity within their gates, but they all know Sam; they all know his story and they all doff their cap and look the other way.

Today happens to be a gem of an October day, a mild Indian summer. The sun is bright, the last leaves clinging stubbornly to the oaks overhead like forks of fire, and the warm sun and crisp breeze are perfect for working up a sweat.

No, the cemetery doesn't bother him, especially today. What *is* bothering Sam is the black cat that has been following him all day.

Sam stands in the middle of the deserted road, his foot atop the skateboard. He cranes his neck up the hill from where he has just come, his green eyes keen, his spiky, dark red hair glowing like a lit match under the cool sun.

The cat is upslope, sitting on the marble step beneath a mausoleum topped with a stone angel with spread wings, watching him. Their eyes meet.

There is definitely something off about that cat, he thinks. Something...

(wrong)

"What do you want from me?" Sam whispers.

The cat, well out of earshot, tilts its head slightly and continues to stare.

"Whatever…" Sam mutters, turning away and mounting his board.

That's when he hears The Crackle.

At first, it is just a suggestion. Then it grows louder, filling his head as it always does this time of year. It builds to a roar, like the crowd from a distant football stadium. Then, he smells the smoke. It's the part of The Crackle that used to throw him off the most, but he's stopped looking for fire when he smells it because there never is one. It's always just in his head. He casts an accusatory glance back up the hill at the cat, but the animal is gone.

Sam turns and plants his left foot – his good one – atop the skateboard and pushes off with the other. This hill is not as steep as the last one, but probably good enough to outrun a cat. He tucks for speed. Rounding a bend, he buzzes a lone sedan parked graveside. From their position on the lawn, a pair of mourners regards Sam with solemn disapproval. Sam whisks by like an apparition, the board's polyurethane wheels whispering on the fresh asphalt. He shifts his weight for the next bend ahead: a plunging dogleg that levels out to the final straightaway at the cemetery gates.

His blood chills. The cat is now in front of him. Beneath one of the stone pillars that mark the exit, it sits motionless, waiting.

Sam's eyes widen, the sound of fire in his head flaring. He teeters on the board for a moment, but he doesn't stop. Instead, he gives the road an extra kick, aiming himself between the two stone pillars that lead to the street. The cat doesn't move, doesn't blink. Sam bends his knees slightly and kicks the ground again. Then he is at the pillars, almost to the sidewalk. Sam and the cat stare at each other as he glides by.

Through the gate, Sam slams his foot on the back of the skateboard again and the deck leaps to his hand. Now, he is on a busy street, his vision not suitable for running away.

"From a cat?" he says to himself. "From a stupid cat…"

(oh, but it's not stupid at all, and you know it)

(it wants something)

No, that isn't right. That doesn't feel right. It doesn't want something...

(it knows something)

Sam darkens. He wonders if anyone else has these kinds of thoughts, and suddenly the sadness is upon him again. Of course they don't. He is different: different in so many ways. The Crackle has grown stronger still, filling his head with the popping and hissing of burning things. His teeth clench, he turns with sickening slowness to check the stretch of public sidewalk behind him and sees what he knew he would see:

The cat is standing in the middle of the sidewalk...

(stalking me)

The animal's head is high and its tail, rigid as a pipe cleaner, is curled into a furry, black question mark. It pads slowly towards Sam, staring.

Sam stops. The cat stops too, stops and sits, and never taking its eyes from Sam's, tilts its head, a thin white stripe blooming beneath its nose. It's...

(smiling)

Sam doesn't even bother to put the skateboard beneath his feet. He just starts running.

-4-

Lucia Winter did not like going into the attic. Even at 17 years old, she would have preferred almost anything else.

"Stupid," she whispered, staring up at the trap door above her on the ceiling of her parent's walk-in closet. "Really? Monsters in the attic? You're almost eighteen."

She bit her lower lip and reached for the brass handle, pulled down and sidestepped. She had been conked on the head by the ladder enough times in the past. Boy, did that hurt like hell, but it was a wonder how it improved your reflexes. She cringed, pressing her back against her mother's soft, winter coats as the hatch above yawned open with a creak and the ladder slid to the floor. thudding softly on the carpet, bringing with it a wisp of spider web that fluttered across Lucia's cheek.

She flapped at it with a convulsive hand. She did not need to be reminded that it was not just old childhood monsters she had to worry about up there. There were plenty of real problems in the attic, crawly, hairy problems that could move a whole lot faster than she could, even if her room was full of trophies for running track, which it was.

"Yuck," she whispered. Then, she turned her head and yelled out of the door of the walk-in closet. "CAN WE WAIT 'TIL DAD GETS HOME?"

From downstairs came her mother's voice: "Avanza, mija!"

Lucia smiled tightly. Telling me to hurry? Her mother was enjoying every minute of this.

"DAD MAY HAVE TO TAKE ME TO WORK!" she yelled back.

Seeing how her father was the General Manager at a cemetery, Lucia thought this was a clever retort. But no reply came from downstairs.

"Okay," she relented. "Fine."

She mounted the ladder and slapped her palm up the cool aluminum rungs. She stared at the dark hole above. One more step up the ladder and her head would...

(be gnawed off by a rat the size of a small bus)

Lucia pursed her lips, swept a lock of her dark hair back with her free hand and crawled into the attic.

-5-

With little regard for the beautiful October day outside, the tiny attic window offered nothing but a small circle of waxy light, leaving the long, low room beneath the peaked roof blanketed with thick shadows. A crow squawked right near the dirty pane of glass. Lucia looked, but the little round window only stared at her, like a milky, dead eye.

Lucia sighed, pulled her legs up, tucked them beneath herself and waited for her pupils to adjust: a planked floor, luggage, stacked boxes. Everything frosted with white dust.

Lucia was fairly tall and fairly certain that standing straight up would result in a nasty conk on the head, courtesy of one of the 4x4 beams supporting the ceiling. So she crouched and scanned the room, moving slowly.

"BLECH!" she cried as a spider web grazed both cheeks. She pawed at her head.

Mercifully she saw what she had come for. Quickly she stooped over further – just to be safe – shuffled over to the two cardboard boxes she had her eye on, and dropped to one knee. Both boxes were striped

with a fat strip of masking tape affixed to the flaps. In black, thick lines
from a marker, each one read:

HALLOWEEN

The flaps had been tucked into themselves in the typical, hasty
cardboard box fashion, and Lucia had to only tug on them gently for the
boxes to yield their treasures. She peered inside.

On top, and staring up at her, was a plastic orange pumpkin
with triangle eyes and a toothy grin. The black, plastic handle had been
torn off. Lucia remembered disposing of it years ago when she was a kid.
One wincing tug and it had popped off easily. At some point she had
become convinced that the flimsy handle was an impediment, blocking
adult hands from placing the maximum amount of candy into the
bucket. Beneath the pumpkin were some ceramic figurines from the
drug store: a moaning ghost votive candle holder, another resin candle
holder in the shape of a haunted castle, and a few unopened bags of fake
cobwebs.

Lucia moved these things aside.

She screamed.

Bolting to her feet, she cracked her head on an overhead beam.
She screamed again, her hand clapping to her head as she backed away
from the box.

"NO! NO! NO!" she cried and began kicking her leg. "YUCK!"

Now bent over, one hand on the knot rising on her head, she
continued running in a circle, kicking her leg. With her free hand, she
reached down and wiggled the denim of her jeans at her calf.

A plump, brown spider scurried from her pant leg and made for
the stack of boxes.

"Gross!" she hissed through her teeth. She brought her palm
down from her head and held it before her face. No blood. That was
good.

Her heart hammering in her chest, she blew her breath out into
the dark. She looked at the floor again to make sure it was clear and
began to sit down. A voice came from behind her.

"Hello, Lucia."

-6-

Lucia stood up, whirling around, almost bumping her head a second time. She ducked, her eyes darting through the gloom, her dark hair a tangled curtain over her face. Across the room, a head was sticking through the floor, lit from beneath.

"Shit!" Lucia cried. "Allison?"

Allison Campbell was peeking through the trapdoor, smiling.

"What's up? There sure is a lot of screaming going on up here."

"A heart attack," Lucia replied, brushing her hair back behind her ear. "That's what's going on. You scared the crap out of me."

"Sorry..." Allison offered, clearly not sorry. Her grin had widened. She crawled up through the trapdoor. "Your mom said you were up here." Allison looked around and began to stand up.

"Watch your head." Lucia warned. "Take it from me."

Allison flinched and crept her way towards Lucia. "Yikes. I bet this place is full of spiders."

"You think?" Lucia said, her mouth a sardonic knot. "Well, I'm glad you're here. You can help."

"Help do what?" Allison asked, inspecting the dusty wooden floor before gingerly kneeling beside her friend.

"I am bringing down the Halloween stuff," Lucia replied, "and my Mom needs the sugar skull molds as soon as possible. She is in a crafting mood. God help us all when she is in a crafting mood. She is freaking out because she thinks she might not have packed them last year."

"Sugar skull molds?" Allison asked, her glasses lifting as she wrinkled her nose.

"For Dia de los Muertos," Lucia said, rifling through the box. "The Day of the Dead."

"What's that?"

"It's a Mexican thing," Lucia replied, still sifting through the box, "I'm half Mexican, you know."

"I know. So what is it?"

"It's a tradition. It was big in my mom's town of Oaxaca when she was a kid. We honor the dead. We go to their graves around Halloween and talk to them, offer them their favorite stuff. Ofrendas, we call it. It means offering. That way they are more likely to hang out with us."

"Sounds creepy."

"It's not as creepy as it sounds. It's so you can still have your family around you, even after they move on. It makes my parents feel a lot better since we lost Carlo, especially Mom."

Lucia's smile began to wilt as she continued: "It's helped us a lot, I think. It's funny. Dad is such a gringo he didn't even know about it, and he works in the funeral business. He only found out when Carlo died and Mom told him about the tradition, about how her parents used to make her go to the cemetery on Dia de los Muertos. Now, Dad really likes it too I think. We go to the grave and clean it, bring Carlo his favorite stuff..."

Lucia stopped, her mouth pressed into a thin line, her eyes wet.

"I'm sorry, Looze," Allison said softly. "He was a cutie. I like the picture on the bookshelf downstairs, the one where he is on his bike? He looks so happy. You know what? I think he looked kind of tough without his hair."

"Yeah..." Lucia agreed wistfully, now digging half-heartedly through the box. "He was tougher than I would have been...tougher than I was at the end."

Sensing the mounting pain in her friend, Allison tried to lighten the mood. "It sounds like a neat tradition. So, it's on Halloween?"

"Close. Technically, its November 1st and 2nd, but we go on Halloween night and stay up until midnight. After midnight it is El Dia de los Angelitos – the day of the little angels. Those two days are when most families go to see their lost children. It is when the dead are most likely to..."

Lucia stopped herself. She was about to go too far.

Long ago she had promised Sam McGrath that all talk of the strange things that have happened to them both would be their secret alone. She had slipped up only once before among friends, but it had been awkward. She never wanted to see that look in someone's eyes again: the look of unease and judgment. Allison was a good friend, but the subject had to be changed now. She knew if she went any further there would be too many questions and there would be hardly enough suitable answers.

Allison seemed none the wiser though. On the contrary, she looked stricken, figuring that Lucia was simply grasping at straws, still floundering in memories of her dead brother.

Lucia sensed her friend's sympathy for her and smiled. "It's actually a very happy occasion. I feel closest to my brother on that day. We picnic on the grave and sing songs and tell funny stories about him and it feels like he is really there."

The two girls fell into silence.

"So, are the sugar skulls good?" Allison ventured.

"No," Lucia grimaced. "They are edible, but not really for eating. You would break a tooth. No, they are for decorating. After we make them, we paint them with swirls of color and stuff and then take them to the grave as part of the decorations. We bring the skulls, candy, food and..."

Lucia gasped, smiled wide and leaned over the box.

"Speak of the devil," she said, holding up a papier mache doll.

The delicate figure was a foot tall, the skeleton of a woman. Her hair was a crown of blood-red roses, her eyes were dark, deep-set in black sockets, and her toothy grin stretched from ear to ear. Her thin frame was wrapped in a red gown with black fringe. In one white, bony hand she held a funereal bouquet of tiny, orange paper flowers.

"Catrina," Lucia said, holding the figure up to Allison and rocking it slowly in the air, "...the Lady of the Dead."

Allison regarded the doll nervously. Lucia shrugged and set it on the floor beside the box. "Weird. All the Dia de los Muertos stuff should be in its own box. Everything is mixed up with the Halloween decorations. Dad probably put it all away last year. You look through this box," Lucia said, hefting the second box and placing it with a grunt in front of Allison.

Allison's blonde hair fell around her face as she lifted the flaps and peered in. With a quizzical pout she produced a much smaller cardboard box from within the larger one and opened it.

"Oh, be careful with that," Lucia said. "That was my Dad's. It was one of his costumes from when he was a kid."

Allison held up a plastic mask of The Fonz, a character from the 70's television show, *Happy Days*. There was an elastic cord attached to both sides of the face. Allison put the mask on. The breathing slit in the mask's mouth poked her lips with its sharp edges and the rims of the eye slits dug into her eyelids. For some reason, the mask smelled faintly of cotton candy.

"This is pretty uncomfortable," Allison mumbled from behind the lifeless eyes and frozen smile that bore only a passing resemblance to actor Henry Winkler. The molded black hair did little to hide

Allison's golden locks and they flared absurdly at the sides of her head, tufted by the elastic cord. "You can hardly breathe in here."

"I know," Lucia conceded. "It's a wonder my Dad is still alive."

Allison peeled off the mask. "Wait," she said, peering into her box. "These look like skull molds." Triumphantly, she held up a pair of plastic trays.

Lucia brightened, "Those are them! Good. Mom can finally cool her jets. C'mon, let's get out of here."

-7-

Lucia's mother, Consuela Winter, went by the name of Connie, but anyone would concede that she looked more like a Consuela. Her dark hair was almost always pulled back from her angular face in a tight chignon. She was voluptuous and possessed of quiet strength. Today her breasts pressed like overinflated balloons at her floral blouse and her thin waist and wide hips supported a yellow apron. She ignored the wisps of grey at her temples and this gave her a confident, unfussy beauty. She smiled at her daughter, her lined face like warm, cracked earth.

"Gracias, Mija!" she said as Lucia and Allison set two boxes down on the dining room floor. Connie plucked the skull molds from the top of one of them, smiling approvingly.

"We're going to go hang out, Mama." Lucia said, offering Allison a grape soda before ushering her friend to the living room. The two flopped on the couch in front of the TV where a brassy female judge was losing her patience with some mousy woman.

"Isn't that Sam McGrath?" Allison asked, peering over the couch and out of the window. "You didn't tell me he lives across the street."

"Since we were kids," Lucia replied, pulling deeply on her soda.

"I miss my old neighborhood," Allison lamented. "I had a cute guy who lived across the street from me, too."

Lucia stopped drinking her soda, gaped at her friend and then snapped close her mouth quickly before her dismay was noticed. Sudden heat had flushed her cheeks. She was surprised by it and she turned her face away slightly, fiddling with a long strand of hair at her ear.

She wasn't jealous was she? Of course not. Nothing could be sillier. Sam was her best friend, always had been. That was all.

"He's been skateboarding," Allison continued. "I thought he was crippled? It's too bad. Otherwise..." She trailed off with a hungry, tuneless whistle.

"He's not crippled," Lucia fired back, a little too peevishly she thought. "He has some nerve damage, that's all. He got hit by a car when he was a kid. He's still a hottie."

She had meant to simply defend him as a friend, but that's not how it had come off, and she knew it. She sounded jealous, and she needed to retract her claws fast or Allison was going to get the wrong idea.

But Sam and Allison would never work out anyway, she was certain of that. No reason to be snippy. After all, Sam was a peculiar guy. Lucia was pretty sure that she herself was the only person who could ever...

(marry him)

...understand him.

She flushed. Did she really feel that way? For Sam? She shook her head hoping it would clear the confusion from her head. It didn't. The strand of hair at her ear was now a twisted cord.

Thankfully, Allison had moved on, commenting on how bitchy the television judge was getting.

Lucia glanced over her shoulder and through the parting window sheers. Across the street, Sam was entering his garage and placing his skateboard on a shelf. He was looking over his shoulder and scanning the ground, as if he had lost something.

"This chick is SO going to lose this case," Allison said, leaning forward at the television.

"MIJA!" Connie Winter shouted from the dining room. "Can you come here?"

"Why does she call you Mija?" whispered Allison.

"It's like 'my daughter' in Spanish," Allison whispered. "She has always called me that. COMING, MAMA!"

Connie was on the floor, the boxes mostly unpacked. Concern clouded her face. "Where is the Catrina doll? It is not broken is it? I want to take it to your brother's grave with his ofrendas."

Lucia remembered seeing it; she had shown it to Allison. She was sure of it.

"It's not in there?" Lucia asked. "I saw it. Maybe it fell out. I'll go look." She raised cupped hands to her mouth and shouted at the living room. "BE RIGHT BACK!"

Lucky me, she thought. I get to go back up there.

When she got upstairs she noticed that she had left the ladder down and the trapdoor open. With a deep breath she clambered up the ladder quickly and through the hole in the ceiling.

-8-

Had it gotten darker in here, she wondered.

On her hands and knees, she padded onto the plank floor of the attic and got into a crouch. It WAS darker. She would swear to it.

She froze.

"Loo...see...ahh..."

It was a voice: faint, barely at the edge of hearing, but it was definitely her name. Dread flooded her. This time it wasn't going to be Allison. No one else was up here. It came again, a little louder this time, and it whispered slowly. "Loo...see...ah..."

She looked behind her. Nothing. Her bladder began to cramp with fear.

The voice whispered again, and it had gotten closer. "For...get something?"

Lucia let out a despairing moan, her skin stippling with gooseflesh.

The voice was unnatural, thin, reedy, and Lucia's mind quickly flashed to when she was younger, when it was hot, when she had spoken into the oscillating fan that cooled the living room in summer. It had sounded so strange, funny even, but this didn't sound funny at all. It sounded...

(evil)

"Loooo...see...ahhhh..." the voice purred.

Still hunched over beneath the attic's peaked roof, her neck craned awkwardly, Lucia's eyes darted, struggling to adjust to the gloom.

Then she saw it. It was the Catrina doll and it was standing in the middle of the attic. Beneath its crown of red roses, the skeleton face grinned wolfishly. One thin, bony arm held out the orange funereal bouquet of paper flowers towards Lucia.

"For your brother..." the thing cooed.

Lucia's blood ran with ice. Her legs wobbled, filling with useless jelly.

"Don't you want to see Carlo again?" the doll pouted. To Lucia's horror, the skeleton face drooped into a frown of mock pity. Then, the doll took a step forward, teetering crazily on its paper legs, the hem of the black and red dress riding up to reveal splayed, white toes on the dusty plank floor. That was when Lucia's mind became a black furnace of panic.

"WELL, DON'T YOU!?" the doll screamed.

As fast as she could, Lucia spun and made for the trapdoor. As she did so, she came out of her crouch. Dull pain knocked her to her knees as her head connected with an overhead beam. Her brain filled with bright stars.

The doll's voice was closer now, right behind her. "Bring your ginger boyfriend, Lucia. Bring him and you can see Carlo again." Then, it spoke in Spanish: "Ahhh...pobre muchacho...yessssssss..."

Lucia could hear its paper feet shuffle up beside her where she lay on the floor.

"He waits..." it said, "we all wait...forever we wait..."

Clutching her head, Lucia made an attempt to get to her feet, but darkness was tugging her down. She had one last, terrible thought before she lost consciousness.

(oh God, it's whispering in my ear)

"The Nowhere," the doll said, its moldy breath puffing cold air on her cheek. "I'll see you in The Nowhere...Mija..."

II.
Black Cats and Ravens

-1-

Father Doctor was in his study, his eyeglasses reflecting blue with the light of the computer monitor. He bit his lower lip in concentration until a presence in the doorway made him jump. He laughed nervously, "Sam!"

"Did I scare you?" said Sam, leaning on the jamb. "Sorry. It's so dark in here. He flicked on the overhead light.

"Dark is good," the priest replied. "It calms me." He rolled his chair away from the computer and swiveled to face Sam. "Did you happen to check the mailbox? We still need that birth certificate if you are going to get your passport in time for your senior trip. Processing alone takes weeks; we're cutting it close."

"I'll go look," Sam replied.

"How was the skating?"

"Good. Nice day. You should go see."

Father Doctor studied Sam, "Anything weird happen?"

"I saw the cat again."

The priest nodded gravely. "Did it follow you home again?"

"I don't think it's here. I didn't see it once I crossed El Camino."

"Smart cat," Father Doctor said, leaning back in his office chair. There was another long pause as he surveyed his charge. As his only guardian, he wished he could help Sam more than by just grasping at straws on the internet, but the answers had to come from somewhere. At least he had found something that might convince the boy he was special rather than just crazy – which he was sure was Sam's leading conclusion.

Father Doctor ventured on, "You got a sec, Sam? I want to show you what I came up with, about how you can see things, feel things. It's an old Irish wives' tale, but I thought you might get a kick out of it. It's not much, but it's something. Mind you, this is only a lark. Of course, I don't believe any of this stuff, and it's especially hard to believe Halloween has something to do with it. Personally, I still think it's a holdover from your accident. Why this stuff only happens in the autumn I'm not sure. Maybe it's triggered by the falling temperature? Haven't you heard that farmers can tell when rain is coming by the way their war wound hurts? Ever heard that?"

Sam shook his head.

"Yep. Their bones ache when it gets cold. Even mine do and I'm only middle-aged. It's a theory at least. Or...who knows...it could be a number of things. The brain is still mostly a mystery..."

The priest paused and watched Sam closely, the boy he had vowed to protect. Sam was still tormented. That was clear, but the boy was doing his best to hide it. It was all so frustrating. Why hadn't the doctors offered him anything? After all those visits? It had to be some lingering brain damage of some kind – had to be. That made more sense than anything else.

Sam was slouched in the doorway and looking at his feet. The priest knew that the best thing to do was not to darken alongside the boy. He had to keep things light. He cleared his throat and went on.

"Anyway," he continued, "have a look. I just came across it when I searched for 'born on Halloween'. Remember last week when you were convinced that it meant you were cursed and I told you that you were being silly? This is all just tales and mythology. Just like our friend the black cat. Maybe it just likes you. It doesn't have to be a witch or bad luck. People can come up with the wackiest theories about anything; I only want you to see what I found to prove that point."

Father Doctor paused and waited for a reaction. Sam only stared at the wood floor, dusting it with the tip of his sneaker. Cautiously the priest went on, but his easy smile was wilting.

"Remember, this is just for fun. Okay, Sam? Anyway...interesting bit of folklore...there is a theory here about those who have extra senses. The word in Gaelic means..."

Father Doctor stopped talking, and although Sam was backlit from the hall light and he was unable to see whether his charge's expression was improving, he could feel that it wasn't. He decided to change the subject quickly before Sam was unsalvageable, retreating within himself as he often did when this subject came up.

"Never mind, it's okay, Sam. You can look at it later if you want. I have to phone the church about something anyway. The article I'm talking about is up on the screen whenever you want to look at it. See you in a bit."

Sam nodded stiffly, "Thanks..."

The priest did not have to phone the church, but he could always tell when Sam was pulling back. It was a fine line to walk: when to indulge the boy, when to guide him, and when to get out of the way were all questions with no clear answers. As he passed Sam, Father Doctor smiled and tousled the boy's hair, "You're welcome."

What was happening to Sam was inexplicable. There was no basis in his faith, and probably little basis in science for Sam's extraordinary perceptions, no matter what he told the boy out loud. Offering Sam this old Irish legend seemed the right thing to do. It might soothe the boy, make him feel less alone and not so different. At least he prayed that would be the case. Convincing Sam that nothing was happening was certainly not working. Somehow, the boy had to find peace. That was what anyone would want for their son.

And, that was what Father Doctor considered Sam: his son. Though, on paper he was only a legal guardian. Sure, he had thought of adopting Sam many times, but it always seemed profane somehow, or presumptuous. Sam had lost his parents suddenly and violently, and at a young age. He knew it was silly, but adoption seemed like taking advantage of a tragedy somehow, gaining an honor from an unspeakable horror.

It was far too late for adoption now anyway. Sam was seventeen already, a senior in high school, and about to go off to college. The time for second guessing such matters was long gone, but as Sam neared the time when he would leave the nest and venture out on his own, Father Doctor still fought pangs of self-doubt and regret.

The granting of the guardianship had been a coup, especially given the state of the Catholic Church. The word around the parish was that the archdiocese was even willing to consider an adoption given Sam's extraordinary circumstances, but Sam got squeamish whenever the topic was broached.

"I love you," Sam would say, "so it doesn't matter. If the church is going to freak out about it then it's not worth it."

So Father Doctor, after all of these years, was left to hope he had done the best by Sam. He considered himself blessed and very lucky. He had simply been the McGrath family priest and since Sam's grandparents were lost somewhere in Ireland and Sam's parents had no siblings, there had been no next of kin to take care of the boy when Sam's parents died. As the one who had administered rites at the McGrath funeral, Father Doctor found that young Samuel had been orphaned at his very feet. Now he had a son that his vows of celibacy would not have allowed, a bright, kind boy who – in spite of his secret troubles – was growing into a fine young man. Sam was too good of a kid to have been left as a ward of the state.

It had been a hard road though. The death of Sam's parents had shaken the little town of Colma. Death was certainly a big cottage industry for the town, but its few residents were not prepared for two of their own to be on the receiving end of Death's sickle with such violence and swiftness.

Little Sam was only six when his parents had been run off the San Mateo Bridge and into the frigid, pitch black waters of the San Francisco bay. The driver and the car that hit them were never found.

-2-

But that was long ago, when Michael Patrick Riordan was just a young catholic priest at Holy Ghost. It was years before he would complete his second doctorate which would earn him the tongue-in-cheek name of Father Doctor.

"You don't have to always call me Father Doctor," the priest would urge his young charge. "That's a little formal don't you think?"

But Sam did. The boy had a wicked sense of humor, even at a young age, and he delighted in the absurdity of such an overblown title for the only parent he was to have. Over time, it had become clearly a term of endearment. So much so that everyone in the neighborhood used the name and always would.

Sam's friend across the street, Lucia Winter, was often a guest in Father Doctor's house. She often compared the handsome, forty-seven year old priest to Clark Kent. This led to her playful conviction that the bespectacled and raven-haired priest harbored a secret identity.

"Where's your phone booth?" she would say.

"Hardly," Father Doctor would reply with a blush. "Do your worst. You will find no tights in this house."

So the years melted away. Sam's childhood was full of what might be expected: ups and downs, bumps and bruises. Until one horrific day, just like his parents before him, Sam was mown down by a hit and run driver. But unlike his parents, Sam survived. That day had changed everything and it had tested them both.

Father Doctor had been stricken with guilt and worry at the news. He was physically ill as he waited at Sam's bedside for the boy to move from critical condition to serious condition, and then finally to stable. It had been the longest two weeks of his life. Finally, Sam's green eyes had fluttered open and Father Doctor cried tears of joy and relief. He thanked God for his mercy.

But all was not the same. The right side of Sam's body was paralyzed briefly, and after much therapy and years of doctor's appointments and neurological surgeries, Sam was left permanently blind in one eye and with limited feeling on the right side of his body.

It was then that Sam's inexplicable torments became even more pronounced. Sam insisted that The Crackle – as Sam called it – was present *before* the nerve damage, before he had ever caught a glimpse of the huge, black car that laid him out on the asphalt beside his elementary school, driving away to leave him for dead.

It took many years before Sam would even mention anything having to do with The Crackle. It was only after he had grown to trust Father Doctor more than anyone on earth that he dared mention it. It was longer still before he dared mention the strangest part of the conflagration that sizzled in his head: it only happened in October.

But there were other odd things happening to Sam, too. There were his visions of ghosts, and his ability to see random bits of the future. These things too happened only in October.

Eventually, Sam would have to brace mentally for the coming of autumn. After many years he got used to it as much as he could. He had nearly accepted his uniqueness, but still he knew he could never accept it fully. In the end, he needed to confide in someone or else lose his mind completely. Only two people knew of his visions – of his contact with what should remain unseen. Only two people knew the truth of the boy his peers called Pumpkinhead, the boy who felt Halloween coming like a storm – a storm that raised every red hair on his head and rattled every bone in his body. Those two people were Father Doctor and Lucia Winter.

-3-

Sam's phone chirped in his pocket. A smile played at the corners of his mouth. It was Lucia.

"Senorita," he said into the phone, turning the corner from the hall and tugging the sliding glass door to the backyard.

"Sam," Lucia said, her voice spiked with alarm. "It's happening."

"What?"

"I was up in the attic. God, I hate going up there. Mom wanted the Halloween decorations down so I went up to get them. Long story, but I had to go back up because I forgot one of the dolls for Dia de los Muertos. The Catrina..." Lucia trailed off.

"You alright?" Sam asked, cupping the phone and sitting on the edge of a chaise lounge. She didn't sound good.

Sam eyed the two large pumpkins sitting on the patio table, awaiting the blade. Sam still insisted on dragging Father Doc to the pumpkin patch and carving the gourds every year. Sam considered it imperative, always had. He didn't quite know why, but having the pumpkins nearby as he listened to Lucia calmed him, made him feel more in control.

"Are you okay, Looze? You sound like shit."

"It came for me Sam. The doll, I mean. It spoke and it came for me."

Sam stared at the pumpkins on the patio table. He gripped the phone tighter. "You're not hurt..."

This stopped short of a question as he began to see something: Lucia flat on her back, dark hair splayed on the dusty floor of the attic. She had bled. The smell was like copper in his nose.

"I cracked my head on a beam," Lucia continued. "I was out for a bit. Allison is here with me. She found me. Mom freaked out and wanted to take me to the hospital. I told her it was no big deal. At least frozen peas are good for something."

"Hey, I like frozen peas," Sam protested. Lucia was okay, but it had been too close.

Sam could hear the rustle of the bag of peas as Lucia shifted the phone from one ear to the other.

Lucia lowered her voice: "It talked to me, Sam."

"What did it say?"

"It said..." Lucia fought back tears, "...it asked if I wanted to see Carlo again. It said it would see me in 'The Nowhere'."

"In The Nowhere? It said that?"

"Yeah..." Lucia confirmed, her voice soft, child-like. She sniffed.

"It said it was waiting for me."

Neither spoke for a long time.

"Lucia," Sam said, "I'm sorry. I really am."

"It's not your fault, Sam. We've talked about this. Just *knowing* you can't be the reason these things happen to me... A lot of people know you. Do you know how many weird things happen in the world? To how many people?"

"I make it worse though."

"You always make it better, Sam." Lucia sniffed again, a fortifying sound that marked the end of fear and the beginning of resolve. "This one freaked me out bad though. I didn't see it coming."

"Shit..." Sam said, chewing it over. "I don't get it. It mentioned Carlo? That isn't something The Woman in the Glass would say. That's evil. The Woman in the Glass is not. No, whoever that spirit was, it was someone else."

"Someone else?" Lucia's voice seemed far away. Although she had never seen it herself, Lucia knew about the woman who appeared to Sam in mirrors, in windows, the blue woman who screamed at him from somewhere far away. She had haunted Sam for years, but Sam had become convinced that whoever it was meant him no harm. The woman was simply trying to tell him something, and couldn't seem to do it.

Sam was right though. The thing in the attic was something else, or someone else entirely. It wasn't good. That was for sure.

Lucia's voice was shaky, "Then what does it want, Sam?"

Hold on," Sam whispered. He was being watched. He could feel it. He scanned the small backyard: a rusty gas grill, the table with the pumpkins – its forest-green umbrella closed and tied, flagstones underneath littered with fallen leaves. Above, a raven stared, perched on the power line that stretched across the sky in the corner of the backyard. Sam kept his eye on it. The bird kept his eye on Sam.

Sam continued into the phone: "I don't know, Looze, but I saw the cat again."

"Really? What did it do?"

"Same thing...stared and followed me. It's not here now though. I don't think."

"Maybe it's just hungry."

"I bet it is. For *what* I don't know."

They laughed without much humor.

"Hey, Sam..." Lucia lowered her voice again, "Allison had to take off. Do you mind if I come over tonight? I can't hold it together in front of my parents. Will you ask Father Doc if it's okay? I kind of need to be around, well...you...right now."

"Yeah. Sure. Ask your mom if it's cool if you eat over. I think we're having burgers."

"Yum. Thanks, Sam."

They ended their call, and Sam – feeling stronger than he had when he came home – went back in the house. He turned, meaning to pin the raven with a final look, but the bird was gone.

(hiding, you mean)

Sam passed the study. Father Doctor still hadn't returned from his "call". He knew there was no call. It was a sweet gesture, trying to throw him a bone, but Sam knew he was...

(a freak)

...more complicated than an Irish wives' tale. His physical limitations were bad enough, but they could be handled, and he did handle them, but in October things came up that only he had a name for: The Crackle, The Thinning, The Woman in the Glass – and any thoughts of living a normal life were put on hold. It was as if a radio frequency would tune in and he could hear...

(The Nowhere)

...another world, another place, another time. It was all of these things, really – none of which he understood. What he did know was that he would not be free from it until November 2nd or maybe even the 3rd. Then it would fade. Then he would get his life back.

Cautiously, he stepped into the office. The computer was still on, the screen casting its glow across the rows of books behind the desk. Sam dragged his knuckles on the cool wood of the desk as he slowly walked around to the chair.

He closed his bad eye out of habit to read the screen:

Celtic Mythology

Sam took a deep breath, moving the mouse pad to his good side. He scrolled down the page:

In Scotland and Ireland, a child born on Halloween is said to have An-dà-shealladh...

Sam mumbled the foreign words, sounding them out. He kept scrolling:

...translated as "the two sights": an ability to foresee events, an uncommon connection to the spirit world, or the ability to see what is otherwise unseen.

So it was true, Sam thought. It's all true. It is all because I was born on Halloween.

His eyes welled with tears as he stared at the screen. He sat there for a long time gripping the mouse as the pointer on the screen shook.

-4-

Sam needed fresh air. This time he left through the front door and sat on the porch. Bob Winter, Lucia's dad, had just pulled up in front of the garage across the street. Getting out of the car and smoothing his tie, he opened the back door of the Volkswagen sedan and hefted a briefcase from the back seat – a briefcase undoubtedly full of glossy brochures of monuments and tombstones.

Turning, Bob Winter happened to notice Sam. He waved. Sam waved back and watched Bob as he mounted the steps to the porch and was greeted at the screen door by Connie Winter. The two kissed, Bob sliding a hand around Connie's waist.

Sam wondered what his mother would have looked like now, or what his father would be doing for work. Sam's parents were forever frozen in time somewhere in their early thirties in a photo album on the living room bookshelf, an album that Sam didn't have much desire to look at anymore. The pictures never changed, new memories were never added. He knew the snapshots by heart anyway. Looking at them was like beginning some movie that started promisingly enough, but had a very terrible ending.

Sam was now lost in thought, staring blankly at the front yard. The shadows on the lawn were tall and thin, cast by the spindly trees. At the end of the lawn, a large, plump raven was sitting on the mailbox. It was staring at him. It flexed its shiny, black feathers for a moment, and then settled. It jerked its head once and looked at the mailbox.

"The mail..." Sam said dreamily.

The raven...

(wants you to get the mail)

The bird flew away as Sam got to his feet. He crossed the lawn, pulled open the creaky aluminum mailbox, shoved his hand into its recess and produced a wad of mail. Flipping through it as he walked back to the front door, he stopped and closed his bad eye and read his name on one of the envelopes. The return address read:

PENINSULA HOSPITAL

"Good," he sighed. "Finally." He threw open the front door to the house. "FATHER DOC! IT CAME!"

-5-

Father Doctor was at the other end of the hall, wearing the apron that Sam had given him last Father's Day. It read:

I WOULD TELL YOU THE RECIPE,
BUT THEN I WOULD HAVE TO KILL YOU

Sam thought it was particularly funny hanging on a Catholic priest. Father Doc – who had a better sense of humor than any priest Sam had yet to encounter – obviously thought it was funny, too. He had already worn it to a fade.

"Looks like you're going to make it to Ireland after all," Father Doctor said. "That's a relief. Why I didn't just go by the hospital and pick it up myself, I don't know. I had no idea they would send it by wagon train. I'll be right there; I have hamburger hands."

Sam tore open the envelope.

Ireland happened to be one of the three study trips he was able to choose from for his senior trip. It could have been anywhere – at least anywhere with a strong attraction for a Catholic school group. Luckily, Ireland was just such a place. Better yet, the trip fell within the week of St. Patrick's Day, making it the most popular choice of the year.

Of course it cost extra, and Father Doctor had to scrounge – his modest pay from his priestly duties was just enough to get the two of them by. It had not been an easy topic to bring up, but Father Doc assured Sam that he could go, that they would make it work and that he believed that nothing could be more important than to connect with one's heritage firsthand.

Sam suddenly felt very lucky, a feeling he almost never had. He smiled and unfolded the copied piece of paper:

```
Legal name: SAMUEL HAIN MCGRATH
Date of Birth: October, 31 1996
Time of Birth: 11:58 p.m.
```

Confusion creased Sam's brow. "Hey! I didn't know I had a middle name!"

Father Doctor overheard, and drying his hands on a dishrag, came into the room. "I didn't either!" Tossing the dishtowel over his shoulder, he took the offered piece of paper. He screwed up his mouth. "Strange. I suppose I never actually laid eyes on this before."

"What about when you became my guardian?" Sam asked.

"True. It must have been required to establish legal guardianship, but Monsignor Mullen arranged for all of the paperwork to be taken care of. At the time, my faith had been challenged by your parent's death. Your parents were good friends as you know. I signed the papers, but neither noticed nor thought much of it at the time. I hardly remember those days..."

Father Doctor ran his eyes over the names of Sam's parents. He felt far away, closer to the younger, more confused man that he used to be. Yet, it felt good to see their names in print. Somehow, it made them seem real again. He handed the paper back to Sam, his bittersweet smile spreading to a grin. "Well, looks like you have an extra name in case you don't like Samuel."

"Yeah, right," Sam said, shooting Father Doctor a horrified look. "Hain McGrath? What kind of name is Hain? What were they smoking? Was I named after underwear?"

Father Doctor raised a cautionary eyebrow, but whatever sternness he was attempting to level was being undermined by the mirthful twinkle in his eyes. "No, that's Hanes, not Hain. So, no, you were not named after underwear, you goofball. But I have to be honest, kiddo. That name isn't the best; I'm not going to lie to you. It's a sin."

Sam folded the paper peevishly and slid it back in the envelope. He looked up at Father Doctor who was still taming his smile with effort.

"Don't tell anyone about this," Sam said. The two stared at each other, daring each other to be the first to crack. Sam lost. He spit out a giggle that set them both to laughing.

A text came through on Sam's phone. It was from Lucia.

Lucia W   Oct 26   4:55 PM
Ready or not here I come.

-6-

"So, someone in your family must have had the name 'Hain'," Lucia said simply, taking a chair next to Sam in the backyard. "It's not so bad. Kind of cool, actually. Different. I don't know, it's kind of growing on me already."

Sam watched her suck on a sports bottle full of water. Her legs were bent, her feet resting on an adjoining chair. Her jeans rode up her athletic calf and her brown skin was set off by the white straps of her sandals. Above that, her long, dark hair pooled at the shoulders of a bright blue cable-knit sweater. But above that a pair of sunglasses was failing to hide a nasty bump that swelled from the top of her eye to the center of her forehead.

"You don't look so good," Sam said. "Father Doc could slap a piece of cold meat on that knot."

"That's a waste of meat," she replied. She flicked her eyes to Sam and then turned away, feigning interest at a finch hopping along the fence. She felt suddenly ugly.

Sam had seen her in all manner of indelicate situations over the years, not the least of which was the recent false fire alarm in her house that had flushed her to the curb at two in the morning with severe bed head, wearing a very old pair of dowdy pajamas. Sam had heard the commotion from his bedroom window and had come out to help. It had not been her finest hour. Still, she had plenty of vanity left. But what was the big deal? Sam was...

(just a friend)

Yes, but a boy none the less. It was always best to pull yourself together in front of a guy whenever possible. Her mother was from the old country and drilled it into her head, still believing decorum to be a good thing. But Lucia knew she had no choice but to try and get over it. She was just going to have to look like a monster for a while.

She chanced another glance at Sam. He was smiling roguishly. He knew what she was thinking, and not necessarily by virtue of his special gifts. After all, she figured she was pretty easy to read. He was turning away, nonchalantly, trying to make it look like he was oblivious to her insecurity. Now he was running a hand through his hair, hair that looked almost bronze in the shade, piled into tufts and spiked at the front. His pixie nose twitched. He was definitely getting cuter as he got older.

Lucia flushed. She settled her glance back at her feet. He was good to her and she was happy to be with him, especially tonight. She pulled again on her bottle of water.

"You're making me thirsty," Sam said. "Be right back."

Sam tugged the glass slider open and stepped into the dining room.

Father Doctor sat in one of the dinette chairs, staring straight at the wall before him. He was bone white.

Something was wrong.

Sam glanced to the right, through the threshold of the kitchen. The ingredients for the evening's meal were chopped, laid out, ready. Looking back at the priest, Sam suddenly became very afraid. Something had happened. Father Doctor looked far away, utterly lost, crushed by the weight of some consuming thought. His shoulders were rounded, his hands limp in his lap. Unconsciously, Sam grabbed the back of one of the dinette chairs, intuition telling him that he may need extra support, an extra something to hold on to.

"Father..." he began, swallowed and started again. "Father Doc? Are you okay?"

"Sao-wen, Sam," the priest said. His dark eyes haunted. "Sao-wen..."

"Sow...when?"

"Yes...Sam. Do you know what it is? Do you know what it means...Sao-wen?"

Sam's mind suddenly crackled with flames. The familiar smoke filled his nose, the unmistakable fumes of wood, roasting flesh and burning hair. It was the sound of a thousand fires, the sound of thousands of years of them. The crackling roar began to meld with a chant, a drone at the edge of hearing, a chorus of voices that were pleading for mercy. It rang through every cell of his body until he wanted to cry out.

Father Doctor removed his glasses and rubbed at one of his temples as he spoke: "It is pronounced 'Sao-wen', Sam, but it's spelled S-a-m-h-a-i-n."

"Sam Hain?" Sam's nerves began to squirm, each utterance from his guardian flaring the sizzling noise in his head.

"Your name," Father Doctor said numbly. "I figured it out while I was cooking. You would figure it out eventually, Sam. I know you would."

"What?" Sam asked, not sure if he really wanted to know the answer. "What does my name mean?"

"It means Halloween, Sam. Your parents named you after a pagan festival. We just call it Halloween now." The priest rubbed his temples harder. "I don't know...maybe it was just a coincidence..." Father Doctor looked up and met Sam's eyes, "but we both know it's not. Don't we, Sam?"

Sam was glad he had the chair to lean on. His legs didn't seem like they were going to work for much longer.

Through the window across the room, and from beneath a thick bush that pressed its dark fronds against the glass, the black cat sat, watching them both.

III.
Omen Of The Tiles

-1-

The sun had fallen into the Pacific Ocean beyond the hills of Colma. The globe light above the dinette was doing little to cleave the ecclesiastical gloom that had always been a part of Sam's home. Most of the time, it was a calming way to live, but tonight the shadows crawling up the walls of the house seemed to be a little darker, and a little too thick.

Normally Father Doctor's hamburgers never stood a chance against Sam and Lucia. Tonight, they were taking longer than usual to disappear.

"I overreacted, Sam," Father Doctor offered finally, picking at a yellow lump of potato salad with his fork. "It's a coincidence. Not everything has to have some ominous meaning. It's not like we're living in some Nicholas Cage movie or a Dan Brown novel." He laughed dully and looked up at the two teenagers. They reciprocated with weak smiles.

Undaunted, he went on, "For all we know, your mother's favorite great-uncle was named Hain."

"No," Sam said glumly. "You were right. My parents knew what they were doing. I mean, no one has that name. No one." He locked eyes with Lucia across the table, his face set in stone.

Lucia knew what the look meant: time to talk about what happened in the attic. She also knew that Father Doctor was having difficulty accepting a lot of what she and Sam had already accepted, and she felt bad for him. He was a brilliant man, but still a religious one, and no matter how much he respected logic, he would always defer to his beliefs first. What was happening to Sam, and what was happening to her with increasing frequency, was not going to be easy for Father Doctor to fit into a box, but it had to be said.

Lucia finally began to speak, keeping her eyes on Sam at first to maintain the will to keep talking.

The words came slowly at first, hanging in the air between silences that were pregnant with the absurdity of it all. But just like a confession, she kept going until she was lost in her recollection, telling the priest everything as her blood chilled all over again: how the paper doll's bare feet had sounded on the dusty planks, how it had smelled like wet, moldering newspaper, how cold its breath had been as it whispered in her ear.

Sam watched the two most important people in his life sitting across the table and grappling with the supernatural horror that he was contagious with. Guilt began to tug at his heart. He had dragged them all into this. They had to deal with him, they were committed. They had said so. He wished he could let them off the hook. He was tired of it all. He was tired of...

(being a freak)

(crippled orphan freak)

He was a liability, at best a nutcase, but at worst?

(a demon)

Could that be true? Was he bad and he didn't know it yet? Was his soul infected? He wasn't sure anymore. Just when he thought he had a handle on it all, just when he thought he was able to tamp down his oddities into tight holes where they would hopefully suffocate, they were always flushed out by a new revelation. This time it was a middle name that just so happened to be...

(an omen)

Maybe. Either it meant what he thought it meant or it just meant that his parents were world-class weirdos. Whatever the case, he felt like he was hanging over a pit that hungered to swallow him, hanging from a cord that was frayed and ready to snap.

Sam Hain...Sao-wen. Sure he had heard of it. There had just been a show on television about it. No wonder The Crackle had been bad while he watched it – so bad, in fact, that he'd had to run outside to clear his head.

Why Samhain was pronounced "Saowen" they didn't explain. What the show did explain was that it was a druid festival to ward off the dead, to appease the Gods with sacrifice, to light fires, and along with the smoke, to send prayers for mercy to the heavens before winter killed all things and extinguished all light.

And he was it. It was he.

And he had always known, hadn't he? But it still didn't make sense: How could someone be a ritual, a time of year?

"Sam?"

It was Lucia. She had finished her story and Father Doctor had reached out a hand, grabbing Sam's wrist – his bad arm, the hand that tingled. The warmth of Father Doctor's touch was lost, the ravaged and broken nerves still unable to feel all. Sam turned his weary eyes to his guardian, his friend, his father, not sure if he could mask his growing despair.

"Sam," the priest said, leveling his eyes at Sam, "this curse thing has gone too far. You were hit by a car. Your parents were hit by a car, too. Why? Only God knows. It's terrible though, it really is. You were dealt a bad hand. You were chosen to suffer in those ways, as we all will suffer to one extent or another eventually. It is part of the human experience and nothing more. Only God knows why they named you Samhain. Maybe it was simply light-hearted, or just some hippy conceit. Maybe it is supposed to commemorate the festival. Perhaps they just thought it was clever. I can't say, but it *doesn't* mean you are cursed and it *doesn't* mean you deserved anything that has happened to you. You can be a slave to your fears and differences or you can master them. In the meantime, give yourself a break."

Father Doctor turned to Lucia. "Lucia, you watched your brother die of leukemia. That is not easy for anyone, especially a fourteen year old girl. Weren't you fourteen?"

He shook his head with disbelief and looked back at Sam, wiggling the wrist he held for emphasis.

"I love you, Sam. God loves you. You are not some mystery that nobody can solve. Neither are you, Lucia. You have both been through a lot for as old as you are. You both deal with it in different ways. That is all."

"But..." Sam began, and couldn't finish. Father Doctor's face was open, sincere, and it prevented Sam's revolt. He deflated, his back clapping into his chair.

"Let's let it go for awhile," the priest urged.

Sam and Lucia nodded. Surrender slowly graced their faces with calm; their appetites suddenly returned, and they ignored the mystery for the rest of the night. They even managed to ignore it for three more uneventful days. Then, two days before Halloween, on a Friday that began like any other, the mystery would no longer be ignored.

-2-

Sam had spent the week growing more and more restless. His studies had always suffered in October, but this year concentration was almost impossible. It was bad this year, worse than usual. It was only by feigning illness that he was able to escape charges of indifference, daydreaming, or even worse: drug use. The priests and nuns eyed him suspiciously during his classes.

He was acting weirder – he knew he was – and it was getting harder to maintain some semblance of normalcy. The Thinning was starting in earnest.

He had always called this time of year 'The Thinning'. He didn't know where he got the epithet, but it felt right. The world of the living and the world of the dead were closer together, and whatever was separating them was...

(getting thinner)

He could feel it. He could feel it the way people can feel a storm coming.

Then there was The Crackle. That seemed to be worse this year, too.

But earlier in the week, while he was watching a varsity basketball game in the gym, hoping against hope that Holy Ghost would finally wipe the hardwood with Sacred Heart, he received his first piece of unwanted intelligence this year.

A boy with the name "Frasier" on the back of his jersey, a forward for Sacred Heart, was driving the lane and was almost certainly about to put another two points on the board for the rival school when Sam saw the tumor growing in the boy's head – saw it as clear as day – right in the center of his mind. It was a living, breathing mass and it pressed at the boy's brain stem, clenched like a bloody fist, writhing like it was eating the kid from the inside.

Frasier was fouled and had made only one of his two free throws before Sam had to leave the bleachers, shaking and sick to his stomach. Hitting the crash bar on the gymnasium's double doors, he stumbled out of the gym in a consuming fog of horror and headed straight for the bathroom where he promptly threw up his guts into a sink, unable to make it the extra ten feet to a toilet.

That was early evening. In the morning, Sister Katherine was placing geometry tests neatly on each student's desk when she approached Sam. She placed the test on the slick, varnished wood of his desk and breezed by, her habit grazing Sam's arm. Sam saw her veins, black and sticky, struggling to pass her oily blood to her sick heart. Sam began to breathe heavily, began to panic, and left the class. Again, he headed for the boy's bathroom and huddled in a stall amidst the foul smells and the bits of toilet paper scattered across the cold tile floor – alone. He cried for Sister Katherine. She was not his favorite teacher, but he cried for her anyway.

He could warn her, but he had tried that so many times and it did nothing but stir the pot, invite more scrutiny and make him crazy with guilt and worry. It had taken years to convince himself that God was in charge of death and not him, and that just because he could interfere didn't mean that he should...but it was a lonely struggle.

Yet another grim premonition was banging on the inside of his skull, and he had to deal with it: the nun would be dead within the year.

-3-

The Woman in the Glass no longer startled him. Long ago, Sam had stopped being afraid of her. She was as much a part of October as the chill in the air. When Sam emerged from the bathroom stall, he saw her in the mirror before him; her face, radiating her own peculiar blue light, screamed at him from behind the glass.

The closer Halloween came, the better Sam could understand her, but words never really came to his ears, only garbled sounds. This year however, she was louder than usual. This year, instead of her words sounding like they were coming through cotton, or from underwater, they were clearer – like the final feedback of a mountain echo. He peered into the glass, tilting his ear. Maybe he could catch a word.

Just one word...

"What's up, Pumpkinhead?"

Lenny Kidd approached the adjoining bathroom sink. Sam jumped, the woman dissolved, and he snapped his eyes to the reflection beside him in the mirror. He had not even heard the hissing of the bathroom door's hydraulic hinge or the approaching squeak of Lenny's sneakers. He had been utterly lost in the vision. He offered Lenny the best carefree smile he could manage.

Since their fight in grade school, Sam and Lenny had become friends. Lenny still called him names, but now that they were both seniors – ostensibly older and wiser – it was mostly just a playful homage to the past. Now the names were pure affection.

"What's up, Ox?" Sam replied.

"You sick, bro?" Lenny asked, primping his hair with his fingertips. Sam knew that Lenny was in the bathroom for no other reason than the simple fact that the guy had just as much of a chance of sitting still in a desk for an hour than he did of sprouting wings and flying to the moon. Sam thought secretly that it was a miracle that Lenny was going to pull off graduation. In the early days, he would have lost money on that bet.

"I got the heebie-jeebies, Oxman," Sam replied. "I'm going to bow out I think. I'm going to play dead for the day."

"Blow in my face, give it to me. Whatever disease you have, I want it," Lenny said. "Father Dunn is going on and on about Hemingway like he wants to hump the guy. It's getting creepy."

Sam puffed a laugh out on the mirror. Back in his grade school days, Sam could have never believed that one day he would come to think of Lenny as naturally funny, but it had happened. Lenny had grown into a hulking linebacker of a boy with an incongruous baby face that was now creased with exaggerated concern. Watching Lenny's comic muggings in the mirror, Sam's heart grew lighter.

Though he considered Lenny one of his best friends, Sam would never tell him about what he was going through – that he had just been carrying on with a ghost of some woman in the mirror. No way no how. It was just too risky. Sam would just have to do his best to hide whatever supernatural crap was happening to him around Lenny Kidd, around anyone at school for that matter. Lucia was it.

Sam turned to Lenny and stretched his smile. "Father Dunn knows a stud when he sees one, Ox. A jock like you may make him leave the priesthood."

"You know you're going to Hell for that, McGrath," Lenny said laying a hand on his shoulder. "I will pray for your soul."

Sam laughed as Lenny turned and left. Mostly he laughed from pure relief. He had not seen any terrible visions about Lenny. Maybe someday he would, and someday he would have to finally tell him. "An-dà-shealladh" the internet had called it, the "second sight".

It was October 28th. Three more days, four at the outside, and he would be free of it along with the phantoms and the constant persecution from some other plane of reality that he couldn't understand. In four more days the black cats, ravens, spiders, rats, the woman-who-appeared-in-glass and even the man in the moon would turn their eyes mercifully away from him again and allow him to get on with his life. Whatever they wanted from him, whatever dark and terrible secret was on their lips, they would just have to swallow it once the winter finally settled on Colma, California.

As he left the bathroom and headed for home he breathed deeply. The fall air had become crisper, the leaves all but shed from the oaks along the street that led to his home. Along the last of the chain-link fence that defined the sports field of the school, a wooden ghost moaned with outstretched arms and proclaimed:

HOLY GHOST HALLOWEEN CARNIVAL
A HOWLING GOOD TIME!
OCT 29 & 30

Staring at the sign as he passed, Sam felt a peculiar sense of importance. He sometimes felt as if he was the one throwing the party called Halloween, and he was the host of it all.

"You think a lot of yourself, don't you now?" he chided aloud as he turned away from the school and headed for home.

At the very least he definitely had a reverence for the occasion that he was certain that few people shared. He knew deep in his marrow that it was important that Halloween continued to happen. Carving his jack-o'-lantern every year 'for protection', dressing up to 'confuse the wandering dead': these things were as important to him as anything could be.

He did not know why he had always felt so strongly about this, why he didn't outgrow what was sometimes considered a holiday for kids. He knew better, but how? That part was trickier, but he knew misjudging the night of Halloween and being derelict in the sacred duties that the living were charged with could lead to chaos: a contagion released into the world that might never be excised or contained. Of that, he had always been sure...

Somehow.

Sam had watched Halloween become nothing but a dime-store holiday. His peers used it as an excuse to dress in a skimpy costume and attempt to hook up with each other. Sam knew this was a big mistake. Halloween was a living and breathing thing, and he was convinced it would wait until their backs were turned, their guard down, and then it would come for them.

It would come for them all.

-4-

Lucia Winter had a nightmare, another one about her brother. But she was sure that she had been awake, that was the worst part. She was sure of it.

She had opened her eyes, gripping her moist bedclothes and scanning the room for signs of the morning, the light that would come to her rescue and put an end to the pounding of her heart. But the darkness in the room was complete, the air still and thick as molasses. Her throat was dry. With a shaking hand, she reached for the water on her bedside table, and that was when she saw Carlo standing at the foot of the bed.

Her dead brother's small, bald head was just high enough to clear her bundled feet at the end of the mattress, feet that quickly jerked away. Carlo's eyes were dark and hollow, and they stared Lucia down with pure malevolence. Then the Carlo thing reached out a white, withered hand and began tugging on the bedclothes. It was freakishly strong, and it was tearing the covers off the bed no matter how hard Lucia's sweat-slick hands tried to fight back. It croaked a single word before Lucia could find the breath to scream:

"Nowhere..."

-5-

Scrabble had been a tradition for Lucia, Sam and Father Doctor ever since the two teenagers were able to put up a good enough fight. The priest won most often, but Sam and Lucia were no pushovers. Tonight, Sam and Lucia welcomed the distraction wholeheartedly. For some reason, this year the supernatural stuff was worse than it had been in previous years, for both of them. This year Lucia was affected like never before, and she and Sam were trying to stick together as much as possible until it all blew over.

Lucia wondered why the idea to spend the night at Sam's had never occurred to her before. I mean, it was not like anything was going to happen. They did have an extra bedroom, and she was on her last nerve.

Father Doctor had been delighted by the idea and offered the 3rd bedroom, apologizing as he cleared his books and study materials that had taken over the small room.

Of course, Connie Winter had raised an eyebrow and Lucia had to assure her mother that there was no "funny business" going on between her and Sam. Though, Lucia was convinced that if it had been anyone other than a priest chaperoning, her mother would not have been so amenable.

Sam looked at Lucia as she chose her Scrabble tiles from the box lid. She had already put on her "cozies" – as she called them – and was pursing her lips in concentration, her dark hair falling over her face and sweatshirt.

Lucia's stay was a good idea, and Sam wished he had come up with it himself, but he also knew the proposition would sound far more nefarious coming from a boy. Luckily, Lucia had little shame – and a good thing too, because Sam needed the company. He certainly wasn't having a better time of things, but he had to keep reminding himself that in just two more days his birthday would come...

(Samhain)

Then he would turn eighteen. It would be a big day. All Hallows' Eve would not only spell the end of his madness, it would mark the end of his childhood. Maybe then he could move on. Maybe then he could have his life back.

Now, as the three sat in Sam's living room, mugs of hot cocoa on coasters sending tendrils of warm chocolate air up their noses, Sam took a long, deep breath of relief.

"You're both in trouble," Father Doctor said, raking up his seventh and final Scrabble tile from the pile and placing it on his rack. "I should read you both your last rites."

Sam laughed, "You're going to be ex-communicated for that kind of talk."

Lucia chose the last of her tiles, her poker face cracking as she regarded it with a frown.

Sam chose his last tile and stared at his letters:

HMRTCAG

Sam had the letter "A". He would go first.

"I have an A," Sam said, waving the tile in the air. The other two did not challenge. Sam returned to looking at his tiles:

MCGRATH

A cool wind blew through his heart, and the room began to swim. He flicked his gaze up briefly. The other two were studying their tiles. Closing his blind eye to make absolutely sure of what he had seen, he looked back at his rack of letters:

MGRH CAT

Cat, Sam thought dreamily. He shot a glance towards the living room window where a stiff breeze was dragging the overgrown bush lazily against the glass. He looked beneath the bush.
Nothing.
Sam tried to shake the thoughts from his head, to convince himself that he was making too much out of...
(the tiles arranging themselves)
Numbly, he lifted the three letters from his rack – the tiles that...
(wanted to be played)
He placed them on the star at the center of the game board, Lucia and Father Doctor watching his hand.
"Cat?" Lucia spat with a grin. "That's the best you can do? You're going down, McGrath."
Sam wasn't listening. He could hardly hear her. He was watching his trembling hand as it floated above the overturned lid, moving through dreamlike air to scrape up three more replacement tiles. He placed the new tiles on his rack:

MGRH UIO

It meant...
(nothing)
Relief flooded him, replacing his cold blood with prickly warmth. He let his breath out. It shuddered slowly down the front of his shirt. He looked up at Father Doctor who had gone next, building "TORPID" from the "T" in CAT.
The feat sobered Sam. It was one hell of a word. Sam caught

Lucia's eye. Lucia looked as pale as Sam knew he must have looked, but only because Father Doctor had thrown down a whopper of a word. Sam had to admit that he didn't know it, but challenging Father Doc was always a foolish waste of time.

Sam glanced back down at his tiles.

"No..." he whispered miserably.

The letters had changed again, and fear roared through him like a passing train. He squeezed shut his eyes and took another look, but the letters remained. Now he could feel the blood leaving his head, and somehow he was able to register one additional and horrible detail before panic made thinking impossible: there was one extra letter that had not been there before. His mind squirmed; his mouth dried and fell open.

He knew this name, knew it from his dreams. It had always been a part of him, lurking in the darkest corners of his mind. It was the mispronounced, bastard version of his last name, McGrath, and all he could do was stare helplessly at the word printed on the bone-white tiles:

MOG RUITH

The last thing Sam remembered was the ceiling filling his vision and then darkness swallowed him.

"Sam!" Father Doctor cried, getting to his feet.

Lucia got to her feet, too. She ran around the table to Sam's side, and as she did so, she glanced at the seven tiles still sitting in his wooden rack:

NOWHERE

IV.
Digital Séance

-1-

A harvest moon had risen, a bloodshot eye hanging alone in a starless sky. The wind had kicked up, sending the dead, papery leaves skittering across the cement of the backyard beneath Sam's bedroom window. Inside, Sam stared blankly at the television.

"It took everything I had to convince Father Doc not to call an ambulance," Lucia said, "but I'm still not sure you shouldn't have gotten checked out. You looked...well...not good."

"Thanks, Looze," Sam shot back.

"Just sayin'..." Lucia muttered, nibbling at a cuticle.

"I'm fine, really," Sam said, "I'm embarrassed more than anything. I have never blacked out in my life."

Sam, still atop the covers of his bed and in his jeans and pullover shirt, lifted the cold towel from his forehead and peered at Lucia sheepishly. "Really, I'm not a fainter."

"It happens," Lucia offered. She sat in the stuffed chair beside his bed, also staring at the television without really watching it.

"Is Father Doc convinced I'm alright?" Sam asked. "What am I supposed to tell him?"

"I vote we tell him nothing," Lucia replied. "He thinks you were dehydrated. Leave it at that."

Sam let his head collapse back on the pillow and he slapped the washrag back over his eyes. "This sucks. He has to think I'm a loon. Might as well tell him what I saw."

Lucia shook her head, "I wouldn't do that. He's just going to send you to a shrink like he did last year."

"He might understand though. We need more help with this whole thing."

"And he might not," Lucia warned. "It's risky. Who knows? He might just draw the line at Scrabble tiles that rearrange themselves. Then he might really think you have a screw loose."

"He might be right," Sam muttered.

A silence bloomed and it made them both uneasy until Lucia finally spoke, "Look, he loves you, anyone can see that, but that's why you should protect him from worry. I mean, there is no way I'm going to tell my mom about the attic. Can you imagine? MAYBE Dad, but Mom? She is Mexicana to the bone. She does not want any part of satanic, ghost shit."

"It's not satanic," Sam muttered from beneath the washrag.

"I know. I know..." Lucia back peddled. "I don't believe it is either. It's not about the devil, but that's just an intuition we both have. But do you want to try convincing them of that. Both are dedicated to a very Catholic view of the world. If you are different at all, even if you're not hurting anyone, they assume evil before any other explanation. That's the problem with being so strongly one thing, one belief, it leaves no room for anything new or different...it doesn't allow for the extraordinary."

"I like that Looze," Sam said. "The extraordinary..."

Lucia smiled wanly. They sat in silence for a while. Then Lucia leaned forward in her chair at Sam who was still supine on the bed, and whispered, "I saw them, too. You don't have to convince me. Sam. I saw what your Scrabble tiles said."

"You cheated."

"Sam, this is no time to be a smart-ass."

"I disagree. This is as good a time as any to be a smart-ass. I got to deal with this crap somehow." He peeked out from behind his washrag, his tufts of red hair like a ruddy crown of thorns. "You saw them?"

"Yep."

Sam considered this for a moment and dropped his head back on the pillow.

What I want to know," Lucia began, "is how long into the game did it happen? Did you see it happen? I mean, were the tiles already an anagram of the word 'Nowhere' or did they just change letters completely?"

"WHAT?" Sam yelped. He rose up on an elbow, the washcloth dropping to the bed. "That's not what it said."

Lucia locked eyes with Sam. "What do you mean? I saw it. Plain as day."

"I never saw that," Sam said. "I swear. First, it was my last name. Then, it shuffled around and took the word 'cat' out of it and stuck it on the end."

"I was wondering why you would play that word." Lucia said to herself.

Sam continued, "Next time I looked...it said Mog Ruith."

Lucia stared at him, her face slack with incomprehension, her mouth working out some silent calculation. "The guy you dream about? I haven't heard you mention that name in years, but wait...that's eight letters...that's an extra letter."

"I never drew an extra letter. And if you saw "nowhere" then I guess the extra letter went away on its own."

They stared at each other's bloodless faces for a long moment, neither one sure what to say.

On the television, a vampire was hocking candy at a local drug store, proclaiming with a farcical Romanian accent that the bags of miniature candy bars he was offering were "full of monster savings".

"Lucia..." Sam began, still propped up on his elbow. He gazed through the window at the bruised moon staring back through a thicket of skeletal branches. "We have to do something...I have to do something, I mean. Everything wants me to. Everything is trying to tell me something...everything is screaming at me from somewhere..." He broke off in frustration.

"What are you supposed to do?"

"I don't know. That's just it. I have always felt that I was meant for something, that I was special somehow. I feel things differently. I see things differently. It's like I'm an observer and not really part of what's going on around me. It's always been like that. It gets super weird in October, but it doesn't just end next week. The weird stuff does, but the rest of the year I still feel like an imposter or something, like...I'm from somewhere else. The problem is, I don't know where and I don't know what I'm supposed to be doing and I don't know where to start. I feel lost." He dropped his head back on the pillow again. "It's frustrating, but it's lonely too. Very lonely."

"I'm here, Sam," Lucia said and swept a strand of hair behind her ear, holding him with her best look of resolve.

Sam appeared much younger to Lucia at that moment, an exhausted little boy who was punch-drunk, but resigned to a life of shadowboxing, his elfin face oddly serene with this new surrender.

Sam rolled over to gaze out of the window as he spoke: "I am not frightened anymore, Looze. Tonight was it. Tonight I decided

something: I'm going to control it. I'm not going to let it control me."
He looked back at Lucia. "Just look at the moon. It watches me. It
watches nobody but me. I know it and I can't run from it forever.
Something or someone is just beyond my reach, pleading for
understanding. I want to hear, Lucia. I am ready to do whatever it is
that I'm supposed to do. I am ready to be whatever it is that I'm
supposed to be. If I am not going to be an ordinary guy, then I guess I'll
be..." he paused, a smile playing at the corners of his mouth,
"...extraordinary."

Lucia lowered her head, smiled and looked back at Sam. He
wiggled his eyebrows at her. She rolled her eyes at him.

Sam sat up and they turned their attention to the television.

"Great," said Sam. "What's wrong with the TV now?"

"Oh yeah," she replied. "What's up? Is the cable going out or
something?"

"That's weird. You never see the picture stick like that. Usually it
just goes black."

On the screen was a very large, very bald man in a dark suit,
filmed from the waist up, blue sky peeking from behind his shoulders.
He was motionless, and there was no sound coming from the set.

"I don't even remember what we were watching," Sam said,
pawing the bed for the remote. "Wasn't it a Western?"

"I know we weren't watching *this*," Lucia replied.

"You are now," said the man on the screen, turning his red-
rimmed eyes to look at Lucia.

Lucia gasped and clapped a hand over her mouth.

Sam, his eyes wide as saucers, jabbed the remote at the
television and started hitting buttons. Nothing worked. The man on the
screen only smiled, purplish lips peeling back to reveal teeth as yellow
and jagged as candy corns.

"Oh no..." Lucia moaned from behind her hand.

Apparently satisfied, the man on the screen brightened, and as if
stoked by some off-camera cue, began speaking.

-2-

"Hello, kids! Has the Thinning got you down? Are you confused?
Well, don't you worry about a thing! Help is on the way!"

The bald man's smile widened into a ghastly perversion of

reassurance, a cold and predatory gesture that looked inexpertly smeared across his face.

The camera pulled back and marble monuments and headstones came into view. The man began to walk with his hands clasped behind him; the camera tracking his casual stroll through some graveyard. Sam recognized the place at once. It was Cypress Lawn - not the area of the huge cemetery where he liked to ride his board, but the big, sprawling part that lies across El Camino Real. Sam's heart began to hammer in his chest.

The bald man continued, that horrid smile still frozen on his face. Sam couldn't shake the thought that the man looked like a jack-o'-lantern in a funeral suit.

"You know, kids," the man said, "sleeping is a lot like death. Your soul is freed from your body and you can direct where it goes. Neato, huh? I bet you didn't know that, did you? You're both smart cookies, but I bet that's news to you. You're welcome. Don't mention it."

The man shot the camera a look before he continued his stroll. "Did you also know that when you're sleeping, your soul, which is much, much lighter and finer than your body, can pass through things? Like closed doors, walls, ceilings and...VEILS."

On this last word, the man's eyes narrowed and he looked at the camera again – his smile falling away to reveal a mask of pure hate. For a moment he stood motionless, staring at Sam and Lucia.

Sam, now at the edge of his bed, reflexively backed away from the television. Lucia was beside him and her hand had flown into his, squeezing it tight.

His smile now reaffixed, the bald man clasped his hands behind his back, and continued his mockery of a lighthearted stroll through the graveyard, stealing glances askance to make sure they were still watching him.

"Who in the hell is this guy?" Lucia whispered, trembling.

Sam licked his dry lips. "No idea..."

"Who in Hell?" the bald man on the television asked. "Who in Hell? No, no, no. You got me all wrong, kids. It's not Hell. Anyone can go there with a little effort. No, this is invitation only, real V.I.P. stuff. I'm talking about The Nowhere. And it waits for both of you. Come on by and stay awhile, won't you? You'll just love it! I know you will."

"He can hear us..." Lucia whispered.

The man stopped in front of a towering obelisk of poured

concrete. Sam recognized it. He had seen it many times. It was the tallest monument at Cypress Lawn. The man leaned on the spire and cocked a foot against the stone and crossed his arms.

"Take this monument for example. It was taken from Laurel Hill Cemetery in San Francisco. You know what else was taken from Laurel Hill Cemetery in San Francisco?"

Sam and Lucia looked at each other blankly.

The man didn't wait for an answer: "35,000 corpses. That's right! 35,000 piles of bones were dug out of the ground, scooped right out of the City by the Bay and piled under this handsome obelisk." He rapped the spire with his knuckles. "They were all kicked out of town. I guess they were considered a bunch of deadbeats. Get it? DEADBEATS!" The bald man grinned even wider at his tepid joke and then looked at the ground in a mock pout. "Rest in peace." A braying, sarcastic laugh erupted from the man: "FAT CHANCE!"

The bald man dropped his smile once again and looked back at the camera, shaking his head with steely sincerity. "All joking aside, kiddos, they don't rest. There will be no peace for them. In fact, they are pretty pissed off, as you would say. But that's neither here nor there. What you should be concerning yourselves with is the fact that The Veil that keeps them where they're supposed to be is getting thinner. Oh, but you already know this, don't you?"

He waited for an answer. Sam and Lucia only stared dumbly. The man shrugged and went on.

"There is one thing you don't know though: The Veil is thinnest where the dead don't rest. Do you know why? Well, I'll tell you why: because we *claw* at it. We claw at it, Sam."

At the mention of his name, the fine hairs on Sam's neck stiffened, his breath freezing in his lungs.

The man walked towards the camera until his sunken, red-rimmed eyes filled the screen.

"We claw at it, Sam. And make no mistake, whoever you think you are. We will claw at it until we get through."

The man peered into the camera, into the room, first left and then right. Sam flinched. For a sickening moment he thought the man meant to crawl right through the screen.

"DO YOU HEAR ME, YOU LITTLE SHIT? UNTIL WE GET THROUGH!"

Then, the screen went black.

-3-

The television lit again and showed a man in dungarees panning for gold as a man on a horse spoke to him from a hill above. The Clint Eastwood movie they had been watching was back on the air.

Sam swallowed hard. His hand, still holding Lucia's, was filmed with sweat, the blood pulsing through his palm.

"Well...that was different," Sam said, his voice shaking.

Lucia blew a steady breath into the air. Her voice was quiet, barely a whisper. "Have you seen him before?"

"No..." Sam said, still watching the television mistrustfully. "Never seen him before."

On the screen a cowboy on a horse was being targeted by a rifle poking through a pile of rocks on the ridge above. Sam reached for the remote on the edge of the bed and flipped the channels, pausing at each one, but there was nothing unusual.

A knock on the bedroom door made him toss the remote aside.

"Yeah?" Sam answered, trying to sound normal, but he felt like he looked, pasty white, and he had only seconds to put some color into his face. He took a deep breath as the door opened a crack, Father Doctor entering cautiously.

Lucia realized just in time that she was holding hands with Sam on the edge of his bed. Guiltily, she tucked her hand to her side and scooted away from Sam. It looked bad. It looked like they were about to commit some sort of carnal sin under a Catholic priest's roof. Her skin, stippled with cold fear just moments ago, was now warming with a blush.

Father Doctor was without his glasses. He was in powder blue pajamas, a robe tied at his waist. "How're you doing?"

"Much better," Sam replied. "You were right. It must have been dehydration. I'm drinking a lot of water." Sam nodded at the empty bottle on his bedside table. Just going to watch the end of this movie."

The priest looked skeptical. "You sure you don't need anything?"

Sam shook his head.

Father Doctor's concern drained away. "Okay, well I'm going to hit the hay. I have that big diocesan meeting tomorrow and then I have a funeral late afternoon." He made a move to leave, and then paused, distraught about something. "Look, I know you always get together with your friends for your birthday at the carnival, but..."

With a grimace, Father Doctor crossed and put a palm on Sam's forehead.

"I'm fine," Sam blushed. "Really."

The priest straightened, continuing his appeal: "But this is your big 18th birthday and..." He paused. He was choking up, biting his bottom lip. Sam began to smile uncontrollably.

(here we go)

Father Doctor was one of the world's leading softies. He was known to cry at funerals he presided over, weddings too for that matter. Not to mention watching baby animals being born on television. Forget it. He would be ruined for the evening. It took a moment before the priest could go on.

"I just can't believe you are turning 18. You will set aside some time for me? I would like to see you, make you dinner. I got a special surprise for you, too."

"Sure," Sam replied, laughing. He crossed the room. "Of course." They hugged one another tightly. "I'll be home at 6, I promise. We are carving pumpkins, right? Don't forget. I won't tell the bishop you are engaging in pagan rituals if you get your hands dirty this year – I mean, really get into it. We have to scare away the baddies."

"Is this blackmail?" Father Doctor asked.

"Absolutely," Sam shot back.

"Then, yes. I will scoop out that slimy...mess, but only because it's your birthday."

"It's always my birthday when we carve pumpkins." Sam reminded him.

Father Doctor ignored this and turned to Lucia: "Oh...and Lucia, I put some fresh towels on the end of your bed."

"Thank you," Lucia said as she stood and gave him a hug. "Thanks for everything."

The priest gave them a final look, a look that Lucia was convinced was tinged with just the mildest concern that maybe Lucia was not going to make it to her room tonight. As Father Doctor pulled the door shut, Lucia tried her best to push the thought from her mind. It was silly. Surely, she was the only one worried about such things.

She surveyed Sam, but he didn't seem to be phased. He was already on to other things, turned away at his bedside table and fiddling with his chirping phone. It looked like he was reading a text. He turned to look back at her. He was starchy white.

"Sam?" Lucia said with alarm. "What is it?"

Without looking up from his phone, he crooked a beckoning finger at her.

"What?" she said, rounding the bed.

"They're not done with us yet," Sam said numbly, his lips pressed into a thin line. With a trembling hand, he tilted the screen so Lucia could see the incoming text.

SIMON   Oct 29 10:13 PM
The Veil is thinnest where the dead don't rest.

-4-

The phone in Sam's hand began chirping maniacally. Texts were streaming in fast. His bad right hand cradled the phone and he tried replying with his left, but was only met with a bell that indicated an error had occurred.

"I can't respond," he said, gritting his teeth, "it won't let me. Man, they are coming in so fast!"

All of the incoming texts seemed to be from two people and they appeared with no associated phone number. Half of the messages were from "Simon" and the other half from "Clara". Sam knew neither of these names.

"Who are they?" Lucia asked.

"Don't know," Sam replied.

Sam scrolled back to the first text and they began to read them in order:

CLARA   Oct 29 10:13 PM
You are in danger.

SIMON   Oct 29 10:13 PM
Sleep is a lot like death.

CLARA   Oct 29 10:13 PM
They have me.

SIMON   Oct 29 10:13 PM

The Veil is thinnest where the dead don't rest.

CLARA   Oct 29 10:13 PM
You must come.

SIMON   Oct 29 10:13 PM
Your parents are here, Samhain. Come see them.

SIMON   Oct 29 10:13 PM
Your brother is here too, Mayan girl.

CLARA   Oct 29 10:13 PM
He lies.

SIMON   Oct 29 10:13 PM
They are here.
They claw at the Veil.

CLARA   Oct 29 10:13 PM
Help me.

SIMON   Oct 29 10:13 PM
Help her.
Her soul tastes like bugs.

CLARA   Oct 29 10:13 PM
We are all in danger.

SIMON   Oct 29 10:13 PM
Come and save her.

CLARA   Oct 29 10:14 PM
The answers are here.
Come home.

SIMON   Oct 29 10:14 PM
Listen to your mother, Samhain

CLARA   Oct 29   10:14 PM
Be careful.
It's a trap.

SIMON   Oct 29   10:14 PM
She lies.

CLARA   Oct 29   10:14 PM
I am the woman who talks to you.

SIMON   Oct 29   10:14 PM
She is nothing.

CLARA   Oct 29   10:14 PM
I am the woman in the glass.

SIMON   Oct 29   10:14 PM
She is the traitor's bitch.

CLARA   Oct 29   10:14 PM
I am Tlachtga, known as Clara to my clan.

SIMON   Oct 29   10:14 PM
Her womb is a fountain of treacherous witches.

CLARA   Oct 29   10:14 PM
I am the black cat

SIMON   Oct 29   10:14 PM
I am the black cat

CLARA   Oct 29   10:14 PM
He lies

SIMON   Oct 29   10:14 PM
Do the sacrificed fill your nose?
Do you choke on their burning flesh?

CLARA   Oct 29 10:14 PM
You must hurry.

SIMON   Oct 29 10:14 PM
Come and get her.
Come and get me.
Pumpkin
Head

CLARA   Oct 29 10:14 PM
Beware.
His magic is strong.

SIMON   Oct 29 10:14 PM
Bring the Mayan girl. Her brother rots here.

CLARA   Oct 29 10:14 PM
Beware.
The Veil is thin.
Simon can reach through it.

SIMON   Oct 29 10:14 PM
Bitch

CLARA   Oct 29 10:14 PM
Trust no one here.

SIMON   Oct 29 10:14 PM
The Veil is thinnest where the dead don't rest.

CLARA   Oct 29 10:14 PM
Laurel Hill.
The night of your birth.
They will let you pass.

SIMON   Oct 29 10:14 PM
Sleep and the dead will drag you to me.

CLARA   Oct 29 10:14 PM
You can beat him here.

SIMON   Oct 29 10:14 PM
You will die here.

The screen went black. Sam shook the phone. The battery indicator was empty and red, the phone was dead.

"Shit," he hissed.

On shaking legs, Sam stumbled to the dresser, yanked open the top drawer and pulled out a charger. His fingers were trembling so bad that the USB only skittered over the slick metal around the tiny hole as he tried to engage the plug. He held his breath and with one more deliberate attempt, shoved the micro plug into the phone. Spinning around, he crouched and pressed the power supply into the wall socket.

"No...no..." he cried at the phone, scrolling frantically through the blank screens.

Lucia knelt beside him.

"Gone," Sam said. "There's nothing here. It's all gone."

-5-

Without a word, Sam ran to the study. Lucia, following behind, pulled out her own phone and began typing furiously, her tongue between her lips in concentration. Both were afraid they would forget the names, the details. There was so much to remember, so much information they still needed.

Sam rounded the desk and wiggled the mouse with his good hand. Father Doctor had left the computer on. Sam sighed with relief as the wallpaper flickered into view: Fall leaves above a glassy lake.

What if Father Doctor heard them and got out of bed for some reason? There would be questions. Sam couldn't answer them, not yet, not until he could translate what he just saw. This was no time for a confession. The information in his head was brittle, and he could already feel it melting like tiny shavings of ice.

Sam looked over his shoulder at the hall. He pricked his ear for shuffling feet on the carpet, suddenly feeling like he was hiding in plain sight. Sharing a computer was usually not a problem, but at this point he longed for a laptop that he could use under the covers of his bed. It seemed like every move they made was making so much noise.

Caught? What was he about to do that required shame? But Sam felt ashamed anyway. Too much weirdness had happened too quickly; the last thing he wanted was to subject Father Doc to it and be forced to come clean. Yet, being this close to finally having answers filled him with such exhilaration that he doubted anything on earth could stop him now.

He organized his thoughts: as much as he wanted to know who Simon was, Simon had given him nothing to go on. Typing "Simon" into a search engine would be useless.

But Sam did remember one crucial thing that had flashed by his eyes. It was from the woman called Clara, the woman in the glass, the woman who always formed in blue light, screaming at him from deep within a mirror. She had another name. She had told him what it was. It was a strange name. She also said she was captured. Was that what she had been trying to tell him all this time?

"God, who is Simon?" Lucia muttered, still tapping at her phone. "I put Simon and Clara together to find some connection. There isn't one."

Sam bit his lip and thought. What else did he know about Clara? He believed her over Simon, that was for sure, and even though it was their first contact with the man, Simon had proved to be a foul presence. So Simon was not a good guy. Did that mean Clara was good? He thought so. Sam had come to the conclusion a while ago that The Woman in the Glass meant no harm. It was only intuition, but it was strong.

 Now, what about that other name she had called herself...
Sam typed his search:

TLACHTA

The computer responded:

Do you mean: Tlachtga?

"Yes..." Sam said. "That's EXACTLY what I mean!"
"You got something?" Lucia asked.
Check it out," Sam replied. He held his breath and read the first entry. It was from Wikipedia:

Tlachtga is the name of a powerful druid priestess from Irish mythology and a festival celebrated in her honor in early Ireland.

Tlachtga was the daughter of Mog Ruith, a druid from Irish legend. She accompanied him on his world travels, learning his magical secrets.

A hill bears her name in County Meath, Ireland, a hill associated with the Hill of Ward, and its celebrations rivaled those at Tailtiu. The major ceremony held at Tlachtga was the lighting of the winter fires at Samhain (pronounced Sao-wen). The ring fort built on the hill was associated not only with the Kings of Mide, but also with Munster as well. The site was known in the popular culture of medieval Ireland as a place where Mog Ruith's flying machine <u>Roth Rámach</u> *had been seen...*

"Wow," Sam said. He ran his tongue across his dry lips. He swallowed hard with a click that sounded like a lock's tumbler popping open.

For eighteen long years he had waited for a moment like this. The answer had been this close all along. The astonishment produced a buzz in his head, as if he were losing reception to reality as some far away frequency began to tune in. All of those years of doubt and fear could have been avoided if only someone had just been able to tell him that there were answers, that it would all make sense someday. No matter how unbelievable and hard to fathom those answers were proving to be, at least they existed.

As he stared at the harmless, one-in-a-million webpage that had always been just a mouse click away, he mourned for his younger self, for the confusion and isolation that marked all those years of his life. It all could have been avoided if only this information could have been imparted sooner. His life could have been different.

It would certainly be different now. Now, there was no going back. He was sure he had a lot left to learn, a lot left to know about what he was and what it meant, but the first tomb had been breached and he was ready to journey further in, where the light of understanding had yet to shine.

Although it was terrifying and unbelievable in a lot of ways, it felt right. His intuition had been validated. The self-doubt that had weighed him down for so long would be shed. He was a part of something bigger. There had always been a reason for his pain, and that reason was not just chaos. It was so much more. It was truth. It was his identity, and now he could finally own it.

As Sam swept his eyes again over the text before him, his vision began to refract with tears. "Oh, God," he said. He laughed with the absurdity of the idea and he winced at the certainty of it. He swiped at his leaking nose and looked at Lucia who was startled by what she saw: a new and singular expression lighting her friend's face: it was fear, it was relief, it was utter disbelief and it was pride.

"Oh God, Looze," Sam laughed again. "I think I'm a druid...I'm a druid in Catholic school."

V.
Day of the Dead

-1-

Of course, there was still the problem of 'The Nowhere'. Sufficient numbers of spirits from the other side of The Veil had insisted on its existence, but the name did not inspire confidence. Now Sam was charged with going to a place that alluded to being no place at all. How was that possible? Not only did Sam have no idea what The Nowhere was, he had but a vague idea of how and when he was supposed to get there. And although he had been relieved to finally have something tangible – a mission, a purpose – the more he thought about heeding Clara and Simon's call, the crazier the whole thing sounded.

Sam still didn't know who Simon was or why Simon was so keen on being hunted. This was unsettling, and there were zero answers on the subject. Sam had little choice but to push the problem of Simon aside for one that might have some traction. Sam was most concerned with Clara. For some reason, he trusted her – Clara, the ghost that had haunted him for as long as he could remember, the woman who appeared in glass, as blue as a gas flame and always desperately beyond reach. She seemed to be on his side. She had terrified him as a child, but now he knew that was unintentional. She was not only harmless, but seemed to be in some kind of distress that somehow affected them both. Sam now knew she was being held...

(in The Nowhere)

Sam knew he wasn't going to get to sleep any time soon. He clicked on his bedside lamp, sat up and stared through the window at the moon.

He could no longer deny that he was probably meant to find this woman. The connection had been laid out in the Wikipedia article; they were both druids – never mind that he didn't know exactly what that was. He certainly knew that he had never lifted a finger to become one. The internet equated a druid to a priest, but the internet also had to admit that next to nothing was known about who druids were or what they did. Sam knew even less, aside from the fact that the vocation would not go over well with Father Doctor, his school, or anyone he knew at Holy Ghost. Moreover, it was quite clear that whatever a druid was, it was soon to become a good ol' fashioned, Grade-A pain in Sam's ass.

Lucia was even more unclear than Sam about her role in all of this as she tossed and turned in the third bedroom. She was convinced now that she had some part to play, but why? All she had to go on were a few mentions of her and Carlo directed at her from the vanished texts. Simon referred to her as "the Mayan girl", like he was hung up on that fact, like it was relevant. She knew the Maya were one of the indigenous tribes of Mexico, but she had never thought of herself as one. Something about these ghosts knowing more about her than she did made her feel very outwitted, and that she didn't like.

Sam returned from the bathroom with a fresh glass of water and sat on the edge of his bed. One thought in particular needled him: Simon had texted "listen to your mother" after Clara had told him to come. What was that supposed to mean? Sam's birth certificate had just come in the mail, and aside from finding out that he was named Samhain – as if that wasn't enough weirdness for a lifetime – there had been no other nasty surprises on the form. Sally McGrath, as expected, had been the name written in the space provided as the mother, not Clara or Tlachtga, or anything else for that matter.

Sam got out of bed again, buoyed by his thoughts, and snuck down the hall to the office. He was not entirely surprised when his internet service provider went down and he lost connectivity with the search results mere seconds after the Wikipedia entry lit his face. He could still read it, but nothing was clickable. It was only a cached page. He chalked it up to more interference from The Nowhere, someone or something trying to prevent access to the answers he needed.

He stared at the woman's name on the page. There was no reference to Tlachtga being known as "Clara". The name must have been a nickname, and one known only to a select few. It wasn't as if Sam could blame her. Maybe Tlachtga – unfortunately pronounced 'clack-ta' in Gaelic according to the page – had been a pretty name in ancient Ireland, but it was quite the stinker in the 21st century. And he had thought "Hain" was bad. Sam winced at the thought.

Sam eventually turned off the useless computer, going back to bed to stare at the ceiling some more. He was certain that the internet was going to be a problem at the height of the Thinning. Clara had warned him that Simon could reach through The Veil, and he was using that reach to knock Colma offline. Or maybe he was just knocking him offline, and if that were the case then it wouldn't matter what computer he used. They would all be down.

So Sam was left with a choice, an absurd choice, but a choice that he had to make none the less. Should he try to gain access to The Nowhere through the methods these spirits had described?

(sleep is a lot like death)

(The Veil is thinnest where the dead don't rest)

Or, he could just let the whole thing go. But could he really? After what Simon had said? After the text that haunted him still?

"Do the sacrifices fill your nose?
"Do you choke on their burning flesh?"

That one would not leave him so easy. That one had been a doozy. It had chilled his bones and stippled his skin with goosebumps. That was when Sam dismissed all thoughts that the texts were a misunderstanding on his part or some practical joke. Only Lucia and Father Doctor knew about The Crackle. Sam didn't even mention The Crackle to the shrink when Father Doc coerced him into therapy last year. Although...

Sam's thoughts sharpened. He bit a nail.

He had made Father Doc promise not to, but there was still the possibility that the Monsignor at Holy Ghost had gotten wind of The Crackle. Maybe Father Doc mentioned it to gain some spiritual guidance. But even so, surely old Monsignor Mullen would never concoct such a plan to save Sam's soul from some perceived evil. The Monsignor was a kind old man whose only fault was that he was woefully behind the times. Sam was expected to believe that the Monsignor got his cell phone number, waited for the Thinning for maximum effect, and then began to torment him with texts? Sam would bet his left one that the man had never texted in his life.

No, a texting intervention from the clergy was probably even more absurd than the concept of a veil between the living and the dead. A veil that was being...

(clawed at)

Sam shuddered.

When sleep finally insisted on taking him he surrendered to it, and to the conviction that whatever was happening was happening for real.

-2-

In the morning he walked a bleary-eyed Lucia across the street. She had not fared any better last night, and she'd come to the same conclusion as Sam. They paused at her front door to look at each other, to commit afresh without need of words what they had decided over breakfast. It was crazy, it was absurd and the very thought of it made their nerves hum like a swarm of bees.

On Halloween night, when the Veil between the worlds of the living and the dead was at its thinnest, Sam and Lucia – God help them – were going to enter The Nowhere.

They both exhaled and gave each other a hug.

"See you at the carnival," Sam said.

Lucia nodded and watched him walk away.

-3-

Lenny Kidd's little brother, Jason, tapped Sam on the small of his back. Sam turned and looked down. Jason Kidd wiggled his crooked fingers and hissed through a pair of plastic vampire teeth. Sam recoiled with exaggerated horror. Jason's smile was wide with pride. His Dracula costume had been effective. It had even scared Sam McGrath, the guy his brother called Pumpkinhead, the guy that seemed to be all things Halloween even when it wasn't Halloween at all.

Surely Sam McGrath was harder to scare than any of his brother's other friends, yet he had done it. Sam had looked scared. Emboldened, Jason grabbed the hem of his nylon cape and drew a forearm across his blood-streaked mouth.

"I'm going to suck your blood," Jason said, his accent sounding unfortunately more Swedish than Romanian.

"Where's your brother?" asked Sam.

Jason deflated slowly, suspecting that Sam had only been humoring him. The costume wasn't working after all.

Sam raised his eyebrows, waiting for a response.

Jason lowered his caped arm and pulled the plastic fangs from his mouth, slurping on them in an attempt to prevent the accumulated saliva from drooling out of his mouth. For the most part, he was successful, except for one frothy tendril of spit that smeared a carefully placed stripe of blood on the boy's chin.

"He's on the Scrambler," Jason said.

"Nice costume, Jay," Sam said. "You scared me good. You got any more blood?"

Jason brightened, nodded and produced a tube labeled "Vampire Blood" from his black pants – obviously his church pants. Sam was tickled by the irony. He took the tube and drew fresh lines of blood on the kid's chin.

"There," Sam said, "no one will mess with you now."

Jason grinned wickedly, shoved the teeth back into his mouth and then ran away, twirling and hissing at the crowd.

It was a good turnout at the carnival this year. The campus was teeming with all ages, even some of the adults were in costume. Sam headed towards the Scrambler. It was popular, the line long. Sam saw Lenny sharing a car with another senior named Gina. They were laughing, weaving in and out as the metal arms above them whipped their car among the others. The weather was perfect, the sun mild. As he stood beneath the rotating Ferris wheel, a patch of sun strobing his face, he listened to the screams of joy. This was his day. He was thankful that he smelled no smoke, heard no flames crackling in his head. He saw no ghosts.

Sam's phone chirped with an incoming message. He tugged it from his pocket, surprised it was working. The thing had become so unreliable since being hijacked by Clara and Simon that he had all but ignored it. He glanced at the screen:

Lucia W.   Oct 30   2:21 PM
Stay away from birthday tent. Not ready.
I'm at the haunted house. I'm alone. Meet me?

-4-

Lucia stood at the corner of a mobile trailer covered in cobwebs and painted in faux, grey stone with black grout. She wore a flamenco dress of crimson taffeta with black fringe. Her hair was pulled back, a blood-red bloom at one ear. She gave Sam a tight, quick wave. Sam suddenly realized he had never seen her in a dress. She wasn't the type, but she should be. She looked stunning.

Sam approached, his lips curling into a devilish smile.

"What?" Lucia asked.

"You do realize that flamenco is Spanish, not Mexican, right?"

"I am multi-cultural."

"That you are...senorita."

A passing cloud moved and sunlight hit Lucia's eyes; her dusky skin like jewelers' felt setting off a pair of emeralds. Sam's wit failed him. He was now squirming in a tangle of confused feelings.

Lucia adjusted the flower in her hair: "Last month I decided I was going to go as Catrina, Lady of the Dead. That was until she came to life in the attic and went apeshit on me. That kind of put an end to that idea." She looked Sam up and down. "And what are you supposed to be?"

"Apprehensive," Sam replied.

"No worries. I have a plan," Lucia said, grabbing Sam's arm and pulling him around the side of the haunted house.

"GO MCGRATH!" came a voice from the crowd. It was a jock named Lars Decker, thinking a tryst was about to take place behind the haunted house.

Embarrassed, Sam grinned tightly, flipping him off.

"Ignore him," Lucia said, unflustered and all business. "I talked to my parents and convinced them that you were into the idea of joining us for Dia de los Muertos tonight. Now, I know you are going to be at home for dinner and presents and stuff..."

Lucia stopped to look around, checking for eavesdroppers, but they were alone. Only muffled screams came from the wall of the haunted house.

Lucia went on: "Obviously, we are not going to Lenny's costume party, not this year. So, after dinner, come by my house. We are leaving for Cypress Lawn at eight o'clock to go feast at Carlo's grave. Dad is driving. It's perfect. I've already stashed the blankets by the Laurel Hill mound, out of sight like you said.

"So, if you come with us you'll have a great excuse to be there. The way I figure it, the only way a white boy can hang out in a cemetery on Halloween night without looking like a grave robber is if you hang out with La Raza."

Sam coughed out a laugh, "Oh, you're La Raza now? The

repressed Mexican brotherhood? I thought your dad was Welsh and made six figures as a funeral director."

"Shut up and listen," Lucia said, socking him in the arm.

Suddenly they were both distracted by an improbable sight: Sister Christine walking by wearing a floppy witch hat.

"NOW I've seen everything," Sam whispered.

"You have GOT to be kidding," Lucia gaped. "Talk about progressive Catholicism."

They watched the nun go by, heading for the table where she sold pumpkin bread.

"She's feeling the spirit," Sam said, realizing that he was feeling pretty good himself. Not only was he turning eighteen, but he was on the verge of something big. Tonight, they were really going to do it, jump in with both feet. He was afraid, but it was a good afraid, a purifying fear, the kind that he suspected drove actors to leave the consuming shadow of the wings for the blinding glare of the footlights.

Sam leveled a look at Lucia: "Are we really going to do this?"

"What do we have to lose?"

"You don't want to know the answer to that."

They fell silent.

Sam said, "You know what I mean. It could be dangerous. Scratch that, it's most likely going to be dangerous. That is, if you even believe it is possible."

"I kind of do and I kind of don't" Lucia replied quietly, kicking at a loose stone with one of her shoes.

Sam knew what she meant. A part of him also found the prospect of passing through some mysterious membrane into another world completely ridiculous. He was eighteen. Wasn't it time to stop playing Star Wars and Harry Potter? But there was another part of him that was far hungrier, a part that needed to know for sure. Now it would be only a matter of hours before he would know which part was right. Either they would wake up in The Nowhere or wake up feeling incredibly stupid.

Sam frowned. "So...if we do go to Dia de los Muertos at the cemetery, how do we leave your parents and make it to the Laurel Hill monument?"

"How do we get away?" Lucia repeated. She considered the problem for a moment. "We will just have to lie. Your parents are at Cypress Lawn too, right?"

Sam nodded. He saw where this was going. "But, their plot is nowhere near the Laurel Hill mound."

"We have no choice," Lucia said. "You'll have to bring *ofrendas* for your parents and fake an interest to my parents in learning about keeping the vigil, learning the tradition. I am going to bring some extra marigolds for you."

"Marigolds? What are they for?"

"The smell of the marigolds is supposed to attract the souls of the dead, help them find their way. My mom said they used to scatter a trail of marigold pedals from the cemetery to their house in the village so that the dead would join them for dinner and not get lost."

"I would like to do that anyway," Sam said. "I mean, put marigolds at my parents grave." Briefly, his face was wistful, but it soon hardened with concern. "At some point we're going to have to go to Laurel Hill and camp out by ourselves. What if they come looking for us?"

"I'll tell them we're going to walk to Lenny's costume party after we visit your parents' grave and then walk home."

"Lenny's house is pretty far away. Are they going to buy that?"

Lucia blushed: "I think they will assume we are lying and that we just want to hook up. My mom is convinced that you are after me. She says she can see it in your eyes."

Sam laughed nervously, blushing to the color of his hair. "That's funny..."

"So...that's the plan..." Lucia trailed off, her voice becoming quiet. She played absently with the fringe on her dress.

"I think it will work," Sam said. "I think you are not just another pretty face. You're smart, too."

A tiny smile curled Lucia's lips as she produced her phone from her dress, glancing at the incoming message. She laughed softly. "Lenny said he's ready to spank you. He said we should head to the tent. So let's go party."

-5-

For most of the day, Sam was able to put all thoughts of The Nowhere aside. The distractions were many. He was surrounded by his friends for most of the afternoon. There was a big cake shaped like a pumpkin – some of which ended up on the walls of the tent during an impromptu food fight – and cheap, token gifts wrapped with good intentions. In short, it was a perfect day.

That night, Father Doctor made Sam bangers with peas and colcannon drenched in onion gravy, and another cake baked from scratch. After dinner the two moved to the living room where, confirming Sam's suspicions, a box too large to sit on the coffee table sat on the floor. Sam tore through the paper to reveal an HP Elite computer, monitor and printer/scanner. He hugged Father Doctor tightly, not expecting such an expensive model. Sam could not stop smiling.

"You're going to need it," said the priest, still in his clerics and collar from his long day at the church. He produced an envelope from his robes. The envelope had been opened. The return address was from Stanford University.

"What?" Sam yelped, fumbling the papers from the envelope, his heart leaping like a jackrabbit. "You've gotta be kidding me...!"

He had been accepted.

They both sprang to their feet and hugged each other again, Sam bouncing around on the balls of his feet.

"Sorry I opened it," Father Doctor said. "Bad timing if they said no. I didn't want a rejection to ruin your birthday. I had faith...but, you know, just in case."

"That's okay," Sam laughed. "You're right. That would have been lame." He sat down hard, staring at the paper. "Wow..."

His smile began to thaw. The financial aid package would not be here for months.

Father Doctor saw Sam deflating. "Don't worry, Sam. Just appreciate what gifts you have. If others are to come, then so be it. I'm sure everything will work out. I couldn't be more proud of you."

Sam's smile returned.

The doorbell rang and Father Doctor jumped up and headed for the bowl of candy. Sam snapped his gaze toward the hallway that led to the front door. Every time Sam heard the bell on Halloween night, he was warmed by a wave of relief. He was thankful for the costumed ghouls roaming the streets.

So important, he thought, more important than anyone realizes.

Sam could hear the front door creak open, could feel the cold draft that carried with it the faint smell of roasting pumpkin, the candle in their jack-o'-lantern slowly cooking the tendrils of meat that hung from its insides. The trick-or-treaters were not in sight, but Sam could see them as they flashed into the center of his mind. It was three girls: a fairy princess, some kind of pop star and a witch. The smell of smoke and the crackle of flames began filling his head.

Sam glanced at the clock on the wall, prickly dread surging through his body where only moments ago there had been nothing but giddy flutter. It was a strange brew, and the heavy rush made him swoon. He pushed his back into the couch.

At the edge of hearing, Father Doctor called "Happy Halloween" into the night. The sound of shoes scraping on the cement walk receded. The front door creaked closed and the door latched with a soft click. In the ensuing silence, Sam stared at the clock on the wall, listening to it tick like a bomb:

7:30

He had to leave in a half hour.

The cemetery was waiting for him.

-6-

Marigold pedals, like golden confetti, littered the grave of Sam's parents. He stood beside Lucia in the darkness, their faces painted as the sugar skulls of Dia de los Muertos: white with black eyes and nose and a row of skeletal teeth stretching from ear to ear. Lucia had abandoned the day's flamenco outfit and was dressed for stealth, as Sam was, in warm layers of all black. The sky was dark and starless. The bright eye of the moon watched them, its face streaked with clouds.

The McGrath plot was near the wrought iron fence that separated the graveyard from the sidewalk. Cars whispered by on El Camino Real. Beyond, faint cries of "Trick or Treat" carried on the chill wind. A few orange flickers from the neighborhood's jack-o'-lanterns lit spider-webbed porches and shuffling packs of giggling specters.

"Your mom seemed suspicious," Sam whispered.

"I know," Lucia said. "I don't think she bought that we were going to Lenny's party. There was no good reason to refuse a ride. Not much we can do about it now." Lucia paused, staring down at the McGrath's headstone. "I think we left too soon. I feel guilty. You know, leaving Carlo..."

"Yeah," Sam said quietly, looking behind him.

In the distance, beyond a gently sloping hill, he could see the candles and the makeshift altar at the grave of Lucia's brother, the two shadowy figures of Bob and Connie Winter huddled together in retrospection, huddled together for support.

"I was going to crack though," Lucia confessed. "I was so nervous about doing this. Still am..." Her words collapsed to a whisper, suddenly sure they were in way over their heads. Panic kicked in her stomach. She looked at Sam. He was quiet. He stared at the sky. In his skull make-up, with his jaw set and his eyes unblinking, he looked fierce. He looked resolved.

Lucia took a deep breath and grabbed his hand. "Okay, let's do this."

-7-

Ducking through trees, they broke cover and passed one of the cemetery's lakes, its waters shimmering silver in the moonlight. They were in the open now, there had been no choice, and if they were going to get stopped, it was going to be now. Walking briskly, their heads down, they headed for the next stand of trees. The trees were getting closer, but not fast enough. Their pace quickened until they finally reached cover.

Then they saw it.

The obelisk of the Laurel Hill Monument was etched against the sky, a bony white finger stabbing the heavens. It was 200 yards away.

They broke cover and ran to it, keeping low. They reached the spire and sat quickly, their silhouettes disappearing from the horizon. Their eyes were wide and alert, their dry mouths puffing steam into the cold night air. The grass beneath them was moist, soaking slowly through the seat of their pants. They held their breath and scanned the horizon. They had not been seen. They were alone.

Alone except for the 35,000 bodies below them, in the mass grave beneath the spongy grass. In a crouch, Sam approached the obelisk and read the inscription in a whisper:

AS YOU STAND HERE, OPEN YOUR HEART TO THE
PIONEERS. THEY GAVE YOU GREAT CITIES, A FAIR
FREE LAND OF MOUNTAINS, A BROAD SEA, AND
THE BLUEST OF SKIES. OPEN YOUR HEART TO THEM
AND TRUST THE BEST THAT WAS IN THEM ALL. AND
THEY WILL ALSO GIVE YOU WISDOM AND HUMOR

AND, ABOVE ALL, COURAGE.
FOR THEY ARE YOUR FATHERS

Sam ran a finger over the words, lost in them. A sizzle of energy pricked the hair on his arm.

"This is not going to be easy," Lucia whispered. Sleeping here, I mean."

She crawled to the low wall that cut between the obelisk and a mound topped by a stone Angel of Death. The cache of neatly folded wool blankets was just where she had left them that morning: behind a sapling and beneath a spindly shrub of impatiens.

"They're here," Lucia whispered around the wall. "Thank God for that."

Suddenly, Sam shushed her, his eyes wide. He indicated the nearby path with a jerk of his head and collapsed to the wet sod, face up. Pressing his body as flat into the grass as he could, he froze.

The night watchman was coming.

Lucia jerked her head back behind the wall. She was okay, but Sam wasn't. He was in plain view. She dared another peek. The man was approaching fast. He was slightly overweight, bearded and carrying a flashlight.

"Shit," Lucia said, pressing her back against the wall. Sam had forgotten that his face was stark white with makeup. If the man saw him, it would all be over.

Sam was lying on a slight incline and could follow the man with his eyes as he lay motionless and spread eagle, the cold moisture on the grass seeping through his clothes. The man kept to the middle of the path, passing no more than twenty feet away. The man wore a hooded sweatshirt. It read:

It's great to be alive in
COLMA

Sam did not dare to breathe.

The man passed so close that Sam could hear him wheezing through his nose, but the man's attention seemed to be occupied by something in the other direction, his beam of light bouncing aimlessly on the path at the man's feet as he scanned the far gates. There was noise in that direction, laughing, probably a group of teenagers. After what seemed like forever, the watchman passed and disappeared between two marble monuments in the distance.

"Get back here," Lucia whispered. "You're going to give me a heart attack!"

Sam got up, absently swatting at the grass stains on his clothes, and hunkered down with Lucia between the start of the wall, the tree and the cluster of foliage.

"No one will see us back here," she said. She tried to steady her voice, but it shook anyway. Spreading the blankets, she made two separate sleeping areas where it was darkest: in the shadow of the wall and beneath the obelisk that towered above them.

Sam checked his watch:

10:15

The exhilaration made it hard to breathe. It was as if he were an astronaut about to board a rocket. He wondered how he was ever going to go to sleep. He hadn't thought of that. Not only was he alert as he had ever been, but this was creepy as hell.

They were really going to do this. They were really going to sleep in a graveyard on Halloween night.

Sam looked at Lucia already snuggled in her blankets, her skull-painted face smeared with nervous sweat. He knew he and Lucia were no different than the early explorers whose bones rested beneath them. Sam could feel the charge from the souls under the squishy lawn where he lay, kicking softly like babies in a womb. They were...

(clawing at the Veil)

Sam's skin crawled. His heart fluttered in its cage. He rolled over to look at Lucia and they stared into each other's black-rimmed eyes.

"Happy Halloween," Sam said.

"Happy Birthday," Lucia replied.

They said nothing else; they only stared at the sky. They stared until their eyes burned and their lids grew heavy. Soon, they began to sink into a woozy quicksand of fatigue. It was an hour before their exhausted minds finally surrendered and sleep took them completely.

Above them, atop the stone wall and in the shadow of the obelisk, the black cat watched. It watched as fingers of dark fog reached for them from below, curling around their sleeping bodies until there was nothing left, until the two forms had melted like black ice into the sodden ground.

PART TWO
THE NOWHERE

VI.
Bone Yards of the Fringe

-1-

Is it sleep or just darkness?

Awake? Dreaming in black?

Or is it death?

Alive. Yes, he can hear his breath.

He hears a noise, like rain, but there is no water on his body, yet the patter comes from all sides. There is only the dank cold, tight upon his crawling skin as he moves.

Forward or back?

Up or down?

She hears the beating of rain on stone, but there is only dirt. The dirt doesn't end, it only parts for her as she glides through the cold silt. She is a warm knife slicing through some rotten cake. There is the smell of decay in the moist soil, the smell of old death: death that has fled this place, but has left behind its resonance to foul each grain of earth. She has smelled this before, in putrid rose water, in dehydrated meat.

He is now motionless. All of his systems are static. He is frozen at a point of suspension, at the overextension of some trajectory, as if weightless in the strap of a slingshot. He can sense that there will soon be a tug within him, as if he could collapse backwards and snap from this zenith to his détente, his point of origin where every cell within him strains to return. Or, he can reach forward, search for purchase and grab for whatever waits for him in the silent darkness. If he does, the means that brought him to this place will surely spring back from whence it came and leave him behind, maybe never to return.

"Sam...?"

It is Lucia's voice. She is here. He reaches for her voice. He claws...

(at The Veil)

He reaches forward, straining, flexing his fingers. As he does, he remembers. They fell asleep, they had to have fallen asleep, and now he's awake. He must be, because there is an awakening within him, his nerves alive and bristling as the earth caresses them.

"Lucia?" he calls through the darkness.

The powdered dirt rains from his skin, leaving only dank air to whisper across his face. Is he standing up or lying down? He'd lost his sense of direction, but his focus is returning. There are shades of darkness now where moments ago there was only black. His hearing is returning to normal. Yes, the sound of rain is louder now, it's closer. Yet he does not feel it on his skin, rather it is falling all around him on all sides, only feet away.

Light, faint light, midnight blue.

He is standing.

No.

It is not rain.

Lucia screams.

Sam stares in horror as the cavern before him comes into focus. Skeletons, hundreds of them, stare back at him, slowly gnashing their jaws. The clicking of their teeth sounds like the patter of rain. It echoes through the chamber that yawns before Sam's eyes, the sound filling the cathedral of luminous granite that rises to meet the stalactites that hang like pearly daggers from the dripping rock high above.

Sam's mind seems to slip a gear, and for the first time in his life, he attempts to run in two directions at once. Standing in place, his feet skitter on loose dirt.

"LUCIA!" he screams. He cannot see her.

"SAM!"

She is above him and to the left.

Sam flicks a quick look upward. His back is to a dirt wall, and ten feet above him Lucia stands on a thin ledge of crumbling soil. She is partially embedded in the wall like a half-excavated statue. This illusion is almost complete, complete except for one of her arms. It has worked free of the earth and is flailing wildly in panic, flailing in mid-air. Her face, still painted like a skull, is smeared and screaming.

Sam looks back at the skeletons. There's an army of them, rows and rows of them. Most are stripped clean of flesh, but some still have some...

(meat on their bones)

One of the tall ones in front seems to have a piece of its burial suit hanging from one of its ribs.

"HANG ON, LOOZE!"

The skeletons seem to be evaluating him, watching him the way a pride of cats would watch cornered prey. Swaying in place, hunched and with limp arms they stare: their eyes nothing but black holes, their yellowed jaws never stopping their methodical gnashing.

Sam chances a look behind him, a quick pirouette, but when he turns he freezes at the sight. The wind leaves his lungs as he sees the moon and branches of trees through the dirt, but the perspective is all wrong. He is standing, but it is as if he were lying down back in Colma, back under the tree by the Laurel Hill monument at Cypress Lawn. His mind swims upstream trying to grasp what he is seeing. The dirt is transparent and he is looking right through it, through it and upwards into the world he has left behind.

"SAM! BEHIND YOU!"

-2-

Sam spins around and claps his back against the dirt wall, facing the skeletons again. They stop advancing at once, freezing in place. They sway slightly from side to side and stare back at him. Sam can't help but flash on childhood games: Red Light/Green Light, Mother May I, Red Rover. Somewhere in his head the part of his mind that is breaking laughs. It is a crazy laugh, a laugh of someone who is losing control, and Sam doesn't like the sound of it.

Even their jaws stop their clicking briefly as Sam sweeps his twitching eyes over the dead, and in that moment he can hear the space before him clearly, the moisture dripping from the cavern's walls and echoing into darkness. The skeletons gained a few feet on him while his back was turned. His stomach clenches. He had only taken his eyes off them for a moment, but...

(they had been waiting for that)

They have all the time in the world to be patient, Sam's mind warns. They have eternity.

More clods of dirt rain down from above.

"LUCIA, YOU HAVE TO JUMP DOWN HERE!"

Fine, moist soil, like coffee grounds, sprinkle Sam's upturned face. Maybe he has misjudged the height. On second look she is a good fifteen, maybe even twenty feet up. Quickly he shoots a steely glance back at the army of dead, his heart hammering. Their gnashing jaws quicken for a moment, apparently frustrated that he had not looked away long enough for them to creep forward.

Sam listens for Lucia's reply, but there is none. Only a moan of despair escapes her. Sam sneaks another peek above him. One of Lucia's legs is now free of the dark earth, pawing at the air. Whatever ledge still remains isn't going to hold for long. Too much moist dirt is pouring onto Sam's head.

"We can't go back the same way!" Sam punches the wall of earth at his back. "It's solid! "You're going to have to jump, Looze! DO IT NOW!"

Lucia falls forward and Sam flicks a glance up to see her smeared, skull-painted face coming towards him from the dark above. He positions himself at the point of impact, arms outstretched, stumbling forward slightly. His mind registers one bit of good news: his forward motion has stuffed his sneaker in to a mound of soft dirt. Beneath Lucia's fall the ledge that had been crumbling from above has left nothing but fluffy soil in which to land. Still, Lucia was too high and she falls to earth hard, past Sam's waiting arms in a blur. Sam and Lucia crumple into a heap in a spray of fine silt.

The watching skeleton's jaws chatter excitedly. Sam leaps to his feet and fixes them with the fiercest stare he can muster, helping Lucia to her feet. She is slow getting up. She winces.

"Are you okay?" Sam asks.

"Ouch..." she says breathlessly. She takes stock of her body. "Yeah, I think I'm okay. Now what, Sam? Look at them. There's so many of them." Her voice trembles on the edge of panic. She grabs Sam's arm, her grip like a vise.

Trying to steady his own voice, Sam speaks from the side of his mouth: "Do you see to my right, at the edge of the cave? Look just below that rock formation that looks like organ pipes. I think that is the mouth of a tunnel. God, I hope so."

"I see it," Lucia says. "You're right. It might be." She strains her eyes, her pupils dilated to the size of dimes. "Are we dreaming, Sam?"

"I don't think so."

"I was afraid of that," Lucia says. "We're below the cemetery?"

"Something like that," Sam replies, still staring down the skeletons with his fiercest look. His heart feels like it might explode as it bucks wildly at his ribcage. He puffs his cheeks and blasts out his deep breath. "So let's head for that tunnel."

Lucia leans across Sam for a better look across the cave. "If it is a tunnel, who knows how far it goes or if it just dead-ends in a few feet. It's so dark. Sam, I'm scared."

"If you weren't, I'd be worried," Sam says. "All I know is that our choices are pretty slim right now."

Lucia stares at the rows of skeletons. "Why do they just stand there clicking their teeth? What do they want?"

"I don't know. Maybe it's good that we are painted to look like them, but they still seem to be waiting for us to turn our backs. We seem to be okay if we don't, but if we do I'm pretty sure they are going to come for us."

Pale light filters through the semi-transparent dirt at their backs, light from the moon over Colma; it casts the skeletons' tall, swaying shadows up the walls of the granite tomb where they dance and ripple across the toothy rock. The light also glints on a piece of metal embedded in the dirt at their feet. Lucia bends and scoops up the object. It flashes as she turns it over in her hand.

"Is it gold?" Sam asks, scanning the ground at his feet and he sees that the metal disks are scattered everywhere.

Lucia flings the object with a yelp of disgust, and panic shakes her voice. "No, it's not. They're brass buttons."

"Buttons from the suits they were buried in," Sam mumbles dismally. "Alright, that's enough for me...time to leave." He grabs Lucia's hand. "Keep your back to the wall, and don't take your eyes off them.

Crab-stepping, the two work their way across the cavern towards the hole in the wall, the skeletons turning their heads to watch their progress, but the dead take no steps forward, they only stare and chatter. Soon Sam and Lucia are positioned in front of the mouth of the dark hole in the wall, but upon closer inspection, the cave's entrance seems a lot smaller.

"The perspective is all screwy," Sam whispers through his teeth. "It's smaller than I thought. We have to crawl, or at least duck, but we have to do it backwards. If we take our eyes off them they are going to..."

(get us)

Sam swallows hard, trying to tame the adrenaline that is pouring into his body.

Lucia steals a glance at the cave opening, a dismal moan escaping her.

"Ass first," Sam says. "You ready?"

"Nope."

"Me either."

The two get on their hands and knees. There is just enough room for both of them to plug the mouth of the cave, side by side, like runners in a starting block.

"On three..." Sam says, "we crawl backwards and hope it leads to somewhere better than this. Not much of a plan, but pretty much the only one we've got."

Lucia only looks at him, her eyes wide. She nods tightly.

Sam takes a deep breath: "One...two..."

-3-

...THREE!"

Their palms slap the earth and they crawl backwards into the darkness.

Lucia can feel the rock above her hunched back, smooth and eroded as a set of molars, glancing against her clothes.

Keeping an eye on the entrance, they keep crawling. There is not much room. The way begins to narrow, and before their fear becomes unbearable – the gnawing thought of wedging themselves into a dead end like corks in a bottle – the rock tearing at their sides widens again. They both voice their relief to the darkness.

Lucia screams.

The indigo haze at the mouth of the cave fills with skulls as the skeletons lean over to peer in. One of them squats at the entrance, jaws clicking, a splayed hand on the earth, and cranes its neck for a better look. Then it does something so natural, so human, that any thoughts Lucia might have been holding on to of this situation being a harmless nightmare shatter in a bath of cold dread. The skeleton raises its other hand and shields its eyes, shields its eyes to peer in at them. It is evaluating its chances. It means to track them like prey.

"NO!" Lucia cries, crawling backward faster. "GO AWAY!" She doesn't want to look anymore. She squeezes shut her eyes and crawls as fast as she can. Jagged rocks, shards of shale, and something else...

(bones)

...cut into her palms and knees. Still her hands slap the earth. She doesn't care if she falls backwards off a cliff or crawls over bodies, she just wants to get away from them, get away before they catch up, before they...

She screams again, a hand falling on her shoulder.

"It's okay, Looze. Look."

It's Sam. It's only Sam and he sounds calm, his voice tinged with wonder. Lucia, still on her hands and knees, looks up. Sam is standing over her looking towards the ceiling, his skull-painted face glowing as if bathed in black light. She realizes that the tube of rock she had been crawling through has ended. She is in an antechamber lit green by some unknown source. She gets to her feet slowly, her breath catching as she sees them: thousands of fireflies fluttering high above them in a cloud.

Sam stares at a fly on his forearm. "Bottle flies, lots of them." He scoops it onto his index finger. "We studied these in Father Christopher's biology class. They are green bottle flies. These have become bioluminescent. They make their own light, like fireflies. They also eat flesh."

"Oh, that's just great!" Lucia's face is a mix of amazement and disgust.

"Dead flesh," Sam corrects her. "They only eat dead tissue. Their maggots were used in medicine long before antibiotics as a therapy. Don't worry. They have no interest in us."

"Still..." Lucia says, staring at the roof of the cave. "Gross."

Sam confirms this with an absent nod, returning his wide eyes to the swarm above. "I guess they've had plenty to eat down here."

Behind them comes the sound of bones scraping on shale. Spinning around, they stare at the mouth of the tunnel. They hold their breath, Sam crouching to listen.

"They're coming. Let's move."

-4-

Sam springs to his feet, scanning the new chamber. It is not as large as the first, but it is also not as isolated. There are two tunnels in the rock wall across the rubble strewn floor. There is also a third, halfway up the wall, accessible by scaling a series of boulders.

Sam jabs a finger towards the one high on the wall: "One of these caves must lead to the topside, and my guess is that one is closest to where we want to go."

"Which is where?"

"Who knows," he replies, running for the boulder. "Anywhere

but here. Let's go!"

"Can't argue with that," Lucia says, and runs after him.

Behind them, the rustling coming from the mouth of the cave grows louder, followed by the hollow echo of chattering teeth. Gooseflesh stipples both of them as they run.

Thanks to good sneakers and some easy handholds, the two scale the first twelve-foot-high rock with a few pumps of their legs. The second boulder is inclined, an easy crawl to its summit.

"Let's just hope skeletons are bad climbers," Sam says, panting. He offers Lucia his hand and she gets to her feet atop the boulder beside the cave's mouth. They take a moment to stare into each other's smeared skeleton faces for fortitude. Now they are almost level with the swarm of fireflies, the light bright enough to light well into the tunnel they are about to take. The tunnel is wide; it is tall, and it will be easy to run through. As they look down to see the first bony hand slap the ground at the mouth of the chamber below that is exactly what they do. They run.

The green light fades behind them, and with it, so do the mottled rock walls before them. Now, they are running in blackness, hands before them to protect their heads. They hear nothing but their own shallow breathing and the pounding of their feet on the packed earth. Finally a green glow begins to light the tunnel in the distance and a sickening thought breaks their stride: they have run in a circle. They are about to run into the bony arms of the army of dead, into their yellowed, gnashing jaws. Panic skids them to a halt.

But they can see that the light ahead is shining from an unfamiliar room, smaller and made mostly of dirt instead of granite. Convinced, they pick up their pace. The light gets brighter as they run towards the opening and into the new chamber.

Before them is a junction. Four tunnels line the walls, roughly the same height and width. Another swarm of bottle flies crawl across the ceiling casting a shifting, ghostly kaleidoscope of green light and shadow across the walls of the cave.

"That one," Sam says, pointing at one of the tunnels.

They enter without haste. The tunnel rises slightly, wends left and then right, uphill again, and then another room is before them. There are holes in the ceiling. Pale, natural light...

(moonlight)

...is breaching the chamber from above, stabbing the floor with silver shafts. But relief does not come, only a strange boiling in the air and the sound of quaking ground.

Lucia cries out as she spins to see the ground behind her erupt in a shower of small pebbles and dirt. A skeleton rises from the floor, soil raining from its ribcage. It faces them, its jaws gnashing. Sam pulls Lucia's wrist, and in the moment before they turn to run, Lucia notices the symmetrical holes in the earth walls. More skeletons are crawling out of them, tumbling to the dirt floor with a hollow clatter of bones.

"Catacombs!" Sam warns, spinning around. "These are all catacombs! This is not good!"

Running back to the junction, they choose another tunnel and run into its mouth. This tunnel is short: up, then down, and then an abrupt left. They stumble into another room and this time it is Sam who screams.

-5-

The skeleton who sits on the throne of rock before them is huge. It is wearing some kind of fur. It takes Sam a minute to figure out exactly what kind of fur it is. But Lucia figures it out almost instantly. She claps a hand over her mouth.

The pelts of large rats are draped over the collar bone of the imposing skeleton that sits before them, stitched together with what appear to be the rodents' own whiskers, and forming a crude cape that drapes over the skeleton's body. The dried-up heads of the rodents are still attached. Stiff streamers of wiry hair and cord-like tails flutter to the skeleton's waist as it begins to rise from its seat.

By Sam's calculations the thing is a good seven feet tall. Lucia is not interested in calculations though. She is shuffling her numb feet backwards into the mouth of the cave she has just come from.

There is a soupy moment of unreality that seems to stop time as the skeleton stretches to its full height under the glow of the flies from above, and just as Sam and Lucia's wits thaw and they turn to run, the oddest sight fills the corner of their eyes: the skeleton is holding out an open palm.

Sam's mouth is dry, his lips as cold and thick as two slabs of liver, but as he gropes for Lucia's arm he manages one word: "Wait."

Tentatively, they turn back around to face the skeleton. It is crouching now, still holding its palm in the air as if to calm them. Once it has their attention it slowly folds its hand into a fist with an index finger pointing at the ground. Sam follows the gesture with his eyes. At the skeleton's feet there is nothing but white dust. In fact, the entire floor of the chamber is covered in it.

Dragging its bony finger along the ground, the skeleton begins to write in the fine, white powder.

WELCOME

The skeleton drags its foot through the dust, erasing the word. It writes again:

I AM LORE

Sam and Lucia stand and gape, speechless. Both of them are thinking similar thoughts: How real this has suddenly become. How the fear tastes like a penny. How the complex smells of dank ground and ancient decay fills their nostrils with such singularity that they know they will never forget its perfume. How the green shadows on the wall dance through the tomb like the reflection of a swimming pool. How this long-dead person before them moves with such grace, conveying both curiosity and patience.

"Lore...?" Sam croaks. He swallows and tries again. "Lore. Where are we?"

Lucia is praying in a Spanish whisper beside him. She squeezes his arm.

The skeleton writes in the dust:

NOWHERE

Suddenly, Lucia knows what the white powder is. After years of pleading with her father not to tell disgusting tales at dinner about mishaps at the funeral home-although God knows she would certainly trade that problem for her current one-she had eventually heard everything she ever wanted to know about the nasty business of dealing with dead bodies. This powder under their feet was lime. It is what was poured into a grave after a hasty burial, to prevent the corpse from stinking and to promote swift decomposition. As if she had any further doubt, the lime confirmed that they were really standing in a mass grave. It was the kind of detail that a hasty nightmare would never have produced.

Suddenly she felt she was going to be sick.

The skeleton had found good use for the powder though, busy with his makeshift chalkboard. Swallowing her rising bile, Lucia watched the word disappear under the skeleton's foot.

"You can't talk?" Lucia said, surprised at the sound of her own voice. She regretted asking the question immediately.

NO LUNGS

"But you can think without a brain?" Sam asked. As soon as the words left his mouth, he realized he was trying to carry on a conversation with the re-animated bones of a dead person. His fear was quickly being replaced by incredulity.

I AM A SPIRIT

I CONTROL MY OLD BODY LIKE A TOOL

Sam was suddenly aware of the cave's mouth at his back. He turned and shot a glance into its dark throat. He saw nothing. He heard nothing.

The scratch of bony finger on powder made him turn back to Lore.

YOU ARE NOT IN DANGER AT THE FRINGE

"The Fringe?" Sam asked.

The skeleton nodded solemnly.

"But your friends," Sam continued, "or whatever they are...they are trying to..." Sam faltered. He wasn't sure exactly what they had been trying to do. The army of the dead could have rushed them both and there was certainly enough of them to do it. Either way, it was probably best not to insult a huge skeleton wearing a rat coat by jumping to conclusions. Sam looked behind once more, sure that he would see a flash of white bones advancing in the darkness, but he saw nothing.

He was confused. This was a perfect opportunity to spring a trap. The chamber was no more than twenty feet around, with no visible exits. If the skeletons back at the junction wanted to block the way out of this room, they would have done it already.

Sam's thoughts were stilled by the sound of more scribbling in the lime:

YOU ARE SAMHAIN

Lucia gasped. "Sam...he knows!"

The skeleton's foot swept through the powder and it wrote again on the floor:

I AM YOUR HUMBLE SERVANT

Sam and Lucia stared blankly at each other.

Sam licked his lips and said: "If we are safe, why do I feel your friends want to hurt us. Why do they wait until we turn our backs and then follow us?"

This sounded petty as soon as it left his mouth, but he didn't know how else to put it. He flashed on a number that the man, Simon, had given that night when he was on the television screen, that night that already seemed long ago and miles away:

35,000.

If they were still under the Laurel Hill mound-and he certainly had every reason to believe that they were-then there were thirty-five thousand piles of bones haunting these caves and tunnels. Those were odds Sam didn't like. His nerves were shot, and he knew Lucia's certainly were. More than anything he wondered if this skeleton who called himself Lore could provide a good explanation.

It turned out that he could.

Lore began to scribble:

THEY WANT YOUR CLOTHES

I TOLD THEM YOU WERE SAMHAIN

THEY WILL NOT BOTHER YOU

Sam and Lucia both screwed up their mouths in confusion. Lore crouched again and wrote:

THEY ARE COLD

Sam and Lucia still did not respond.

THEY HAVE NO SKIN

They both sighed with incredulity, Lucia speaking out of the corner of her mouth, "Ask a stupid question..."

Sam grimaced at the barb, and stepping forward he steadied his voice as best he could: "Lore, how do I get back to...my world?"

THIS IS YOUR WORLD SAMHAIN

Sam didn't think it possible for a skeleton to look confused, but this one did. It tilted its head quizzically.

"How do I get back through the wall?" Sam insisted, remembering the correct term. "The Veil I mean, how do we get through The Veil?"

Lore sat back on his throne of rock and folded his arms in a recalcitrant slump.

He was pouting, Sam thought. He had no intention of telling them how to get out of here. Now it had become a stand-off, Sam, Lucia and Lore saying nothing for upwards of a minute. They all just stared at one another, until Lucia sighed and said: "Fine, we will find our own way."

Lore bent down and scribbled:

I THOUGHT SAMHAIN KNEW HOW TO SAVE US

"Save you from what?" Sam asked.

THE NOWHERE

"I don't even know what The Nowhere is, or where I am, nothing!" Sam said irritably. "None of this makes a whole lot of sense to me. This was a huge mistake."

Lore stared, motionless.

"Is this Hell?" Sam continued. "Is that all this is?"

Lore shook his head.

"It's different?" Sam asked.

Lore nodded, morosely.

"You're bumming him out." Lucia whispered.

"Bumming him out?" Sam snapped. "We're the ones stuck in a moldy mass grave with no way out! And HE'S bummed?"

Lore turned his head, stung by the comment.

"Lore," Sam pleaded. "I have to figure out how to get back eventually. I can't live here, right? I'm not dead, at least I hope not. Look, maybe I can get you out of here too, but I can't do it running around in caves. You have to throw me a bone here."

Lucia groaned and ran a finger across her neck. Lore slapped a palm over his mouth, clearly appalled.

"Oops," Sam said. "Sorry. That was totally insensitive. Look, Lore, please...is there a top side to The Nowhere? We saw light in that other room and it wasn't made by flies, it sure looked like moonlight to me."

Lore nodded. He bent over and scribbled:

SECOND CAVE ON THE RIGHT

Lore gestured vaguely at the tunnel they had just come through, dismissively waving them away with a bony hand.

"You're kidding," Lucia whispered. "The second cave on the right? The only one we didn't try."

They turned to leave. Sam paused and looked back. The big skeleton sat hunched on the natural promontory of rock that served as his throne, pulling the coat of rat fur tightly across his body. His jaws chattered a few times. He looked up slowly.

"Sam," Lucia urged. "He's all sad now. Say something."

"Lore," Sam said. "Thanks. We will figure this out. You'll be okay."

Lore nodded and looked away.

They started to leave when they heard a scribble behind them:

GOOD LUCK SAMHAIN

BE CAREFUL

They know you're coming.

VII.
The Knolls of Ceaseless Midnight

-1-

Back to the junction cave they went, only now all of the exits were blocked. Moreover, there was hardly any room at all left in the chamber. It seemed that all the fleshless denizens of this place had converged on this spot. They kept a respectful distance however, making no move towards Sam and Lucia as the two entered tentatively. It was as if the skeletons only wanted to see for themselves the living beings from the world they once knew, to marvel at them as one would a rare and exotic species. Then, the throng of skeletons parted to reveal the tunnel Lore had told them would lead to the top world, the second on the right.

San and Lucia walked stiffly towards the center of the room. They looked around at the empty eye sockets of the skulls that watched them. Somehow the watchers conveyed varied emotions: sadness, hope, respect and longing. Maybe it was the wistful tilt of their heads, or the way some stood tensed as if in expectation, others slouched as if in despair.

Whatever they were trying to convey, Sam and Lucia were no longer afraid. Instead, it was a blend of pity and wonder that made them stop in their tracks to look at each of the dead in turn as they swayed beneath the ghostly green light of the fireflies that swarmed above. For some reason, the spirits of these long departed men and women refused to leave their bones. Sam and Lucia did not understand why, but it made them feel suddenly very sad. The skeletons all seemed utterly lost. As Sam and Lucia cautiously gained the center of the chamber, the teeth of the dead began to chatter softly, only this time it did not evoke rain, this time it sounded more like applause.

A skeleton standing nearest the mouth of the tunnel that lead to the top world stepped aside and swept an arm towards its entrance. Overcome, it walked hunched into the mass of its kin, bony arms patting its shoulders as they ushered it to the back of their number.

Sam paused for a moment to address them: "We're sorry. We don't know why you all are not at peace, but we will find out." He wanted to say more, but no words came. His own skull was crowded with conflict, questions screaming for answers, not knowing what he should say and what was better left unsaid. He hung his head, turned, accepted Lucia's waiting hand, and together they entered the cave that would lead them to the new world above.

-2-

Father Doctor rubbed his eyes, his vision starring. It was silent in the den, but for the ticking of the wall clock.

11:40 PM

He had not planned to spy on Sam. He had never done so in the past. Tonight had started innocently enough: a little bout of insomnia and a mild pang of loss. After all, his time with Sam had been so brief, especially for such a big day, but he had ended up in his study and one thing had simply led to another. If it hadn't been for the small sheet from his notepad sitting atop the pile of litter in the little wire wastebasket by his desk, his hope for a different outcome for Sam may have been preserved. From where it lay in the wastebasket, the hastily crumpled piece of paper had revealed only the letterhead:

HOLY GHOST SCHOOL
COLMA, CALIFORNIA

Why he had plucked it from the wastebasket he could not say. It was simple curiosity from a groggy man sitting in the dark, hypnotized by the ticking of his wall clock, a man who had found himself with idle time – found himself on the devil's playground, or so the proverb cautioned. But he had picked it up. He had smoothed it out on his knee. It was Sam's writing, scrawled absently the way one might write on a notepad while they were consumed by many thoughts at once. As the priest stared at it, he was forced to accept that the day had come, the day he had feared, the day that would put to rest any thoughts of either he or Sam ever being set free from this awful legacy.

On the page, in faint pencil, it read:

mcg rath

mog ruith...

Sam had been drawing conclusions, keeping things from him. Hadn't it been inevitable? He supposed it was. No thanks to that damned birth certificate. It had started all of this. He cursed the oversight and chewed the end of a pencil until he tasted lead.

So, the two were not going to a costume party. Dia de los Muertos? Since when was Sam interested in that? Sure it was a popular tradition south of the border, but that's where it should have stayed. It smacked of occultism even more than Halloween did. The dead should be left to the comforts of Christ, and they should especially be left alone tonight. The church had devised All Saints Day to compete with all of this, but the observance never did gain much traction, falling mostly on deaf ears. It seemed everyone wanted to play with fire tonight, and his son was right in the middle of the blaze.

Father Doctor slumped as hope drained from him as if by a puncture in his heart. This year was going to be the year. The boy knew too much. The puzzle pieces had filled in, and now something was staring back at them both, staring back with a hungry smile.

Yes, Sam and Lucia had made other plans, plans that made his stomach wring with worry. Sam was too close to the truth, so close it could lunge out of the shadows and bite him.

Raising Sam as a child of God had not been easy. The signs had tested the young priest's faith early on. Now his faith was in danger of being blown apart by the compounding evidence. There was no place for any of this under God. How could there be?

Now, as he sat in the dark, it was the memories of the boy's real father that chilled him afresh. He remembered the words of Sam McGrath, Sr. – the last words the man had said to him before the Rolls-Royce Phantom had run him and his wife off of the San Mateo Bridge only hours later. It had been in the confessional, and in October.

Father Doctor had listened with his blood running cold as the elder Sam McGrath raved and cried uncontrollably from the other side of the confessional's partition. "Father, he is after me. He calls himself a slayer of druids. He says we are the last of treacherous blood. Oh Jesus, oh Jesus...he can reach through the Veil, he *can* reach through it now!

You have to help me! After he gets me, after he gets my wife, he will come after you. He will come after all of you..."

The man's voice broke, wracked with sobs. Suddenly, his glistening face filled the confessional's mesh partition, his hot breath puffing through the grating, his swollen eyes wide with terror. "PLEASE, FATHER! You have to save my boy! He will come after Sam. He will come after my son!"

Father Doctor remembered that day in vivid detail: the smell of lemon-scented polish on the rosewood of the confessional, the chill coming off the slab stone of the church's floor, and how he had been compelled to ask the next question even though he didn't want to – didn't want to because the answer was not going to be good. No, it wasn't going to be good at all.

At that moment he knew with a sudden sickness of heart that he was not qualified to ease this man's delusions. This man needed a psychiatrist, not a young priest. Bracing himself, Father Doctor asked Sam's father the question anyway: "Who? Who is after you?"

"Simon," the man hissed, his eye still pressed against the mesh screen. "Simon Magus."

-3-

The tunnel before them narrowed and ended in a curtain of vines.

"Dead end?" asked Lucia, her voice plaintive.

"No," Sam replied. "Feel that?"

They stared at the barrier. Cool, night air was seeping into the cave from between the tendrils of crispy ivy.

"The way out," Lucia said.

Past that tangle lay a new world. They could see nothing past the vines, but they could feel it. They could feel the rest of this alien world waiting for them – feel its patient, panting breath. It was as if they were about to enter the mouth of a sleeping dragon.

The two had walked almost straight uphill in pitch dark to get to this place, and keeping an eye on the curtain of ivy before them, they tried to catch their breath. For a while their labored breathing was the only sound they could hear, the silence thick until a wolf howled somewhere beyond the vines. Somewhere close.

"Did you hear that?" Lucia asked.

Sam nodded, his lips curling with concern. The two stood unresolved for a long while. These last steps would be the hardest steps to take, the steps Sam imagined astronauts must face.

"Well," Lucia said, "this is it."

"This is it..." Sam returned, but he looked distant to Lucia. Something was wrong. Lucia figured it was the sound of that wolf howling somewhere past the vines – it was certainly not what she wanted to hear either. But on second look he didn't appear apprehensive. Instead, he looked as if he were trying to comprehend a private thought, work out the solution to some puzzle.

"What is it?" she asked.

"I didn't tell you," he replied. "I wanted to make sure it wasn't wishful thinking first, I guess." Sam flexed his hand, staring at it suspiciously. When he looked back at Lucia, his face seemed to surrender to something, and it went slack with revelation. "It's gone. The numbness in my hand, the numbness in my leg, and my right eye..." Sam looked away, overcome, choking on the last words "My right eye. I can see. Lucia, I'm...whole again."

"Sam," she touched his shoulder. "Really?"

"Yes. It's true." His face lit with joy, his eyes wet. He was suddenly giddy, his voice racing. "I am normal for once in my life!" he laughed. "Sure, I may be standing under some graveyard in some other world, freaked out that I'm going to be eaten by something or someone behind every turn. And sure, I just talked to a huge skeleton who has been dead for over a hundred years, but I've never felt this good in my life."

Lucia laughed, cautiously at first, and then with abandon. She hugged him tight.

Sam pulled back and looked at Lucia again, this time gravely. "Lore knows how to get us back, I know he does. He's a pretty bad liar. So, just say the word and we will go down there again and tell him that you want to go home. I could tell he was disappointed about me wanting to turn back, probably because he figured I knew something he didn't, some way to help him and his dead buddies. Of course, I don't, but he did not seem to want to believe that.

"Anyway, I don't think he would put up much of a fight if you wanted to go home. I think he only cares that I stay. I don't know this for sure, but it's a hunch. What I mean is...you don't have to do this. This has gone too far. I don't know what is beyond that..." He cocked a thumb at the cave's mouth and the tangle of vines. "But you do not have to follow me. I will still...

(love you)

(say it)

...love you."

"I love you too," Lucia said, "I love you too, Sam, but I'm not going anywhere. I'm staying. Are you kidding me? This is amazing!" She twirled, her hands outstretched. "I always knew something like this was going on, just beyond my reach. I've known it my whole life, ever since we were kids. Do you remember the first time you told me about The Crackle? How nervous you were? You thought I would call the men in the white coats!"

Sam laughed.

"But I've always believed you," Lucia went on, "and we've been waiting for this, this validation. I always knew you were something special. I wouldn't leave you now for anything."

Sam's smile melted into a mask of fierce determination, the face of a man going to war, and Lucia's feelings for him flared in her, hot and dizzying. Even with the chill in the air, it was as if she had been hit with a beam of summer sunlight.

"This is not a good place," he said.

"It might not be, but it wants us here. It always has," she said.

"We may not ever get back home."

"It's not our design, so who knows, but it let us in. It can let us out. Sam, Carlo might be here like they said. Your parents could be here, too. Look, all I know is that we never had much of a choice. We were always going to end up here. It was only a matter of when."

Sam nodded. That was certainly true. Here was inevitable—wherever "here" was.

He thought back to something Father Doctor said the night they all had dinner a week ago, the night he had discovered his middle name: "Not everything has to have some ominous meaning," he had said. "It's not like we're living in some Nicholas Cage movie or a Dan Brown novel."

Father Doc was not often wrong, but that time he had been.

"Then let's do it," said Sam, turning to face the end of the tunnel. He grabbed Lucia's hand, and together they walked through the curtain of vines.

-4-

Even from downstairs she could hear her husband snoring. Bob had been nodding off at Carlo's graveside and Connie let him for awhile, but then it had gotten cold. Bob couldn't stay up too late anyway. He had a funeral home to run.

"People never stop dying," he had mumbled when they got home, clomping up the stairs to bed.

Now, Connie Winter was alone. The trick-or-treaters had stopped coming and the pumpkin on their porch had been blown out.

A good thing too, she thought. The troublemakers would finally go home.

Lucia had carved the pumpkin, both Bob and Connie finding little reason to deal with pumpkin guts anymore now that their daughter was a senior in high school, but Lucia had wanted to. No, more than that, she had been adamant about it, claiming it was "important". She was sure acting strange lately.

"It's the boy," Connie Winter said to the gloom. Unable to sleep, she had made herself a cup of hot apple cider and had settled in the living room. She parted the sheers behind the couch and peered through the darkness, across the street to the McGrath house.

"*El diablo esta en el trabajo*," she muttered. Yes, Satan was definitely at work tonight.

Sure, the boy Samuel seemed like a nice enough kid on the surface, but he was hiding something. There had been a strange energy surrounding him tonight at the graveyard. She remembered looking at him once and the oddest thought had come to her. She didn't know where the idea had come from, but it had entered her head like some parasite and had lodged there, replicating itself, refusing to leave.

(he does not celebrate Halloween)

(it celebrates him)

She rubbed her eyes. She was tired. That made no sense at all, but even as she recalled the thought it felt accurate.

(it celebrates him)

What it could possibly mean she did not know. Regardless of all her punchy thoughts, the boy was still involved in something shady, that was for sure, and now he had dragged Lucia into it. Why was Lucia so obsessed with him? She wondered if they were having sex.

"*Claro*," she confirmed. Of course they were. That's what

teenagers did. And before she knew it, Lucia would be knocked up and married, a Mexican and Irish grandchild? Weren't the Irish responsible for this satanic holiday in the first place? She didn't want any part of it.

She glanced out of the window again. The pumpkin on the McGrath's porch still flickered.

And since when could a priest afford a Rolls-Royce? Yet, there was one parked in front of the McGrath house now, a big black one. She had never seen it before. Maybe it was a visitor – had to be. She let go of the sheers.

Why hadn't Father Michael – or Father Doctor as he was called by most of the neighborhood, although Connie refused to use the name herself, finding it a little too irreverent for her orthodox taste – why hadn't he seen that his boy was hiding some secret? He had to know that his boy was up to no good.

Maybe the priest did not know what she knew: there was a group of them, possibly a cult of some kind. Well, at least one other boy involved that she did not know, a boy Lucia had never mentioned before.

She debated whether to wake up Bob and tell him about this other mystery boy, but more than likely Bob would be cranky and tell her she was just overreacting. It was Halloween night. Teenagers were up to all sorts of things.

Still, Connie glanced again at Lucia's cell phone and her stomach panged with worry. Ever since it had chimed over 15 minutes ago with an incoming text she had been lost in conflicted thought. Connie had not wanted to pry, betray her daughter's trust, but the phone was sitting in the living room and in plain sight. It's not like she had gone upstairs to rifle through her daughter's drawers. And why had Lucia left her cell phone anyway? The girl would have the thing surgically attached if she could.

Because, wherever she was going tonight had made her nervous, nervous enough to leave her phone. A costume party?

Connie laughed to herself. Not likely.

She stared at the phone, the text still lighting the screen:

Simon   Oct 31   11:15 PM
Come, my little lamb.
We wait.

-5-

Father Doctor stopped staring at the phone and decided it was time to call in for help. He glanced at the clock on the wall:

11:42

It was late, but Monsignor Mullen would probably still be awake. Ever since seminary, Father Doctor had been amazed at just how little sleep his friend required.

He jerked up the phone and dialed the rectory. Crestfallen, his tired eyes glazed as he listened to the phone ring over and over. Suddenly, he felt very alone. Help was drifting further and further away with each ring. He was about to hang up when the Monsignor answered.

"It's me, Michael," Father Doctor said.

"Is everything okay?" Monsignor Mullen asked, alarmed by the tone of his friend's voice. Sensing the need for discretion, Monsignor Mullen hunched and cupped the receiver to his mouth, his voice falling to a whisper. "What's going on?"

"It's Sam. He went off with the girl across the street. I think tonight is the night. He knows about Mog Ruith. That means he probably knows enough."

A pause and a disapproving grunt from the Monsignor.

Father Doctor went on: "The McGraths even thought far enough ahead to leave him a clue on his birth certificate, just in case. The church admin missed it. Get this...his official name is Samhain, for the love of God. Sam Hain McGrath. It's as if they knew we would try and steer him away from all of this so they made his name the failsafe. Now, they are reaching out from the grave to undo everything I've worked so hard to accomplish. He is my son now, Danny. He's my responsibility!"

"Slow down, Michael. Where did he go?"

"He left with the Winter family."

"Bob and Connie?"

"Yes. Their daughter, Lucia, has some part in this too, or maybe she only thinks she does. They went to Cypress Lawn to visit the grave of the Winter boy, the one that died of leukemia. They celebrate Day of the Dead; the Winters   probably do it every year, but this time Sam went with them. He came up with some story about going to a costume party afterwards, but he's not. He's going to try and pass into The Nowhere."

Monsignor Mullen was silent.

Father Doctor continued: "I should have sat him down and told him what we knew. I should have armed him with as much information as possible. He is playing with forces he cannot possibly understand."

"You mean forces that WE cannot understand."

They both said nothing.

The Monsignor continued: "It's frustrating, I know. At least he is stronger now, much more capable. If he had pursued this when he was younger, less developed, his soul may have been in danger. Michael, we knew this could happen. He is armed. He is a good kid. His head is on straight and his allegiances are unassailable."

"You really think his spirit can pass The Veil and get back?" Father Doctor asked. He felt sick with worry, dizziness forcing his head into his hand. "My boy..." Father Doctor trailed off miserably, fighting back tears. "He just got accepted to Stanford. Now this crap..."

"Easy, Michael," the Monsignor soothed. "If any of us on this side are allowed to do such a thing as pass The Veil – and keep in mind we still can't be absolutely sure – it is Sam who has the ability. There is not much doubt about that. Maybe the Winter girl can, too – maybe only because she is with him. Either way, there is a reason for all of this. A gift like that would not be given without purpose."

The Monsignor paused and sighed, grappling with the significance before he continued: "This is the part we just don't know much about. As far as we are concerned, Limbo – or whatever you want to call it – has lost recognition from the Church, as you know. It is speculative. The Bible does not have much to say on the matter."

"Much to say?" Father Doctor asked. "You mean, nothing to say. It wasn't until we met the McGraths that we could even conceive that death was not a requirement to visit these places, to travel between realms freely. Someone granted that family the ability to do this long ago. But who, Danny? For what reason?"

The line was silent except for the controlled breathing of two men trying desperately to control their nerves.

"Sam has a far better chance than we do of understanding who he is and what he is supposed to do," the Monsignor offered finally. "I prayed that this could be avoided, Michael. I hoped that it would all go away, but I was wrong."

"You know what I can't reconcile?" Father Doctor asked. "Why does this situation even exist? Why would a boy like Sam, a good kid, a smart kid be saddled with such a burden? Was he born on the wrong side of God? Will his nature, whether he acts on it or not, prevent his salvation? Do you know how many times I have asked myself that? What if he is an agent of the Devil?"

"Do you believe he is an agent of the Devil?"

"No," Father Doctor replied. "No more than you or I. I love him like no one else."

"Then trust in God," the Monsignor said. "This is God's design. This is what He wants. This is what He has planned for Sam. Look, Michael, did you think the Bishop would have allowed you to take guardianship of Sam and maintain your duties as a priest if he didn't think that you were the right man for the job? If he didn't think that sending Sam out into the world, rudderless and unloved, would be a disaster? It would have been."

Father Doctor was silent.

The Monsignor continued: "Since when does the Catholic Church allow priests to live alone with children? Almost never. Back then the sex abuse scandals were just breaking. It wasn't easy. The public had their torches lit. The Bishop had to fight for you. He went all the way to Rome on this one."

"I know, I know..."

"You did what you were supposed to do. You were charged with a sacred task: to raise him as a child of God, to teach him values, to understand his inherited nature and love him anyway. The Bishop knew a foster home was never going to do that for Sam. That's why he chose you. He knew you were a special servant. You have helped him, Michael. You have protected his soul, fortified him with the tools God has given us. All of these things you have done."

"I was lying to him."

"No, you were giving him a chance."

"But...as you said, God decided on his nature, on his purpose. What good did I really do?"

"You are right. You were never going to change him. What you did influence is the outcome, only the outcome. That was all you need do. It is out of our hands now."

Father Doctor moaned with frustration into the receiver.

"It must be hard, I know," said the Monsignor, "but you have done right by him. All we can do now is wait. Only the dawn will end this, so pray for the dawn."

-6-

Sam and Lucia emerged from the cave and onto a hillock overgrown with vines beneath a starless sky. It was dark, but the moon was full and high. Was it their moon? Neither of them could be certain.

Quickly brushing off, the two turned in a quick circle, expecting new dangers, but they seemed to be alone. To the left: more mounds of earth covered with decaying vegetation. To the right: more of the same. A chain of low hills, each no more than 15 feet high – like tumors on some sleeping giant – stretched in all directions, rolling towards the indigo glow of the horizon.

Sam was about to speak when he was forced to swallow his words. They weren't alone after all. He put his fingers to his lips and Lucia held her breath to listen. They heard an all too familiar sound: clicking teeth. Spinning around and stepping back from the thickets of ivy and the dead branches of listing and rotting trees, they looked to the top of the knoll at their backs.

Hundreds of skeletons were jostling at the ridgeline above, their backs turned, their bones rattling as they crowded into one another. It was a hollow, musical sound that floated down the hill on crisp and still night air. Stepping back even further, Sam and Lucia saw what was preventing the dead's forward progress. It was an invisible barrier, a continuation of the one they had seen below ground.

With every mindless charge, the thin air before the skeletons only acknowledged their efforts with a mild distortion of rippling, concentric rings as if a breath of wind had blown across the glassy surface of a lake set on end.

And beyond this barrier of rippling air was a sight for Sam's restored vision, a sight that made them both hunger momentarily to quit all of this nonsense and run towards its promise.

"Colma..." Lucia whispered.

As if seen through an impossibly wide and tall movie screen, random bits of their home town – interiors and exteriors alike – formed a patchwork of shimmering images. They were all mostly familiar scenes, but as a whole they were completely out of context and perspective: an angel of death above a grave at Cypress Lawn cemetery, another famous marker at Hills of Eternity cemetery, the inside of someone's living room where the resident lady was reading a book in a wingchair. Strangest of all was the brightly lit parking lot of a Ford dealership on El Camino Real.

"Where the dead don't rest..." Sam said dreamily. "Those must be all the places where The Veil is the thinnest."

"Colma Ford," Lucia wrinkled her nose.

"Apparently," Sam replied.

A sigh of wonder leaked from Lucia's mouth and she grabbed Sam's arm. "They're trying to get through..."

As the two watched, one of the skeletons at the front of the crush bristled with ultraviolet light. It released its spirit through the barrier, its abandoned bones crumpling into a heap at the feet of its brethren who began gnashing their teeth faster as if celebrating this small victory.

Sam and Lucia watched the ghost as it swirled through the unseen barrier and down a familiar Colma street, elongating into the illuminated form of a woman, her mouth stretched in a silent scream of triumph.

"It was a woman," Lucia gasped. "She made it! So that's where ghosts come from. They come from here." A chill was working its way down her spine and she gripped Sam's arm a little tighter.

"I'll be right back," said Sam and he scrambled up the steep knoll for a better look, grabbing a bone-white branch for support. He looked down over his shoulder, his voice hushed: "So the Veil is not just underground. It cuts right through this place, from sky to core like an axe blade or something. It's a wall. I bet it doesn't have any edges or these guys would have found them." Letting go of the branch, he slid back to Lucia on the side of his shoes: "No sense in letting them know we are here. I know Lore said they have no interest in us, but just in case."

"You think we could just walk through The Veil?" Lucia asked.

"I don't know. Do you want to?"

"No," Lucia said, biting her lip. "Not yet at least. We are here – so far so good. We should figure out why we were even let in."

"Agreed," Sam said.

They turned around to plot a course. It was dark, but they took note of what they could: more knolls topped with trees that scratched the night sky with barren branches. Little valleys between them filled with narrow paths that zigged and zagged amongst crispy bushes and brambles.

They kept low and threaded their way among the hills until they were out of sight of the skeletons, out of range of their rattling bones and clicking teeth. Sam paused to remove his cell phone from his pants pocket. He held it up to his face. He turned it to Lucia. "It doesn't work."

"Not surprised. This is a dead zone."

"Good one, skull face," Sam said.

Lucia's painted face smiled back at him.

"Oh wait!" Sam went on, "Thank God. Some of the apps work, like the flashlight." He flashed the light briefly. "I'll save the battery. We may need it later."

Lucia pawed at her own pants. "Shit. I left mine at home. I guess I'm not surprised. I had a lot on my mind."

Sam shoved the phone back into his pocket and they continued walking. Rounding another short hill, a "U" shaped valley stretched before them, its ridges crowned by birch trees, naked and white, their scraggly branches etched against the moonlit sky.

"Ouch," Lucia kicked something and stumbled.

"What is it?" Sam asked.

Lucia crouched and then looked up at Sam: "Pumpkins!"

Sam focused on the dark, undulating valley floor. Scores of plump gourds littered the dell, their stems still attached to thick, snaking vines. The two walked in wonder, side by side through the vast pumpkin patch, marveling at their discovery until Sam paused to look back.

Far away, like waving blades of white grass, the skeletons on the horizon still lined the crest of the far away hill. A duplicate full moon...

(the real moon)

(their moon)

...hung in Colma's sky beyond The Veil, and Sam suddenly felt very far from home. But he turned his back on it and continued walking, threading between the pumpkins until they reached the far side of the valley. It seemed to be a dead end, or at least there was no obvious path. They would have to go straight up the incline before them, a slope choked with prickly thistles.

As they caught their breath, Sam said, "I don't know where to go, I don't want to get lost. We should wait until it's not so dark."

The voice from behind them froze the two where they stood, "It's always dark here."

The voice sounded like a stone slab being pushed off the top of a crypt, rough and gritty, and it made the fine hairs on the back of their necks dance. When it came again it was much closer, and it had fallen to a whisper, "Dawn will never come to this place."

VIII.
Jack of the Lantern

-1-

Footfalls on dead, crunchy leaves were approaching from behind. Turning slowly, the first thing they saw was the pumpkin: a glowing jack-o'-lantern floating at the level of their eyes, its face carved into a broad, toothy grin. It took a moment for them to realize that it wasn't floating at all, but was being carried in some kind of contraption. Wrought iron chains held the grinning pumpkin as it hung from the top of a long, black staff. With a crunch, the owner of this lantern planted the staff into the pile of dead leaves at his feet and leaned forward, the reddish light from the pumpkin streaking his face.

"You have been minglin' with the Skinnies," the man said. His accent was thick, unmistakably Irish. "You even look like a pair of 'em."

The light danced freakishly across the man's face, the chains holding the jack-o'-lantern still swaying. The man was impossibly old. The sinewy tendons in his craned neck were covered with stretched skin that looked like bleached leather. His beady, cataract-clouded eyes flicked between Sam and Lucia, and as if enjoying their reaction, the man offered them a grin that rivaled the one he had carved in the gourd: toothy, crooked and yellow. A dingy pork pie hat was crushed on his head and his wiry white hair sprayed from under it in all directions.

"Well?" the man asked.

"What?" Sam managed. He and Lucia stepped back, Sam stumbling into the hillside.

"You've been fraternizing with the Skinnies," the man said again, "and you look like 'em, too."

Sam and Lucia looked at each other. Although their makeup was smeared, they still looked like they were attempting to pass themselves off as skeletons. Was it the worst thing they could have done?

"It's...just make-up," Lucia said.

"I know it's make-up," the man spat, "I ain't stupid, ya'know. Well, I might be, but you ain't privy to such information as of yet, are ya'?"

They both shook their heads.

"Who are you?" Sam asked.

The man cackled. "I was wondering how long ya' would bug at me before yer curiosity worked those painted lips of yers."

He walked out into the pool of light cast by his pumpkin lantern and thrust out a hand. "They call me Jack o' the Lantern."

Extending from the frayed cuff of the man's coat was a gnarled arm that looked like a tree root. At the end of it was a claw-like hand, human, but worn to the bone, parchment-like skin stretched around it. The course lines on the man's face deepened as he frowned, awaiting a handshake.

"Oh, come on," Jack said, "there are a lot of things that will bite ya' out here, I can assure ya, but I ain't one of 'em."

Sam tentatively offered his hand. "My name is..."

"I know," Jack interrupted, gripping Sam's hand and giving it a pump. "Oh, I know who ya' be, Samhain, and I am at your service." He doffed his cap and patted it back onto his tangle of hair.

Sam looked confused.

"But where are ya' manners?" Jack continued. "Does your pretty little wench have a name?"

"Wench?" Lucia railed. She turned to Sam and whispered: "No he didn't just say that."

"Oh relax, lassie," Jack said, winking at Sam. "I mean no disrespect, Samhain." He dropped his voice to a confiding whisper and leaned into Sam. "I understand that your women have become quite a handful. My condolences, lad."

"Watch it old man," Lucia said.

"OHH!" Jack cackled and danced a brief jig. "That bird's got the spirit, don't she just? I know I'm mingin', but it ain't no fault of me own. I'm rotten through and through, I am."

Lucia looked at Sam again, her eyebrow cocked defiantly. It was clear that her patience was getting thinner than The Veil.

"Look," Sam reasoned, "we don't want any trouble. We are only passing through. We aren't staying."

Jack of the Lantern peered at them, his eyes glittering with amusement. "That's what you think."

-2-

A wolf howled close by, very close by. Slowly, they cocked their heads in the direction of the sound and peered through the dark, listening intensely: a snapping branch, the distant crunch of dead leaves. Then, on a knoll across the dell the moon shone on a large wolf strobing between the white trunks of barren birch trees, its long, red tongue lolling from its mouth. As it loped, it swung its heavy head to glare at them, eyes flashing moonlight before it disappeared down the far side of the hill with a crash of brush.

Lucia moaned quietly, a dismal sound, and Sam suddenly regretted subjecting her to any of this. In fact, he was becoming increasingly unsure by the moment whether he should have subjected himself to any of this. The wolf was big – bigger than he thought a wolf could get – and now it had seen them. Sam knew a little about how wolves worked. The wolf would call his pack. Then, the pack would come and stealthily surround them. And that was about as far ahead as he wanted to think.

Lucia resumed, trying not to appear shaken in front of the stranger: "Are you going to stop us from leaving? Is that what you mean?"

"You got me all wrong, Lass," Jack said. "I'm here to help."

"I do have a name," Lucia said, and she told him.

"What kind of name is that?" the man asked, screwing up his face.

Lucia looked stung: "I'm Mexican. The name came from Rome, to Southern Spain to Mexico. It means 'Light', as if you care. You could use a little around here."

Jack only stared at her. Lecherously, Lucia thought.

Lucia folded her arms and looked away. "So, are we going to small talk out here in the open until we end up as wolf shit or do you really plan on helping us like you say?"

Sam gaped at her. His eyes were wide, suggesting caution. She was wound up. Sam had seen this many times before. This was how she sometimes dealt with fear.

Lucia was on a roll, her hands on her hips: "In case you didn't notice – which I find hard to believe – a wolf the size of a delivery van is circling us at the end of this pumpkin patch. You live here right? Is it going to eat us? Are we just going to stand here in the dark and wait for it to call for backup and a wine list?"

Jack looked at Sam for guidance, but Sam only shrugged.

"Come with me," Jack croaked, wrenching the staff from the ground. He turned and beckoned with his free hand. Sam and Lucia followed cautiously, the man's pumpkin still swinging from its iron chains, its light dancing across the tawny leaves. At the foot of one of the knolls surrounding the dell, the light fell on a trail head. Looking up, they could see that this knoll was higher than the rest. It was a proper hill, and the neatly blazed trail led to its crown in tight, steep switchbacks.

Sam liked to be quiet when he was nervous, preferring to observe and evaluate any time he felt he was off his game. Lucia was the opposite. "So is this Halloween Land or something?" she asked as they leaned into the steep grade, making their way up the trail.

Jack's voice was surprisingly strong as it came from over his shoulder, not the least bit winded, whereas Sam already felt a stitch developing in his side. The old man was sharper and fitter than he appeared. They would have to be careful with this guy. He could be playing them for fools.

"No," Jack replied, "you're Nowhere. Try and make it somewhere if ya' like, if it makes ya' feel better, but yer Nowhere, lass. It only seems familiar 'cuz this place has leaked into yer world for centuries. Everything here has become part of ya', acquired by glimpses from the corners of yer eyes. When The Thinning happens, we breathe our rotten air into yer world, and sometimes it works the other way, sometimes ya' Thumpers can see in. Aye, some of ya' have even treaded these haunted grounds. Ya' ain't the first to set foot here."

"Thumpers?" This time it was Sam who asked.

"You," Jack said, "your kind, the living. Your heart beats at your ribcage. It thumps like a bodhran, like a drum. You're used to it, but it's louder than ya' think. We can hear ya comin', lad. We can hear ya' comin' from far away."

Sam and Lucia's gait slowed at this last comment, Jack pulling ahead around the last switchback so that they came face to face with the warbling light of the pumpkin and the ghostly glow that it splashed across Jack's face.

"You mean...you're not alive?" Lucia asked.

Jack, leaning into the hill, looked up at them, his cracked lips stretching into a grin. "Lass, I haven't been alive for hundreds of years."

-3-

Jack's hill was taller than any of the ones surrounding it, affording the old man a panorama of his dark world. Sam and Lucia marveled once again at the strange and disconcerting sight of the second full moon lighting the night sky past the ripple of the Veil. The distant skeletons – now far enough away to look like wind-up toys – were still at its barrier, jostling along the crests of the little hills and into the narrow valleys between.

Behind them and in the direction they had been heading before meeting Jack it was too dark to see much of anything, for on that side of the knolls only a single moon splashed its pale offering over the land. Only at the horizon could they see anything: the ridgeline of a mountain chain scraping the violet crest of sky like a yawning mouthful of jagged teeth.

"Rest yer duffs, I'll get ya' some gargle," Jack said, planting his staff into the ground with a grunt. He waved at the glowing remains of a fire on the clearing and shuffled over towards a wall of piled stones. The wall of stones enclosed a wooden shack, its tumbledown roof just visible over the fortification.

Tentatively, Sam and Lucia sat.

"He's creepy," Lucia whispered.

"I think everything here is going to be creepy, Looze."

"I know, but he's REALLY creepy." She craned her neck and saw Jack hunched over what looked like a misshapen cauldron sitting on glowing embers. She turned back to Sam. "He called you Samhain." she whispered. "It means something to him. I think he's afraid of you. You must be the shit around here."

"I don't know about that," Sam replied modestly.

"Well I think you should work it," Lucia said, jiggling his shoulder. She cupped her hands to her mouth and called to the old man: "What are you doing?"

Sam poked her.

Jack looked over his shoulder peevishly. Soon, he shuffled back, carrying two small pumpkins that were hollowed out and filled with liquid.

"What is it?" Sam asked, cupping the little gourd to his nose. He recoiled, coughing.

"Pumpkin Mash," Jack replied. "Ingenuity, lad." He tapped a bony finger to his temple. "I took the hollow trunk of a hag tree – durable things the hag trees be – a couple of hollowed-out crypt vipers for tubing...oh, not to worry, all of their venom is in their piddle and they ain't piddlin' no more, I assure ya.'" He gestured at the two gourds, smiling with pride. "Add a little heat and you get hooch good enough to wobble the dead."

Lucia hadn't noticed before that Jack's gums were as black as a thoroughbred dog's, but she did now. She put down her pumpkin.

Flummoxed by the lack of a reaction, Jack went on, sweeping a gesture over the land below: "You might not be able to see 'em, but pumpkins grow here like weeds, and they got plenty o' sugar to make all the gargle you could ever want. You can even drink it from the bloody things."

Sam stared at his own pumpkin and put it down as well.

"We're not very thirsty," Sam said. It was a lie. He could use a drink of something, but he was not about to drink anything that required the use of a hollowed-out crypt viper to create – whatever that was.

Jack shrugged, plucked up Sam's pumpkin and drained its contents in a single draught, his Adam's apple bobbing like a piston in his leathery neck. He panted his satisfaction and wiped his lips with his tattered sleeve.

Lucia had dipped her own sleeve into her own supply and was using the grog as paint thinner, wiping the make-up from her face. Sam reached over, dipped his sleeve, and started to do the same. Jack looked at them confused, snatching Lucia's pumpkin from her and draining its contents down his throat while she wiped her face.

Lucia gave the man the eye, a flip of her head, and began scrubbing the make-up beneath her ear: "So, how do pumpkins grow if midnight never ends?"

"Pretty thing," Jack said, staring at Lucia's revealed face. "Even with skin as brown as shite."

Lucia sprang to her feet. "That's it! We're out of here, Sam!"

Sam stood.

Jack cowered. "I meant nothin', Samhain! Please! Don't light me on fire! Don't kill me pumpkins! It's all I've got! I'm a sorry sod, don't I know it though! Me heart is black, me tongue is blue. Have mercy! Mercy..." He broke off, miserable and beating his forehead with an open palm.

Sam and Lucia exchanged glances. Lucia nodded stiffly.

They sat.

Jack peeked at them from behind his hands. He grinned: "There ya' go," he soothed, poking the fire with a gnarled branch sending sparks dancing into the air. "Remember...ya' have questions and I got yer answers."

"Maybe," Sam said, "but if you disrespect her one more time, I'll knock what's left of your teeth down your stringy throat."

Jack cackled, but his laughter withered under Sam's stare and he swallowed hard.

Sam sprang up and Jack flinched, but it was the horizon that had drawn Sam to his feet. A distant skeleton had broken through The Veil in a flare of purplish light. Sam watched the spirit spin into the far away sky. Whoever it was, whoever it had been once, they were now haunting his hometown.

Jack had relaxed a bit and was now slurping from his own pumpkin, peering at Sam over its rim, the fire lighting his face: "Please, sit..."

Sam did.

Jack continued. "So...what is yer first question?"

-4-

Sam had so many questions, his thoughts as tangled as the brambles that strangled the hillside below. He looked at Lucia, but she was staring contemplatively into the fire, prepared to accept whatever question he asked and whatever answer it was to yield. Sam concluded that she was losing steam and fatigue was setting in.

He looked at his own clasped hands and wondered again if he were dreaming. He flexed the hand, the restored nerves fired; the muscles were warm and alive in spite of the chill in the air. He wondered if his spiritless body was safe back in Colma, back under the bushes of the graveyard. Or had he actually taken his body with him? He couldn't tell. Was he an approximation of himself or had he been transported: mind, body and soul? Whatever the case, he could stay awhile, just to feel this completeness a little longer. That is, if the answer to his first question was the one he wanted to hear.

Staring at the horizon, he let the question fall from his lips: "This is Hell, isn't it?"

"Not even close," Jack replied. "You still want to be somewhere, don't ya'? Well, ya' aint. Everyone who ya' will find here is not welcome in Hell, and they certainly ain't welcome in Heaven neither. Everyone here has to make their own way."

"So are you really dead? Like you said?"

"Indeed."

"You look dead."

Jack laughed until he began to choke. He leaned to the side and spat an oyster of phlegm onto the dirt. A shiny black spider crawled from the glob and scurried to a nearby rock. Lucia had turned her head in disgust immediately and hadn't seen the spider, nor did she see that the glob was not phlegm at all, but rather a cluster of spider's eggs. That was very lucky for her. She would be spared the thought that Sam was now burdened with:

(he's full of spiders)

Sam swallowed hard and it took him a moment to regain himself. "So why aren't you trying to get out like they are? Why aren't you a skeleton like they are?"

"Why aren't I a Skinny?" the old man grimaced. "I tried it once, we all have. Don't care for it."

"What do you mean?"

"You don't even know how it works? The great Sao...wen..." He drew out the name with mock reverence, "don't even know how it works?"

"Stop calling me that," Sam said. "My name is Sam. I don't go by Samhain. And who told you about my middle name anyway?"

"Everyone here knows who you be," Jack replied simply.

This stung Sam. Suddenly, he felt naked, violated. He knew he was working off very little information, but it seemed everyone here had a huge advantage. They knew who he was, and according to Jack, they could all hear him coming. That was not good.

A wolf, maybe even their wolf, howled at the moon somewhere below.

"So, you're not Samhain then?" Jack teased. He took a deep sip from his pumpkin, peering over its rim with distrustful eyes. "Well, I'll tell ya' how death works anyway, if you insist – at least how it works on this side of The Veil. It has many sides, The Veil does, not just two. There is also the side that looks into Hell, the side that looks into

Heaven, and more sides than that I suppose, but I only know how it works from this side. This side is all I've ever known. I've known your side too, but long, long ago. So, to answer your question, yes, I've been a Skinny – once or twice. I don't like 'em, they are all conniving lit'le fiends, thinkin' they will have a better eternity somewhere else, but they ain't, I can tell ya that."

"Then why do they try?" Sam asked.

"Just like those who love their drink, love their drugs, they are hooked. But here, they be addicted to nothing but an idea, only an idea. Oh, but it's a doozy of an idea."

"What idea?"

"Being *alive* again," Jack said. "Thumpin' again. You didn't lose your flesh did ya', on the way in?"

Sam looked puzzled.

Jack went on: "I suppose ya didn't. 'Cuz ya ain't dead. A corpse like me can't get any closer to The Veil than this. If I do, my flesh melts off me like candle wax, puddlin' at me feet. Then, it gets cold, freezin' cold, it does. Me teeth chatter somethin' terrible. Then, The Veil draws me to it. The thought of turning back seems impossible once yer standing at The Veil, yer face pushed against it. Yer so close you can almost touch the world ya' knew once. Life is right before yer eyes. You can see the Thumpers, you can smell 'em, the blood, it smells like...an electric storm, it smells like life, it's the smell of hope, it is.

"Then, you wait 'till The Thinning comes. It's your best chance, The Thinning is, but even if you make it through, it is only your spirit you take with you. It's all that will fit. You can't take your flesh nor your bones. A ghost, a specter, it's all yer ever gonna be. Make no mistake. All the talk on the Thumper's side of the dead coming back to life lookin' like meat puppets is a bunch of malarkey. The body ya bury in the ground will rot 'till there aint nothin' but bones, but the bones aint never comin' back through The Veil. Never..."

"So why do you have flesh?"

"It's a costume, on loan from the powers that be. It's an approximation of who I was. That's all it is. But there ain't nothin' to me. I'm nothing but spirit."

(and spiders)

(black shiny ones)

Sam shuddered.

Jack gestured at the horizon. "If those Skinnies start walkin' this way, their flesh will grow on 'em like mold until they are whole again. Only one problem with that: they will have to turn their backs to The Veil, and accept that they are nowhere at all. Forever. And that ain't easy, lad. No, it ain't."

Sam stared at the horizon. Even now, at the height of The Thinning, not many of the skeletons' spirits were getting through. The odds seemed pretty low for such meager results. Yet, the skeletons still fought for their spot at the rippling barrier.

Lucia broke in: "So the closer you get to our world, the less solid you become? So what is the point of getting through at all?"

"Ahhh..." Jack said, leaning forward, "you aren't dead yet so you don't know how bad it feels to be unwanted for eternity. Just to be a ghost among the living would be better than The Nowhere where everything is nothing and all is meaningless. I ain't gonna be a Skinny no more, but I like to keep an eye on The Veil, just in case."

"Just in case what?" Sam asked.

Jack's eyes narrowed. "Never mind that, lad. I have a question of my own. What is your business here, druid?"

"I'm not a druid," Sam replied, exasperated. "I'm not even sure what a druid is. I'm Catholic. And, as far as what it is I'm supposed to be doing here...well...I don't know that either. I'm looking for some people; that's all I have to go on. Do you know any people here named McGrath? Or Carlo Winter? Or a man named Simon? What about Tlachtga who goes by the name of Clara? I think she is in trouble."

Jack shook his head, pursed his slug-like lips and looked away "You druids are all alike, up to no good, ya' are. Ya' know more than you let on."

"We don't believe you either," Lucia fired back. "You certainly know more than we do. If this isn't Hell, then why aren't you there? Or why aren't you in Heaven, if you deserve it? Surely, you qualify for one or the other? And, obviously pumpkins can't grow without sunlight. And your real name is not 'Jack of the Lantern', that's ridiculous. So, what good is it trying to convince us of this crap? Why not tell us the truth? How many visitors can you afford to bullshit, seeing as how you probably never have any?"

Jack stared at her. So did Sam. Evidently, Lucia had gotten her second wind.

"Everyone calls me Jack o' the Lantern now," Jack said, his voice low and far away. "It wasn't always that way, but it's me name now, I assure ya'. And I'm not welcome neither place, Heaven nor Hell, like I said. Soon ya' will know why."

Jack got up, took the glowing pumpkin down from the chains that held it aloft on his staff and gazed into its flickering face. For a moment he was lost in thought. He sat back down with the gourd in his lap, a flat palm stroking it as if it were a pet. The smell of its roasting flesh came to Sam and Lucia's nose on a cold breath of wind.

"So then why are you named after a jack-o'-lantern?" Sam asked.

"I'm not," Jack said. "It's named after me."

Sam and Lucia stared at him, searching for signs of cheek, but there was none. On the contrary, the two began to think that the man might be telling the truth, for in spite of the amount of pumpkin mash he had consumed, his face had gone suddenly steely sober, haunted by some distant memory.

"If ya truly want to know how I came to be here," Jack said, "I'll tell ya' me story. If ya think yer tender ears be ready."

-5-

"They called me 'Stingy Jack'. Not at first, but soon enough. I was the lowest, low-down, rapscallion me village had ever seen. Robbin', stealin' and beggin' until I had shaken down every last one of 'em for their silver. So they called me Stingy Jack, 'cuz I took a lot and paid for nothin'. I didn't mind their name callin'. What did I care? I was drunk most of the time anyhow, drunk on them buggers' coins. That is, if I chose to pay the barkeep at all, which was mostly never. I'd slither out while their back was turned. So they called me Stingy Jack. 'Go ahead,' I would say, 'have yer laughs. Who needs ya anyway', I would say.

"I lived in County Meath, on the isle of Eire, spittin' close to Tara – where the kings were crowned. That was until they ran me out, and ran me out they did. Even the children threw rocks at me, all the way to the county line they did. So I went on to Dublin, to work the big game, where nobody knew what I was up for. They called me a 'bogger' like they were wont to do – them city ruffs thinkin' they were so clever. But they were fish in a barrel for the likes of me. To them I was nothin' but a country sod wand'rin' the streets, nothin' but the butt of their jokes, and they let me be, paid me no mind. And, that was their greatest mistake it was. 'Let 'em laugh,' I would say. I might have been blootered the long part of the day, but I was a wiley one, I was.

"Dublin had plenty of strangers comin' and goin', and plenty who were only stoppin' by. It was good huntin' for a long while, and a long while before I was noticed by a soul, but then word got out: word of a man who was quick to cut your purse and quick to cheat ya' at Twenty-Five.

"And, wouldn't ya know it? Someone from my old town of Navan was at Grafton Street selling bolts of wool from his cart to some highfalutin haberdasher when he spotted me right there on the street. His eyes got wide as saucers and he yelled: 'Stingy Jack ye bastard!' He dropped his wares right in a puddle, and came chargin' at me. Well, I ran and ran, not lookin' back, not knowin' how I had wronged that man, but damn sure that I had done. I ended up in a pub, one of the few that could still stand the sight of me and there I sat with me back to the door and me beard dippin' in whisky.

"Suddenly and very quiet like, a man sat on the stool beside me – a man I had never seen before – and just starin'... starin' like I was a mouse and he was a hungry cat. I flicked my eyes to see 'im and saw his collar was turned up, his beard was long and his eyes were...well...not *right*. Somethin' was wrong with 'em. Very wrong.

"'What 'ya bloody starin' at?' says I. 'Mind your own damn business,' says I. At first, the man said nothing, just kept starin' like he was enjoying the squirm. And squirmin' I was. The man smelled of rotten eggs somethin' terrible, like the sulfur gas that would fume up the wells back home. I wanted to stare him down, but I didn't want to see those eyes again, those eyes that had nothing but yellow slits for pupils. Finally, without lookin' at the man, I says, 'Who are you and what do you want?'

"'I'm the Devil' says the man. 'And I'm sure you know what I want.' I started shakin' like a dog shittin' blackberries. 'The Devil me arse,' says I and I took a sip of whiskey, but I knew he was. I knew it if I knew anything at all.

"'I've heard a lot about you, Jack,' says the Devil. 'You are quite the scamp.' Then he smiled, and it was a terrible thing, it was, that smile. My voice was tremblin' and I tried to keep it steady as me blood ran cold.

"To my surprise, I managed a few words. 'Why is the Devil drinkin' in Temple Bar?' says I. 'Surely, you have some bigger fish to fry than little ol' Stingy Jack?' 'Oh, don't you worry, Jack,' says he. 'There is plenty of frying to go around.' I gulped, and then reached for me whiskey and gulped some of that. My courage back, I says to the stranger, 'But how do I know you're the Devil for sure?' Oh, but I knew. Between you two, and I, and that moon above us that will never wane, I knew it to be true. I was only stallin' for time.

"The man, that awful smile still on his face, looked down at the floor and I followed his eyes. He wore black breeches, and he yanked up the hem. Then I saw it, a goat's leg stickin' out from the cuff, covered in grey, wiry hair, and at the end of the leg a cloven hoof that the man had not even bothered to hide with shoes. The sight was so horrible, so terrifyin' that I jumped back from the man. I knocked over me whisky and it poured into me lap, a lap that was already wet with piddle.

"'I've come to take your soul', says the Devil. 'I could use a man like you, Jack.' I stared, me eyes buggin'. 'Now?' says I. The Devil nodded. Then, m' smarts began kickin' in. This ol' brain was chuggin' through the whiskey fog, gettin' sharper and sharper. That instinct to survive cleared me thinker and I knew that all that mattered was more time, stallin' for more time. Lord knew I had gotten m'self out of sticky situations before.

"'Wait,' says I, trying not to let my voice quiver with fright, 'if you are going to take my soul, then at least let me finish me drink. I spilled the last one as you can see, but I have no more money. So, if you're the Devil, like you say, then you can turn yourself into a coin and buy me a whiskey.' 'Why should I do that?' says the Devil. 'Why not?' says I. 'When the barkeep comes to take the coin, you can change back and scare him out of his skin. Scare him so his heart stops.' The Devil considered this, and a mischievous smile – far better than the predatory one that had been aimed at my sorry arse – played on his lips. 'Why not?' says the Devil. 'I like your style, Jack. Yes, let's have a bit of fun first.'

"With one hop, the Devil sprang onto the bar, and in a flash he turned into a gold coin. As the coin spun in place on the pocked wood, I snatched it up as quickly as I could and shoved it into the inside pocket of me coat. And, do you know what was in the pocket of me coat? A silver cross. A silver cross I had nicked only hours before from a rich old lady's carriage while it was parked, while her randy footmen's eyes were busy followin' a pretty young skirt swishin' by.

"I wasn't much for church goin', but even I knew that the Devil was powerless around the cross. From my pocket, where he was pressed tight against that cross, the Devil began fussin' and beggin'. 'Let me out,' says he. 'Not a chance,' says I. 'You can't keep me in here forever,' says he. 'But I can try,' says I. The barkeep eyed me suspiciously, figurin' I was drunk enough to be talkin' to me clothes. I waited for the barkeep to turn his back and start washin' glasses, and then I ran from the pub and into an alley.

"'LET ME OUT!' the Devil cried from me pocket. 'No way!' says I. 'You're going to send me to Hell,' says I. 'I won't,' says the Devil. 'Not yet. If you let me out, I'll give you another year. That's all I can give you. You are going to Hell though. Your soul is mine, make no mistake, but you'll have another year, a full year. Think about it – a full year with no hard feelings. You tricked me fair and square.'

"I considered this. I figured I could repent. I could clean up me act and repent. Then, the Devil would have no chance at me soul, not in a year, not ever. 'Okay,' says I. 'You have got a deal.' I plucked the coin from the pocket of me coat and threw it in the alley. It spun in the cobblestones and then before me mind could comprehend the change, the Devil was starin' me in the face, his sulfur breath waterin' me eyes. Oh, the hate twistin' his face, I wouldn't have wished it on my worst enemy. I heard the patter of my piddle as it left the leg of me pants and hit the cobbles. 'One year,' says he. Then, he was gone.

-6-

"Time went by, and I meant to repent, I really did, but it never happened. I was havin' too much fun. I passed a few churches, but I never set foot in any of 'em – not when there was a whole world to be had. After all, I was an expert in me field, an expert cheat and swindler. If I did repent, then what? I would be good for nothin'. So, on I went until one day I robbed a blacksmith's shop, a little shop that he had beside his forge. He was busy bangin' on some piece of somethin' or other and I nicked a dagger and a pocketful of doornails that I could sell on the streets.

"Unfortunately, someone saw me and gave chase. Others joined, and before long I was a fox to their hounds, runnin' out of Dublin proper and into the fields beyond, into an orchard of apple trees. Pantin' like a dog, I paused to rest, peekin' from behind one of them tree's trunks. I had lost the mob, or they didn't have the piss and vinegar to chase me all the way out of the county. Either way, I was safe. I turned to go and tripped on a root. Only, it wasn't a root, it was the

Devil.

"There he was just lyin' in the leaves and looking up at me with that smile, that horrible yellow smile frozen on his face. I screamed and jumped back so hard I smacked me back against another tree, lost me breath, and then fell to one knee.

"'It's time,' says the Devil, already on his feet and looking down at me. 'You scared the shite out of me,' says I, getting up and dustin' off me quakin' legs. 'Then,' says the Devil, 'I imagine there is not a whole lot left of you.' Me face soured at this, me eyes flickin' around like a cornered lamb. 'It's been a year already?' says I. The Devil nods, his goat eyes gleaming with lust, lust for me very soul. I'll never forget that look, for eternity I won't.

"'I meant to repent,' says I, but I didn't mean to say it out loud. 'I know you did,' says the Devil. 'But, you didn't. And I also knew you wouldn't. Not a man like you.' Me mind was spinnin', tryin' to think of some way out, tryin' to buy some more time. I glanced above me at the boughs, heavy with shiny, red apples. I reached for one, jumped for it, but they were too high. 'Mr. Devil, sir,' says I, 'if I must go, can I at least taste one more apple before I go?' The Devil shook his head, but it was the kind of shake that did not exactly mean 'no', it was the kind of shake that meant I was pathetic. 'Yes, I am pathetic,' says I. 'I know it, but just one more sweet apple for the road? Then I will go quietly to where I belong.'

"With ease, the Devil scurried up the trunk and plucked an apple from a bough. Quickly, I took out the dagger I had nicked from the blacksmith and began carving crosses all around the trunk of the tree. 'NO! NO! NO!' cries the Devil. 'You slithery bastard!' 'Yes,' says I, 'and you're not gettin' off so easy this time.' 'What do you want?' the Devil pleads, peerin' down at me through the branches, those yellow goat eyes chillin' me bones. 'I want you to leave me alone,' says I. 'Forever.' 'But your soul is rotten,' says he. 'I don't care,' says I. 'That's the deal. You are not going to take me to Hell ever. Agreed?'

"The Devil's eyes disappeared into the leaves for a moment. He was fuming, I know he was. The leaves were shakin' with his rage. After a moment, his face appeared again, a single leaf fluttering down from where he stared at me, stared at me with such hate that me twig n' berries crawled up into me stomach and turned to stone. 'You have a deal,' says he. I began to pry off the bark where I had made the crosses, and as I was workin' the last of 'em, a hoof came down on me head.

Look, you can still see the scar..."

Jack pulled back his pork pie hat and a lock of his hair. A black crescent scarred his head, the shape of a glancing hoof.

Sam and Lucia gasped in astonishment.

"Anyway," Jack continued, "the Devil flew out of that tree as quick as a flash, and just like that he was gone. I didn't see him again, not for the rest of me life. But I did die eventually, about five years later, and not at the gallows neither. It was me liver, it exploded. I could feel it. I don't remember dying much, but I remember the next part, I remember it all too well.

"I stood at the gates of Heaven, blinded by the light, every fiber and every nerve shrinkin' from it in shame. There I knelt, eyes squeezed shut against it, an arm over m' face. A voice purred in my ear, as sweet and warm as syrup, 'Do you deserve to play in God's garden, to be in His sight, to be close to His light?' 'NO!' I sobbed. I wanted to say 'Yes'. After all, eternity depended on it, but I could not. A wretched howl and that single word: 'NO!' was all I could wring from me cold and black hollows. The voice did not speak again. Soon, the light faded, and I dared to look up.

"Now, I stood at the gates of Hell, the Devil standing before me in all his fierceness. 'Well, well, well' says he, 'if it isn't Stingy Jack.' I tried to look at him, but I could not hold his gaze. Oh, those terrible eyes! Just thinkin' of 'em now gets me to shiverin'. 'I know,' says I, hangin' me head, 'I belong here. I am ready to go with you. It is surely where I belong. I will fight you no longer. Take me.' The Devil only stood, arms crossed. 'I will do no such thing. We had a deal. I am not to take you to Hell. Ever. Weren't those your words?'

"I didn't know what to say. I began to panic. 'But,' says I, 'I can't go to Heaven. I am not worthy.' 'Not even close,' he agreed. 'Then where am I to go if you won't take me?' says I. 'Not my problem,' the Devil answers. 'But I have to go somewhere!' says I. 'You will go Nowhere, like you always have,' says he, and with that, I was suddenly in darkness, darkness so complete, so thick that I could feel it crawlin' on me skin like bugs. I know now it was the Pitch where I had been sent, the entrance of this place. The Pitch is the part of The Nowhere that nobody ever goes back to once they have made it through. And, if ever ya' do go back the Wraiths – the guardians of that place – will eat yer soul, they will. Nay, more like digest it slowly. Oh, it's a horrible darkness, and that's where I ended up, on m' knees, and cryin' like a baby.

"I don't know how long I cried in that blackness, but at one point, I looked up and the Devil was standing over me. For a moment, I thought he had changed his mind. 'No, I didn't change my mind,' says he, 'you're not getting into Hell. Make no mistake, you miserable worm,' says he, 'did you think you would have the last laugh? Even a fool like you should have known. However, because you served me so well in life, I have a little gift for you – a little token to remember me by. It's an ember from the fires of Hell.'

"He dropped it at my feet – an ember the size of a potato – and it throbbed in the dust, throbbed with crimson light. 'Don't worry,' says he, 'nothing can put it out. You will wander the darkness of The Nowhere forever. And, now you can see all of its horrors when they come for you.'

"He disappeared, and I was left in the darkness, the ember at m' feet. I could not touch it, it was too hot. So, I kicked it before me as I walked, walked forever it seemed, through The Pitch until I made me way out. Finally, I saw others. I saw that this place was like a dark version of home. There was a moon, but no sun. There were vegetables in the ground, but everyone was dead and there was no need to eat. There were animals around, but only ugly and horribly misshapen ones. And the only people here were the people that for some reason or t'other both Heaven and Hell had rejected. Then I understood: It truly was nowhere at all. It was close enough to make you remember your own world –which is the worst part, the part that gets to you – but full of nothin' but a whole lot of wrong.'

"After kickin' that ember for what seemed like forever, I plucked a turnip from the soil and hollowed it out with a sharp branch from a hag tree – a tree that only grows in The Nowhere – and put the ember inside it so that I could hold it before me to light me path. I carved a thousand of 'em, I did, for the ember would eventually burn through the turnip and scorch m' feet.

"Then, I found the pumpkins here in The Knolls. They were easier to carve, and bigger too. I carved holes in 'em so that the light would do me some good and shine upon the endless paths I've walked in this place. Eventually, and mostly out of sheer boredom, I began to make more than just a hole in 'em. Finally, I settled on carvin' faces. Turns out the faces scared the bejeezus out of all of these godforsaken creatures of the night. They can't understand what's makin' the light, or maybe they know what's makin' the light, maybe they know very well, and that's a whole lot worse. Either way, it scares the baddies. So, faces it became.

"Before too long, many of these cretins slinkin' around The Nowhere began to call me Lantern Jack, or 'Jack of the Lantern'. Now, it's just Jack-O'-Lantern. And as the most reprehensible dead wander through this place they give me a wide berth, they do. Cuz out of all 'em, I am the only creature that has been given a lantern from the fires of Hell, given to me by the Devil himself."

Jack lifted the lid from the pumpkin in his lap and tilted the gourd towards Sam and Lucia. There in the bottom, surrounded by charred and blackened pumpkin flesh, was a chunk of glowing brimstone that made both Sam and Lucia lose their breath and recoil from it, for when they laid eyes on it their souls defined it immediately. It was Hell's Ember.

-7-

"So," Jack said, "I understand ya' mock me plight on your side of The Veil? Puttin' gourds on your porches to scare off that baddies, too? And I bet none of ya' know who brought back me tale from The Nowhere, but somebody sure did once upon a time. I can't tell ya' who, could've been one of many. Good thing for your kind though. Now, there are thousands, maybe millions of lanterns keepin' away the baddies during the Thinning. Somebody knew. Somebody saw that it worked here, and figured it would work there, too. Somebody is lookin' out for ya' Thumpers."

Sam and Lucia sat, stunned, and could not take their eyes off Jack's pumpkin. The thought of that ember having come straight from Hell and having been touched by the Devil himself had turned their blood to a frozen river. Peeling her eyes away from it with difficulty, and in a hoarse whisper as she was not yet able to find her voice, Lucia said: "Wouldn't you rather be here than in Hell?"

"Why would I?" Jack replied.

"Because," Lucia went on, "at least you're not burning for all of eternity."

Jack's laugh startled them both. "And where did you get that notion? Are they still feedin' you that line? So, you think the Devil would have burned me forever?"

"Of course," Lucia said. "You told us yourself how bad you were."

"Have you ever thought about it usin' your own thinker?" Jack said, tapping his skull.

Sam's stomach flipped at the sound. Jack's head had sounded sickeningly hollow, like it was nothing but an eggshell. Like it was...

(full of spiders)

Jack leaned towards Lucia, speaking as if to a child, his breath sweet with pumpkin liquor and sour with rot: "The Devil is the enemy of God. Why would he punish ya for doin' things that God doesn't like? Does that make any sense to you? How would he get anyone to do his dirty work if word got out that he was punishin' sinners? Tell me that. He's been the victim of a pretty slick double-talkin' from Heaven. No, lass, the only punishment in the afterlife are the absence of God's love or, in my case – and in the case of all of us crawlin' through The Nowhere – the absence of God's love as well as the absence of the Devil's appreciation."

Lucia said nothing.

"Now," Jack said, "if ya' insist on staying, you will wander where I have wandered, and ya' will meet wretched creatures whose stories will make yer pretty, dark hair turn white as frost, they will. Aye, but don't ya' forget one thing: they were like you once, alive and thumpin', and they all came from your world. We are the forsaken, and most of us are in a very shit mood."

Jack got to his feet. He hung his pumpkin from the chain on his staff and pointed to his hut behind the stone wall. "You can stay here. There is no mornin' to speak of, but you can rest yer bones if ya need to."

"No," Sam said numbly, "we should go. If you don't know of any of the people I mentioned, then we need to find someone who does. Thank you anyway."

"Where should we go, Jack?" Lucia asked, getting to her feet and peering off the knoll and into the darkness.

"If I were you," Jack said, "I would appeal to some that are far more social than I. Ya' see, I prefer keepin' to m'self and I don't get involved in the bellyachin' and the treachery around here. Ya' need to speak with the old, wise ones, the ones beyond the bog."

"Fine," Sam said. "Beyond the bog. That's good. How do we get there?"

"At the bottom of m' hill, go through the dell and up the far side and head left. There, you will see the path. Follow the ruts in the path.

They will take ya' through the Bog of the Covens and that will lead ya' to Hex. Those in Hex are most foul, they are, but they know much. And I suppose, like all of us they've been expectin' ya'."

"Who?" Lucia said. "Who lives there?"

"Witches," Jack replied, heading for his shack, "and lots of 'em. Oh...and good luck. 'Cuz even if you are with Samhain, lassie, luck is what you're gonna need." Jack looked over his shoulder a final time, "Aye, a whole lot of it."

With that, he disappeared into his hut and slammed the door.

IX.
The Blackened Man

-1-

After an unsettling hike scored by howling wolves, Sam and Lucia cleared the Knolls, but as they now gained a heavily furrowed trail of packed earth, new sounds surrounded them. These sounds were even worse because they could not be identified by either traveler.

Suddenly, Lucia shrieked, stomping convulsively in place and flapping her hands at her ears: "YUCK! That was a big, BIG bug!"

Sam dusted her off, but could see nothing. It was so dark. Even with his restored vision he could barely see his hand in front of his face. Glancing up, he saw that the alien moon was just beginning to free itself from a tangle of gauzy cirrus clouds that reached across the sky like old hair floating on black water.

Sam walked backwards for a moment. He couldn't see The Veil anymore. "We're in deep," he muttered.

"Sam, did you see that bug?"

"I can hardly see anything." Sam replied. "But we've got to keep our heads. If we freak out, we're never going to make it."

"Make it where?" Lucia asked. "We don't even know where to start."

"I know, and I'm not all that happy about having to appeal to a bunch of witches for information either, but Jack said he didn't know anyone we were looking for. So, it's either this or we go back."

"He didn't say he didn't know who we were looking for," Lucia corrected, "he just never answered the question. He changed the subject. You asked him about your parents, Carlo, and Simon, and Clara, and he never answered."

Sam considered this, "You're right...but later he said he kept to himself and he didn't socialize."

"That's what he said," Lucia agreed, "but do you believe him? I don't. I think he knew. In fact, I think he knows exactly what we are here for even more than we do. He called you Samhain the whole time. Then, he said 'everyone knew you were coming' and that 'everyone knew who you were'. It sounds to me like he gets around and that he's pretty clued in. No, he was hiding something. What bothers me is why he isn't talking."

Sam was quiet. They walked in silence for a while before he spoke, "You're probably right. He might even know where Clara is being held. I could force him to tell..." He stopped walking, put his hands on his hips, looked at Lucia and blew his breath into the darkness. "What am I doing? Force him? How? And for Clara? I don't even know her. All I've seen of her has been a reflection, yet here we are in the middle of nowhere – literally, I might add – risking our lives when we have our whole lives ahead of us. This is crazy. Why do I care what happens to a ghost...or...whatever she is?"

"I can't disagree with that," Lucia said. "It was exciting at first, but now...I'm not so sure."

She looked around her. From what she could see by the feeble light, the land had flattened in all directions. Still, the strange noise surrounded them. It was a resonant flutter and it was coming from both sides of the road.

(bugs)

Yes, it was as if hundreds of huge wings were beating the air in place, waiting for a signal to charge. As she listened, a low, rumbling drone began, like the cicadas that Lucia remembered as a child visiting Mexico, but much deeper and thrumming with predatory purpose. The flesh on her arm began to stipple into goose flesh.

"And whatever just flew past my head," Lucia whispered, "whatever is out there...there are a whole lot of them."

They started walking again. Soon, the ground began to get muddy. At times the fluttering would get very close to the road, the deep drone rising and falling like some Buddhist chant, and Lucia would grab Sam's arm. Sam didn't mind this at all. He didn't like the sound either, and it felt good being closer to her. They tried to keep quiet, listening for any sound of ambush, but the less they talked the more their imaginations took over. It was in the silence that they could almost see the bugs watching them from the bog: hundreds of eyes clustered like larvae on stalks, glossy black carapaces crouched within the sodden cattails, wings beating the air as the things waited for the right moment to tear large bites out of their faces with mandibles the size of needle-nose pliers.

"Sam," Lucia asked, her voice quavering, now grabbing his arm with both hands, "did you mean what you said when we were in the tunnels?"

"What did I say?"

She looked at him. His hair was in silhouette, sticking up from his head like licking flames, and only the glittering whites of his eyes shone through the night.

"You said you loved me," Lucia whispered.

For a terrible moment, Sam said nothing. But this was only because he had been distracted by a sound to his left. Something had been crashing through the reeds. Whatever it was, it had stopped. He turned back to Lucia, "Of course I do, I've known you my whole life. You're my best friend,"

"I know," she said, "you're my best friend too, but that's not what I mean. What I mean is..."

Lucia shrieked and her hand left Sam's

Something very large had buzzed past their heads. Sam crouched and pulled Lucia down towards the ground with him. The creature zipped past their heads again, hovered in the air about ten yards from them and began banking in a slow, wide arch for another pass. It was at that instant that Sam could see it clearly as it hung against the cloud streaked moon. It was a bug of some kind, but it was huge, the size of a bird of prey. Before he could comprehend it, the thing charged. With a sound like the choking of a chainsaw, it went straight for Sam's head.

-2-

Sidestepping, Sam sprung upwards, and with a flattened palm swung a roundhouse in the direction of the buzz. He connected. The thing had hair: thick, wiry hair. Sam yelped with disgust. The thing screeched like a rusty door hinge before falling out of the sky to the muddy ground with a wet thud.

Sam and Lucia stepped back, both of them stumbling in the puddles of muck on the shoulder of the road. Sam drove his hand into his pocket and produced his cell phone. He scrolled to his lamp application and hit enter. The phone's flashbulb turned on, the small pool of light dancing across the muck.

"Oh, my God," Lucia gasped.

The wounded insect was crawling slowly over the furrowed dirt.

It was a spider, a flying spider the size of a small dog. It was light brown and covered in white hair. Sam's imagination had been correct. Its eyes were clustered on stalks, like inky, blind mirror balls. Its broken cellophane wings were lined with red veins, but now they only dragged the ground like deflated parachutes as the thing stumbled sideways, its drunken lurches punctuated by short bursts of that droning buzz. Sam flashed on the gas powered weed whackers that the gardeners used to tend the cemetery grass back in Colma.

"Oh, God," Lucia said again, slapping a hand over her mouth.

The spider-thing dragged itself into the weeds leaving a trail of black ichor in the dust.

"I think its family is pissed off," Sam said with a shaky voice as the drone around them rose to a din. "We have to find cover."

The sound surrounding them was now even lower, steadier and decidedly angry. Lucia spun, trying to retreat from every direction at once. The flying spider things were...

(hungry)

Lucia knew there were hundreds of them crouched in the dark, flexing their crab-like legs in the weeds, watching them and drooling. They were surrounded, with nowhere to go and suddenly Lucia could picture their bloated, hairy bodies crawling all over her corpse, the popped whites of her eyes stretching like pizza cheese as they tugged them from her skull.

Lucia screamed. Sam jumped and trained the light on her. He saw nothing. She was only screaming in panic as if the wind from her lungs could blow away the darkness. The sound made Sam's blood run with ice. It was the sound of Lucia losing her mind, and it was the worst sound he had heard yet.

"Looze..." he pawed for her arm, but she was still twirling in a circle, trying to watch all sides of her at once. Her breath was a shallow rasp. He caught her shoulder and pulled her to him.

"I hate bugs," Lucia cried into his chest. "I hate spiders the most!"

"Wait..." Sam implored her, "listen, just listen..."

"No..." she mumbled miserably into his shirt, her hot breath chugging through his clothes heating the skin of his chest. He grabbed her head with both hands and stroked her hair. "Listen," he said, hushing her. "It worked. They stopped."

"They stopped?"

"Yes. I think they realized you meant business."

She listened for a moment to the silence and then laughed. It wasn't a real laugh, only an optimistic sob, but Sam was grateful to hear it anyway. She was thawing. Her tense body began to relax a little against his.

"You're okay," Sam said.

She looked at him. He could see the wetness in her eyes, but not much else. He could no longer see that familiar, emerald fire that always twinkled with such humor and intelligence. It had been extinguished by the blackness of this godforsaken place. He almost forgot about the phone in his hand and its little flashlight. He held it above their heads.

"What?" she asked him, her voice skittish. "Is there something on me?"

"There's nothing," he replied, "I just miss seeing your face."

She looked into his eyes. He smiled at her and then kissed her, kissed her gently in the little pool of light, in the middle of that dark and barren land that had known no love before. She kissed him back, and in that moment the impenetrable darkness around them no longer mattered. They had formed their own world and they were safe and warm beneath their own sun. They pulled back and just stared into each other's eyes under the pool of light, savoring the sight of one another, marveling at the power that flooded into them as if they had plugged into a live wire.

The buzzing across the bogs started up again, cautious at first, and then with insistence.

"We run," Sam said, "and we scream. They don't like it. If we do that, they won't hurt us. I think I see trees in the distance."

"I think I do too," she said.

"We can make it."

"I think we can too."

"I have to save these batteries. We will need them."

"I know..." She reached up to steady his hand to look at him for just a moment longer. "Okay. Let's do this..."

Sam shut off the light.

-3-

Their feet pounded the earth as they yelled battle cries into the air. It was working, at least for now, but both of them were sure that they would soon feel bursts of wind at any moment – the flying spider things whizzing past their heads in flesh-tearing sorties. First, the bug's bloated bodies would bounce off of their heads like mindless water balloons until one of the awful things finally grabbed onto one of their scalps with their spider legs. Then, the real horror would come: the bug's white, wiry hair pressing its swamp stink into their face, the clicking mandibles groping blindly for their necks.

The two wanderers screamed, they flapped their arms, and they ran. They ran until their hearts felt as if they would burst, their hot breath puffing white into the cold, moonlit sky. It felt good to run. It felt good to scream, to make a stand in this place instead of cowering and waiting for the next thing to attack them.

They slowed their pace and dared to turn around. The flying spider things might have looked like their worst nightmare, but evidently they were as easy to scatter as a flock of pigeons. Soon, the two were trotting uphill, too tired to run anymore, panting and grabbing their knees.

Their breath steadied as they realized they were now entering a forest, and they stopped when they saw a torch in the distance through the trees. They both eyed it suspiciously. It was glowing at a bend in the trail ahead, and looked to be stuck in the ground. Naturally, they thought of Jack o' the Lantern, but this was not a pumpkin. It was a real torch, stuck in the forest floor. It appeared to be unattended. They approached slowly, eyes darting, scanning the darkness for the torch's owner. Soon, they were beside the light. They held their breath but could hear nothing but the sputter of the flame.

"Nobody here," Lucia whispered.

"I see another one," Sam said, pointing further up the trail.

"You really shouldn't leave torches unattended in the forest," Lucia said. "Just saying..."

Sam smirked.

They walked slowly towards the next torch and they noticed how foggy it was getting the deeper into the forest they went. Fronds of white vapor curled through the air beneath the orange glow of the flame and licked the trunks of the ancient trees.

"Someone must be close by," Sam whispered.

"I feel like we're being watched," Lucia whispered back.

As they approached the second torch they saw the sign beside its pool of light. It was a fog-soaked plank lashed to a pole, and in thick red letters it read:

H E X

-4-

Lucia figured that she should have been scared by the sign, that it was a harbinger of bad things to come, but she wasn't. During their hike she had given some thought to what Jack had told them about how this world had colored their own over time, about how the associations that she had made with Halloween had simply been The Nowhere "leaking" into her world over centuries of the Thinning.

So, all of those years of lining up for haunted houses, haunted hayrides and the like had reduced the atmosphere of The Nowhere to a cartoonish familiarity, an old, worn hand that held hers as she took in the pastiche of sights and sounds. It was as if she were now touring the paradigm of eeriness, the world that countless set designers, artists and Halloween impresarios painstakingly recreated year after year.

The sign before her was just as it should be. And the forest was just as she would expect: rising and falling on gently undulating hills, blanketed with tawny leaves, the ground fog wrapping around the trunks of the trees like cotton batting, trees whose arms were bare and arched over the torch-lit trail before them like arthritic claws poised to grab the next traveler by the throat.

True, there was nothing charming or redeeming about the flying spider things. Aside from that, she considered the majority of what she had been experiencing to be more exhilarating and wondrous than terrifying. In short, she was bearing witness to the most perfect setting that a holiday could ever have.

But just like a rickety roller coaster that you were not sure would make it back to the gate before flying off the tracks, this place did little to guarantee that her thrill ride would end with the relieving click of a rotating turnstile or an overpriced souvenir photo. No, this was definitely the real deal. The worst part of it all was that she didn't know the rules, and a misstep could have real consequences, not just for her body and mind, but for her soul.

She could die here. Sam could too. Then what? If they died here, did they remain here? Would God come and pluck them from these haunted grounds? Had He ever deigned to cast a considerate glance in this direction?

These thoughts dissolved quickly when she heard a sound behind her and Sam tapped her on the shoulder to suggest that they hide behind a tree. But this new sound was finally one that did not stroke her spine with fear. It was a gentle and familiar sound. It was the distant nicker and blow from a horse. Peeking from behind the tree she saw it, a black stallion back at the first torch, a cruciform silver marking stretched across its brow and down its nose. On the horse's back was a very large and very black man.

The man gathered the reins and the horse began to close the distance, cantering towards their circle of torch light.

"Salut," said the man. His voice had some kind of accent. "Come out from your hiding place for it is not a good one." It was the deep, hearty voice of a middle-aged man.

French, Sam thought, and he cautiously stepped out from behind the tree with Lucia in tow. The man approached, his mount parting the ground fog, and as the horse and rider entered the pool of torch light, Lucia gasped, clapping a hand to her mouth. Sam stiffened. The man was not African as they had assumed from afar. He was burnt beyond recognition.

The charred rider performed a full pass as he came upon the two, moving the horse sideways and looking down on them with bemused interest. A flowing dark beard tangled with his long salt and pepper hair, setting off his charred and blistered face. His eyes were hard and grey.

"Samhain," the man said. "Bienvenue, Monsieur. I am Jacques de Molay."

"How do you know my name?" Sam asked.

"Why wouldn't I know your name?" the man replied.

The Frenchman was dressed in robes, his hands obscured by gauntlets, but Sam knew that beneath the garments this man had been burned from head to toe, and for one terrible moment, Sam swore that he smelled the man's cooked flesh in the wisps of fog that were gliding lazily past his nose like ghost fish in a spectral aquarium. The orange light lit the purple blister that was once the man's face. The flesh of the nose seemed to have melted and dripped at some point only to solidify again like old candle wax, rendering the appendage bizarrely elongated and misshapen.

"What happened to you?" Lucia asked, trembling. She had been studying the man. Even the revolting sight of his condition could not hide that he was still possessed of a bygone elegance that moved him about with an antique brand of poise. Yet, when Jacques de Molay's saddle creaked and he turned to look directly at her, Lucia had little choice but to look away.

"I was burned alive, burned at the stake," the man said, "six hundred years ago."

"Sorry..." Lucia offered clumsily. She regretted it immediately. It was not only a feeble thing to say, it also showed weakness, and that was something she vowed she would not do anymore as long as she was in this place. But she was sorry. The man was a tragedy. He reminded Lucia of a great work of art that had been carelessly ruined.

"Not half as sorry as I am, Mademoiselle," Jacques said.

"Do you live in these woods?" Sam asked.

"I don't live at all," Jacques replied crisply.

"Where do you stay then?" Sam asked.

"Passing through," Jacques replied, "that is all. The question is what are you two doing here?"

Sam hesitated, not sure how to answer.

"You don't know do you?" Jacques teased. "But when you finally do, they will be sorry. You are the one he believes can stop him, and until he could get you on his own turf, he had no chance of beating you. He has wanted you here for a long, long time. Now, he can face you on his terms. You should have stayed home and carved your pumpkins, young prince."

"So WHO can face us?" Sam asked.

Jacques de Molay sat back in his saddle. His eyes were like two chips of granite and they fixed on the two travelers. When he finally spoke, he spoke suspiciously, as if he believed Sam to be testing him by way of a tiresome and insultingly easy riddle, "Who will face you, you ask? Well, that would be Simon Magus, and all the cretins that serve him."

The horse champed at its bit and tossed its head.

"Yes!" Lucia blurted out, "Simon! That's right! Wait...Simon who?"

"Magus," Jacques said.

Lucia continued: "That must be who we are looking for, or that is one of them at least. Where is he?"

Jacques de Molay only pursed his blistered lips.

"Is he the one who burned you?" Sam asked.

"No," Jacques replied. "These are my mortal wounds. I wear them as further disgrace."

"Do you know Clara, known as Tlachtga?" Sam asked. "How do we find Simon?"

"He will find you, Monsieur, I can assure you of that," Jacques replied. Then, under his breath, the blackened man rattled off something in French before he uttered one distinct phrase in English that made Sam's heart buck in his chest: "The priest has sheltered you far too much for your own good."

"Father Doc..." Lucia said. "Are you talking about his...his dad?"

Sam had gone pale and he stayed Lucia with a hand to her shoulder.

Jacques de Molay's eyes remained keen and steady. He held Sam's sharpened gaze before reining back his mount with haughty resolve, making as if to leave, "I will not talk with you anymore, for if you fail, I will be the sorcerer's plaything, I will be Fley's monkey boy. All of us will surely suffer. So far, you are not inspiring confidence. You may be a legend, the great druid among the Thumpers, the last of your clan and the first line of defense for your world, but you may also end up on the bottom of Simon's boot. I am no soothsayer, I am only a Templar. And as long as my soul wanders this place, I would rather it belong to nobody in particular than hand it to Simon Magus. I will not gamble it away on the proficiency of a mere boy."

"I'm eighteen now," Sam shot back defiantly.

Ignoring him, Jacques continued, "Therefore, I must bid you adieu."

"Wait!" Lucia stepped forward. "Who is Fley? What sorcerer?"

"What sorcerer?" Jacques asked in disbelief. He sighed. "*Simon bien sur, mon petit fluer*. Pray, what other sorcerer is even worth talking about? And Orace Fley? You do not know of him either? Has he not graced you with his presence on your side of The Veil? I would wager that he has. Either way, mademoiselle, you will know him soon enough. The word in Hex is that Magus has enslaved all the Leeches of Black Fang and has put the centurion Fley in charge of them all. And they have but one purpose..."

"What's that?" Sam asked.

Jacques laughed heartily, as if he finally concluded that he had been the victim of a well-crafted prank. Surely, this fabled boy had to know the answers to these questions. Surely, he had to know that much.

"Who is Orace Fley, you ask?" Jacques said, his eyes glittering. "He's your executioner! And what is his purpose?" Jacques' smile widened as he leaned towards Sam from his saddle. "To destroy you, of course."

-5-

"Wait!" Sam called as Jacques turned his horse. "If you won't tell us where to find Simon, can you tell us where to find Clara?"

Jacques had no eyebrows left to raise. His blackened forehead rose instead. "Certainly not."

"Why?" Sam asked.

"Because Simon does not want you to know," Jacques replied curtly.

"But we are on the same side, aren't we? If we weren't, then you would have tried to kill us. Wouldn't you?"

"There are no sides here," Jacques said, "Good and evil has already been decided. Here, there are only those who believe The Veil can fall, and those like me who do not. However, those who want to return to your world to live among the Thumpers as living dead, reigning over you all without fear of death will stop at nothing. Simon will lead them. If he and his army succeed, we are all free, but if they do not, those who have stood in their way will surely suffer most."

"So, this Simon Magus plans to destroy The Veil," Sam asked, "and you're not going to get involved? You are not going to help us?"

"Correct," Jacques replied.

"Nobody here seems to want to help us," Sam said glumly. "Jack O' Lantern told us the same thing. He doesn't want any part of it either, but someone has to help us or we are not going to be able to stop Simon. Is that even what I'm supposed to do? Nobody will give us a straight answer and nobody cares: Is that what you're telling us?"

"The souls in The Nowhere have one thing in common," Jacques replied, lowering the reins, "they have all been abandoned by both the Shepherd and the Betrayer. We are the most unlikely of all souls to choose a side. We lived sitting on a fence, and we will all spend eternity doing the same. It is too late for us, Monsieur. If you are waiting for us to dazzle you with our ability to make a sound and moral decision, you will be waiting for eternity as well."

"You're all cowards," Lucia said.

"We are all self-serving," Jacques conceded. "That is our primary function. Cowardice is only a charge leveled by those who get in our way so that they may find comfort. Others may call us "evil" or "crazy". Those epithets also lack accuracy. In reality, we are quite the opposite. Au contraire, it takes quite a bit of courage to thumb your nose at both God and the Devil."

"Or stupidity," Sam spat. "I thought you said you were a Templar? Weren't those the knights that protected the Holy Land and went on Crusades against the non-believers? And you aren't in Heaven? How is that possible?"

"Oh it is possible..." Jacques said, his voice trailing off. For a long moment they heard nothing but the torch sputtering at the trail's edge. It was barely visible now. The fog had thickened around them where they stood. Jacques looked up at the moon.

"What happened to you?" Lucia urged. Her voice had become tender and almost maternal. "You said you were burned alive? Why?"

Jacques turned to look at her. His grey eyes were now distant and they had softened from granite into wet pools of quicksilver. "You are not safe in the open. These woods have ears. These trees listen for the witches. Come with me."

-6-

Following the horse and its charred rider along the torch-lit trail, the three ducked into a clearing off of the road where the interlacing arms of the barren trees formed a small, natural amphitheater. In the clearing were a series of benches fashioned from the hard, silvery-black trunks of hag trees. Jacques dismounted, then motioned for Sam and Lucia to sit before he gathered his robes and did the same.

"This is the meeting place for the Covens of Hex," he said. "Doesn't it remind you of the oak forests of Rouvray? I think you call it the Bois de Boulogne now? Have you been to Paris? No? *C'est une honte.* It is a shame." He clicked his tongue. "Anyway, it looks like this place, remarkably so. That is why I haunt these woods."

"Um..." Sam began, "if this is where the witches meet...shouldn't we...?"

"No, monsieur," Jacques smiled thinly. "We are safe. This is only where the hags hold their Council of the Sabbath – purely symbolic at this point since there is no Sabbath left in this place – but that is not impending. Still, you are correct Mr. Samhain, we should not stay long.

"Now, I will help you by telling you my story, so that you understand the nature of The Nowhere and how the souls here do not align strictly with good or evil. I tell you because whether you succeed here or not, whether or not you can rescue the mother of your clan and stop Simon from destroying The Veil, I will be safe only if my neutrality in those matters remains unassailable. Is that correct? Is my English good enough?"

Lucia tapped Sam, "Doesn't unassailable mean..."

"Wait!" Sam held a palm out to Lucia. "Sorry, Looze, hold on a sec." He looked back at Jacques, "Clara is the mother of my clan? What else do you know about her?"

The question made Jacques flinch and he continued without answering it, "I will tell you my story for one other reason: your world has sown these haunted grounds and continues to do so still. It is for this reason alone that I will recount my disgrace. Perhaps, I can save your souls. Not that I assume your souls are endangered, nor do I question your goodness, but neither did I question mine...until the end.

"I lived in France at the turn of the fourteenth century. I was the last of the great Grand Masters of the Knights Templar. And yes, as you correctly put it, we were charged with protecting the Holy Lands. We were an army in the service of Christ, but we became so powerful and wealthy that we became a threat to both the King of France and the Pope in Rome.

"Nobody understood the influence of the Knights Templar better than my King, Philippe 'le Bel'. He was very indebted to us, and that he did not like. He was a proud man, and rather than concede that France's power and influence was overshadowed by that of the Knights Templar, he set out to destroy his competition. He set out to destroy us.

"At first, he tried to get the Pope to do his dirty work, to disavow us, to cut off the support of Rome. Somehow, he had planted spies within our ranks to dig up whatever dirt they could. He charged us with unholy and unspeakable practices during our initiation ceremonies, claiming that we trampled the cross and denounced God. Soon, the Pope was questioning his support and public opinion was also turning; all the while, I was being portrayed as a heretic.

"Without warning, I was arrested on Friday, October 13th, 1307, just as that year's Thinning began in earnest. Of course, at that time, I knew nothing of the thinning of The Veil, much less The Nowhere, but my arrest was obviously orchestrated with help from someone from these realms. As you must know by now, The Nowhere's reach is long.

"Anyway, I was dragged off to prison along with sixty of my best Knights. We were tortured in terrible, terrible ways. For years I was imprisoned. Eventually, I confessed my crimes against God. I later recanted, but then came more torture and I confessed again. It became clear that there would be no way out for me. The King was not going to let me wiggle from his grip no matter what I said, no matter what I did.

"Finally, even the Pope had fallen into the King's way of thinking and they both decided that it would be best if I were out of the way. It had all become far too messy. So, on a small island in the middle of the river Seine, I was lashed to a stake and slowly roasted alive as my countrymen lined both banks of the river to jeer, their spit falling far short of my person, but not from lack of effort.

"I have seen that there is a plaque commemorating my death at the Pont Neuf in Paris, the old bridge over the river. I have seen it myself at the part of The Veil that lies east of here, a part that looks onto my homeland. Of course, The Veil is particularly thin there, and for good reason I should think.

"I remember making one final request at the stake, a request that would serve as a statement of my innocence and my piety. The King's executioners happened to have tied me up facing the great cathedral of Notre Dame. Maybe it was on purpose? I do not know. Anyway, I requested that my hands remained untied so that I could clasp them in prayer as I died.

"My final words were a curse upon the two men who had been responsible for my death: King Philippe and Pope Clement. I am glad to say that both men died within the year: the Pope of a terrible illness and the King by way of a hunting accident. As for me, I ended up here."

"Why?" Sam asked, leaning forward on his stump. "You dedicated your life to the Church, right?"

"It would appear that way," Jacques conceded, "but it is not so."

"I don't understand," Lucia said. "You were a Templar knight. So some insecure King didn't like the fact that you were rewarded well for your job and made up a bunch of charges about you trampling on the cross and defaming God? Why would anyone believe that?"

"It didn't matter," Jacques said simply. "The King of France was jealous, and no one on earth has perfected jealousy like the Kings of France. I would have been executed for some other reason, it hardly mattered. Anyway, the leveling of false charges was not my undoing in the end."

"Then what was?" Sam asked. "Why are you in The Nowhere?"

"Because, Monsieur, the charges were true. They were all true."

-7-

Lucia looked stricken, "But why? Why would you betray God while your job was to champion Him?"

"Because I believed in the power of the Templar," Jacques confessed, rubbing his long beard absently. "I believed we were gods among men."

As Sam and Lucia watched, all traces of the man's arrogance, and whatever poise they had once perceived was now evaporating before their eyes. Regret now consumed the knight-along with the wraith-like fog that now engulfed them all. The blackened knight had now begun to hug himself and rock slowly on his bench, the movement becoming more pronounced as he recounted his treachery, as if the inconsolable spirit still within him was shaking the prison bars of his borrowed ribcage. Sam and Lucia were now staring at a simple wretch.

"We even taunted God," Jacques said. "We dared Him to strike us down."

"Then why did the Devil not take you to Hell?" Sam asked.

"Because, I dedicated my life to God and that is not something the Devil takes kindly to. Worse, in a desperate attempt to save myself, I prayed to God at the very end. The Devil did not approve of this either. He did not believe I was truly his servant, and of course, neither did God."

"I thought God was forgiving," Lucia said.

"Reputedly," Jacques said, "but obviously not always. Read your holy writ more closely. His jealous streak is well documented."

Sam and Lucia fell silent. The ground fog had thickened around them so that only their heads and shoulders could be seen. It looked as if they were all stewing in a cauldron. Sam figured it might not be figurative if they stayed for much longer. These woods gave him the willies. He wondered if there were witches creeping towards them, somewhere past the banks of fog. He suddenly felt claustrophobic and vulnerable.

Somewhere above the group, an owl hooted mournfully.

"I was arrested on Friday the 13th," Jacques said, suddenly breaking the silence. His cracked lips spread into a wintry smile. "That is how it came to be considered an unlucky day. Did you know that? It is true. That is the only claim to greatness I have left. I am the enduring symbol of misfortune."

"Really?" Sam asked. "Friday the 13th is all because of you?"

"*Absolument*," the knight replied. "We all affect the world. Even here we do. You see, The Nowhere does not have a god. We are all our own gods. All laws in this place are defined only by its inhabitants. Did you know that time moves thirteen times faster here than it does in your world? It is true. For every thirteen minutes that pass in The Nowhere, only a minute passes in your world. That is my contribution. It is homage to me, Jacques de Molay, last and most disgraced of the Knights Templar."

Jacques smiled weakly and got to his feet, the fog stirring around him. "Now, I must go."

"What do we do now?" Sam asked. "You have a chance to save the world you once loved, and you still won't help?"

"I have not misled you, Monsieur Samhain," Jacques said. "Nobody here will help you. We all have different stories, but they are all alike, as you will soon learn. We have no allegiance to idealism. That kind of foolishness is bait for those who pine for a rewarding existence. Ours is only existence and that is all it will ever be. The only hope you will find here is The Skinnies at The Fringe, banging their heads against The Veil. It is *pathetique, n'est pas*? No, hope is not for me. I do not desire such a prudish mistress."

"But there is an opportunity here," Lucia said.

Sam grimaced. Lucia was getting frustrated and she was winding up. There was no telling how Jacques was going to take it. She stood with one hand cocked on her hip, her other hand roiling the fog with wild gestures. "You can finally pick a side and do what is right, perform a selfless act. How hard is that? If you are right and Simon's whole purpose is to regain entry in our world, to enslave it, and to destroy us in the process, then do something to help us because I take that kind of shit personally!"

Jacques looked at Sam, stunned. Sam could only offer a shrug.

Lucia went on, "And Clara? You called her the mother of Sam's clan. Then, she must be good because Sam is good. I am good too. So we have been called here to prevent some ancient maniac we have never met from taking our world hostage? And you're going to do nothing?"

"I admire your spirit," Jacques replied, "but it is too late. Anyway, this is not my fight. If you and Samhain succeed I will be free of this place. If you fail, I will be hunted and enslaved if I helped you. You think I should ride with you both and destroy Orace Fley and his Leeches? I should ride to Black Fang, storm the tomb and face Simon, the greatest sorcerer who has ever existed? Even if that were possible – and it will only be possible if Samhain is as great as the legends say – I still would not help. Jacques de Molay is, and forever will be, non-aligned. "

"You are going to play both sides again," Sam asked, "even when you are suffering for eternity for doing so?"

"I never said I was suffering," Jacques replied. "I do not want Heaven. I do not want Hell." He gestured wide with his arms, the fog parting at either side of his robes. "If anyone belongs here, it is I. It is far from pleasant, but it is just."

Sam and Lucia fumed and looked away in frustration.

"However," Jacques continued, "I can tell you one thing. You should follow this trail into Hex. The witches care little for repercussions. They believe in their magic. They believe it will protect them even against the likes of Simon Magus. There is one among them that will point you true. She is the most ancient of them all and you will know her because she flies across the moon in a mortar fashioned from the clay of the Bog of the Covens. She uses the pestle to wipe away the tracks that she leaves in the sky. And you will know the hut in which she dwells, because it is already hunting you."

Sam and Lucia looked at each other blankly.

"Did he just say what I think he did?" Lucia asked.

"Yep," Sam confirmed. "We are being hunted by a hut. I don't think that's what he means though." He dropped his voice to a whisper. "It must be a language problem."

"He speaks better English than I do," Lucia protested.

"You can think what you like," Jacques said, "but she is coming for you. Know that I have done you a favor just in case you are on the winning side in the end."

"At least he doesn't mince words," Lucia whispered to Sam.

Sam managed a smile and a frown at the same time.

Jacques approached his horse at the side of the clearing and reached into a saddle bag, producing what looked like a jagged leaf of paper. Returning to them, he said, "I do not make it a habit of visiting The Fringe, as I've said. Further, I am proud to say that I have never succumbed to the temptation to follow The Skinnies, but I have found that the flesh shed in piles at the border of the Fringe – when pressed and properly cured by torch light – makes for fine parchment."

"Ewww," Lucia exclaimed, recoiling from the paper. Sam nudged her.

Jacques unrolled one of the tanned leafs on the hag tree bench, batted away some fog, and then dragged his index finger down his burned face. With the soot on his finger, he wrote:

O HUT O HUT

TURN YOUR **BACK** TO THE **FOREST**

TURN YOUR FRONT TO ME

I SAMHAIN COMMAND YOU

Jacques folded the parchment in half carefully, and handed it to Sam with a bow. "You must say it exactly or you will be eaten."

"Eaten?" Lucia said. "This just gets better and better."

"Say it to who?" Sam asked, "Say it when?"

"It will be most obvious," Jacques replied, mounting his horse.

"Why can't anyone just tell us things without riddles?" Lucia asked the sky.

"Mademoiselle," Jacques replied, reining his horse, "I am not going to tangle with witches, even dead ones. I have told you too much already. I do not fear death, for I am already dead. It is magic that I fear. And I have already helped a druid to find a witch. That's more than enough for me. I do not want to be anywhere near here when you meet Baba Yaga, when your sorcery greets hers."

Jacques kicked his horse to a trot.

"Baba who?" Sam called, "I don't know any magic!"

"And I am not a barbecue-ed Frenchman!" Jacques called over his shoulder. "*Bonne chance, mes amis!*"

Sam and Lucia watched him go as he entered one pool of torch light, and then another, until he disappeared into the fog-laced forest.

The hoof beats died away. For a long time Sam and Lucia stood, unresolved, the silence and the fog thickening around them until they heard the cackle. It was a faint, knowing snicker and it came rolling towards them through the fog to splash icy water on their spines. They both held their breath. The sound came again, this time from the tangle of woods at their back, from somewhere in the dark.

X.
Hex

-1-

The trail snaked ever deeper into the woods. The two travelers could see no settlements. The only signs of life were the torches stuck into the trail, beckoning them towards the next bend with warm pools of orange light. But as they walked further, the dark spaces between these torches became farther apart and more unsettling. The two began to move more quickly, convinced that the ceaseless night in this place was crawling on them, threatening to swallow them if they stayed within its black throat for too long. The crunching leaves underfoot betrayed them with each of their hurried steps.

Worst of all, the witch still followed them. The cackle they had heard earlier had been tracking them just to the right and just above the tree line, but neither Sam nor Lucia could see the owner of that raspy snicker. The witch did not spring, nor did it offer a glimpse of its person. This seemed to imply that the two wanderers were right on course and heading for some trap up ahead.

"It's like we're just walking into a trap," Sam said.

"Maybe it's just some kind of bird," Lucia offered, but the note of hope in her voice convinced neither of them. She didn't really hear her own words anyway. She was busy conjuring images of being slammed into an oven in some gingerbread cottage by a maniacal hag with a taste for children. She was seventeen, soon to be eighteen within a month, but did that qualify her as a child? Witches ate children, right? Surely her meat was not as sweet as it once was. Any witch with a taste for children would pass on the two of them for more tender fare, right?

Kidding herself was not her strong suit. She was making up rules that made sense and The Nowhere had its own set. For all she knew, witches here ate nothing but Mexican girls.

The watcher in the trees seemed to hear her thoughts and it snickered faintly, yet so close to Lucia that it was if the witch had a freakishly long neck and had leaned down from the branches to purr the laugh directly into her ear. She wanted to ask Sam if he noticed how close it was, but her answer came when Sam grabbed her arm and quickened their pace.

The undulating hills rising and falling all around them had now obscured their trail. There was nothing left to do now but concentrate on locating the next pool of light and making it there, hoping they were not going in endless circles as if they were spiraling down a drain.

"We should be leaving breadcrumbs," Lucia joked. She wanted Sam to know she was okay, that she was unaffected by whatever was following them through the dark, that she was strong. But her voice had sounded thin and young, and she wished she could take it back so her words didn't just hang in the fog like a desperate prayer in a bad dream.

Lucia's heart began to sink. She told herself to concentrate on the next pool of light, then the next, and then the next. This worked for awhile. It worked until she heard snapping branches, something crashing towards them through the underbrush, something very big. It worked until the ground began to quake beneath her feet and an impossible sight filled her vision. It was the gingerbread house she had feared. Yet, even her fevered imagination never anticipated what she saw. Somehow...

(oh God, somehow)

...the house was crashing towards them through the brittle, leafless trees and spraying branches into the moonlit fog on both sides of its shingled face like a buzz saw.

Lucia screamed.

Then, all of the torches went out.

-2-

Just before it went dark, Sam saw something that seared into his mind and danced in its center like the ghost image left by a flashbulb: the house was not just coming towards them; it was running towards them, running on what looked like the bones of chicken legs, maybe hundreds of them.

Before he could make sense of what he saw his body had already decided to leave. It moved fast, abandoning his gawking head and grabbing Lucia as it turned to run. Crouching, the two scrambled upslope and away from the oncoming house, their feet slipping on the fog-soaked leaves. They saw the thick trunk of a nearby tree and dove for it just as a severed branch whistled past their heads and struck the tree with a smack, sending a spray of bark pattering to the ground. Slamming their backs against the trunk, they froze, trying to catch their breath – breath that chugged like a pair of runaway trains. Sam's heart was on fire. It felt as if a branding iron was being pressed to his chest.

He cursed himself for regarding skateboarding as proper exercise. His vision starred white. He closed his eyes until controlled breathing finally replaced his panicked rasping. His heart calmed slowly to a dull thud as he listened. He heard nothing, nothing it all. He tried to gather enough spit in his mouth to speak.

"It stopped," he said. "The house, it stopped."

Lucia was against him, her hot breath on his neck as she peered over his shoulder and around the tree.

"*No puede...*" she mumbled dreamily into the night.

"I don't know what that means," Sam whispered, "but I have a feeling I agree."

Lucia mumbled more Spanish into his chest. She was clutching a wad of his shirt.

"Maybe this is not the time to tell you that the house has chicken legs," Sam said.

"What?"

"Oh, yeah. It's walking on chicken bones."

"Holy shit," she groaned. "What? Why? Really? That's just...wrong."

"Yes it is," Sam conceded and took a deep breath. "Yes it is. And I suppose we are going to have to take a closer look? Right? Fine. Great. Okay, but let's not stray too far from cover. I'm no expert on outrunning houses. You're the track star. You go first."

Lucia glared at him, horrified.

"I was kidding," he said, smiling weakly. "Really."

Lucia beat a fist on his chest and moaned.

Sam took a deep breath. He fixed Lucia with a steely look. "We both go. You ready? On the count of three we leave this tree and check it out. Okay? One..."

"LOOK!" Lucia cried, jabbing a finger into the sky.

They were only able to catch a glimpse, but the sight rooted them to where they stood. A shrill cackle drew their focus to a patch of indigo sky framed by a canopy of interlacing braches. There, in front of a moon that was as full and wide as their eyes, they saw the witch. Yet, this witch was not riding a broom. Instead, she was streaking and spinning over their heads in some kind of bowl as if she were piloting a flying saucer, silver hair flapping wildly around her head. She was a small woman. Her conveyance was no bigger than the tire of a truck.

She flew quickly past the patch of sky and the two were forced to break cover to follow her trajectory. The shadow of the witch streaked towards the cottage. The small house had come to a stop just shy of the trail, slightly below them and to the left. Sam could not see the legs beneath the house, but he knew they were there, waiting to lift the dwelling at any moment and sprint after them.

The cottage sat hulking in the clearing that it had made, two upstairs dormer windows staring at them, the front door yawning darkly like an open mouth.

The witch sailed over the slate roof in her bowl.

"Mortar..." Sam whispered dreamily. That's what Jacques had told them. She was sitting in a mortar and that stick she was holding – the one sticking out behind her like a rudder – was a pestle. Her flight had left a contrail of parted fog, but she was busy wiping it away with the stick, scattering the thin haze behind her, covering her tracks. The knight had spoken the truth.

"It's Baba Yaga," Sam whispered.

With a final cackle the witch hovered for a moment above the house, spun in place, and with a whoosh of air plunged down the chimney and out of sight.

Sam and Lucia were left in silence to listen to their runaway breath. The house was still. The woods were deathly quiet.

"What do we do now?" Lucia whispered.

"I don't know," Sam replied. "If this is Baba Yaga, then Jacques said she would help us."

"Nobody here is worth a shit," Lucia said, "and it might not be worth the risk."

"True," Sam agreed, "but the knight said that witches don't care about politics. They are not afraid of Simon. She may know something about Clara. After all, Clara is a witch...of sorts...I guess. Maybe they used to hang out."

"Used to hang out?"

Sam bit his lower lip and peered at the house, unresolved.

"Is that what druids are?" Lucia whispered. "Witches?"

"I don't know for sure. Maybe. The internet only said that they were priests of sorts. Anyway, even if I am connected to Clara and the other druid, Mog Ruith, I certainly don't want to be a witch. That shit is a little too goth for me."

"Sam, if YOU aren't goth then who is? You are the guy who brings a Halloween vibe to a 4th of July barbecue, whether you mean to or not. You OOZE goth, dude."

"Well, I don't want to be a witch!" Sam insisted, still peering at the house. "And, I don't know any magic. Even though everyone seems to think I do. I can't even do a card trick."

"Maybe you should start faking it," Lucia said. As the two kept talking they slowly approached the house. It was not very big now that it wasn't coming at them through the woods like a charging bull. Wistfully, Lucia thought of the small cabin where she and Sam – along with Allison, Lenny and a few others – had stayed in Lake Tahoe on spring break a million years ago and a million miles away. Spring suddenly sounded very good to Lucia: pastel colors, blooming flowers, mild sun, life.

"What I mean is," she said, her whisper becoming even more discreet as they crept ever closer, "if everyone assumes you to be Samhain, the bad-ass druid, then why not just go with it? Especially if you plan on knocking on that front door which I'm pretty sure you are planning on doing, right?"

Sam nodded resolutely.

Lucia continued, "In fact, from now on, it would be a good idea to bluff. At least until you understand what it is you are and what you are capable of doing. So far, the weirdoes we have met have been mostly uninterested in us, but the closer we get to where we are not supposed to go, the closer we get to Simon, the more likely we will be unwelcomed. All I'm saying is that this witch may be the first who has other plans for us. If she knows you are a bad-ass, maybe she will think twice before she messes with us."

"You're the bad-ass, Looze," Sam said. "I wouldn't have done this without you." He turned to look at her and grabbed both of her hands. "I only wonder if we're doing the right thing."

"Sam, we've gone over this." Exasperated, she wiggled her hands free of his. "The Nowhere wants us here tonight. It was screaming for us to come."

"No, I mean about us."

Lucia stalled and looked at the ground, embarrassed.

Sam continued, "When this is all over, are we going to regret that we did not remain just friends? Am I taking advantage of your fear, or of you being stuck in a strange place with me? I mean...am I having some lapse in judgment? I've known you for so long; I don't want to mess this up."

"You know what I don't want?" she asked, fishing for his hand again. "I don't want to be stuck in the "friend zone" with you, Sam. I never did."

"Good. Then kiss me."

She did, long and passionately. Their lips parted, and they stood for a moment looking at each other, their noses touching. Again, power had returned to them, the power to do anything.

"Okay," Sam said. "Let's pay that witch a visit."

They took a deep breath and continued their walk down the hill to the house that waited patiently for them, waited crouched in the swirling fog.

-3-

With a roar, the torches along the trail ignited at once. As the orange heads of fire sputtered back to life, they splashed their pale, flickering light up the shingled face of the cottage. Sam and Lucia pumped a squeeze into each other's palms. Fear snapped their eyes wide and slowed their approach.

The little cottage was pink and yellow, like some birthday cake laid away in a foggy walk-in freezer. There was something mockingly perverse about it: those cheerful hues in the middle of such darkness and decay. Lucia's nerves pricked into a low hum. She thought about Brother Christopher's biology class last year, learning about venomous snakes and how nature often warned you of danger ahead of time, usually with bright colors.

Sam was finding it very hard to take the final steps to the porch. More than ever, the house looked like a face to him: the two upstairs windows a pair of dead, staring eyes beneath the arched eyebrows of its peaked, dormer roofs. The front door was like the slackened jaw of the dead. And the paint, the paint was like the grisly illusion that a mortician would attempt, slapping some make-up onto the face of a corpse so that you would be comfortable getting nearer to it.

But they had to get nearer once they could get their feet to move. If it took one dragging step at a time, they had to get nearer. As they did, the light of the sputtering torches behind them cast their tall and crazily deformed shadows up the house's staring clown face.

The house lifted up with a groan, the chicken bone legs beneath it scrambling for purchase and finding it.

Sam and Lucia jumped back.

The house was kicking up moist soil and it was screaming with the torque of its wood and straining of its nails. It was going to come for them again.

Sam and Lucia cried out, and as they turned to run, Lucia's left foot came down wrong. She buckled and fell to one knee, and before they could regain themselves and run, the house had settled back down again with an earthshaking thud. Sam craned his neck around. The house was motionless. It had only spun in place. It had turned 180 degrees.

"Shit!" Lucia said, standing slowly, Sam helping her to her feet.

"You okay?" Sam asked.

"Yeah," She wiggled her foot. "I can walk it off."

Now, the two were looking at the back of the cottage. There were no windows and no doors, only a wall of candy striped clapboards.

Sam's voice was distant, "What is it up to?"

"It's that witch in there," Lucia whispered, "she's commanding the house...or something. She's messing with us."

Giving the cottage a wide berth, but not daring to take his eyes off it, Sam took the lead and made his way around the side of the house. He put his finger to his lips and motioned Lucia to join him. They were almost back to the front door when the house lurched into life, standing up on its legs again.

Lucia yelped and headed for the trees. Sam followed looking over his shoulder.

The house lifted and spun in place again, spitting dead leaves and a vortex of fog from its foundation before thudding back to the ground. Again, it had turned 180 degrees. Again, they were now facing the back of the house.

"The paper," Sam said, patting his pockets.

Jacques de Molay had seemed like a long, long time ago, and Lucia had all but forgotten about the paper the blackened knight had given them.

"Found it," Sam said, holding up the paper. "Let's go."

The two headed up the trail to the nearest torch. Beneath its pool of light he carefully unfolded the parchment. They both stared at the words. No, not just words, it was a spell. It was a spell if there ever was one, and Jacques de Molay had written it on a piece of cured skin with his own burnt flesh for ink.

"This actually isn't dabbling in witchcraft," Sam said. "It's jumping in head first."

Lucia's stomach wrung like a dishrag when she thought of her mother finding out what they were doing. She squeezed shut her eyes really tight and then opened them hoping that maybe she would be home again. She even flashed on the Wizard of Oz, glancing down at her shoes, but they were free of rubies. They were only dirty sneakers.

"Well," Sam said as he stood facing the house, holding the tattered page out before him, "here goes nothing."

-4-

"Wait!" Lucia cried. "You have to say it exactly..."

"Or we will be eaten. Yes, that part I remember. Now, don't interrupt me."

Lucia wilted and stepped back, hugging herself.

Sam held up the page before his eyes. His hands were trembling. He cleared his throat and bellowed at the house: "Oh Hut! Oh Hut! Turn your back to the forest, turn your front to me! Ss...

(don't say Sam Hain. Say it how it's pronounced)

...SAO-WEN COMMANDS YOU!"

To their utter astonishment, the cottage before them promptly complied, lifting onto its strange, bony chicken legs. The house whipped around, blowing their hair back, before crashing back to the earth. There was a weird, breathless silence, the displaced fog drifting towards them and then over them like a passing procession of ghosts.

The front door clicked and groaned slowly open on rusty hinges.

The two stood agape.

"Okay," Sam said, panting with relief. "That went well."

Lucia wasn't listening. She was staring through the open door. She could see clearly inside. The innards of the house were lit with flickering light. Past the open front door a short hallway dead-ended at a wall. Above its wainscoting, the wall was papered with yellow and pink stripes, and centered on the wall at eye level was an ornate Black Forest cuckoo clock, its pendulum swinging slowly and steadily like a hypnotist's chain. The violent movements of the house had not affected it at all. In the silence she could hear it tick. The clock had no hands.

Then the wall beside the clock began to darken with a shadow, spreading and lengthening into a human figure crawling up the yellow and pink stripes, a hunched figure with crooked, arthritic hands kneading the air. The owner of the shadow was coming from some side room to the left, its form eclipsing the clock's face and blackening out the carnival wallpaper.

It was coming to greet them.

Both Sam and Lucia's breath froze in their lungs when they saw the first point of a shoe enter the distant hallway, then the hem of a black dress, and then...

Tiny, she was tiny.

Sam and Lucia exhaled, swooning with relief.

The witch was three feet tall at the most, and she was young. More than that, she looked improbable, like a child's doll that had come to life; a well cared for heirloom with dark, lifelike eyes.

"Won't you come in?" she cooed from the distant, flickering hallway. Her voice was high and sweet.

Sam and Lucia looked at each other. They walked forward, hesitating at the front step.

"Don't be afraid," said the witch-girl, "I won't eat you. I don't think I could. You are both SO big!"

Sam and Lucia studied her. Her alabaster cheeks were flamed with circles of rouge. Above the modest neckline of her black dress, she wore a cameo on a ribbon of blood-red velvet. Her dark, round eyes were framed by a bob of raven-black hair.

Neither Sam nor Lucia could manage a word.

"You must be Samhain," said the witch-girl. She turned her doll head to Lucia, "And you must be Lucia, the Mayan girl. My name is Baba Yaga." She pronounced her last name Jay-ga. She beckoned them forward insistently with a chubby arm. "Please, come in. Your time is short. I will answer your three questions."

"Three questions?" Sam asked. Lucia nudged him hard, all the while fixing the witch with a plastered-on smile.

Sam stiffened, "Oh, yes, that's good. Yes, we have a lot of questions."

"But I will only answer three," Baba Yaga admonished, holding up a cautioning finger and wagging it before her raised eyebrows. "Only three. You see, I get older every time I assist a traveler. At least, in your world I did, but old habits die hard. Underneath this skin is a five-hundred-year-old soul and a five-hundred-year-old skeleton to match. That, I cannot change. Old bones still hurt here, and I don't hurt for just anyone. Ah, but you, you are a special case. You might just be able to beat him."

"Simon?" Sam asked.

"Yesss," Baba Yaga replied, savoring the word. "But let's not stand here in the doorway. It's dangerous out there. Come in, won't you?"

-5-

They sat on tiny furniture in the witch's tiny living room. It was essentially a doll house and it wasn't long before a realization slammed into Lucia, drawing a palm to her open mouth: the place looked familiar. She had played with a doll house just like this place when she was little, although hers had been no bigger than a hat box. It had split in the middle, opening on a hinge like a book to expose its two-level cross section. Yes, she would swear to it: the pink and yellow stripes, the little ceramic teapot clutched in the witch's hand...

Baba Yaga settled in her chair, "Your questions?"

The witch poured steaming tea into little cups that sat on little saucers that sat on little doilies.

"None for me thanks," Sam protested.

After all of this time, Sam was finally lit by something close to normal lighting and Lucia took the opportunity to drink him in. His ruddy hair was a mess, sticking up in tufts. There was a smudge of something on his cheek: probably a missed streak of his old skull make-up. He looked adorably uncomfortable on his little chair, his knees higher than his lap and Lucia was finding it hard to tame the smile on her face as she watched him.

"It's not poison," the witch said, the pot poised above Sam's cup. "You read too many fairy tales. If I wanted to kill you I would have done so already. I'm only being hospitable. Just because I am a witch does not mean I am an animal." The witch's cherry red lips pouted.

Sam looked skeptical.

"I AM from Europe," the witch said slyly, raising her fine little eyebrows as if she thought this might make some difference. "Don't you find that fancy in your part of the world? So...none of my fancy tea?"

Sam nodded reluctantly. Delighted, the witch poured the tea.

"You would be foolish to try and poison him anyway," Lucia said simply as the steaming tea poured into her own cup. "Samhain does not take attempts on his life too kindly."

Baba Yaga paused in mid-pour, her lips now a thin line. Her eyes met Lucia's. They were as black and dry as raisins, "I'll remember that."

Lucia knew she had either scared the witch or had made an enemy. As if to make up for her insolence, Lucia quickly raised the cup to her nose. "It smells yummy. Thank you."

Sam eyed the witch, waiting for her to drink. When she did, he took a sip from his own cup. It wasn't half bad: sweet and floral.

"Enjoy," Baba Yaga said. "It's bat piss and peppermint."

The tea had had barely passed Lucia's lips when she spit it out in a fine spray, her cup clattering back to her saucer. Sam put down his own cup and glared at the witch.

The witch laughed hysterically, but it was no child's laugh. It was the gurgling, congested cackle of a very old woman and it was bone-chilling as it brayed from the witch's baby face. Sam's neck hair stood on end and he edged his cup and saucer away with walking fingers.

"You two are too easy," she said, her child's voice settling back into its place. "It's night-blooming ghost vine. That's all it is. We get a lot of it here."

Lucia cast down her eyes, trying to recover her nerves.

"Are our family members here?" Sam blurted. His nerves were shot too and he felt he had precious little patience. "My parents? Lucia's brother, Carlo?"

"Ahhh, the first question," Baba Yaga said settling back in her chair with a creak and peering over her teacup. "No."

"No?" Sam asked.

"No," the witch confirmed. "Why would they be? This is The Nowhere. This place is for those who are special." She drew out the last word, giving it a bitter emphasis.

Lucia looked stricken. She pressed her lips together, but still they trembled. Her eyes became wet.

But..." Sam leaned forward, "Simon told us that they were here."

"Simon Magus is a liar," Baba Yaga said simply. She eyed Sam suspiciously. "You should know that, Samhain. That is the first thing you should have known."

Sam clapped his back into his chair and simmered. When he had regained himself, he straightened and asked, "Then who is Simon Magus?"

"Question two?"

Sam looked momentarily unsure, and then he nodded resolutely.

"Don't you both go to Catholic school?" the witch mused.

Startled, Lucia straightened in her chair as well, "How do you know that?"

"The Veil is thin, dear," replied the witch, "and my reach is greater than most. It is true of most witches..." she turned to offer Sam a cursory nod, "...and druids, but particularly with me because I am the font of many witches of history. I am the patron saint of Hex. Just like your clan mother, Clara, I reach through The Veil and I can bend many to my will."

"You know Clara?" Sam brightened.

"A third question?" the witch smiled.

"No," Sam said hastily. "Maybe, but not yet."

The witch nodded and sipped her tea, "So you go to catholic school and you know nothing of Simon Magus. And, you are surprised at his lies? Surprised that a man who once tried to pass himself off as Christ – quite successfully I might add, even gathering a fair share of disciples throughout Rome – would lie to you about such a small little thing? Simon Magus is ancient. He is the first real sorcerer, and undoubtedly the greatest. Even the word 'magic' is connected to him. And lucky you, he is also the one who means to destroy you."

"But why?" Lucia asked.

"Is that your last question?" the witch snapped, turning to glare at Lucia. Just for a moment, Baba Yaga flashed her true form: a wrinkled, shrunken head that looked like a rotten apple topped with white, wiry hair, the sunken eyes no bigger than chips of flint and just as lifeless, the smile wide and hungry, teeth like wads of chewed gum stuck at random angles into her moldy jaw.

Lucia recoiled, upsetting the tiny sugar bowl.

"NO!" Sam cried, "That's not our last question!"

"Very well," Baba Yaga said, her placid doll face now returning as she looked back to Sam. Once again, her voice was sweet as syrup, "more tea?"

Sam ignored her. He had caught Lucia's eye and he could see

that there was something very wrong with her. He had missed something, but it was clear from Lucia's bleached face and darting eyes that she was suddenly very afraid. It was time to wrap up this little tea party.

"Oh, and one more thing about Simon," the witch said, pouring herself another cup. "He killed your parents."

Time stopped. The world had smudged away and soupy unreality filled the dead space left behind. How long Sam sat there breathlessly he did not know. How long he was suspended in cold jelly he could not tell either. Finally, his woozy mind fixed on a distant sound. It was the witch. She was slurping at the hot liquid from her teacup, tasting it, savoring it, her dark eyes glittering keenly at Sam above the rim.

"Yes," the witch continued. "Ran them down. In a Rolls-Royce, no less. He certainly has taste, wouldn't you say?"

Sam stared at her, his breath chuffing steadily from his nose. His vision was tunneling. Now, only he and the doll thing before him existed. Only he and the filthy, lying doll thing...

"You lie," Sam said through his clenched teeth, but he had no wind left in his lungs. He had to take a deep breath to continue. "It was an accident."

"Whatever," Baba Yaga said dismissively, and she slurped her tea.

"You expect me to believe that?" Sam asked. Even as his mind fluttered like a shuffling deck of cards, his voice remained steady. "You expect me to believe that Simon can come and go through The Veil at will? That he can DRIVE A CAR! YOU LYING BITCH!" Sam stood up, knocking over his tiny teacup on his tiny saucer, spilling its contents onto the tiny doily.

Baba Yaga set her cup down gently and nodded in a parody of understanding. She was...

(in control)

Sam knew he had to keep it together, but his vision was clouding with a thousand emotions.

"No one was driving the car, Samhain," the witch continued. "Did they catch anyone?"

Sam had meant to go for the little thing's throat, to throttle her until she admitted that she was a liar, until she apologized and begged for mercy, but he wavered. Now he was confused. She was right. They had never found the driver. Why had they never found the driver?

"Sam," Lucia pleaded, reaching across the table to find his hand, "please..."

He flicked a glance at Lucia. She looked even more scared now, and he was probably the one scaring her. He sat very slowly; his hands clenched on his lap, staring a hole into the doll thing.

Was Baba Yaga nervous? She looked it. Although it was little consolation, Sam thought that maybe she feared his magic, his non-existent magic, but Sam knew this creature before him was no fool. So, if she feared him at all, even a little, then maybe she knew something about him that he didn't: he was worthy of being feared. Cautiously, and with his palms flat on his knees, Sam deflated.

Baba Yaga leaned forward, and in a conspiratorial whisper said: "Simon's reach is long, but you have come in time. He means to go after the priest next."

"Father Doctor?" Sam asked. Gone was his fierceness of only moments ago and to his ears he now sounded like a homesick little boy.

"Yes," said the witch. "The priest knows everything. He knows you are here. Taking out the priest would clear a nice path for Simon, prevent further complications. Even now, the priest is trying to figure out a way to intervene."

"He knows?" Lucia asked Sam. "Father Doctor knows?"

Sam could only return Lucia's question with a blank stare.

"Once his path is clear," continued the witch, "he will destroy The Veil. The dead will have free reign over the living. But only you can stop him, you and the Mayan girl. Clara will help you."

"Then where is he?" Sam asked. "How do I get to Clara?"

"The last question," the witch said. "and a good one. You will have to follow the ridgeline behind this house, follow it around Hex. Then, you will head for the mountain of Black Fang. Simon's tomb crowns its summit. The sorcerer spent quite a bit of time holed up in Hadrian's tomb in Rome during the second century. He has recreated the tomb here. It's quite the tourist attraction for the lost souls who are stupid enough to get anywhere near it. I guess its construction here was a sentimental choice. It was built by the Leeches, Simon's slaves. Great location for a last stand, don't you think?"

Sam and Lucia said nothing.

The witch went on, "The sands of time are not piled in your favor – you must go. The centurion, Orace Fley, hunts you. He may already be licking at your heels."

"Fley..." Sam repeated, searching his memory.

"You know of him?" the witch asked.

"He works for Simon?" Sam asked without much hope of getting a straight answer. His three questions had been used. The witch grimaced, her eyes twinkling. She knew Sam was trying to sneak another one in, and he was letting him know that she was amused by the attempt, but not fooled by it. However, as they all stood, she answered. "They are old friends from Rome. Orace Fley fed on the blood of the living in his day. Although he needs no such sustenance now, those juicy hearts of yours will surely make Fley hungry for old times. Do you realize how loud your hearts beat? I heard you coming a long way away."

"Yeah, we've been told that," said Sam.

"A vampire..." Lucia mused under her breath.

"If you like," the witch said.

"Vampires are not so bad," Lucia considered. "Usually they are just a bunch of overly dramatic metrosexuals with relationship problems and gym memberships."

"Not even close," the witch cautioned. "Fley is a monster and he embraces it. He is a warrior and he commands a rather large army of his more...shall we say, defective brethren.

The witch kept talking as she led them to the door: "We call that brand of bloodsucker a Leech. There is no blood around here for them, and lucky for you that hunger is gone, but what has replaced it is far worse. They are insane creatures. During their lives, they never got used to the idea of being bloodsuckers, infected humans, vampires, or whatever you want to call them. So, something in them snapped long, long ago. Now that they're stuck in The Nowhere, their worst fears of being abandoned by God and the Devil alike are fully realized. The whole thing has made them as crazy and depraved as a bunch of shithouse rats."

Baba Yaga opened the front door. For the first time, Sam noticed that the keyhole in the door was full of tiny little gnashing teeth.

The witch leveled a final, humorless grin at them as they walked onto the porch. "So, best of luck, kiddies. Bye, bye then."

As soon as Sam and Lucia cleared the threshold, the witch slammed the door.

-6-

The two walked through inky shadows cast by splayed branches of massive oaks that were draped in Spanish moss. The moon's silver knives were only able to cut an occasional, feeble gash into the forest floor before them. There was no path to speak of; this was wilderness. The civic-minded torches of the trail they had cause to abandon were far over their shoulders now. The witch had suggested they keep to the deepest shadows, to keep off the main trail to Hex if they wanted to thwart Orace Fley.

When finally they saw the city of Hex, it was from the crest of a ridge and from between two trees. It looked as though the long lost sun were rising far below. Approaching a cliff's edge, they kept low and crawled on their stomachs for a better view. The sight astonished them.

A wide valley, framed by low hills, spread below them like a sparkling blanket. Above them, witches – Sam figured there must have been hundreds of them – criss-crossed the sky on brooms, in kettles, on carpets. They were obviously witches from many cultures, from many epochs and they had all congregated here to form their city, a city lit by thousands of orange flames that sent wisps of black smoke towards the face of the moon.

Sam ducked lower into the cover of a thick bush as a witch flew past at eye-level. The old hag, dressed in laced robes and a bonnet tied at her chin, turned her ashen face towards them as she streaked by, her eyes tracking Sam.

(spotted)

Sam's heart sunk. If he had been seen would the witch sound an alarm? Sam watched as the witch swooped left, and in a graceful arc, plunged into the valley below. Sam figured there was not much he could do about it now. He decided not to tell Lucia.

"Wow," Lucia said, lost in her amazement. "They formed their own city."

Thousands of hovels dotted the valley floor in pools of flickering light. Most were simple wooden structures, leaning at boozy angles and clustered in patches. A few, however, were grand. Left on the horizon was a black renaissance chateau with capped towers that stabbed the sky. In the heart of town was a public square where dark figures milled about, traversing the square and spilling into the adjoining veins of cobbled streets. A low, industrious murmur rose from the city along with the tendrils of black smoke.

Lying on her stomach, peering between the branches of her sheltering bush, Lucia listened to this distant hum of thousands of far away voices, the occasional cackle percolating above the din and rolling across the orange glow of the valley.

She opened her eyes. She wondered...

(how long she had been asleep)

She must have been more exhausted than she thought. It felt good to lie on the ground, on the soft down of the forest floor, and she had to stretch wide her eyes to keep them from falling shut. With a yawn she pondered the sight below her. What had all of them done to end up here, to be abandoned in The Nowhere? Was it just witchcraft that landed them here or some deeper betrayal of the gods? Below her were thousands of stories that she would never hear. Thousands of them...

She opened her eyes. She had fallen asleep again.

The city of Hex came back into focus, and again she was dazzled by the sight. She realized what the streetlights were. They were pumpkins on stakes, and they gave the entire city a flickering orange glow. They were far away, but she fancied that she could even make out the frightening faces carved on them. She thought briefly of Jack of the Lantern, of old Stingy Jack.

"Jack was right. This is where we get Halloween," she whispered to Sam. "It's true. This is where it comes from. It has all leaked into our world from here. Isn't it amazing? Isn't it just amazing?"

With a grunt, she pulled herself off of her stomach and onto her elbows so that she could turn and look at Sam.

But Sam wasn't there.

"Sam?" Lucia asked the emptiness beside her. She sprang to her feet, whipping her head around. "SAM!" Cold dread flared in her heart and spread to her limbs like an infection.

"SAM!" she cried at the silent woods. Only a distant cackle from somewhere in the far away city of witches came to her ears. "No...." she moaned. "No..."

(of course)

(the tea)

They had been set up. This was not the way to Black Fang. It was an ambush, it was nothing but an ambush and she had slept through it. They had left her and they had taken Sam. There was no need to call his name again. Lucia sank to the ground, her hand pawing the trail of packed dirt where he had been dragged away. Just like that, she was alone in The Nowhere.

Just like that, Sam was gone.

PART THREE
THE TOMB OF THE FALSE PROPHET

XI.
The Phantom

-1-

Lucia had almost convinced herself that Sam would return. She was suddenly sure that she had been hasty leaving the spot on the ridgeline. Sam was probably wondering where she was. He had simply heard something and had gone ahead to investigate, not wanting to wake her. It had to be that simple. It had to be. If she just would have been patient, she would have heard his voice, the snapping of twigs, his tufts of spiked hair etched against the moonlight. He would wonder how long she had been awake. He would tell her that they were safe. He would kiss her and flood her with relief and happiness.

But even as these thoughts burst and fizzled in the center of her head like little fireworks, she knew they held no real promise. They were only ghosts, like everything in this place, useless remnants of a world that had once made sense. No, she had waited, staring at the place where he should have been for a long, long time. He wasn't coming back.

She found herself walking slowly downhill through brush and the low branches of trees, some of them cracking loudly to allow her passage, some of them stubborn and sweeping past her face, grazing her numb skin and leaving marks. She didn't care. Even when one claw-like twig drew blood, a thin line of sticky warmth cutting a trail down her dirty cheek, she didn't feel it. She walked without purpose, without feeling, without any idea of what to do next, or of where she was going. She simply walked, the dark world refracting with her tears.

(alone)

Why was she even here? Why had she come? She had convinced herself that she was part of this, part of some great mystery, but The Nowhere did not need her. It had simply chewed her up and spit her out. Not even the great and terrible enemies that haunted this place had thought enough of her to kill her, or to even detain her. They had simply let her sleep as they dragged Sam away. She had been of no more consequence than the dirt she had been laying on.

Simon had tricked her, telling her that her brother was here. Sure, Clara had warned them in the texts that everyone would lie, that everything here was a trap, but the seed had been planted. Even the remote possibility of her being able to see Carlo again had been too delicious a carrot not to chase. Simon had used her pain and her loss to lure her into The Nowhere, but why? Why did she have to be here at all?

It was clear now that both Simon and Clara wanted Sam here to force some kind of standoff. Clara must have thought Sam had a better chance of stopping Simon on this side of The Veil. And Simon? According to the witch, Simon fancied that he also had a better chance at stopping Sam here, but again, why her? It was obvious now that she meant nothing in all of this. Was it just a cruel amusement for Simon?

Then, the answer came to her. The simplicity of the answer was so revolting to her, that her teeth clenched so that her jaw began to ache: Simon had only used her as insurance, and now that he had gotten his prize, she was of no concern anymore. She was just a girl who had feelings for Simon's prey. Who better to talk Sam into delving deeper into his strange nature, to urge him forward, to devise the plan and get him to the cemetery on time? She was a pawn, the pawn of some ancient madman, and she had placed Sam into the hand of doom, right in the center of its meaty palm. All Simon had to do was sit back, sharpen his claws, and wait for the one Sam trusted most to deliver Sam on a silver platter.

Had Sam been hurt? Had they dragged him kicking and screaming? How did she know he was even alive? This final thought scared her so badly that she stumbled, falling to one knee and tearing a slice in the leg of her black jeans. She groped in the darkness for something to prevent a fall down the steep slope and found a handful of gummy tendrils.

(ivy)

Her mind flared with loss. She remembered entering The Nowhere, out through the mouth of that far away cave. They had walked into this place through a curtain of ivy. They had walked hand in hand. She yearned to feel his warmth again, that simple gesture of enfolding her hand into his that could erase all of her fears and recharge her will.

A noise to her left shattered her thoughts. It was the feral call of some godforsaken creature. It sounded like a huge door opening slowly on rusty hinges; another thing denied entrance to Hell. She heard whatever it was crash through the thick brush and scurry up the hill far to her left.

(it wants to come at you from behind)

For a moment, Lucia resigned herself to death. Maybe it was better than what her future had in store. It could only save her from other horrors, maybe some that were far worse.

She stopped to listen. The thing was receding, its alien call being swallowed by the forest somewhere up the hill. When she was sure it was out of range, she moved through the woods again, pawing at the dark.

Suddenly, anger flushed her torn cheeks. Look at what she to deal with now: thoughts of surrender, thoughts of death and the slow dismantling of her spirit. The callousness, the cruelty of her abandonment made her heart begin to beat like a war drum. Would she have preferred that they killed her when they had the chance? No, of course not, but they should have. The fact that she had been discounted – left asleep on the ridgeline as an inconsequential heap of garbage – began to stoke her indignity until she wanted to hurt someone, wanted to hurt them bad.

She stood looking at her flexing hand, the one that still gripped a wad of ivy, a hand trembling with adrenaline. She was alive, and as long as she was alive she would make someone pay. They had taken Sam. There was nothing left to do but take him back, and as she paused to look at the moon in that tangle of dead forest she made a vow: whoever – or whatever – took Sam from her would wish they had never come across Lucia Winter. By the time she was through with them, they would be beating at the gates of Hell, pleading to be let in.

-2-

(wake up)

Someone was stroking his hair.

(Lucia?)

His eyes fluttered open.

It wasn't Lucia.

He saw nothing but teeth above him, yellow and craggy, tucked into white and wrinkled lips. They were cadaver lips, split at their edges and fouled with grave rot. He shrank away as the lips parted in a hungry smile. The thing leaning over him was vaguely human, but it was panting like an overheated dog. A drop of drool hit him on the cheek.

His freezing mind could make no sense of it. The thing had materialized from nothing, from the bark of the trees, the forest rippling through it as if the world were merely reflected on water, until finally its spectral camouflage began to bend to the will of whatever laws still remained in this place and it turned solid. It turned solid and grabbed him before he could take a breath, before he could scream.

Now there were four of them, six of them, a dozen. The cloaking, ethereal plain from whence they had come began to reject them, pushing them forward into their stark and perverse sacks of assumed flesh, their forms coagulating before Sam's wide and unbelieving eyes. The last thing he saw clearly was the almost transparent white of their faces pocked by sunken black eye sockets, faces that caught the moonlight as if they were lit from within.

Then, something cold and wet pressed down on his face, and darkness came.

-3-

"Sam...?"

(Lucia?)

No, it was another trick.

Behind his closed eyes he was fully awake now, and in a fetal ball. In a burst of memory, he recalled a pastiche of random moments of consciousness: swirling orange fire, heavy footfalls surrounding him, strange sounds from the mouths of those who hoisted him above their heads, sounds like panting dogs, depraved and thirsting. There had been a wall, a great wall that filled his vision followed by clanging metal, keys, iron gates.

"Sam, can you hear me?"

It was a trick. It was not Lucia. It was not her voice. It was older. He kept his eyes closed and flinched from the thing's touch.

"It's okay. You're safe now."

The voice was kind, maternal. Even in a whisper he could hear the accent. It was Irish. A smooth palm stroked his cheek.

"It's me, Sam. It's Clara."

-4-

Father Doctor tried Sam's cell phone one more time without much hope of him answering. It went to voicemail. The priest listened to the boy's recorded voice again, praying desperately that it would not be the last thing he would ever hear him say.

He flicked his eyes to the clock on the wall. In fifteen minutes Halloween would end and it would be New Year's Day – at least as far as the druids were concerned. What was going to happen, he didn't know, and he didn't know if time even existed in the same way in the place where his son was now, but he did know that midnight was not called the "witching hour" for nothing. Whatever was coming was on its way.

He had tried to heed the Monsignor's words, to let fate play its hand, to let Sam follow the path that he was meant to follow, but it felt like a dereliction to do so. Sure, he had always known this day would come, but that was little consolation.

A thought cleaved suddenly through the gooey mess of hot anxiety in his head. Why hadn't he tried calling Lucia Winter? He had the girl's number in his phone. Sam had given it to him a long time ago when they had gone away to Lake Tahoe. "Just in case my phone craps out and you really need to reach me," Sam had said.

Quickly, he plucked the phone from his desk, wiped a hand across his bleary eyes and scrolled for Lucia's number.

-5-

Connie Winter awoke to the sound of soft music. She had fallen asleep in her chair in the living room. The tinny, Latin jazz ringtone galloped from Lucia's little cell phone speaker, then the measure repeated. It wasn't until the third ring that Connie's thawing brain registered what was happening. Collapsing the footrest on her Lay-Z-Boy chair, she lunged for the phone, her heart hammering. Lucia was calling.

Yet, even though her mind was still not free of sleep's fog, a dismal conclusion formed as she fumbled for the talk button: Lucia would not call her own cell phone. But it was when she held the phone to her ear that she swooned with a revelation that was far worse: the voice on the other end was a man's voice – not a boy's...

(the police)

(she's dead)

"Lucia?"

"This is not Lucia. This is her mother. Who is this?"

"I'm so sorry to...I thought...it's Father Michael Riordan – Father Doctor? I was just...I didn't know where Sam was. I thought he would be back by now. Again, sorry to call so late. Are you with them by any chance?"

"No Father," Connie sighed with relief. "I am not with them. I am home. Lucia left her phone in the living room. I am worried about them too. They said they were going to Lenny Kidd's costume party after they left us at the cemetery, but then this boy texted her – a boy I don't know – and told her he was waiting for her. It makes no sense. You have not heard from Sam?"

"No," Father Doctor replied. "No, I have not. If you don't mind me asking, what was the boy's name? The one who said he was waiting for her?"

"Simon. Do you know who this boy is? Is he a friend of Sam's?"

The priest's stomach clenched. Beyond his rising nausea he was vaguely aware of the woman's tone of accusation, the sharp edge that indicated her assertions: Sam was a bad influence. This was all Sam's fault.

Maybe it was, but Father Doctor was far too busy breaking out in a cold sweat to assuage this woman's fears or to defend himself as a father or to defend Sam's quality as a friend. Large beads of sweat were making their way from his armpits to his waist like crawling beetles. He felt as helpless as he had ever felt in his life.

"Father? Are you there?"

"Yes..."

"So, do you know this Simon?"

(do you know the false Christ?)

"No..." he said, the lie falling from his lips like a shot squeezed slowly from a revolver by a reluctant assassin. Did she have the right to know what was happening? Did she have the right to know who Simon Magus was and what he might want with her daughter? Of course she did, but he was not going to tell her. Not now. It would do no good. What he really needed to do now was to reconcile himself with his two dismal options: either develop a taste for liquor quickly so that he might get some sleep, or else begin wandering the streets calling Sam's name as if the boy was a lost dog.

Connie Winter was still going on in his ear, her tone prickly: something about worry, something about not approving, something about nice boys and not so nice boys. Through the glut of words one thing she said clawed its way through his private thoughts and snapped Father Doctor to attention: "...and I've never seen that car before, the one in front of your house? It's big. It's a nice car. Did you buy it? I didn't think priests made so much money. I don't mean to be nosy, but it's Halloween and you can't be too careful. A lot of mischief, y' know? At first, I thought you might be having company, a party maybe? But then, I didn't think a Catholic would have a Halloween party. Someone visiting from out of town? It's none of my business..."

(car?)

The priest snapped his eyes to the office window.

(nothing)

Only the shrub at the bottom of the window waved in a light breeze. He stood, approached the window, and craned his neck to see the street beyond the lawn.

Father Doctor was a simple man with simple tastes and had a very limited knowledge of luxury cars, so he had little chance of recognizing that the make and model of the car parked at the curb were Rolls-Royce and Phantom, respectively. All he knew was that it was very big, very black and so out of place on his working class street that the sight of it filled him with dread.

"Are you there, Father?" Connie asked.

"No party..." Father Doctor mumbled into the phone.

"I didn't think so," Connie Winter went on. Her accent seemed to be thickening as she perceived her admonitions to be silencing the priest. She started talking about Halloween, about evil, about "the devil's night".

"Mrs. Winter," Father Doctor said, keeping his eyes on the car and summoning the well-honed, ecclesiastical tone that had saved him on many occasions, the one that both drew on his authority and calmed the listener. "Mrs. Winter, I will let you know if I hear anything from Sam or Lucia. Please do the same? I'm sure they will be okay. After all, they are adults. Midnight is not that late for such a holiday. We should not worry ourselves sick."

Connie Winter tapered to a few mumbled words in Spanish, and then said: "Okay, Father. Goodnight."

"Goodnight," Father Doctor hung up the phone, his unblinking eyes still leveled at the enormous black car on the street. An ethereal, bluish light glinted from its chrome.

He looked out the window, left and then right. There were no other cars on the street except for the white pickup that Brad Gould used for his fly-by-night plumbing work. It was in its familiar spot on the street two houses down, but he'd never seen the black car before. Maybe the neighbors on either side of him had company. Then why was the car not parked in front of their houses? The street was empty. Why was it parked directly in front of his own house?

(because the car came for you)

The thought pulled him away from the window. "Ridiculous," he mumbled. There was no reason to dread a car. His nerves were shot, that was all. He decided it couldn't hurt to take a closer look, perhaps make a note of the license plate. Pulling on a coat from the hall closet, he scolded himself: "You're turning into an old man already."

Still, the fresh air would do him good. His empty house had become stifling, his skin tacky with sweat. He tugged open his front door. The night air hit his face with a bracing slap. He stopped at the bottom step of his porch.

The car was a hearse.

He had not noticed the back windows before. From his office window, the mailbox had obscured this detail, but sure enough, in the back window, there were curtains. Currently they were swept to the sides and fastened with tie-backs. The sedan had been altered slightly, the back end elongated and fixed with clam shell doors, also with lace curtains drawn back from their tinted windows.

Father Doctor approached, his slippers crunching the bronze-colored leaves on the cement walk. It was dead quiet.

(dead quiet in Colma)

Father Doctor smiled weakly, trying to make light of this, but his body was sounding alarms. His heart began to race. He could feel his carotid artery bulging with hot blood. He was scared, very scared. Something was very wrong and the wrongness seemed to thicken the closer he got to the car.

"Relax..." he whispered to nobody. "Chill," Sam would have said. He tried, but his feet were dragging as he neared the end of his cement walk. The car...

(was patient)

...was in very good shape, not a ding, not a scratch. Its black armor was waxed to a mirror finish. It was the kind of car that you would see at a car show, rotating lazily on a mirrored turntable, a velvet rope protecting it from your impulse to reach out and touch it, to prove to yourself that it wasn't just a dream or a carving in black ice.

He reached the sidewalk. It was as close as he wanted to get. From a distance, he crouched and peered through the passenger window, casually, as if he were adjusting his slipper.

The car was empty.

He really didn't want to be near the car anymore. As pretty as it was, it was a pernicious beauty, like the streamlined body of a shark or the symmetry and gloss of a black widow spider. Now that he was close to it, it seemed to be secreting bad intentions.

But he had one more task: just glance at the license plate and make a note of it, then he would go. A small bush was in the way. With his hands in his pockets and a deep breath, he stepped off the curb. He glanced at the plate:

SAMZDED

His legs buckled.

The car roared to life, the headlights splashing him with blinding light.

-6-

Lucia stumbled and grabbed at the air for support. She had been crying again, her tears drawing from an endless well. Her hand found a wad of foliage that steadied her for a moment before it ripped from its source and sent her sprawling forward.

She heard a human voice.

Her eyes widened and she got to a crouch, pain flaring in her knee.

It was a man's voice, deep and sonorous, and it was coming from above her, somewhere in the woods. She tried to control her body, her mind, but they were all writhing in their respective agonies. Clenching her teeth she pricked her ears and held her breath, her eyes straining to see something, anything through the blackness, through the impenetrable forest that had swallowed her.

"PERHAPS YOU WANT THE WRAITHS OF THE PITCH TO CHEW ON YOUR SOULS?" the man roared from somewhere above.

The sound of pleading followed from a group of raspy voices, maybe twenty or thirty of them, all clamoring for mercy.

The man lowered his tone to one of menacing patience. Lucia had to strain to hear, but she could still make out the words: "Leeches! How do you mistake a Thumper for dead? You're telling me her heart stopped? You are as full of lies as you are full of bugs. If she was dead then whose footprints are these? Tell me that you worthless, blithering idiots!?"

There was no answer. Lucia's pain and fear had been replaced with wonder. An acoustic effect of the ravine was making it possible for her to hear this far away exchange. As long as the man with the deep voice remained somewhat heated, she could still make sense of it all, even if now she were only getting bits and pieces on the wind: the witch had given her too much. The witch would have to deal with Simon. The Mayan was alive. For once in their godforsaken lives, the Leeches were lucky. Find her now.

Then the bits and pieces stopped and a lunatic battle cry shook the woods. As Lucia stood rooted, the cold sweat trickling down the small of her back, an army began crashing through the underbrush above, heading straight for her position.

-7-

The Rolls-Royce lurched forward with a squeal as its tires bit into the asphalt. It happened so fast that Father Doctor had little time to react. His hands had flown to his face to protect his eyes from the headlamps' searing light, and before he could register that the car had somehow started, it was already running him down. Its enormous grill, like the cow catcher on a freight train, was inches from biting into his stomach and sending him into the sky as a lifeless ragdoll.

Stiff-arming the hood and spinning, he avoided being run over, but the car had clipped his hipbone. Sharp pain brought even more white light to his already blinded eyes.

As he twirled, the arch of one of his slippered feet struck the curb and he was sent sprawling. His hands slapped the sidewalk, just to the side of the driveway, his body landing mostly in the strip of crabgrass and ice plant beside the curb. One of his ankles was still hanging into the street, and as the car's engine gunned behind him, he quickly tucked it under his body. He rolled onto his side, his palms burning from their contact with the cold cement. He flexed a stinging hand. The pain in his hip was searing.

The car turned into the driveway mere feet from his prone body, and with another squeal of tires, threw itself into reverse.

(it isn't finished with me)

Father Doctor had only seconds to spare. With mounting horror and confusion, his bulging eyes searched the car's front window for signs of life, but there were none. His feet began to kick at the ground, trying to get under his body, trying to lift his gelatinous weight. He got to one knee as the car stopped its reverse motion in the middle of the street with a squeal of tires. The hearse was shifting into drive. Something unseen was in charge of it and Father Doctor knew now who it was.

It was Death. It was Death and he had been very patient, but now he was hungry, eager to have his prize, to finally feast.

The priest's mind seized up with the horror of it all. Now that he could see the hood ornament, the golden wings spread, the figure tucking for speed, it all came to him in a flash. This was the car that had run down Sam's parents so many years ago, the one that had sent the McGraths into the icy waters of the San Francisco Bay. It was the car that had never been found. It was telling him; somehow it was telling him with each firing of its goddamned cylinders, bragging about it as he writhed on the ground. He had to get moving or he would be next. The thing gunned its engine.

His legs weren't working. He tried to get up, his feet slipping on the plants slick with dew. It was now his turn to die under this thing's wheels. He was making it all too easy. Death would not even have to break a sweat. Death would roll back and forth over his body, open the shiny black driver's door and stretch his legs before strolling casually over to the freshly mangled corpse. Would he then cock one of his robed feet on it proudly like a big game hunter posing for a picture?

"No..." Father Doctor said, clawing at the grass. He heard the tires behind him squeal, but he did not look back again. He had managed to plant one foot on the cement, a foot planted like a runner in a starting block. He sprang from the patch of ground with a groan of pain. He ran with everything he had. He ran straight for the door to his house, his hip emptying scalding hot fire down his leg and buckling his stride. The car roared behind him. He heard it jump the curb, the suspension protesting with a shriek.

His front lawn was not very big, but now it stretched before him like a football field. His foot dug into one of the perennial beds that bordered his front walk, sending dark, fertile soil spraying. He wasn't going to make it. The roar of the car behind him was too close, it was too close. He could feel the car's hot breath on his back. It was pouring from that massive grill of chrome teeth. It was going to chew him up, swallow him into oblivion. His lungs were burning now, his legs pumping, heedless of the pain.

The front door was only 12 feet away.

He had to jump a shrub, a slight left turn to gain the porch. The car would have to do no such thing. It would shred the plant like a combine, just like it would shred him. He jumped. He came down on a wobbly leg. Had he lost time? Was that all it would take? The car was so loud, so close. It was at his heels. Feverish begging filled his head as he bargained with the God he had given his life to.

(not like this)

(not so close to the front door)

For a moment, he flushed with relief. He had left the front door ajar. If he hadn't left the door cracked, the few seconds it would have taken to twist the knob...

(a few more feet)

The car's bumper grazed the back of his left leg just as his right foot hit the porch. He aimed and launched himself at his front door with both arms stretched before him. He crashed into it and it flew open with a violent smack, the handle smashing into the plaster of the foyer wall with the force of a bullet. He went sprawling headfirst onto the tile floor, skidding on his forearms and crashing into the door of the hall closet in a heap.

Behind him came the terrifying sound of destruction. Rolling over, he got to one elbow fast, blood trickling into one eye from a gash on his forehead. Wide eyed and panting hot knives from his burning lungs, he saw the grill of the Phantom filling his front door with its clenched teeth. With a roar it reversed, a severed 4x4 that supported the covered porch grinding a livid scar down its hood. Part of the covered porch collapsed.

The car roared with frustration. Through the door, and down the length of shredded lawn, Father Doctor and the car stared at each other over the purring idle of its engine.

The priest wiped the blood from his brow with the back of his shirtsleeve. He was trembling all over, numb and hot. Still, the car watched him, idling.

"Go to Hell," he whispered. His eyes flicked to the thing's license plate:

CYASOON

With a screech of tires, the car backed onto the street, shredding grass and casting off lumber from the porch overhang. It gunned its engine, bit into the asphalt and howled away, disappearing into the night.

XII.
Tale of the Sorcerer

-1-

"Clara?"

"Yes."

"You are the woman in the glass?"

"Yes. How I've waited for this moment. I have waited so long, Samhain."

"Who are you?"

"I was given the name Tlachtga by my father, Mog Ruith. I am the earth spear. I am the mother of your clan, but I have taken a modern name for this age. You can call me Clara. How do you feel, Samhain?"

"Not good," said Sam. "And you can call me Sam. I need to find Lucia. Where is she?"

"She is not here. They did not bring her here. There is the possibility that she is no longer alive."

"WHAT?" Sam got to one elbow, but his head swam.

"Be still. You are weak. There is nothing you can do at this moment."

"BULLSHIT! I have to find her." He tried to rub the stars from his eyes, but he could see nothing. "Where am I?"

"You are in a cell, in Simon's tomb, on the summit of Black Fang."

"How did I get here?"

"Orace Fley and his army of Leeches. They brought you here. They meant to bring the Mayan girl as well. There must have been...a complication."

Sam winced and gripped his stomach. He began to retch, but he produced nothing.

Clara, who had been stroking his cheek, began to massage Sam's shoulders and neck. Her voice was low and soothing. "You will regain your strength. Try and relax. You were knocked out with a drug, a form of nightshade."

"Nightshade?" Sam's retching had stopped, and again he tried to focus.

"Yes," Clara confirmed. "It is a deadly hallucinogenic. You ingested a variety that is not found on your side of The Veil. The Devil himself grows it in Hell's garden of ash. Long ago, the Devil seeded The Nowhere with it and it is one of the rare drugs that can addict the spirit as well as the flesh. So many here are fiends for its bloom, and they have become enslaved by the promise of more. The Devil finds it amusing when mortals and the dead alike hand over their free will. Here in The Nowhere, Simon Magus controls the supply."

"I can't see."

"Your vision should return soon."

"Leeches? That's who brought me?" Sam asked. "The vampires?"

"They were vampires once, yes. But the creatures that brought you here have lost their terrestrial need for blood. Now, they have the taste only for promises, the two promises offered by Simon Magus. The first, that they will again walk among the Thumpers and again partake in the pleasures of the flesh, and second, that they will be flush with the devil's weed. Hopefully your friend survived the dose, but there is no guarantee. I'm sorry."

Sam moaned with frustration. Clara peered at him, knitting her brow. "Your eyes are clearing. You should feel better soon. The effects do not last long."

"Lucia...I can't...I have to find her..."

"You are locked in a cell. If she is alive, she will have to find you. Perhaps the Leeches left her for dead. Simon would not be pleased if they had. Simon wants her alive."

"Why?" Sam got to one elbow again, and this time he was able to support himself. "I have to get out of here."

"You cannot."

"So why are you here anyway?" Sam asked. His head was pounding. "I thought you were on my side."

"I am," Clara replied. "I am not free to leave. I am locked in here with you."

"How long have you been here?"

"Hundreds of years, I suppose."

"If you are so good than why are you in The Nowhere?"

"I am here for the same reason you are here. I am meant to be. I was supposed to stop Simon Magus, and I failed. I only hoped you would find your way through The Veil. You are the last of our clan. You are also the first to be able to bring beating hearts into The Nowhere. You can walk The Fringe without shedding flesh. You are Samhain, the last of the gods of the Death Realms. This place cannot bind you with its laws."

"This can't be happening," Sam muttered and rubbed his throbbing head. "This seriously cannot be happening. I don't want this. I just want Lucia back. I NEVER should have come here!" He let his head sink back down to the cool stone beneath him. "You haunted me my entire life. Why me? Why am I the only one who has to deal with some ancient lunatic? How come I couldn't have a normal life?"

"I'm sorry for your burden."

"I've been a freak. Most people stay clear of me. I am Halloween Boy. They all called me Pumpkinhead my whole life and they didn't even know why! Do you know how WEIRD AND STRESSFUL MY EXISTENCE HAS BEEN?" Sam's hands had been trying to rub the life back into his face as he lay on the stone floor and now he let them drop to his sides. "Everyone knows. They don't really know, but they do – my teachers, my friends, Lenny. And Father Doc, he...doesn't know what to do with me. It's been hard on him, too."

"Samhain..." Clara began.

Sam interrupted her. "So, you scream for help, you convince me to come here and now you're telling me that my best friend – my girlfriend now – may be dead?" He managed to sit up and he turned away from her, his voice breaking. "This sucks...this is not fun anymore. This is not an adventure. This is a nightmare and I want to wake up from it. I want to wake up from it now. Just leave me alone."

There was no response from Clara and silence filled the cell until Sam finally turned towards her. His eyes had healed enough to see her clearly now. The sight of her was astonishing and it took his breath away.

Clara was lit from within, with her own blue light, the edges of her being crackling and dancing as if she were made of pure electricity. She was waifish and beautiful. Her gossamer hair was auburn and as silken and delicate as a spider's web in a ray of sunlight. Her large, green eyes stared into his, unblinking and kind. Her delicate hands were folded in her lap amongst her puddles of robes. She smiled a smile that was both sad and understanding.

"I waited a long time to meet you, Samhain" she said softly.

When Sam could find his breath again, he appealed to her as gently as his frustration would allow. "But I am Samuel McGrath. I am not a druid. I'm just a guy from Colma. I'm not...qualified for this. Everyone seems to think I'm special somehow."

"Everyone but you."

Sam looked away.

Clara reached out and touched him gently on the shoulder and it sent a warm, bracing shock down Sam's spine. His eyes widened.

Clara leaned towards him and whispered in his ear, her breath like ozone. "It's time for you to learn who you really are."

-2-

"Samhain, you are descended from my father Mog Ruith. I know that name must mean something to you. You have dreamt of him, have you not? Your surname was never McGrath. It was always Mog Ruith. An immigration officer did not understand the heavy Irish accent of one of our ancestors when they arrived in the New World, so someone gave you a typical British Isles name that sounded similar. The name of my father was given as a surname to my descendants so that they would know who they were. As for your first name: Samhain has been the name of every male descended from my father for the last 100 generations."

"My father was named Sam, too..." Sam said dreamily.

"He was called Sam," Clara corrected. "But his father named his Samhain like his father before him. It means the end of summer. You are the last stand before death. You have all been Guardians of The Veil."

"Oh great..." Sam muttered into his hands. "This just gets better and better. Then what does Mog Ruith mean?"

"Mog Ruith means "Slave of The Wheel" in the old tongue, and my father took the name to celebrate his connection to "Roth Rámach" his flying chariot, one of the greatest of his many fetishes."

"What?" Sam's brow furrowed. "Isn't fetish a sex thing, like being into someone's feet or something?"

"There are similarities," Clara explained. "But a fetish is a term in sorcery. In your example, sexual desire is being intensified by the presence of an object. So, in the same way, a fetish of magic is an object that distills and focuses a spell, and a spell is simply a desire. A fetish can be anything, but a fetish is always required. The "magic wand" became the proverbial fetish, but many things have been used throughout the centuries: talismans, amulets, rocks, human bones, animal bones, feathers, weapons of all kinds, and in my father's case, conveyances – although this last form of fetish requires great control.

"As an example, suppose you are a sea of endless water, but you are contained within your shores. You may toss and roil, but you will never soak a faraway desert. But, if you have access to a river, an aqueduct, a hose, or even a bucket, then you can bring your nature to bear in very specific ways and with extraordinary extension."

"Do you have a fetish?" Sam asked.

"I preferred a sickle of gold," Clara replied. "How I got it is another story. It has been taken by Simon. I can feel it calling to me. Mine resides in Simon's reliquary. It is somewhere in this tomb. Of that, I am sure."

"So," Sam began, "you're telling me that we are related, that I am a druid like you? There is kind of a problem with that since I don't even know what a druid is."

"A druid is simply a magic user," Clara replied, "a sorcerer if you like. Eventually, we gravitated to one another over time and passed our knowledge and power on to our clan. This gave us social status, and we were perceived as close to divine as any human could dare to be. As a result, we were employed by kings, consulted by the wise, and revered by the rest. We became disciplined in our trade, sober with the responsibility of our calling, and ended up a priestly caste, guarding and protecting our knowledge and power from those who might exploit it to the detriment of nature or mankind. Do you understand so far?"

"I AM going to college," Sam grinned sardonically.

Clara acknowledged this with her own thin smile and slow nod: "You are a bright light, Samhain."

"Look, Clara," Sam said. "I want to help. I mean, I thought I wanted to help. Right now, I just want to find my girlfriend and get out of here."

Clara suddenly flared. Her eyes fixed on Sam, her aura sizzled and her voice became spiked with anger. "You have the priorities of a child. This goes far beyond what affects only you. Listen to me and listen close because time is shorter than you think."

Sam deflated and glared at her.

"Simon is going to tear down The Veil and release the forsaken among the living. That, you probably already know by now. What you may not understand are the consequences. They will feast on you all, they will covet your bodies and they will take them, they will thirst for your blood and they will have it. The only reason that what you now call Halloween exists at all is to confuse and deter the dead from gaining a foothold during The Thinning. It is very hard to tell where The Veil begins and where it ends when all of the Thumpers are dressed as the forsaken. The mayhem, the ghouls moving through the dark night, the lanterns in the gourds, all of it looks identical to The Nowhere. It has worked to blur the lines until now, but without The Veil in place at all, there is no hope. But we are finally together you and I. We have a chance to stop him. Until we do, it is doubtful that you will ever see your side of The Veil again."

-3-

"And how are we supposed to do that?" Sam asked. He was careful to measure the impudence in his tone. He didn't want to see Clara burn again with anger like she had. It had made his guts crawl with a strange combination of fear and shame. "All I mean is that we're trapped in a cell and I don't know the first thing about magic."

Clara narrowed her eyes. "You underestimate yourself. Yes, we may be trapped now, but until the last chapter is written, we have as much chance of success as he does."

"That's one way of looking at it." Sam muttered.

"It is the druid way." Clara said.

"So, if you are a powerful druid, then why can't you get out of here?"

"Simon is no fool. This cell is lined with lead. He tricked me into entering this room once. Here I am powerless. As you may know, not much can penetrate lead. It is one of the few elements that can stop magic. I can do small things for my magic is strong. For instance, I was just barely able to communicate with you on your side of The Veil, but I certainly can do nothing to battle Simon while I'm in here. Neither can you. But this is not over yet, Sam."

Sam was disarmed by Clara using his familiar name. Her tenderness and patience had returned. As intolerable as this situation was, he was grateful for her company. Otherwise, he was sure that he would have gone crazy with his thoughts and let them eat him from the inside. He could not imagine what Lucia must be feeling, what she might be facing. He implored Clara a final time, every nerve reaching out to her as a tender, young shoot would bend for the light and warmth of the sun. "Clara, if she is still alive..."

"We can do nothing in here," Clara replied. "But I don't think she is dead. I will call to her when the panel opens for it shouldn't be long now."

Hope enriched Sam and he craned his neck around. "What panel?"

Clara pointed high on the stone wall and Sam's heart leapt. He saw it, but it was not as big as he would have hoped, and it was too far up to reach. "What's it for? When does it open?"

"As I said," Clara replied, "this cell is lined with lead. They have to open that panel to allow you to breathe. It is also how I was able to communicate with you. I pried it open a few times before Simon reinforced it."

"How did you get up there?" Sam asked.

"No laws bind me here," Clara replied. "Not gravity, not anything."

Sam's eyes widened as Clara continued, only now she was sitting three feet above the ground. "The panel is facing a cliff. We are very high up. A steady wind always blows at that wall from the north. It will fill this room with oxygen when it opens. The panel was made especially for you. I died 1,900 years ago. I don't need to breathe."

"Wow, do I feel special," Sam quipped.

"You are."

Sam's eyes quickly made note of the rest of the cell as well. It was big – as far as prison cells went. Sam had only seen them on television, but he was sure that this one would be considered roomy. He figured it was twenty by twenty feet or so, but rounded. It was lit only by Clara's luminescence – her own generated light. He noticed one other detail: it was completely unadorned and there was no place to...

Sam's cheeks bloomed red.

"There is no place to..."

Clara smiled, "You don't produce waste here. You do not hunger or thirst here. If you do have any earthly needs, they are only as strong as they were the moment you entered The Nowhere and they will not increase or decrease. You are not bound by laws of nature either. Remember that."

"I can fly?" Sam brightened.

"Eventually, it is something you could master, yes."

Sam was grinning now and he continued looking around. There was a door without windows or bars on the cell's only flat wall. The door had no keyhole. Sam figured it locked with a bolt. He turned his attention back to the panel situated perhaps 20 feet up in the center of the curved wall surrounded by stone – a small exposed panel of dull metal. It was the only visible indication of the cell's lining. The panel was round, and perhaps the size of a car's tire. Sam marveled at the construction on his behalf. "So, why go through the trouble? Why not just kill me? I mean...what a pain in the ass."

"He has his reasons," Clara replied, "The first is that he wants to meet you. You are the last of our kind and he is fascinated by the mere idea of you. The other reason, I suppose would be to convince you that you are much better off joining him. He has no more disciples, and even the slight possibility that you would follow him has to be explored. It would all but guarantee that his plans would succeed."

"Wait! What?" Sam gaped at Clara. "You have GOT to be kidding. He obviously hasn't seen Star Wars."

"Star Wars?" Clara asked, wrinkling her nose.

"It's a movie," Sam said. "Never mind. It has SO been done before. And, guess what? It NEVER works. Does he honestly believe I am going to instantly become evil?"

"He only thinks that you will be subject to human frailty. If you are not, he feels it's a risk worth taking. You may not be as immune to his influence as I would like. We have a lot of work to do to prepare."

"That's what I've been trying to tell you!"

Clara looked down at her lap.

"Never mind," Sam said. "Okay he wants to toy with me. Fine, but why is there oxygen here at all if all the residents are dead? Why is the atmosphere here even suited for life?"

"Because," Clara began, "The Nowhere is part of your world and part of no other. It shares the same breath. It is just one of the many dimensions of your world that most cannot see."

At this, Sam chewed on his bottom lip, "So, when will they open the panel?"

"It should open any minute. Once it is determined that the oxygen level in here is deficient it will open just long enough to keep you alive. So, when it opens, I will search for your friend. You can do the same. All you need do is call to her. Reach out to her with your spirit."

They both stared soberly at the panel until Clara spoke again: "It took Simon over a hundred years to build this cell. You see, there are no metals in the ground in The Nowhere. This land is devoid of any deposits of natural resources. The only things that are here were put here by God or the Devil – mostly either as concessions or afterthoughts. Most things here are just failed experiments. Some things are here as gifts from God, like gourds, trees and a moon. Some things are here for caprice, and some things are here because of an absence of oversight – abominations that could not exist within natural laws. In short, this cursed ground is not veined with anything that anyone in the Death Realms has perceived to be of any value."

"Then where did Simon get the lead?"

"From years and years of combing The Fringe for Skinnies with bullets lodged in their bones. He doesn't do it personally, of course, he leaves that kind of trench work to the Leeches. You see, the most prized materials in The Nowhere are simply the things buried in your world. The Fringe has turned into quite a salvage yard. Since the sixteenth century, a surprising number of residents in The Nowhere ended up here after being shot, all for good reason I'm sure. Simon painstakingly collected the bullets, one at a time, and melted them down. Some Skinnies were suspicious as to why the Leeches were after the bullets, but all Simon needed to do to quiet the Skinnies was to promise them salvation. After all, that's what Skinnies care about most."

"I know. I've met some."

"So, in the face of such a promise, they swallowed any suspicions quick, even prying the lead out of their own shattered bones. The Leeches are no different. Promise them another hit of nightshade and they will pile atop any uncooperative Skinny and do it themselves. Either way, all Simon had to do was wait for the sacks of lead to arrive.

"So, to make sure I get this straight," Sam said. "If magic doesn't work through these walls, then, what are we going to do?"

"We wait for him to make a mistake," Clara replied. "I wish I had more options, but we can only wait for an opportunity. I only hope the opportunity comes before The Veil falls. Because, once it does, he will be unbeatable. I think our best chance lies in the reliquary."

"What's that?"

"Simon is a god who has lost the faithful, so he is destined to weaken. Until he can once again derive power from followers he must come up with another means of power, and I know what it is. He has built himself a reliquary somewhere in this great tomb, stocked with magic fetishes that have been buried with the dead in the world's cemeteries over thousands of years. Combing The Fringe, Simon has found a great number of these burial sites and a lot of these powerful items. He has become the most prolific grave robber the world has ever known, robbing from beneath – from this side of The Veil – and he has had nothing but time to amass his arsenal. The items he has collected are imbued with the sorcery of ancients. Their combined power can focus magic in a catastrophic way. Simon believes, especially when it is at its thinnest, that The Veil can be destroyed once all of these treasures are his to command."

"And God – the real God – won't stop him?"

"The real god?"

"You know...GOD? God, the Father?"

"No. The God of all Gods, to whom you refer – The Creator of all Creators – would best be thought of as Nature, and Nature does not allow for intervention. Lesser gods are generally just talented sorcerers who briefly seize control of specific aspects of nature. Simon is cut from that cloth. The God of Gods is not inclined to intervene in the nature he has set in motion because He has created perfection and part of that perfection is chaos. We are only agents of that chaos. We are encumbered with struggle as a means to maintain balance. We are constantly trying to impose our will onto Nature as it does the same to us. That conflict is the essence of the universe. But at this time, I am confident that the influence of our clan is what is now best for all of humanity."

"So are you a god?"

"Yes," Clara replied, "and so are you."

"ME?"

"It is not a sacrilege. Do not worry. There is still a hierarchy of angels and demons. All I mean is that you are eternal and capable of great acts of creation and great acts of destruction. You are different than most because of whom you are and where you came from, but then again so are others similarly different from each other. All this philosophy can grow tiresome and I don't blame your eyes glazing over; it is a lot to handle, Samhain. I know it is."

Clara was no longer floating above the stone floor of the prison cell. She was now standing and looking at the panel high above in the wall. "How are you feeling now?"

"Better, I guess," Sam replied. "I'm tired."

"Oxygen in here is low," Clara agreed. "The panel will open soon. I hope it does. I hope Simon hasn't changed his mind."

"Yeah, me too."

"Samhain," Clara began, approaching Sam and sitting beside him. "Now you must learn the most important thing of all. Ready your ears. I must tell you the story of the false prophet. It is as amazing a story as it is blasphemous. This is the story of your enemy. This is the story of Simon Magus."

-4-

"Simon is a Samarian. He was born to wealthy land owners who produced wine and olive oil, in part of the land that is now known as Israel. He lived well in a house of ivory, but he was a restless spirit, and he wanted more of everything. In his travels he visited Egypt many times. While there, one of the last of the Star Race that settled in Egypt – a younger and certainly undisciplined type – became enamored with the young Simon. Just before this son of the Star Race was called away to leave for good, he imparted the knowledge of sorcery to Simon Magus in a last act of disobedience."

"Star Race?" Sam interrupted.

"Egypt was built by a race of humanoid beings from another galaxy."

Sam laughed, "Oh come on! You have GOT to be bullshitting me now!"

Clara looked stung. Her aura prickled.

"Really?" Sam asked, his smile fading. "I mean, really?" He wrinkled his brow and screwed up his mouth, but still, Clara did not flinch. She returned his gaze steadily.

"Who did you think built Egypt?" Clara asked.

"Fine..." Sam surrendered, "I shouldn't be surprised, I guess. It's not like everything in my life hasn't been SUPER weird for a SUPER long time. Okay...sorry. Go on."

Clara did. "Now pay attention, Samhain. Sorcery comes from the Star Race. Elemental magic, however, does not. That discipline is purely terrestrial: a manipulation of existing laws by force of will. I prefer it. For instance, my Irish name, Tlachtga, means "Earth Spear" and is in reference to my ability to command atmospheric energy: to cast bolts into the earth."

"Like Thor?" Sam asked eagerly.

"The Norseman?" Clara frowned. "I suppose, but he was an awful man, a real horse's ass. He had no feminine energy, no redeeming qualities. He also wasn't fond of bathing."

"You knew THOR?"

Clara looked perturbed.

Sam figured that maybe the two had not gotten on well with each other. Obviously something had happened between them.

"Did you have a thing for Thor?" Sam teased.

"You certainly have the mouth of a soldier," Clara shot back.

Sam decided he would have to drop the subject for now – as hard as it was to do so – but not without vowing to himself that he would bring it up again later, if there even was a later.

"As I was saying," Clara continued unabashed, "I prefer elemental magic. The sorcery brought by the Star Race is dangerous because it violates the balance of nature by introducing foreign laws. I, however, have command of this type of sorcery as well. I use it sparingly, but Simon prefers it as he has little regard for the balance of nature. Unfortunately, Simon was a quick study in Egypt. He learned fast.

"Through the years, Simon honed his skills, and before long, he started displaying his newfound power and attracting a lot of attention. Sometimes I think that young soul from the Star Race knew that humanity might confuse Simon with a real prophet, the real coming of the Messiah, and decided to watch the results of his mischief from a safe distance. Maybe even the Devil influenced this turn of events for his entertainment as well. I should ask him next time I see him, though he has never been one for a straight answer. Anyway, Simon returned to Samaria and began his mission to gather faith."

"Gather faith?"

"Yes, faith is the currency of the gods. The ones who have the most of it are the most effective. When one loses the faithful, one loses their power. Many religions would like this to not be true, but all one need do is look at history. It would be nice if a god's power was derived from an endless font, but a god relies upon the faithful just as much as the faithful rely upon the god. It is really just two sides of a coin. Do you understand?"

"I don't know," Sam replied. "I'm a Catholic and my God is not dependent on me, I don't think."

"Then why are many gods – hundreds, if not thousands – no longer worshipped? Some are even dead. Is the newest god always the correct one? Should a god be treated as fashion? God is nature and nature has remained unchanged. Only what we call God changes. Never mind, it is not important right now. By all means, continue to believe in your concept of God. Both you and your concept of God will be stronger for it, and that is why faith is mutually beneficial. But back to the story..."

Clara continued, "Simon was a celebrity long before that term was coined. He became quite skillful in his newfound sorcery. This may have been enough to draw the attention he needed, but he also had something else, the other attribute that always seems to compound evil: charisma.

"Soon the admiration of his audience began to harden to faith, and the better he got at his new craft the more he was revered, until finally he was widely considered to be divine. In fact, he spawned his own religion called Simonism. He is even mentioned in the *Acts of the Apostles* by Luke, although Luke never actually met Simon. I believe I can recite the passage for you, it's one of the advantages of being thousands of years old, I have inadvertently memorized just about everything.

"It is written in chapter eight, starting with verse nine: '*But there was a certain man, called Simon, which beforetime in the same city used sorcery, and bewitched the people of Samaria, giving out that himself was some great one: To whom they all gave heed, from the least to the greatest, saying, This man is the Great Power of God. And to him they had regard, because that of long time he had bewitched them with sorceries.*'

"Acts also tells of Simon meeting with Philip the Evangelist, and then trying to offer money to the Apostles in exchange for miraculous abilities, like the power of the laying on of hands. As I have said, Simon was obsessed with knowing all things and becoming all powerful, and since his family had money he had convinced himself that even the rare powers dispensed only by God were for sale. The sin of simony, or paying for position and influence in the church, is a term still used today and is named for Simon Magus."

"I've actually heard of that," Sam said. "I had no idea..."

Clara went on, "Simon brought his trickery to Rome. After all, it was the place to be in the early centuries. Its audiences were always hungry for the extraordinary and it wasn't long before Simon gained even more followers as well as the attention of the Caesar. Finally, the debate as to whether this dark and mysterious man was a prophet of consequence, a divine messenger, or even a direct descendant of the one true God, was brought before the Emperor Nero. The event is well attended. The Apostles Peter and Paul are present as well and they begin to pray as Simon begins his demonstration of power. The rest of the crowd holds its breath.

"To the astonishment of the gathered, Simon levitates from a high wooden tower built upon his request. Many are frightened, many are enraptured, and many are simply frozen with disbelief. But then Simon suddenly crashes to earth. How or why this happens, we do not know. Simon dies instantly and his legs are shattered in three places. Peter and Paul – who were obviously convinced that the Christ had already visited them in their lifetime, and who were vocal skeptics of Simon Magus – were then put in prison by Nero so there would be no meddling in what was to follow.

"You see, the Emperor seized this opportunity to conduct an experiment that would put to rest, once and for all, any doubt as to whether the citizens of Rome were in the presence of a God figure – other than Nero himself, of course. The emperor ordered that Simon's body be kept under lock and key for three days to see if Simon might rise again, but he did not, for he was not the Christ.

"The church of Santa Francesca Romana in Rome has been built on the spot where this happened. Within this Church is a dented slab of marble that bears the imprints of the knees of Peter and Paul as they prayed that this false prophet not be allowed to lead mankind into darkness. It's now a tourist attraction."

Sam stared at Clara, speechless. It began to worry him that this kind of truth was the kind that was imparted only when you were dead. Wasn't it? Maybe he was dead after all. Maybe he was a spirit just like Clara was.

Clara kept talking, but she seemed to be drifting further and further away, speaking to him through a long, dark tunnel.

(goodbye...Clara)

(goodbye...Lucia)

(goodbye Father Doc...)

(so...)

(...tired)

A clang jerked Sam awake. High on the stone wall the panel had opened. Howling wind was swirling into the cell. Sam gasped for air, the cold wind flooding into his lungs.

"Breathe!" Clara commanded, her robes bristling with light. She left his side in a flash, flying up the wall, fighting the gale, her garments filling with air so that she became a blooming blue rose of fierce light above his head. She screamed as she approached the panel, she screamed into the howling wind.

Sam shielded his eyes from the wind, from her searing light. Clara was almost at the panel. Was she going to fly through it? Could she? He squinted. Clara moved closer to the hole in the wall. The wind beat at her, sending her hair blowing back like a licking gas flame.

"CALL TO HER!" she cried, looking down at Sam. "CALL TO HER NOW!"

-5-

Sam did not know exactly how to call to Lucia. Desperately, he gulped air and tried to focus. He centered Lucia in his mind; he spoke her name, fighting fresh pangs of loss. He thought of her face, he thought of her eyes, keen with mischief and passion.

The panel slammed shut. The wind stopped.

"Shit..." Sam muttered dismally. It had not been enough time, had it? He was clenching his fists. A trickle of warm blood traced along his palm. His face flushed as he breathed in the fresh air.

Clara slowly fluttered back to Sam's side like the spore of a dandelion. Her legs folded beneath her, her robes settled and her hands returned to her lap.

"She is alive," Clara said. "And, she has heard you..."

XIII.
Fley's Hunt

-1-

Orace Fley scanned the wooded ravine below. The girl was somewhere down there, had to be. There was little chance that she could have scaled the far side of the densely-wooded gully without him spotting her on one of the upward slopes. It was only a matter of time before he would have her.

The drooling Leeches flanking him twitched and watched Fley like a pack of dogs waiting for a bugle to sound. Their eyes – black marbles of hunger set deep in their pale faces – could not help but flick to the leather satchel bulging with nightshade looped through Fley's belt, but the centurion let them cringe without so much as a castigating glance. Fley had long ago resigned himself to the perversity of their natures. He had little choice.

Fley's bald head reflected the moonlight as if it were another celestial body hovering far too close to the ground. Rolls of white skin at his neck were bunched and stuffed into the leather neck hole of his tunic, a blood red tunic that creaked as he turned away from the ravine and swept his eyes over his troop of rabid fiends.

This was not a legion of Romans by any means, but what the Leeches lacked in training, tactics, intuition, swordsmanship, common sense, decorum and hygiene, they made up for in absolute mercilessness. Plus, they were far from human anymore, and far from alive, so the worst that could befall them was that they would have to wait for a new sack of flesh to regenerate around their ancient bones. In short, they were a squad leader's secret war fantasy: disposable grunts. There was no need to deliberate before sending them into battle, to weigh losses versus gains, no crisis of conscience. Moreover, there was no need to worry about allegiance or treachery either, often the most insidious danger to an officer. The nightshade took care of that.

At first, Fley had concerns about being overtaken by the Leeches and his supply of nightshade seized; after all, they possessed a singular brand of brute force and there were a hundred of them under his command at any one time. These concerns were quickly put to rest when he realized the extent of their addiction – it was more profound than any physical addiction that he had ever seen in Rome. Their dependence was a spiritual one. It was religion. They would not attack him because their supply line would be at an end. Simon would see to that. Next, they would all suffer the devil herb's extraordinary withdrawal before being cast into The Pitch by Simon, where the Wraiths would chew on their souls for eternity – gnaw on them like ghastly dog toys. The thought of such an ignominious end made even Orace Fley shudder.

Fley was 6'5" and two hundred and fifty pounds of solid muscle, so he was confident that he would hack most of the Leeches to pieces before that ever happened. After fighting two Punic wars and countless other skirmishes with "real" soldiers facing him across the battlefield, a bunch of preternatural junkies would be no match for his sword. Still, the nightshade's unyielding tether was a rare blessing in a land bereft of such mercies.

The girl, on the other hand, would not fare so well against the Leeches – would not fare well at all. With a smile, Fley peered into the ravine, looking for the slightest movement.

Yes, the girl would find them fiends most unreasonable. She would be torn to bits before she could even comprehend them. As hardened a warrior as he was, Orace Fley flinched somewhere inside his calloused skin when he thought of what the Leeches would do to the Mayan girl. He had seen how the Leeches hunt. He had seen their bloodlust many times. It was some aberrant instinct that even the Devil wanted nothing to do with, a holdover from when they actually subsisted on blood. It was not an easy thing to watch, even for a man like Fley who had seen his share of torture and brutality on the battlefields of Europe. The horrific death of the German, Peter Stumpp, was a prime example.

Stumpp was a werewolf and had been buried in the 15th century with his fetish, the wolf belt. Simon wanted it, and Fley had been sent to The Fringe to recover it. Stumpp must have fancied himself a brutal monster, but he was to get a final lesson on brutality from a breed of true abominations. Stumpp had been spotted not far from The Fringe, in a cave at Ravenscroft. He had been swarmed by the Leeches. They tore him apart. They ate every bit of his flesh, dismantled his skeleton and sucked the marrow from his bones. Stumpp's homeless soul was quickly vacuumed into the Pitch by the greedy inhalations of the Wraiths, who Fley supposed were probably still slowly feasting on it to this day.

That was what was in store for the Mayan girl, and much sooner than she thought. Fley now saw movement in the ravine. He smiled.

-2-

Fley's keen, grey eyes locked onto the distant shadow below as it flickered between trees. It could be the girl, it could be some monster. Whatever it was, it wasn't going to get far. He and his vampires had their chance to nab the two intruders once, but they had bungled the job. Fley vowed that would not happen twice. This mission was to be of the highest priority.

At first, it seemed it would be a short and unchallenging hunt. The two Thumpers were lost and unsure. Fley, on the other hand, was a seasoned soldier of the Roman legion. Also, the initial intelligence had been promising. Early reports had them crossing the Fringe somewhere by the Knolls, heading towards Hex – this according to Jack o' Lantern.

Old Stingy Jack had been an easy interrogation: drunk, as usual, and loose lipped. One raised sword above his still of pumpkin mash, coupled with the hungry grins from the fanged Leeches surrounding him, had been all that was needed to convince the old sot to cooperate.

But the hunt certainly hadn't gone as smoothly as it should have. The two intruders had disappeared from sight for long periods of time, and they moved fast. Once, Fley had them surrounded in the Bogs of the Coven, and he wanted very much to release the Leeches and be done with it, but Simon's directive had been clear: keep them alive.

When later it was learned that the two Thumpers were heading into Hex, an update of the sorcerers' orders had been sent by courier bat: let the Thumpers enter the city of witches. Simon had come up with a better plan to take the boy alive.

After combing the Fringe for centuries for history's baubles, Simon's stranglehold on the fetish trade made it easy to bribe the witches of Hex – even the great Baba Yaga who might have fancied herself to be above such material lust. The thought of getting her hands on one of the great Simon Magus' fetishes was irresistible to the greedy witch. The drugging of the two would insure that no sorcery would be leveled at Fley or his troop of monsters. It was unclear to all exactly what the boy was capable of doing, and it was Simon's goal not to find out. The rumor making its way around The Nowhere was that the boy was a god, and maybe even more powerful than Simon. But no one dared voice such conjecture aloud.

Even if this hunt for the Thumpers wasn't going as well as he would have hoped, Fley would not be returning to Black Fang empty handed. On this tour he had nabbed the Seal of Solomon – one of history's great fetishes – before this aggravating diversion had taken him away from his salvage operation at The Fringe. Fley now fingered the silver ring, felt its comforting weight in his pocket. They were close to victory now. The boy was captured; the Seal of Solomon would soon be added to the reliquary. Then, Simon would shatter The Veil and Fley and his army of the dead would be masters of the world they left behind.

But the girl was still a problem. She had been slippery, dragging them over hill and dale right to the swamps at the foot of Black Fang. Fley had to end this now. The Thinning was at its apex. Time was running low.

If it were up to him he would forget the girl. What about the Seal of Solomon? They never expected to find such a powerful fetish in time for their plans and it needed to be in the reliquary before the end of the Thinning. The ring could imprison demons, and this would be important cover for Simon. Hell might have access to the world of the living if the Veil fell and demons were sure to have their own ideas on who was to be in charge of the enslaved Thumpers. Surely, the girl was not even close to being that important.

But it was not a soldier's place to question a commander, and especially if that commander was Simon Magus. So if the sorcerer wanted the girl he would have her, if only for one reason: Simon was the only man in history that truly frightened Orace Fley.

Fley unsheathed his gladius from its scabbard with one hand and crooked a beckoning finger with his other. The Leeches, drooling and panting, gathered around the centurion eagerly. First, hits of nightshade were dispensed, and then Fley began to draw in the fine soil at his feet with the tip of the short sword. They would flank the Mayan girl on all sides and descend into the ravine. The girl had walked into a perfect trap.

-3-

Lucia stopped to catch her breath and looked up the slope at her back. She had been ducking through the woods for what seemed like hours. Her pursuers never got too close, but she never got far enough away for comfort. She knew that if she had been less agile she might never have gotten this far. All those years of practicing track and field had paid off, all those afternoons at school...

(home)

The homesickness was sudden, overwhelming and clear. For a moment she could feel the warm sun of spring shining on the red clay of the track at Holy Ghost, feel the light May wind combing through her hair and flapping the number on her singlet and she could almost hear the roar of her peers as they cheered her on.

But that bright sunny day faded all too quickly and the relentless darkness of the endless woods replaced it. There was no beaten track beneath her feet. Thankfully, the ground had leveled off, but it had become sodden. She shifted her weight and the ground sucked at her sneakers. Was there a source of water close by? Maybe, but though she was thirsty she would be damned if she was going to drink anything here again. She was finally feeling normal after running off the effects of the damned witch's poison.

Oddly, her thirst was no worse than it had been when she first entered this place, even after intense exertion. How was that? She didn't know, but the bigger question was why she had drunk tea offered by a witch? It was just about the stupidest thing she had ever done, and she vowed it was going to be the last mistake she was going to make in The Nowhere. If she wanted to see Sam again, or feel the sun of her world again, she would have to be stronger and wiser than she had ever been.

She stole one more glance behind for any sign of her pursuers. It didn't do much good. There was nothing but inky black. Even the alien moon did not deign to shine here. So she walked, walked until her scorching muscles were tight as drum heads.

After a while the thick trunks of the species of gnarled, evergreen trees that had sheltered her and scraped her with their rapier branches were giving way to swampland; the moon's pale fingers were now poking feebly at umbrellas of willows. She looked back again. She had outdistanced her pursuers. She could not hear their voices anymore. That was a good thing, but what was not a good thing was the sound that had replaced the chatter from upslope.

In the relentless dark she caught her breath, grabbing the tops of her thighs, her eyes flicking through the blackness   to find the source of the sound. It was a low throb and it seemed to be coming from all sides.

She spotted a weak puddle of light ahead, a clearing. Exhausted, she stumbled forward. It was colder in this new place and she could see her breath in the moonlight's pale offering. Moving into the center of the clearing, the sound grew louder until its steady throb beat a tattoo in the center of her head.

Something wet and heavy plopped on the ground behind her. She stiffened, her heart leaping, and slowly she turned around. She clapped a hand over her mouth to stifle her scream. Whatever it was, it was the size of a large dog, sitting motionless behind her. It was watching her, but it was no dog. She scanned it desperately to make some kind of sense of it, but she just couldn't. In the end, it was the thing's eye – a black slit for a pupil, like an axe wound throbbing in the middle of one huge, jaundiced pool of cornea – that finally made her jump backwards. As she did so she stumbled, her hand coming away from her mouth. Her scream rolled away into the dark swamp.

The giant, one-eyed frog did not blink, it only squinted its membranous, translucent eyelid cunningly for a moment before retracting it again into its warty head. Carefully, Lucia lifted a foot from the sucking ground and backed away. The frog did not move, it only sat crouched on its...

(one?)

...one leg.

Her mind revolted. The thing was balancing on a single, fat piston of green flesh. Lucia snapped shut her mouth with difficulty. What happened next would have surely made her scream again – a far louder and far more out of control scream – but it happened so fast that she had no time to do so.

With the sound of a cracking whip, the giant frog's tongue flew past her ear and tightened in the air like a bright-red rubber band as it struck something behind her with a thwack. Then, the tongue slackened in the air beside her face, a buzzing sound racing past her head from behind. The tongue flew back into the frog's mouth with something attached to it, something with segmented legs as shiny as patent leather. The morsel disappeared into the frog's mouth with a crunch.

The frog's throat swelled to the size of a beach ball and then it blew out an ear-splitting croak.

"Holy shit..." Lucia said reflexively. She had backed away from the giant half frog. Her feet seemed to be doing this without her knowledge, but she had no intention of resisting. At this point, she was simply along for the ride. If her feet started to run, that would be fine too. In fact, that would be optimal. Because, if this huge...

(it has purple warts)

...frog jumps at her with that one leg, if it springs into the air and the last thing she sees is that dinner plate of an eye coming down on her, she will go insane. She knows it.

"*Loco para siempre...*" she muttered, her white breath puffing into the air.

Now it was clear what was throbbing through the swamp. It was this thing's family, its brethren. The darkness was trembling with the deep, sonorous sound of hundreds of these croaking mutants. They sounded like the steady beating of timpani drums, a heartbeat pulsing from the swamp's dark throat.

Still, the huge frog before her watched her and she watched the frog. She did not chance another move. After what seemed like forever, her eyes widened. She flicked her eyes to the sky and sickening dread poured through her.

A thick cloud was passing over the moon.

"Not now..." she whispered.

The frog's staring eye began to stripe with a ribbon of shadow and then the world around her disappeared into pitch black.

-4-

When the ground had finally leveled out, Fley came to a stop, halting his troops with a raised hand – though a Leech never truly stilled. The best that a Leech could do was to shuffle in place, writhing, twisting and panting with raspy breaths. One of the hunched and lurching vampires missed the signal completely and was still advancing with glazed eye determination until it was brought to its knees by a swift crack on the head with the hilt of Fley's gladius.

"Halt!" Fley hissed. "Shit for brains..."

The Leech's black gums writhed in confusion, one of its long, white hands pawing the top of its head as it shrunk back into line.

"Stay quiet," Fley whispered to the rest.

The centurion and a score of his most lethal and depraved Leeches were now standing at the rim of the swamp. Scanning the wooded heights on all sides, Fley grinned as he watched his remaining Leeches flickering in the light falling through the weeping branches above as they fanned out.

Fley peevishly lifted one of his feet, the moist ground slurping at his sandal. With a frown, he replanted his foot on a drier patch of land.

"She is close," Fley said, peering across the swamp. "Use your senses. She is a Thumper. She can't hide for long. Her heart will give her away. Now, we stay very quiet. If you spot her, if you hear that juicy little pink heart...sound the alarm, but only if you are sure. Otherwise, you will give away our position."

Fley wasn't looking forward to the alarm. The "alarm" was a bloodcurdling screech that only a Leech's rotten throat could produce. Even Fley did not like hearing it, it made his skin crawl and he wasn't even wearing his original skin. That sound could still stipple his borrowed flesh and turn it as cold as the grave dirt he had once remembered. Though he would grit his teeth and bear the sound if only it would come, if only she were spotted. This was taking far too long and Simon would certainly be losing his patience. Fley had already lost his. The girl was cornered and it was time to end this.

Fley raised his arm high to ready his troops and then let it fall. "Forward," he commanded.

-5-

It seemed like forever, but the frog had finally hopped away. Lucia had hardly noticed, for while she crouched motionless, waiting for the eclipse to end, waiting for the frog thing to finally lose interest in her, she had been struck with a revelation: Sam was alive. She knew this suddenly and with certainty. The relief had made her giddy. Even while crouching in the dark with a huge, amphibious nightmare that could suck her into its warty mouth, she had almost laughed. Sam was okay.

For a second it was as if he were beside her. But then it passed. Where only moments ago there had been his warm and soothing presence, now only the absence of him remained, and that took up more space than she felt her mind could ever contain. But his whispered gift was hers to keep: he was alive. He was with the woman in the glass.

They both had called her name. They were...

(trapped)

She wasn't sure how she knew this either, but she knew that it was up to her to find them.

The frog had hopped away, its thunderous splats receding into the swamp. Tentatively, her back came off the tree where she crouched. She peeked around the trunk, half expecting to see that huge eye again, glinting with mirth that it had played her for a fool, had tricked her and made her break cover. Then, that bungee cord of a tongue would attach to her face and the frog would suck her into its slimy throat.

It was gone, but her relief was brief. She may have avoided the frog thing, but now she had her pursuers to deal with. At least there was reason to go on. Sam was alive.

She weighed her options. As much as she didn't want to, she had to move forward, she had to go further into the swamp. She left the clearing and kept low. The throbbing croaks of the one-eyed, one-legged frog things pulsed through her, her bones vibrating like tuning forks with the drone as she crept forward. Why did these horrible creatures even exist? For only one reason she knew, and it was no consolation: no reason at all. This place had no balance, no purpose, no oversight, and she was lost in it.

A branch snapped somewhere on the hill to her right.

She dropped to one knee, turned her head towards the sound and caught the profile of a paper-white face hunched forward on a spindly neck. It was an older female Leech, fifty yards away and just upslope. Matted black hair with shocks of white clung to its head like moss. The thing was such a bizarre, translucent white that it seemed to glow as if under black light. The Leech's face was long, sallow, and stretched like melted wax, like a fright mask hung on a nail. Lucia was rooted with fear. It was only when the vampire's black, inhuman eye began to roll towards her in its deep socket that her reflexes kicked her into motion. She spun on her knee and clapped her body against the trunk of a nearby willow tree, her heart hammering.

She peeked around the trunk and scanned the slopes. There was nowhere to go. She was sitting in the bottom of a bowl and the vampire things were everywhere. At least a dozen dotted the hill at her back, and the moonlight caught the white faces of dozens more crawling around the slopes across the swamp from where she had come.

(surrounded)

Above the weird, deep croaking that vibrated the tiny leaves on the umbrella of willow branches that drooped above her, she could hear their number, the thirsty panting of the Leeches as they closed in. She chanced one more peek. Further into the center of the swamp was her only choice. She had to stay away from...

(the exits)

A new sound on the slope at her right snapped her head around. It was a man's voice, a human voice cutting through the feral wheezing of the Leeches.

"I am going through the center..." the man said.

She had to look. She peeked around the tree again. It was him; it was the man who had appeared on the television in Sam's bedroom, the man who had been walking through the graveyard in Colma a thousand years ago and a million miles away. But he was not in a suit this time. He was dressed like a Roman soldier. She had assumed this man was Simon, but it was clear now that she had been wrong. This man was no sorcerer. This man was clearly a soldier, a commander of some kind. His bulk was tucked into a red tunic beneath his bald pate. He had a large sword in his hand, and he was coming down the slope and heading straight for her.

-6-

"I am going through the center," Fley said. "Fan out and secure this slope. Three of you come with me."

Leeches had names, but no one knew what they were, least of all the Leeches. They had all come from somewhere, from some epoch of history, but those details had died with them. For reasons unknown their particular strain of vampirism had made them rejects of the Devil. Why God had abandoned them was clear, however. Fley could certainly understand the revulsion of spending eternity with these monsters, because he had the unfortunate distinction of being the man who was doing just that. Fley supposed he may have carelessly slaughtered innocent women, children and thousands of unarmed men in his time, but did anyone really deserve to spend an afterlife with these craven morons?

Fley raised a finger, vacillating between the pasty-faced troops before finally stabbing the air in front of one of them. With a grimace and a dispassionate sweep of his hand, he selected his final lieutenant from the assembled rabble without a second glance. He was losing heart for this mission and he knew it, but there was a sure-fire way to make sure the Leeches did not. Opening his satchel, Fley flicked the vampires each an extra plump morsel of nightshade as if they were trained seals. He could actually see the murderous intoxication fill them, their eyes bulging with the lunatic desire for destruction as they chewed up the blooms.

They were unstoppable now, juiced and ready. On the Roman's command, they began to head down the hill and into the heart of the swamp.

-7-

A Leech blazed Fley's trail, loping indelicately through a puddle of mud and sending a rooster tail of muck spraying inches from the centurion. Fley halted just in time to avoid being doused, rage twisting his face. He was considering burying his drawn sword up to the hilt in the vampire's head when the creature suddenly shrieked the alarm. It had heard something, seen something.

The Leech turned to Fley and the other Leeches, its dead, black eyes wide with alarm. It crooked its fingers in a gesture of greedy pursuit, its raspy breathing increasing as it hunched into a burlesque of stealth.

"Halt," Fley said, holding his gladius out to his side to stop the advance. "Just...wait a goddamned moment."

The cadre of Leeches at his sides was already frothing and lurching towards the spot that their analogue was indicating with its craned neck and its bulging eyes.

Suddenly, the Leech on point lunged into a thicket of brambles, the sleeve of its already tattered burial suit tearing on a row of thorns.

Fley watched, continuing to still the Leeches as his side with the outstretched sword. He wanted to see which way she would run. There was no sense in more than one soldier flushing her out of her hiding place. The girl was unarmed, and even if she had fashioned some form of weapon from her surroundings, the Leech wouldn't care. It would lock its teeth onto her like a rabid dog and drag her kicking and screaming into the muddy clearing at his feet. Or, if worse came to worst, a nod of his head would give the order to rip her apart.

His eyes watched the thicket. The bushes were tall and deep, but the edges were visible. She could squirt away on the far side where Fley could not see, but the pursuing Leech would indicate her position with another shriek and the girl would quickly be swarmed.

Finally there were snapping branches, splashing mud, another shriek and then the Leech exploded from the tangle of thorns with a look of horror on its already horrible face. It shrieked again.

"What?" Fley commanded. "And stop that shrieking! Where is..."

Before he could finish, a long, pink band sprang out of the thicket and attached itself to the Leech's face. With a sickening suck and a pop, the tongue retracted back into the brush like a whip, taking with it one of the Leech's eyeballs.

The Leech shrieked again, clapping a thin, white hand to its vacant eye socket, little white spiders pouring from between its splayed fingers.

Something crashed through the brambles and landed with a wet and meaty plop in the sodden clearing, sending a spray of mud across them all. Fley and his Leeches cringed and then straightened quickly, bracing for a fight.

A giant amphibious eye perched on a single plump, green leg swept its gaze over them once before leaping into the distant swamp with a perturbed croak.

"YOU HALF-WITTED LUMP OF BUG SHIT!" Fley roared at the one-eyed vampire as it slinked back into the rank and file. "It's a goddamned monotoad! Did I tell you to indicate on a MONOTOAD? DID I?

The Leech shook its head, tossing greasy long hair about its shoulders.

Fley stepped towards it: "You shrieked like a bat caught in a chariot wheel and gave away our position because you spotted a monotoad? They live here, dumb shit! They are everywhere! Do you hear them? LISTEN! THEY'RE EVERYWHERE!"

With a lunge and a lightning fast thrust of his sword, Fley buried his gladius into the Leech's chest. Pulling backwards on his sword, he jerked the vampire to his side, raised a muddy, sandaled foot, placed it squarely on the vampire's stomach and tugged his weapon free of the thing's ribcage. Bugs, lots of them poured from the gaping wound.

A wailing spirit, transparent and ultraviolet, leaked out of the carcass. It was the figure of a middle-aged man, and it spiraled upward, screaming towards the face of the moon. There, it elongated like pulled taffy, tugged by some unseen force, before it was inhaled feet first towards the center of The Nowhere, towards The Pitch – the maw of anti-matter that no one wanted to mention, much less contemplate. The gathered watched soberly as the dispatched spirit streaked away to have its soul digested by the Wraiths.

"Fan out!" Fley commanded. "She must have been flushed from her cover by now! SO GET HER! And, unless you want to wind up as toad shit, try not to bother the monotoads. Is that too much to ask, you witless crap heaps?"

The Leeches were still transfixed to the spot in the sky where their cohort's spirit had been.

"MOVE!" Fley roared. "Or you can join him!"

The Leeches' bloodlust returned, their panting quickened and they lumbered forward. Fley planted a foot in a swampy pool, its edge masked by clusters of cattails. He almost lost his balance as the cold mud sucked at his ankle. He jerked his foot from the clouding water and shook it peevishly. In the distance, a pair of monotoads watched this before hopping into a cave made of weeping branches.

"Shit," Fley hissed. "Go around you dolts! This is deep water! You three come with me! The rest of you head to the right!"

It was clear that whatever advantage Fley thought he had in pursuing a Thumper was extinguished by the din of booming croaks. They would never hear a heartbeat with this racket.

A few yards to his left, Fley spotted a monotoad the size of a pig fattened for slaughter keeping pace with him. It moved with a series of blundering hops that were only able to lift the thing's girth a foot or so from the ground. Fley stopped. The monotoad stopped too, balancing gawkishly on its one splayed foot. Fley locked eyes with the giant thing as he continued on. The toad squinted its membranous eyelid in response and matched him step for step, lumbering through the muck.

Fley had a pleasant thought: Maybe it had eaten the girl. The fat creature certainly looked like it had. There would be no way to know short of attacking it. An idea widened Fley's eyes and quickened his step. Suddenly, he sprinted towards the enormous toad and quickly fell upon it just as the thing attempted to leap away. With a flash of his sword, Fley lopped off its trunk-like leg at the ankle. With a monstrous croak the toad hit the ground with a meaty thud, rolling onto its ridged back. The sticky tongue shot from its mouth. Fley expected this and somersaulted, landing clear and skidding in a puddle of the dark, jelly-like fluid pulsing from the thing's severed leg. He came to a stop beside the creature as the searching tongue snapped back into its mouth. Raising his sword, Fley brought it down hard and gutted the toad from belly to gullet. A blossom of black filth bulged from the wound, pouring onto the muddy ground. With his sword, Fley sifted through the mess. No human remains.

"Shit!" he spat.

Standing, he plunged his sword into the murky pool beside the body, cleaning the gore from his blade. He sheathed the weapon, and with steely eyes scanned the ridges above the swamp. On the hillsides, the lifeless black eyes and white faces of the Leeches stared back. They were absurdly overdressed for the occasion in their tattered burial suits, swaying and drooling, but all empty-handed.

"SHE IS NOT HERE!" Fley roared, stepping into the center of a clearing and turning to address the ranks dotting the slopes. "Somehow, she made it out of here! She made it past one of you useless pieces of shit! To the top of the ridge, all of you! I HAVE NOW LOST MY FUCKING PATIENCE! PERHAPS YOU CAN FIND THAT? MOVE OUT! NOW!"

-8-

A black figure began to rise from a pond at the edge of the clearing. It stood slowly, mud and moss falling from its form and plopping back into the grimy water.

Lucia took the hollow reed from her mouth and blew out a mist of brackish gunk and coughed violently. Her breath was racing out of control. She tried to still her lungs, to find some kind of rhythm. It was as if she had forgotten how to breathe. She stood shivering, the mud continuing to crawl down her frame to its home in the black depths at her feet. Her eyes, skittish and wide, flickered with panic, expecting at any moment that she would be seized.

There was a good chance that she had not waited long enough, come up too quick. She didn't care. She could not stay down there a second longer, not a second longer. If they were waiting her out, then they won. She had her limits. She had done her best, her absolute best, better than she ever expected. She managed to catch her breath and she listened, turning her head to scan the hills, the mud stiffening on her neck as it dried.

(oh, thank God)

They were gone.

Near where the sword had dipped into the water, dangerously close to her feet, one of the giant frogs had been torn open. She looked away. A brief wave of sadness tugged at her. She was convinced that these mutants of nature had let her live, had covered for her somehow.

Gritting her teeth, she took a shaky step and stumbled onto the bank, her every nerve stinging with cold and shaking with fear. She hugged her sodden body, and alone she climbed out of the ravine.

XIV.
Guardians of the Veil

-1-

"She knows I am alive?" Sam asked. "She heard us?"

"Yes," Clara replied.

"And she is okay."

"Yes."

"Lucia..." Sam spoke the name as if it were an incantation. He turned his eyes upward, towards the panel in the wall of the cell. It would open again soon, and when it did he would make the most of it. He knew he had connected to her. He had felt it, but what good it would do he did not know. The confusion and kaleidoscope of images was too short and now it was over. Now there was only an aching emptiness, an emptiness and two stark revelations that had been borne on that swirling wind: Lucia was alive and Father Doctor had been attacked.

"I saw that too," Clara said, coming to his side. "Simon made a final try for the priest, but his injuries are minor. He will be fine."

"I saw red light," Sam said, looking up at her. "Fire?"

"No, it is the lights of the traveling healers. They are at his side."

"Ambulance..."

"Yes."

"But he will be all right?" Sam asked, his eyes welling. "Are you sure? Don't lie to me, please."

"Yes, Sam," Clara replied. "He will be all right. I do not lie. The healers have already left him. They have given him medicine. Now, he sleeps."

"I miss him so much," Sam said, his jaw setting against his tears. "It's all my fault."

"He misses you too," Clara said, touching Sam's cheek.

Sam tingled with her energy. "He knew more about us than I did. He knows everything, doesn't he?"

"He always has."

"Then why didn't he tell me? Why did he keep it from me?"

Clara's ghostly form dimmed as she thought, dimmed until she was barely visible. "He believed he could save you from who you are. He believed that who you are was not a necessary function of nature and he set out to change you. He meant well, and his efforts were gentle, but who you are cannot be changed. It is God who creates the uniqueness in us all, the uniqueness that some consider beautiful and others dismiss as aberrant. But in the end, that uniqueness is part of a whole. It is part of God"

Clara folded her luminous hand around Sam's. "You are dark and mysterious to many. This is to be expected. You are Samhain, you are transition. To me, you are powerful and you are hope. You are made of stars like everything else, but the necessity of your existence is greater than most and it is   beyond the understanding of most. Heeding the call of your   desire, especially when it is a rarified voice can be lonely and you always suffer in its pursuit. But that desire is the wings that bear you to your fulfillment, the wings that have brought you to me, and I am grateful. And soon, the world will be grateful for you, too."

Sam peeled his eyes away from Clara's and pinned a longing glance to the panel in the wall. When at last he turned his eyes back to the shimmering woman at his side, he was grinning slyly.

"Were you the black cat?" he asked.

The apparition that was Tlachtga, Clara to her clan, sparkled like a sapphire as she laughed softly. "Not exactly," she said. "In ancient Ireland we used to believe black cats to be good luck, and somehow they have become considered quite the opposite over time, but to us they are really quite useful. Druids are masters of assimilating with animals. We can shape-shift into them, shape-shift objects into them, and we can use their eyes as if they were our own.

"Black cats have always been favored for a few simple reasons: they are particularly effective spies because they are able to move quickly and quietly, and their dark color makes them stealthier still. So yes, the black cat was making sure you were okay. It was my eyes while I was trapped here."

"And the ravens?" Sam asked. "I am pretty sure a few of them were spying on me, too."

"I commandeered no birds," Clara replied.

Sam frowned, "So, Simon can control animals, too?"

"Of course. He is a great druid."

"And things too, like computers and my phone." Sam mused.

"Yes," Clara confirmed. "Unintelligent things, objects with energy fields unshielded by a spirit can be manipulated from here, but only during The Thinning. It is far too difficult the rest of the year, for any of us."

"I knew it. I knew all this stuff was happening, but part of me just didn't want to accept it."

"You are human. Skepticism is an effective safeguard against foolishness."

Sam brightened with a recollection: "You know what? I haven't had flashes of things that are going to happen since I have been here. I just realized that. Not once have I seen the future here."

"Ah," Clara said, "dà-shealladh – the second sight. That is because nothing here has a future."

Sam considered this before he went on, "Did you know I was healed when I came here, from the accident I had when I was a kid? I regained my vision when I passed The Veil and I got all the feeling back in my leg and arm."

"You are whole here," she said, "and not subject to your imperfections. Here, you are perfection."

Sam considered this too. He stared at his renewed hand and flexed it. The next question was one of the most important, and he was frightened to ask it. It was the source of most of his anguish for most of his life and the answer would either liberate him from it or sentence him to more of it. He looked at Clara. "What about The Crackle?"

"That is what you call it?" Clara asked. A smile played at the corners of her mouth. "It has been with you always, hasn't it?"

Sam nodded.

Clara continued, "It is the astral echo of thousands of years of fires burned on Samhain, the festival at summer's end for which you are named. They are a part of you and they always will be for you are the embodiment of the transition between life and death. The bonfires were the last light before winter, the final attempt to ward off the denizens of The Nowhere at the time of the Thinning. You hear them and you smell them because all of those fires, through all of those ages, blazed on your behalf. The people who set them were aiding you."

"Me...?"

"Yes."

Sam grew very quiet. He could feel the last threads of his

resistance fraying. "It's so unbelievable, but..."

"But it feels true, doesn't it?"

"Yes. I always wanted to help them. I didn't know how. They all wanted protection from the darkness, from all that they could feel clawing at The Veil."

"Yes."

"And we are the only ones who can insure that The Nowhere doesn't get through."

"Yes," Clara replied, "The Nowhere has leaked through enough to help us blur the lines and make our job easier, but if Halloween dies, if the lanterns go out, if the living do not dress as the dead and continue to blur that line between the two worlds, then The Nowhere will have an advantage. This dark place will gain its foothold. That has already begun to happen."

"I know," Sam said gravely. "Most people don't care much for Halloween. It means nothing to them. Some even think it is an evil holiday."

"Strange," Clara said, "because it is the exact opposite. It is simply bringing the fight to evil's doorstep."

"And that," Sam said, "is exactly what I want to do."

It was at this moment that the change swept through Sam. The surrender had happened, and it happened completely. It showed on his face. Since he had come into The Nowhere, Sam had worn the dazed look of a foreigner, shackled by doubt and encumbered by fear. Now, his visage hardened like drying cement into a mask of unbending will. His fine, elfin features sharpened with resolve. His eyes glittered fiercely and he leveled them at the mother of his clan.

"You are not finished with your story, Clara. There is one more piece of information, something else I need to know. You said I am descended from you, and your father, Mog Ruith, the great druid, but you said I was descended from another. Tell me who."

"I will," Clara said, "but the story begins long before us, and you should know it, though it will not be easy to hear.

-2-

"I suppose you have heard the names of Herod and John the Baptist? That is where the story starts in earnest, in the time of Christ. I wasn't there of course, but my father told it to me many times because it involves him. I have also found the story in the Synoptic Gospels. I too was like you. I found my own history hard to believe and had to confirm it for myself. But I have found it to be so.

"As the story goes, Herod had imprisoned John because he reproved Herod for divorcing his wife and unlawfully taking Herodias as his new lover – the wife of his brother Phillip. On Herod's birthday, Herodias' daughter, Salome, danced before the king and his guests. Her dancing pleased Herod so much that in his drunkenness he promised to give her anything she desired, up to half of his kingdom. When the daughter asked her mother what she should request, she was told to ask for the head of John the Baptist on a platter. Although Herod was appalled by the request, he reluctantly agreed and had John executed. Mog Ruith, my father, was the executioner."

"WHAT?" Sam cried. He had turned white, his mouth falling open. "He killed John the Baptist? St. John? The man who baptized Jesus?"

"It is true. In his youth he was an executioner for hire. To be fair, he knew nothing of the future importance of John or Jesus for that matter. The execution happened at about the same time as Jesus was establishing his ministry."

"Oh, God," Sam groaned. "This is not good." He clapped a hand to his forehead and rubbed his temples. "I'm screwed."

"You are not doomed, Samhain," Clara soothed. "Remember, I only visit The Nowhere, but my home is with God."

Calmed for the moment, Sam dropped his hand to his lap.

Clara went on: "At the time, Mog Ruith was a new student of Simon Magus'. Simon was not known to take many students, but the ones he did take on were required to pay him a fee. Mog Ruith paid this fee from the money he received from his executions. Simon chose Mog Ruith as a student because Mog Ruith was already powerful. He had been born at the peak of the Thinning – this is true of all of our clan – and therefore, he had the second sight. His pedigree was also traceable to a storm god of the Gauls. In short, Simon deemed him to be a worthy recipient of the sorcery handed down by the departing Star Child in Egypt so many years before.

"Simon was reluctant to take on any students at first, but he also knew that he would need successors to do his bidding once he had passed on to the Death Realms, for even his sorcery would not afford him immortality in the flesh. He wanted to be a god. He was already delusional enough to think himself divine, but he had no disciples, and only disciples produce the sustenance of the gods: faith. So, he began to share his knowledge.

"At the time of Mog Ruith's tutelage, Simon Magus had only one other student, a Saxon named Bairen who was also visiting Jerusalem from Ireland. Bairen knew some magic already. He was a student of Kabbalah, the Jewish magic, when he became Simon's pupil. Bairen had similar traits to Mog Ruith, traits that made him a desirable disciple of Simon's: intrinsic power and divine pedigree. Mog Ruith told me that Simon favored my father at first, helping him to construct the great flying chariot that would be known throughout Ireland as *Roth Rámach*, although it would be a century before Mog Ruith could pilot such a powerful fetish.

"Slowly however, tension began to mount between Simon and my father, a moral tension. Mog Ruith was all but abandoned by Simon in favor of Bairen, his newest apprentice. Simon saw something in the young Bairen that he liked, something that Mog Ruith did not possess: a willingness to blur the lines of morality in the interest of acquiring power.

"But Simon's infatuation with Bairen was short-lived. Simon had become convinced that his blood was divine and that only a direct descendant could ever truly be worthy of his knowledge. He returned to his homeland. There, he had three sons with a peasant woman. She was killed by Simon soon after so she would have no influence over the children."

"He killed his wife after she gave him three kids?" Sam asked. "This guy is a real asshole."

"Yes," Clara agreed, smiled thinly and went on: "Simon and his three sons soon started plotting their enslavement of the world. It was then that Simon traveled to Rome to begin acquiring disciples. After his flying demonstration where he was struck down and killed in front of the Caesar, shattering his legs, Simon was cast into The Nowhere, abandoned by both God and the Devil.

"Without a master, both Mog Ruith and Bairen returned to Ireland, but the two took very different paths. Bairen became a master druid for the King of Tara and commanded a sizable and well-funded guild of his own sorcerers. Mog Ruith, on the other hand, became a hermit on the isle of Valentia and led an almost monastic life, repenting for his former line of work.

"It was during this time that I was born. I never knew my mother, for she died during my birth. I grew up learning from my father, learning his magic. Later, I left the island and moved east. It was there that Simon's reach from The Nowhere touched our family, a touch that would stain us forever.

"One night, when the fires that marked summer's end burned bright on Ireland's hills, I was raped by the three sons of Simon Magus. I brought the child into the world, an enchanted and beautiful boy he was. Instead of looking upon him as an unwanted child, I encouraged him to be an agent for good. He was the first Guardian of The Veil. He became the first soldier in our cause, the first to be called, Samhain."

Sam started, his eyes widening. "But...that means..."

"Yes," Clara confirmed. "You are a descendant of   Simon Magus."

-3-

Sam shot to his feet, but he sat down again hard. His head throbbed. The oxygen in the cell was running low again, his legs numb and useless. His swimming vision tried to find Clara.

(it can't be)

His eyes found Clara's, and they pleaded for a different truth, but Clara only returned his stare, her mouth curling into a sympathetic frown.

"That is why you are so powerful," Clara said. "That is why our clan has lasted for millennia. In the end, Simon will find that it was a mistake to mix his blood with ours. In the end, his own powers will be used to destroy him."

Sam's brow was cold with sweat, his mouth dry. He sat silently, listening to the rest of the madness, staring at his own hands as if he had never seen them before, as if they belonged to a stranger.

"I died during childbirth," Clara said softly, "just like my mother. I was never able to hold my own child. I have always guided our clan from this side of The Veil."

"What about your father?" Sam asked. "I can't imagine how pissed off he was. What did he do?"

"He had his revenge," Clara replied. "There was a great war in Munster. Bairen – who had become known throughout Ireland as the Red Druid – had enchanted the king of Tara and had seized command of his army. Bairen launched an attack on Munster to find and kill my son. He did this during The Thinning so that Simon could influence the outcome from The Nowhere. Bairen killed many innocent children, but he never found my son. My father was summoned by Munster's king. Mog Ruith raised an army of the dead and destroyed Bairen. The battle is still legend in our homeland."

"I've dreamed of this," Sam said distantly. "Where is Mog..."

"Alive," Clara replied, "but he is over 2,000 years old. His fighting days are behind him. The duty falls to us."

"To us..." Sam muttered, his chin drifting towards his chest.

Suddenly, a blast of cold wind whipped him to attention.

(the panel)

In a flash, Clara's form soared up the wall, flaring indigo as she screamed, "CALL HER NOW! CALL LUCIA TO YOUR SIDE!"

-4-

Sam stood sucking in the cold air, steadying his legs, the wind rippling through his tattered black shirt and pants as he stood staring up at the hole in the wall. He centered Lucia in his mind, and as the wind howled, he reached out for her, for Father Doctor, for the only family he had ever known. He told them both that he was okay. He told them both that he was safe, that he was ready to do what he was put here to do, that Simon would never hurt them again, that he was...

(Samhain)

His eyes grew hot, and his vision tunneled. Red, all he could see was red. All he could see was...

(fire)

"STOP!" Clara shouted at him from somewhere above.

The panel snapped closed. Sam lost his balance, reeled backwards and fell to the ground. With a trembling hand he pawed at his face. His vision cleared and he got to his feet.

His breath froze when he saw what he had just done.

Two black trails singed the stone where Sam's line of sight had traveled up the cell wall. Around the lead panel, fine tendrils of smoke drifted lazily from the charred rock.

"Shit!" Sam cried, his eyes wide and fixed on the blackened wall. "What...what happened?"

"The fires of Samhain," Clara said, fluttering down from the ceiling. She was smiling with pride. She approached Sam and took his still shaking hands. "They are yours to command. You have found the well within you, and it is full."

"Full? You're not kidding!" Sam cried. "Did you see that? I just shot fire from my eyes! From my eyes! HOLY SHIT!! How bad-ass is THAT?"

Clara said nothing, her smile in danger of spreading. For the sake of propriety, she was taming it with effort. There was nothing quite like the first time, and she envied Sam. She remembered the first bolt of lightning she had ever cast, setting fire to a tree when she was a little girl, in a rocky field with her father. The memory was as fresh as if it had been yesterday.

"Can you feel the well at your core now?" Clara asked. "Can you reach for what you need?"

"YES!"

"Sorcery is nothing but will, and if you have it, magic happens"

"Wow, does it ever." He had run to the wall and was feeling the black trails on the stone. They were still warm to the touch.

"But without a fetish, "Clara warned, "it may be hard to control. I am acting as your fetish for the moment."

Sam, beaming with amazement and pride returned to Clara's side, "I can call the fires up again?"

"Yes."

"There's nothing to light on fire in here," Sam said glumly.

"No," Clara confirmed, "and you must control it for now."

"Yes," Sam agreed, his grin wide. He gripped his head with both hands, "WOW!"

Clara watched him with pursed lips, her light billowing calmly.

"Nothing that cool has ever happened to me," Sam said. "Okay...I have to get a grip. Holy smokes..." He ran back to the wall to study the singed stone again and scampered back to Clara's side. "Alright...I'm gonna chill out now...I swear. Could my father do this?"

"Not only your father, but all of your ancestors," Clara replied. "However, the laws that govern your world do not allow it. You are the first to pass through The Veil and thus you are the first to call up the fires."

"Simon should have killed me," Sam said. "The bad guy always makes the same stupid mistakes. I can't BELIEVE he had the balls to call me here. He killed my parents. He's going to regret that, and he's going to regret that his sons raped you, I'll see to it."

Fire licked through Sam's eyes.

"Control," Clara urged. "Your time is coming."

A loud, clanging sound snapped both of their heads to the heavy lead door of their cell. It was swinging open, hinges protesting with shrieks. Sam leapt to his feet. He squinted, shielding his eyes from the orange torchlight that flooded the chamber.

Standing in the doorway was a single silhouette. Sam's bravado drained and he backed away from the intruder, his heart hammering. It was only when the figure stepped forward that Sam could see who it was.

It was Lucia.

-5-

Sam's brain slipped a gear. His head turned and he looked out of the corner of his eye, the place where apparitions hide. The panel above had just recently opened and he was flush with oxygen, but maybe it was too late, maybe he had already suffered some brain damage and this was nothing but a hallucination.

"Sam..." whispered the Lucia figure in the doorway, its voice full of wonder.

Sam blinked hard, but the figure remained.

"It's me!" the voice cried. Then a measure of Lucia's sweet and familiar laugh coated Sam like warm syrup.

"Looze?" Sam croaked. His mind locked into gear and began to race. His heart leapt. She approached with arms outstretched and he fell into them. "Looze!" Sam cried. "Oh, thank God..."

Tears, hot and salty, sprang from his eyes and traced down his cold and dirty cheek. He stroked her hair, pawing it away from her face where it had plastered with mud. His eyes swam, drinking in all of her, searching for the deception, the unreality that he was sure would soon be exposed, but she was real, and she was in his arms again.

"Sam..." she said, and her emerald eyes blazed.

"Senorita..." Sam laughed. Their arms flew around each other's necks and they kissed. They held each other tight, the heat of their embrace weakening them and strengthening them at once. They swooned in each other's arms as love's power took its familiar place, enriching the cold and empty hollows that had longed for its return.

Slowly, their lips parted and they caught their breath.

"Looze, what happened? You look like shit. Are you okay? Are you hurt?"

"I look like shit?" Lucia said. "You're such a romantic." She kissed him again. "I'm fine – long, weird story. Is there any other kind in this place? But we are out of time."

"How did you...where did you...?" Sam could not find the words. Standing before him was a miracle. He had felt a connection over the wind, had known that she was okay, but he never expected this, never expected her to be the one to throw open the door of his cell.

Lucia turned to Clara and stared at her as if she was seeing a ghost, which of course she was. Sam watched Lucia in the same way, giddy with the unreality of it all.

"I am Clara," said the blue ghost in the luminous robes.

"I am Lucia. You were the one Sam talked about; you are the 'woman in the glass'."

Clara smiled and nodded once.

"But your spirit has no body," Lucia said, suddenly alarmed. "The Wraiths..."

"They have no power over me," Clara assured her. "I take no flesh or bone here because my spirit is tethered to Heaven. I have only donned these robes to give me form. They are garments from The Fringe, and they are all I need to walk among you."

"You're beautiful," Lucia said.

"And so are you," Clara replied.

Lucia grimaced and plucked a strand of her long dark hair from the drying mud on her neck, "Thank you, but I've looked better."

Sam's head oscillated between the two women as if he were watching a very strange tennis match. Lucia had asked a question that was not only wise in the ways of The Nowhere, but one that he had not even thought about asking. Lucia was a marvel, and he still could not believe she was standing in front of him. Even with her hair plastered with mud and her clothes torn and dirty, she was the most beautiful thing he could ever hope to see.

Lucia turned to Sam, her eyes stoked with amazement, "I heard you, Sam. I heard you call to me, and I found you. I don't care what happens now. I'm with you, and I don't want to leave you ever again."

"I was just thinking the same thing," Sam said.

"I hate to seem impatient," Clara said, "but we must find the reliquary."

"Yes," Sam conceded. "Lucia, I don't know how you got in here, but now we need to get out. What's it look like out there? Does anyone know you are here?"

"Oh, that's right," Lucia said. "I should have mentioned it. I was just so glad to see you. I brought help."

"Help?" Sam asked.

"Outside," Lucia added. "He is guarding the door. He insisted."

"Who...?" Sam insisted.

"Wait," Clara interrupted; her voice stern. She pulled the cell door ajar and then glided closer to them and held them both by the hand. Lucia stiffened as Clara's energy sizzled and popped on her skin. "The cell has been breached. Before we utter another word, and before we leave, there is one thing that we need to remember. Simon will know that we have escaped only if someone tells him or if he senses us." She speared Lucia with a grave stare, the whites of her eyes blazing like tiny lamps. "Did anyone see you come in?"

"Not anyone whose soul remains here," Lucia replied coldly.

Sam gaped at her. She was a warrior now? Whatever had happened on the way to this cell, whatever she had gone through had changed her for good. His childhood friend was clearly stronger now.

He knew he had been changed too. Aside from now being able to shoot pillars of fire from his eye sockets – which he thought to be an extremely awesome development – he'd gained something even more important than superhero sorcery. He'd gained what he had always wanted, and it was a gift that he had always been free to give himself, but had never dared: acceptance. He was now unafraid to embrace who he was and all that it meant. He could tell that she had come to the same junction in herself and had chosen the path that led uphill, the one that would be toughest to climb, but the one that would yield the better view of the life that stretched before her.

In a way, he and Lucia were now two strangers, strangers born in this haunted place, and the irony of it all was that they would stop being haunted because of it. The Sam and Lucia that they once were had been left somewhere out there beyond the stone walls, somewhere in the endless midnight.

Clara continued, "If no one remains that saw you come in then the only way Simon can track us is if we think of him or mention his name aloud." She turned to Sam, "The same method you used to call

Lucia is also the method by which Simon will track us down." Clara looked at them both, "From this point forward, clear him from your minds. It won't be long before he finds out we have escaped, but this should buy us a little time."

Sam and Lucia nodded gravely.

Clara turned to Lucia, "Where is Orace Fley?"

"On his way."

"How many Leeches?"

"I don't know," Lucia confessed. "Maybe a hundred."

"And there are at least that many here," Clara said, "We must move fast. Let's go."

"You brought help?" Sam asked.

"Yeah, he's an old friend," Lucia replied, heading for the door. "It's a little messy out here. Dead Leeches everywhere, so watch your step."

Lucia led the way, and all three of them walked out of the cell and into the torch-lit maze of Simon's tomb.

XV.
Reliquary of the Fetishes

-1-

Standing outside of Sam and Clara's cell, his back to the stone wall of the narrow corridor, was a large man dressed in a leather jerkin, chainmail and cape standing very still, both hands on the hilt of a broadsword. In the flickering light of the torches, Sam could see only the whites of his watchful eyes as they scanned the hallway, flicking to either side from within his blackened and blistered sockets.

"Jacques?" Sam whispered.

"Salut, Samhain," Jacque de Molay returned, teeth flashing in a grin. The knight offered a bow to Clara, "Madame Tlachtga."

"Jacques?" Clara said with surprise, before turning to Sam, "You know each other?"

"I was going to ask you the same thing," Sam replied. He frowned suspiciously at the knight, "You helped Lucia? I thought you were not going to get involved. You said you cared only about yourself."

"I changed my heart, as you say," Jacques offered.

"Any more of the welcoming party show up?" Lucia asked Jacques.

"No," the knight replied, "only the two from before." He gestured to the piles on the ground at either side of the cell door with a curt nod of his head, "These guards do not need to be relieved because they need no sleep or food so it is unlikely there would be a pair of replacements on the way. Though I suspect nightshade is dispensed throughout the tomb every so often to keep them happy. So, whoever distributes the devil's weed may come soon, and they may come in pairs."

Sam was staring at the fallen Leeches on the stones. There had indeed been two of them, but they were no longer recognizable. They had been two 18th century men from the looks of the burial clothes. The heads had been struck from the vampire's necks where only the yellowed lace of cravats remained. Sam supposed the heads had rolled far away down the darkened corridor.

As for the bodies, they had been split open from breastbone to pelvis with a clean sword stroke, the cavities crawling with thousands of bugs that looked like writhing pools of shiny oil. Dotted throughout the black and pulsing mounds were a few white and fuzzy arachnids. Sam knew they must be relatives of the flying spiders that infested the marshes past Jack of the Lantern's place, only smaller, larval perhaps. These white bugs made Sam panic somewhere deep inside, somewhere he had little control over. One of them was clicking and feeling its way blindly over the canvas of his sneaker, heading for the cuff of his pants. He kicked it off sharply with a yelp of disgust.

Sam looked back at Jacques, "You led us to the witch. She tried to kill us. Why would I trust you now?"

Lucia put her hand on Sam's shoulder to calm him, to assure him, but she recoiled when she saw...

(flames)

They were dancing through the whites of Sam's eyes like tiny pilot lights. For a moment she thought maybe it was a trick of the light, a reflection of the torch sconces on the wall, but somehow she knew better, and words failed her.

"No..." Jacques protested, raising a flattened palm, "I knew nothing of it, Monsieur. *C'est vrai.*"

"I don't speak French," Sam said crisply, fire licking at his eye sockets, "and neither will you when I'm done."

Now it was Clara who laid a gentle hand on Sam's shoulder. The fire extinguished immediately and it was simply Sam's limpid green eyes that turned to her with expectation.

"See the truth, Sam," Clara urged, "See it..."

Sam turned back to Jacques and stared.

Lucia spoke, "He was trying to help us. Jacques told me that Baba Yaga has always had a reputation for being independent and uninterested in alliances with anyone. He told me she kept to herself, and it was very unlikely that she would be able to be bribed. The destruction of The Veil must have been too great a temptation. She chose sides and Jacques didn't know."

"Then tell me this," Sam said, his voice still wintery, "why is this knight not interested in his freedom as well. Why would he help us to prevent the Veil from falling?"

"Because," Jacques de Molay began, staring past Sam with eyes that seemed to be weary with the endless search for what can never be found, "I know you can win. And, I do not believe that my soul can ever be at peace among the living. What I do believe is that my broken soul can be healed, if only for a moment, by doing what is right. There are not many opportunities to test one's purity around here, and it was once my religion to do so. I was a knight, a knight of the Templars." Jacques looked straight into Sam's eyes, "Although I know God has washed his hands of me, I will do his work once again only because it is right to do so. If my broken soul heals even a little, then I will be grateful for it. Either way, I will destroy the false prophet if you will fight beside me, and I pledge my allegiance to you, Samhain."

Jacques bowed before Sam.

Lucia grabbed Sam's arm, her eyes bright and imploring, "Fley would have caught me for sure if Jacques had not been waiting at the top of the ravine, watching everything."

"Ravine?" Sam asked, still not taking his eyes from Jacques.

"There were giant one-eyed toads," Lucia said. "Gross swamp. Long story. It sucked, trust me. I thought you were dead."

Sam looked at the knight again and now he could see it; he could see the truth, just as Clara had said. The knight was covered with it: a faint lemon-yellow haze that curled around his body like clinging smoke. Sam offered his hand. "Sorry to doubt your intentions. Thank you for taking care of Lucia. Thank you for saving her life. I love her."

"I know you do," Jacques said, pumping Sam's arm before returning his hand to his sword and sheathing it. "I can see it in your eyes. She is a remarkably brave woman. She insisted that we find you. I warned her of the dangers, but she would hear none of it."

"So we go on," Clara urged, "but one more thing..." She looked at Sam and Lucia, her glowing eyes stern. "The living have never died in this place. If you were to die; if you were to lose your flesh and release your spirits here, you would be the first. If we were closer to The Fringe, your spirits would stand a better chance of returning through The Veil for proper judgment, but here...here I'm afraid the Wraiths of The Pitch would have something to say about that. Here, God is not watching."

Sam and Lucia shuddered; their eyes met. There were moments when both of them could forget how deep they had gone into this alien world, merciful moments, moving forward as if in a dream, but the unspeakable reality of this place could not be ignored now.

"I just want to make sure that you know that the danger is still real," continued Clara.

The two nodded, their faces set.

"It is getting more real by the moment I'm afraid," Jacques whispered. "Listen. Someone is coming."

-2-

"We can't run. We must intercept them," Jacques insisted. "If they come upon the empty cell they will sound an alarm."

The four looked to both sides. There were only torch-lit stone corridors curving away into the unknown.

The sound was getting closer, but the acoustics were strange in the curved and narrow space. The hollow echo was definitely the steady scrape and clop of footfalls, but how close they were and of what number was not easy to tell. The sound bounced off the stone and it swirled around them, coming from all sides at once. They held their breath. The echo rose and fell as they listened, ghostly and steady.

"Two of them," Sam ventured. "Maybe even three."

"It is coming from where we came in," Jacques whispered. "There is a spiral staircase and then a row of empty cells before they get to us. I will go further down the hall, just beyond the curve in the wall. I will take Tlachtga with me. Sam and Lucia, you remain in the cell with the door open, standing to either side of the door and out of sight. Whoever comes will see that there has been a breach, and they will enter the cell to investigate. We will then ambush them from behind. Now go."

It was a good plan and they all moved quickly.

"He knows what he is doing," Sam muttered as he and Lucia re-entered the cell and pressed their backs to either side of the door.

"He was a Templar knight," Lucia reminded him. "He's done this kind of thing before."

"Well, I haven't," Sam whispered back.

"What are we going to do?" Lucia asked, her whisper now reduced to a panicky hiss. "Kick whoever it is in the balls? I don't have a weapon or anything."

She lifted her head from the cold stones of the cell wall and chanced a peek through the open door. There was nothing but pale orange light and the steady, methodical sound of approaching footsteps. Her heart began to drum in her ears.

"Sam?" she asked, her head now firmly against the wall.

"What?" he whispered.

"What happened to your eyes a minute ago? I swear I saw them light up with fire. I can't explain it..."

"I can't either," Sam replied, "but it's true. I have a feeling you'll be seeing more of it."

"Did Clara teach you how?"

"Not exactly," he replied, searching himself for an accurate answer. "She just taught me about who I am, and that was part of it."

They fell into silence, waiting for whatever was coming to hurry up and arrive. The approaching footsteps were unhurried and it was maddening. It was as if that insouciant echo was taunting them – letting them know that the menace clomping down the dark hall had not a care in the world, that there was no need for haste because their slaughter was imminent.

"Is it a turn on?" Sam asked.

"WHAT?"

"The fire..."

"I...don't... Sam! This is not the time to try and get some!" Lucia scolded. "I'm a little busy having a heart attack."

"It is, isn't it," Sam concluded. "I knew it."

"Shut up," she hissed. "They are close. I'm freaking out."

"So am I," Sam admitted. "Tension breaker."

"It isn't working."

Sam had to agree, but he said nothing. Instead, he turned his head to offer her an impish grin. She caught it and smiled weakly, grateful for the effort, but her eyes were still as wide as saucers.

As they waited, their labored breathing mixed with the echo of the approaching footfalls and filled the cell with nightmarish sound. Sam stared straight ahead at nothing. His heart was beating a crazy rhythm, sickening adrenaline pouring through him, making his limbs quake.

But still they waited, the footfalls coming ever closer until the steps dragged with hesitation. It sounded like two of them. They were right outside the door. Then the corner of Sam's eye darkened. With a slight turn of his head, he saw the pale light on the stone floor under the threshold vanish. A looming shadow replaced it.

Someone was coming through the doorway.

-3-

The first thing to cross the threshold of the cell was the toe of a riding boot, grimy and caked with grave dirt. The boot paused – the heel planted, the toe wavering in the air – before it came down on the stone with a soft click. Then the second boot appeared bringing with it a barrel-chested man in a dark grey suit, double-breasted and chalk striped – the one they had buried him in. As the dead man's bloodless face cleared the threshold mere feet away from Sam's own it was already staring at him, a crazy grin frozen beneath its dried, black eyes.

The Leech's face was long and waxen, the skin melted from rot and tugging the deep eye sockets into elliptical horrors. The dead eyes did not blink or widen with surprise. They were shark eyes, the cold eyes of a predator. With a slow scrape of its boot, the thing squared itself before Sam, its fingers raising and twisting into greedy claws. Then with freakish speed it lunged for Sam's throat.

Lucia screamed. Another Leech darkened the doorway and was heading for her. Its face was...

(coming off)

The face was hanging over the collar of its shirt like it had slid from the thing's skull at some point and had stopped for reasons she would never care to know. The Leech was tall and gangly and it came for her with jerking limbs like some crazed marionette. It lunged for her. She jumped back and struck at it blindly. Her fist connected. The thing's skin was cold and rubbery and she saw the imprint of her fist in its neck before her feet began to move. She was running. She ran into the darkness, to the back of the cell.

Both Leeches shrieked from behind her and the sound made her hair stiffen and her stomach twist. Fear buckled her stride; one trembling knee, threatening to turn to jelly, dipped towards the ground. She fought this, stumbled forward and kept heading for the back wall.

The sound of the shrieking was unbearable, disorienting. The stone walls rang with it. Her head rang with it. She had just reached the far side of the darkened chamber when a different sound, a metallic clang, snapped her attention upward. A roaring wind ripped through the cell. The bracing cold slapped her face hard, the gusts whipping her hair. Confused and terrified, she wheeled around with fists up at the level of her eyes, but she dropped them quickly, amazed by the sight playing out before her.

The Leech that had been coming for her was standing in the middle of the cell with the point of a sword sticking out of its belly, the blade dripping with gore. The Leech was screaming. In a flash, the blade retracted with a juicy suck. The ghoul fell straight forward and hit the stone floor with a meaty slap, revealing Jacques de Molay behind. The knight brought the sword down again and slit the body. Lucia watched, frozen, her hair whipping at her face as the howling wind coming from the panel in the wall above ripped the bugs from the thing's yawning body cavity, sending them high into the air in a funnel.

Beyond this, still pressed to the wall by the side of the door, was Sam. His eyes, nose and open mouth were lit from within, red as a jack-o'-lantern's, his clothes flapping on his body. Beside him, the other Leech was stumbling in a tight circle, as if involved in a private moment of dancing drunkenly with himself. Its head was engulfed in roaring flames, thick smoke pluming to the ceiling. It pivoted once more, took a step forward, turned on a boot heel, and then began to shuffle backwards.

Suddenly, the wind stopped. There was another clang from above. There was silence, silence except for the popping hiss of the dancing Leech's burning skull. The bugs that had been suspended in the maelstrom of wind now pattered to the ground like frozen rain. In the hail of insects, the flaming Leech twirled clumsily once more to face Sam sending thick globs of liquid skin from its melting skull splattering to the stones.

Sam, bracing himself on the wall, kicked the Leech in the chest, kicked it hard. The Leech fell straight backwards, its head exploding on the floor in a shower of sparks and spreading over the cold stones like a half-baked cake.

An ultraviolet form rose to the ceiling, joining one just like it already floating there. It was the souls of the two Leeches. Lucia, her face numbed by the cold wind and her mind numb with horror, watched the two spirits pirouette upward like fizzling fireworks before suddenly stretching into figures from a funhouse mirror, silent screams twisting their faces. In a flash, their forms were sucked out of the room, right through the front door where Clara was standing.

Clara did not flinch as the forms passed her head, nor did she give then a second look. "We're clear," she said. "Let's go."

-4-

The walls were all stone and none of them straight. The dimly lit passages bowed in the distance so that you could never be sure if someone, or something, was lying in wait up ahead. The halls were narrow, claustrophobic and seemingly endless. The four ran, doing their best not to send the echoes of their footfalls too far ahead.

"This is how we came in," Lucia informed Sam. "There were stairs up to the prison level. They must not be far."

"I don't like the curving hallway," Sam said. "There is not much time to react."

"This is a recreation of Hadrian's tomb, at least on the outside," Clara said. "We are at the outer wall and towards the top of the structure. I believe the reliquary to be subterranean. I can sense that much, but where the entrance is exactly...I can't be sure."

"Did you hear that?" Lucia asked, alarm shaking her voice.

"Yes," Jacques replied. He had taken the lead, and he now stretched out his hands to bring the group to a halt.

They stopped in a patch of darkness between two pools of torch light in the narrow hall. They listened, their labored breathing shaking.

Somewhere far below them, somewhere in the heart of the enormous tomb, they heard the unmistakable crash of a heavy iron gate. Had it opened or closed? They moved forward, more cautiously now, approaching the mouth of a staircase spiraling downwards into darkness.

Jacques turned and met the eyes of the group, eyes that were solemn and conveying the same simple message: this is likely to lead to something very unpleasant.

They made their way downward, the stairs narrow and slick, worn at their edges. Sam's foot slipped forward and his heel glanced down five steps before he could stop his fall by slapping a flat palm on the wall.

"Shit," he hissed through clenched teeth. All paused to listen, but they heard nothing. It was quiet below.

(because they were waiting)

(waiting at the bottom of the stairs)

Lucia grabbed Sam's arm. Slowly, they continued, spiraling ever downward until finally the stairs ended at a landing and a wooden door.

"That's where we came in," Lucia said. "That goes to the

outside."

"What's out there?" Sam asked.

"The outside of the tomb," Lucia whispered. "It's a side entrance. We're up on a cliff. It's pretty close to the edge. There is a big field in front of the place and then it just drops."

"We should go this way," Jacques suggested, indicating a low archway opposite the exit. "This should lead us to the heart of this place."

Another corridor, long and curved stretched before them. It swept left. Their senses piqued, their nerves on end, the four walked until another low archway was before them.

Clara, her light dimmed to almost nothing, had taken the lead. She peeked around the corner. She motioned the rest forward and they entered a large room, the ceiling disappearing into shadow, the walls rising unadorned and windowless.

"An auditorium," Sam whispered.

Rows of benches faced a proscenium stage. The room was empty. No torches burned on the walls.

"Hag tree," Lucia said, running a hand over one of the closest benches. She thought of the place in the foggy woods of Hex where Jacques had taken them when they had first met, the clearing in the woods where the covens gathered. These were the same style of bench, probably from the same maker.

A loud clang at their back made them jump. They all whirled around, Jacques' hand flying to the hilt of his sword. Behind them was an arched entry, beyond that a closed set of heavy double doors, lashed with iron hardware. There was a shallow foyer in between, and it was from this antechamber that footsteps were approaching.

"From the left," Clara said.

The footsteps were coming fast.

"Down!" Jacques commanded, and fell between two rows of benches. The benches were solid and knee-high. The cover would work, provided that whoever was approaching only passed by and did not come down the center aisle.

Sam cursed and dropped to the floor beside Lucia. Clara flew to the ceiling, like the spark from a campfire, disappearing into the darkened eaves.

The intruder was already in the room and heading for...

(the center aisle)

Sam's mind groaned, his limbs tingling with ice. He was flat on his stomach with hands splayed before him, ready to spring if he needed to. Lucia was by his side and Jacques was in the next aisle, but he could not see Clara. He guessed she was watching from above.

Someone was approaching his row of benches. It was a large man. A sandal planted mere inches from Sam's nose. The foot was attached to a thick leg, the ankle wrapped in leather straps. Sam held his breath. The sandal was gone just as fast as it had appeared, and with a creak of leather, the man passed. A stirring of air whispered at Sam's neck. The footsteps continued down the center aisle.

Lucia, her dark hair hanging in her face, lifted her head off the floor, her wide eyes peeking over the bench. Clara watched from above, tensing, as Lucia's head came up from the floor. As Lucia's eyes cleared the bench, the man froze in his tracks. Lucia jerked her head back down. The man had heard her. Lucia cursed herself and pressed her head back onto the stone floor.

From her perch in the rafters, Clara watched as the man turn around and took several slow steps back to where the three were lying on the floor. Clara stiffened. It looked like he was going for the sword at his hip. Instead, he scanned the room once and pulled a ring from his pocket, a metal ring, and held it up to admire it. He turned it with his thumb and forefinger before palming it and continuing briskly toward the stage.

Lucia released her breath. It rattled from between her lips and onto Sam's neck.

"Fley," she whispered. "That was Orace Fley, the man we saw on your television, the man who was hunting me."

-5-

Slowly, the three got to their feet, Clara floating down from the eaves.

"That was him," Jacques confirmed. "That means the army is assembling on the field beyond those doors." He gestured at the double doors through the archway where the faintest moonlight was leaking from its cracks.

"They only need to distribute the fetishes now," Sam informed Lucia. "Armed with those, they'll march to The Fringe and destroy The Veil. With that much sorcery in their hands they can pull it off."

"Are they all sorcerers?" Lucia asked. "The Leeches?"

"They don't have to be," Sam replied. "The magic comes straight from…"

(Simon)

He had almost spoken the name aloud. Still, he had thought it, and maybe that was enough to give away their position. Shaken by his mistake, he offered all a sheepish glance before he went on, "Anyway, the fetishes will work like cell phone towers, like relays, y'know? Repeating whatever is sent through them. All the Leeches have to do is hold the objects and point."

Lucia looked at Clara and who nodded gravely.

Lucia said, "We have got to be out of time. What time is it back home? The Veil should be at its absolute thinnest at midnight, right? Well, it must be…"

"Four minutes to midnight," Clara offered. "Thirteen times slower here. That's less than an hour."

Clara turned to Sam – the only one among them who had not seen the outside of the tomb – and began to explain their position: "We are on the summit of Black Fang. The site of this tomb was chosen because the summit overlooks a small section of The Veil that stretches between two outcroppings of rock, just across the proving grounds and down slope about a half kilometer. It's an isolated piece, almost free of Skinnies. That is where the army – the one assembling through those doors – is headed, and they don't have far to march. We have to move fast. Fley was holding a ring in his hand. I think it's a fetish. If I'm right, he is heading for the reliquary."

"Let's go," Sam said.

Fley had disappeared backstage and to the left. Cautiously, the four mounted the creaking planks of the stage. Sam looked up. Gauzy curtains were parted above their heads. Just by looking at them – tattered and yellowed with age – he knew at once that they were the wrappings from ancient mummies. Between these curtains hung a sign of branded wood:

TEATRO DELLA ABANDONATO

"What does that mean?" Sam whispered to Clara.

"It's Italian," she replied, "Theater of the Forsaken."

They entered the darkened wings at the side of the stage. Turning a corner, Sam was surprised to see the trappings of a working theater: wigs and masks piled on long tables and racks of costumes along the walls. Threading between the costumes, Sam picked up a red silk robe with Japanese characters on it.

"Stolen off bodies from the world's cemeteries," Clara said.

Sam dropped the robe, screwing up his nose.

"He must have gone this way," Lucia said, standing in a hall between two tables of scattered props. The rest joined her and followed her to a junction.

"I hear him," Sam said.

"This way," said Jacques, breaking left.

Sam glanced at the ground. There was white powder on the stones. He knelt, running his finger through it and holding it to his nose.

"Lime," Clara said. "It must have come off one of the Leeches."

Lucia whispered to Sam, "That's the same stuff the big skeleton wrote in at The Fringe,"

"Lore," Sam nodded, and without knowing quite why he knelt and ran the rest of his fingers through the white dust and then through his hair, spiking it up until it was frosted white. The powder tingled on his scalp.

"It's a dead end," Jacques said, dismayed. "I don't see another way out."

They all looked around. There was no door; only a full-length mirror hung on the wall before them. Sam approached it and gasped. The other's approached the mirror and they too fell into shocked silence. The mirror was not reflecting their image – not exactly. Instead, it reflected another version of them.

Lucia's face was painted again for Dia De Los Muertos with the skull of Catrina: black eyes and white face with a set of painted barbed wire teeth. Her hair was tied back, a blood-red rose at one ear and swirls of black at her cheeks. Her black clothes were form fitting and iridescent, the limbs striped with thin white bars.

Clara was a worldly being once again, a druid priestess in flowing robes, auburn hair cascading over her shoulders and framing the pink flesh of her face.

Jacques' cape and leather jerkin were vibrant and unsoiled, a bright red crucifix over one breast. His dark and flowing hair and beard framed his restored face. It was rugged and handsome, the face of a proud and noble knight of France.

Sam was dressed as a Celtic warrior, layers of bronze scales were at his breast, a dark cloak falling from his shoulders and emblazoned with the mark of his clan. His hair was spiked and white, his eyes fierce and set.

"What is this?" Sam muttered, transfixed by the image of them all.

Clara reached out and touched the mirror and the glass rippled like water.

"A quicksilver mirror," Clara replied. "It reflects your spirit. It's an old trick, and an old way of disguising a door." Effortlessly, Clara stepped through the glass and disappeared.

The other three watched their reflections ripple crazily before the glass settled back to a wobble. Clara's head poked through the silvery haze from the other side, startling them all.

"Come," she commanded.

-6-

Stepping through the mirror, they saw a hallway with a low, barrel ceiling stretching before them. At the end of the hall was a set of heavy double doors made of hag tree wood. Dangling from one of the doors was a length of iron chain. The doors were unlocked; one of them was ajar. Jacques approached and pressed an ear to the crack in the doors, then an eye. Slowly, he tugged on the door. The others grimaced, but there was no betraying creak of hinges. Jacques' face slackened with relief. Beyond the door, a spiral staircase wound precipitously downward. They froze at the top step as a distant clang floated up from below to wash over their blanched faces.

The sound died and Jacques nodded sharply. Quickly the four entered the narrow stairwell and descended, Jacques taking the lead, shuffling down the slick steps. Rounding the final curve, Jacques stopped so suddenly that Sam's nose mashed into the knight's back. Jacques snapped up a halting hand, and the group retreated a few steps, huddling in the stairwell. Jacques nodded again, a finger to his lips, and as carefully as they could, the four peeked around the corner. What they saw astounded them.

It was a large room, rounded at its back and full of rows of stone tables. The room was not lit, but the objects on the stone tables were somehow giving off their own light, each of them perfectly distinct with illumination as if the surrounding darkness could not suppress their intrinsic brilliance.

Orace Fley was standing in the center of the room, his back to them. He began to turn around. The four retracted their heads, staring at each other and listening, the two mortals trying to suspend the tell-tale hammering of their hearts. A crushing silence followed.

Fley spoke: "I know you are there." His voice was casual, matter-of-fact.

In the shadows of the stairwell, the four gritted their teeth and widened their eyes.

Fley took a step, his footfall echoing through the chamber. He took another. "I don't bite – not anymore at least."

Silence.

"I am outnumbered at the moment," Fley continued, taking another slow step, "so there is really no need to hide from me."

A sound, deep and sonorous, started from somewhere above and the four all looked up through the dizzying heights of the spiral staircase. At first the sound was nothing but a cacophony, but it soon smoothed into one steady bass note that shook the stone walls. Sam's bowels twisted. It was an awful sound. In fact, it was just about the worst sound Sam could imagine: a choir of moaning voices, bass voices, thousands of them – all sliding up and down a run of soul-wrenching minor scales. Instinctively, Sam knew what it was, the way any human would know if they ever had the misfortune of hearing such a miserable, bone-chilling perversion of music.

(the choir of the dead)

"Listen," Fley called towards the stairwell. "The Dirge has begun. You are too late. I may be outnumbered now, but not for long. The generals are on their way down here now. They are coming down the stairs behind you to get these." Fley swept his hand over the tables of fetishes. "You are surrounded. It's over."

With Clara taking the lead, the four walked out of the shadows of the stairwell and into the room.

-7-

Fley's smile was cold. His gladius was unsheathed and in his hand. He spotted Lucia and his smile faltered, his eyes flashing with rage before the smile could reaffix. "So...the Mayan girl is with you."

"Her name is Lucia," Sam blurted and then snapped closed his mouth.

Fley approached him, "Samhain..." He raised his blade to caress Sam's chin with its tip. "What an honor."

Sam did not flinch. He returned Fley's stare, but his stomach cramped. The tip of the centurion's blade was sending tremors of ice down his spine.

Fley turned to Lucia and cooed in her ear, "You were in the mud weren't you, you filthy girl? I thought so, but I thought of it too late." He plucked a tiny clod of dirt from the top of her head. "Losing my touch. No matter. Soon, you Thumpers will be praying to me. If Simon is God of The Nowhere, you can consider me the Holy Ghost."

"Simon is hardly a god," Clara said. "He is all but forgotten."

"That will change," Fley snapped. "These..." He swept a hand over the glowing objects in the room, "...hold the magic of the ages, the power of all civilizations." Fley turned into the room to survey the treasures. The four followed, eyeing each other and fanning out.

"Careful..." Fley cautioned, turning around once more to face them before continuing his stroll down the aisles. "Sure, you can destroy me at the moment, but what good would it really do? I will only miss the glory of our triumph over the living for a while. The Nowhere will be freed anyway. Even if my soul ends up in the hands of the Wraiths, they will spit me out like a sour grape and head for the broken Veil just like everyone else here. This will become an abandoned Death Realm. So, do your worst."

Clara picked up a spear on the stone table closest to her and hefted it in her hand.

Fley noticed her and said, "Rhongomyniad: King Arthur's spear, enchanted by Merlin. His sword, Excalibur, is over there."

Sam sucked in a breath and followed Fley's finger with wide eyes. Just laying his eyes on the weapon was enough to convince Sam that it was the real thing. It was as if it was telling him so. It was beautiful. It took every bit of will to not run over to the sword like a little boy and touch it, run his hands over the fabled blade, even heft it into the air and peer up its length. Instead, he tamed the wonder that was spreading on his face by clenching his teeth and bracing himself with another sharp breath.

Fley kept strolling down the aisle, away from them to the back of the room. Clara followed at a distance, her hand glancing over the tables.

"And that's not all," Fley continued, sensing Sam's reaction to the treasures and baiting him. "There's the Golden Fleece..." He flung a casual gesture at another table. "Maybe Jason found it once, but we have it now. In fact, we just staged the legend in our theater. I played Jason, of course. I was brilliant. Everyone said so."

"Yeah, about that..." Sam ventured. He could tell Clara was up to something and he needed to bide some time. "what's with the theater?"

"Magic shows mostly," Fley replied. "We have been collecting hundreds of history's most powerful talismans. Might as well have a little fun with them. After all, waiting for The Thinning every year is such a bore, but the wait is now over...permanently."

The rumbling drone of The Dirge continued from the tomb above. Sam winced, the damned sound made it hard to think and he was suddenly sure it wouldn't stop until it shook his organs to liquid. If it wasn't for the objects glowing on their slabs – by far the most fascinating things he had ever seen – he was sure he would go crazy.

Fley was staring at the four, resting a hand casually on one of the tables.

"Should we kill him?" Sam asked.

"No," Clara replied coldly, not taking her glowing eyes from the centurion, "I am more interested in the head of the snake, not its ass."

Fley glared at her.

Lucia spun to look at the stairwell. Even over the din of the moaning voices of the dead, she could hear footsteps coming for them.

Fley approached slowly, his sword drawn, "This is where the tour ends. I think you know who is waiting for you upstairs."

XVI.
Midnight

-1-

They did not fight, they did not struggle. Four generals armed with bronze lances and short swords filled the stairway behind them. Two of them were lycanthropes – wolfmen with long leathery snouts twisted into snarls, eyes yellow and feral beneath their deeply furrowed brows. The other two were human, but absent were the depraved countenance and nightshade-glazed eyes of the Leeches. Theirs was a steady, piercing gaze, pupils pulsing with cool vigilance. One of them looked to be a former Confederate general of the civil war, judging by his worm-eaten uniform. The other was Asian, Chinese maybe.

One of the wolfmen raised a tarnished Tommy gun, the cracked wooden stocks gripped by hands matted with wiry brown fur. The wolf jerked the muzzle of the gun at the staircase.

"Does that even work, Chewbacca?" Sam asked, though he was not keen to find out.

The Confederate soldier disarmed Jacques, but the knight hardly noticed. He was eying the wolf's weapon with poorly concealed curiosity, tilting his head to peer down the muzzle. He had never seen anything like it before.

"That's where the boom comes out," Lucia informed him stiffly. She glanced at Sam, and then they all looked at Clara who nodded and began to climb the stairs. Resigned, they followed.

Long hallways and another flight of stairs brought them to an antechamber of ornate arches. Two grinning Leeches stood by either side of an ivory door. When they saw the approaching throng the Leeches swung wide the door and stood aside to allow the group to pass.

Before ushering his captives through the entrance, Fley addressed the four generals: "The Dirge has summoned the damned to your ranks. We are legion, and we will not be stopped. These druids we have feared will soon face their insignificance. Leave them to me. It is our time of victory. Return to the reliquary and arm your troops. Stand by. We march to The Fringe in one hash of the moon dial." Fley swept his eyes over his captives with a tight smile, "This shouldn't take long." Then, Fley extended his arm to them in a mockery of gentility, "After you."

Clara took the lead, whispering to Sam as they entered, "Two minutes to midnight."

The generals stayed just long enough to make sure the four captives were through the ivory doors. Sam turned to see the generals leaving in a trot. Mercifully, The Dirge had stopped, but that meant the ranks were in place. If there were only two minutes left until midnight at home, that meant there was less than a half hour here.

(not enough time)

Sam's heart bucked with panic as he was ushered through the threshold, the heavy doors swinging shut behind him.

-2-

The grandeur of the great room was breathtaking, every surface dripping with opulence, and Sam felt insignificant in the face of it. The room was longer than wide and vaulted like a cathedral. Marble walls soared upwards to gothic buttresses that supported a ceiling caked with colorful frescoes of cherubs, nymphs and demons. High up the walls were friezes depicting animals, warriors and unidentifiable symbols. Above that, clusters of green bottle flies provided illumination. The unearthly light tinted the expansive marble floor underfoot a ghostly, purplish-green.

To the left, suits of armor from different periods of history stood sentinel amidst a colonnade. To the right: fluted pedestals hoisted urns and classical sculptures in marble and bronze. Beyond these treasures and several rows of thin, elegant columns, Leeches watched them from the shadows. They were grinning and as still as the statues themselves.

"Leeches," Lucia whispered nervously at Sam. "A lot of them."

Sam raised his eyebrows at Clara and Jacques. They indicated with solemn nods that they had seen them, too. Lucia was right; there were a lot of them – too many, in fact. The four descended three smooth marble steps and the creatures lining the back walls tracked them with their eyes as they passed. Sam's heart felt like a lump of ice in his chest. His legs refused to move him forward. Fley poked Sam in the back with the tip of his sword.

Far across the room, perhaps 150 yards away, another set of wide, shiny marble steps led to a chancel capped with an altar of slab marble. To the right of this altar sat a mausoleum. The Corinthian structure was the size of a small house, decorated with *bas-reliefs* and slender columns rising to a capitol scrolled with Acanthus leaves. The mausoleum was open, but its black mouth revealed nothing.

Fley's gladius urged them forward across the expanse. The floor was as fascinating as it was terrifying. It was comprised of thousands upon thousands of tiny tiles. At first it was too vast to take in the entire image, but the composition revealed itself as they walked: a dark, hulking man on a throne was holding a woman by the arm. The woman was recoiling in horror. Far below the pair were scores of naked people with eyes pleading for mercy, their hands reaching up, flailing through a swirling red fog. The whole image was...

(alive)

Sam blinked hard, but still the image moved, the withered arms of the damned swaying like sea grass in a lazy tide.

"A mosaic from ancient Carthage. Second century," came a voice from the altar.

Fley halted the group at the bottom step.

A slapping sound echoed through the room, then another, and then another. A hand emerged from the shadows of the mausoleum, splayed on the ground at the mouth of the structure. The other hand appeared, slapping the marble, and then a man came crawling out of the crypt.

He was dressed in a black robe, dragging his limp legs behind him. He slapped the marble again, then again until he was moving fluidly across the chancel like a reptile. Thin arms lifted his chest from the ground, dark hair hanging over his bearded face, and his eyes peered through the tangle, eyes as white as spider's eggs.

"It depicts Hades, god of the underworld, and his captive love, Persephone," the man continued. "Her absence meant endless winter for the world above. It touches me.

Sam knew at once that this was Simon Magus. The story of his flight over Rome, the fall and the shattered legs all came flooding back to him. Sam's breath seemed to freeze in his lungs. Those white eyes were holding him. The worst part was that the man looked so much like...no, exactly like...

(Jesus)

Sam's soul squirmed with the thought. He supposed many looked like Christ at the dawn of the first century, but this was disturbing, uncanny. All of his years in Catholic school and in Catholic churches had given him plenty of exposure to a wide range of depictions of Christ, and this man looked like most of them, only his hair was darker, his complexion duskier.

The very presence of the slithering form on the white floor chilled the vast room. Sam found himself backing away unconsciously until Fley poked him forward again. He could see how this man could have once been mistaken for the messiah. Even encased in crippled flesh, even on all fours and crawling, he was mesmerizing, otherworldly. He was Christ just fallen from the cross. He was indeed the false prophet and every cell in Sam's body revolted.

Simon continued speaking, his voice silken and low. "It is complete, not missing a single tile." He crawled to the edge of the step. "It was buried just outside the capital of Tunisia. You see, it is not only flesh that ends up in the ground. We have found many things that have been choked with earth, forgotten by time. The pieces of this mosaic were collected by the Skinnies and reassembled here by my children." Through the hair that hung over his face, Simon Magus swept his white eyes lovingly over history's madmen: the Leeches that lined the walls. "The whole process took more than a hundred years, but we had...plenty of time."

Simon looked at Clara, "Tlachtga, it's been a while."

Clara said nothing.

"You take no flesh in The Nowhere," he stated plainly. "You are free to travel through the Death Realms. Why is this? God approves of druids?"

"The good ones," Clara replied.

"Ah...the good ones. Of course. So subjective, don't you think?" Simon stared at Clara silently for a moment before a smirk curled the corners of his mouth. "My apologies about the rape. Bad kids, they don't listen. All three of them had you? Over and over?" He clicked his tongue in a parody of disgust. "Boys will be boys. Again, so sorry."

"Not as sorry as you're going to be," Clara replied thickly.

Unfazed, Simon speared Sam with his milky eyes. "Samhain..."

Sam stiffened.

Simon smiled, "I understand you are here to destroy me."

-3-

A river of ice was coursing through Sam. His legs were trembling. He wondered if Simon could see it. But Simon could sense it, that Sam knew. Suddenly, Sam regretted everything; he regretted ever coming here. All of this could not possibly be expected of him. It was too much. He wanted to go home. He wanted to skate, let the long-lost sun beat on his neck. He wanted to see Father Doctor's warm smile, to see him tapping at his computer in his little office that he kept so dimly lit. Sam searched for him in his mind. Sleeping, he was sleeping, the bandage on his head glowing white with the moonlight pouring through the window.

"I almost got him," Simon whispered.

Sam saw the scene before his eyes, and he knew Simon had put it there, installed it somehow right in the middle of his head. It was as if a projector had flicked on in his mind: Father Doctor running across the lawn, the screaming, black car crashing into the porch.

"Do you recognize it?" Simon asked. "You should. It is the same car. It was the same car that killed your parents."

Sam was shaking. Anger, fear and sadness roiled within him like a foul stew.

"I understand your eyesight is better in my world," Simon went on, "and the feeling in your leg and arm have been restored. Even if you made it home – which you most certainly will not – you will have to live with your injuries, and they will get much worse. All injuries get much worse as you get old, because that's God's world past The Veil. It's unfair, I know. You see, I can be a lot more merciful than Him." He crawled down a step with a slap of his hand and peered at Sam through his tangle of hair. "Your injuries...they were from an accident you had when you were young, yes?"

Sam said nothing.

"You were hit by a car, too. Did you see it?"

Sam shook his head numbly, hoping he still appeared in control, that he appeared unafraid. Though he didn't see how that was possible. He felt sick to his stomach, his skin clammy and crawling with dread.

Simon grinned, "Surprise. It was the same car. Did it ever occur to you that it was all the same car? Believe me, I know because I was driving it. I'll solve the mystery for you: It was a black hearse. A Rolls-Royce Phantom, to be exact. I do get around, don't I?" Simon laughed softly, but then his eyes narrowed and he darkened. "You should have died then. Your clan has been wasting my time for centuries, but it ends now, boy. It ends here."

Sam tried to hold Simon's stare, but it was too much, and his eyes fell to the floor. The God, Hades, stared back from the tiles below.

"Hades is not real," Simon said. "Never was. I am, and this is the REAL underworld." Simon rose on his arms and surveyed the four before him. "I am the only God here. No one watches over you but me. You would do well to remember that in your remaining moments. Your praise is welcome." Simon looked around and sighed theatrically. "I love my kingdom, but it is time to expand."

Jacques spoke: "What makes you think that once you are in the land of the living that you won't be subject to God's laws and judged again?"

"How sad, Templar," Fley spat. "That is what you long for? Another chance? Not I. I make my own salvation. You still believe that past The Veil the living are the flock watched by the Shepherd? Maybe He will intervene, maybe not. I believe He is a bit too...overextended to care much about Thumpers, much less the forsaken. There are millions of universes. How much do you care about what the ants are doing in your vacant grave?"

Jacques said nothing, his fists clenched, his lips a bloodless line.

Simon turned his head to stare at Lucia, "The Mayan..." he cooed.

"You're a creep," Lucia shot back.

"At the very least," Simon confirmed, "but I am also your judge and executioner. So bite your insolent tongue before I have it removed and shoved up your ass. By the way, did you find Carlo?"

Lucia said nothing, her guts wringing out like a dishrag at the mention of her brother.

"He may be in Hell for all I know," Simon mused. "Chances are good. After all, he was related to a disrespectful little shit. You serve only one purpose, Mayan. Do you know why you are here?"

Lucia said nothing.

"Of course you don't. You just followed your boyfriend like the slut that you are. Are you a god-fucker? Are you hoping some of his card tricks will rub off on you while he's rubbing on you?"

"Watch your mouth, Samarian," Clara warned.

Simon swiveled his head to Clara, "I will give you credit for one thing: naming every generation of our clan Samhain was a brilliant move. The kid owns the faith of legions. Every Thumper who celebrates the festival is making him stronger." Simon looked at Sam. "That has caused me a lot of headaches, Pumpkinhead."

Sam flinched at the mention of his nickname.

Simon continued staring down Sam, a burlesque pout on his face, "The mighty Sow-wen..." Simon chewed the words in mock reverence and then turned his head to Clara in disgust. "He didn't even know how to pronounce it last month. Now, he is your best hope? Pathetic."

Simon returned his attention to Lucia, "So, Mayan, you have had time to think. Have you guessed your purpose? You aren't going to say anything now? Lost your nerve? Well, I'm not going to tell you. I am going to show you instead." Simon snapped his eyes to Fley and barked an order in Latin.

Clara understood it. They were taking her to the altar.

Sam started and his paralysis broke. He turned to face Fley. Clara reached out a hand, "Easy," she whispered. "Patience."

"LET GO OF ME!" Lucia screamed as Fley dragged her by one arm to the altar beside the mausoleum.

Sam stared at Clara, eyes wild.

"Trust me," Clara soothed. "Soon..."

Sam gritted his teeth as Lucia was dragged up the steps, her free hand beating the centurion. Fley hardly flinched. Two Leeches appeared and helped Fley tie her down to the marble slab with leather straps. Lucia kicked and screamed.

Sam's eyes flared, fire licking at the sockets.

"Steady..." Clara whispered. She lifted her robe off of her chest to reveal two long, thin pieces of gleaming metal within the folds. "My sickle," she whispered, "and my father's trident. They were buried with me when I died. The bastard robbed my grave too."

"Mog's trident?" Sam asked, hardly able to keep the amazement off of his face. Sam's mouth opened to ask the questions "how and "when", but he knew the answer. Clara snatched the weapons from the reliquary during those brief moments when Fley had strolled down the aisles with his back turned, lost in the fantasy of his coming triumph. The repossession had been executed so quickly and so deftly that even Sam had not noticed.

Now they had fetishes, good ones.

Sam smiled with hope and relief, but it didn't have a chance to spread. Fley and the Leeches had backed away from the altar and now Simon was slapping his hands on the marble floor. He was crawling his way to Lucia.

-4-

"What is your name, Mayan?" Simon asked, looking up at the altar.

Lucia did not answer. Instead, she craned her neck to gain sight of Sam, Clara and Jacques, her eyes wild and afraid. What she saw made her relax, if only a little. The three seemed strangely calm, Sam nodding at her ever so slightly. Something had changed. They knew something that she didn't – at least she hoped so.

Confused and desperate, she tried to find this new intelligence herself, scanning everything in her line of sight: a frescoed ceiling high above lit by a swarm of the glowing flies, Simon leering up at her from the marble floor, Leeches lining the far walls. There was no advantage that she could see. On the contrary, the situation was just about as grim as it could get. She looked back at the three again. Stoic and calm, they returned her stare. If they were waiting for something, waiting for the right moment, she wished it would come sooner than later.

"I asked your name," Simon demanded crisply. "Now you are shy? Where did your bratty little temper go? Fine, save your breath. You don't have many of them left. Your name is Lucia, Lucia Winter." Simon lifted himself high on his arms, peering up at her. "And what does Lucia mean? Did your mother ever tell you? ANSWER ME!"

"Light..." Lucia cried. "It means light."

"Yes," Simon continued as if enlightening a child, "and your last name is Winter. Do you see now? Light before Winter – the last offering before darkness falls. It's all very simple. It always was. You are just another bonfire on a hill, another flame dying within a gourd. You are the sacrifice. Just like the Mayans before you, your blood flows to feed the gods. That is your purpose. That is why you are here."

Lucia screamed. Gritting her teeth she tugged at the restraints, the leather cutting into her arms.

Simon, his hands slapping on the marble, crawled around to the back of the altar. "Until you came, there was no blood to spill in The Nowhere. It has been such a long time since a blood sacrifice has been offered to me. The wait will make it all the sweeter."

Suddenly Simon rose off the floor, his shattered legs dangling within his black robes. Lucia watched in horror as his white eyes came level to the altar and then hovered above it, Simon staring down at her as she struggled vainly to get away. He stretched out a papery white hand to caress her cheek. "My lamb..." he whispered.

"HEY, PSYCHO!" Sam shouted.

Simon looked up.

Sam stepped forward. "Touch my girlfriend again and it will be the last thing you ever do."

Narrowing his eyes, Simon assessed the threat. Then his lips tightened into a dismissive grin. He pulled a dagger from within his robes and nodded at Orace Fley.

"NO!" Sam cried.

Fley, his voice booming, addressed the far walls where the Leeches waited in the shadows.

"KILL THEM WHERE THEY STAND, AND THEN JOIN YOUR BROTHERS AT THE VEIL!" Fley ran down from the altar, coming at Sam with his gladius drawn.

At the altar, Simon raised the dagger over his head with both hands. "*E lux tenebris!* From light I bring darkness..."

-5-

A column of fire shot from each of Sam's eyes. Fley, just off the last step, ducked and tucked into a roll, the fire streaking over his head and slamming into Simon's chest. Lucia, her face lit by the blaze, screamed as Simon's robes ignited with a roar. The dagger fell from his hands, bounced off her chest, and clattered to the marble floor below. Lucia craned her head to look at Sam just in time to see his face lit like a jack-o'-lantern before the jets of fire receded, leaving only tiny flames to lick at the sockets of his eyes. He began running towards her.

Simon, still floating above the altar, screamed with rage. He was a pillar of flame, wrapped in a fire ball of burning robes. He came crashing to the ground, tearing at the blazing clothes that were melting into his skin.

Fley completed his tumble, sword still in hand, and sprang to his feet. Jacques broke left behind Sam and ran towards a suit of armor beside one of the pillars of the colonnade. The armor was English, but it would do. It displayed a well-honed sword. A row of Leeches rushed to meet him.

Just as Jacques reached the suit of armor, a Leech bit into his shoulder. Jacques elbowed the thing in the throat and kicked the suit of armor squarely in the breast plate. The armor fell into the approaching line of Leeches and crashed to the ground, the armor plates scattering in all directions.

Jacques made a dive for the sword. He and the sword skittered across the slick floor, his hands trying to get a grip on the hilt. He grabbed it and rolled onto his back. Fley was over him in an instant, the centurion's sword poised above his head. Fley's blade came hissing downward; Jacques parried the strike with a clang of metal, rolled away and kicked to his feet just in time to see Fley's sword arching through the air, coming right for his head.

-6-

Clara's robes dropped to the ground in a puddle of wool, a golden sickle in one of her hands, a bronze trident in the other. Her naked body blazed with blue light, fine tendrils of electricity radiating from her and probing the air with pops and sizzles. She thrust the trident at Sam, just as a line of Leeches fell on them both from the right.

Clara raised the golden sickle. It whirled like a helicopter blade above her head, before the shaft slapped into the palm of her waiting hand, the cutting edge whistling through the air at the pack of Leeches. The heads of four of the drooling monsters detached, seeming to float in the air above the decaying cravats of their funeral suits for a moment before they all thumped to the floor; their insane black eyes staring up from the ground watching their headless bodies sink to their knees and fall forward. From the gaping necks of the Leeches' bodies, ultra-violet spirits drifted to the ceiling.

Sam, with trident in hand, ran to the altar. Simon was still rolling on the floor, growling in frustration, still ripping the last of the burning rags from his body. Sam had surprised the sorcerer, but the fire would only be a temporary distraction, and it was unlikely that it would work again. He knew he didn't have much time.

"LOOK OUT!" Lucia screamed, eyes wild, as she watched Sam running towards her.

A Leech flew at Sam from the right, teeth bared, claws reaching.

Sam had no time to react. The Leech got a hold on Sam's throat. Its head reared back, yellow jaws bared. Sam turned and sank the trident deep into the thing's side. It shrieked in his ear and as it looked down at the wound, Sam drove an elbow into its collar bone and yanked the trident out of its body. The Leech bent over. Sam kicked it in the face. He looked towards the altar.

"HURRY!" Lucia screamed.

Simon was rising and heading for Lucia.

-7-

Jacques and Fley stared at each other over their locked swords. Fley was big. Jacques figured he must have wrestled at the coliseum in Rome, maybe wrestled lions by the looks of him. Jacques knew he could not win a show of strength. He had to get out of the bind. Fley might be stronger, but a Frenchman knew how to use a sword, and if he was going to survive this, sparring was the only way to win. The locked swords quivered between them as the two gritted their teeth.

Quickly, Jacques sprang backwards, breaking the bind. The tip of Fley's gladius flashed downwards to graze Jacques' forearm, leaving a livid stripe of torn flesh. A Leech lunged from the left. Jacques spun once and plunged his sword into its belly, kicking the vampire in the groin to free his blade. The Leech fell on its back, bugs blossoming from its gaping wound.

Standing in the back guard position, his sword behind him like a wagging tail, Jacques raised his hand, and with two fingers, waved Fley forward. "Your grave misses you, Monsieur."

-8-

Just as Sam gained the three steps to the altar, Simon floated up from the floor and turned to face him. Again, Sam was struck by the Christ-like resemblance. Simon was suspended in the air before him, naked, arms to his sides, palms out. Only moments ago, the man had been a flaming and cursing ball of smoke, but now the sorcerer was strangely calm – beatific even – his head tilted, watching Sam with those white, spider-egg eyes, watching him with curiosity. Sam came to a halt and stared back at the surreal figure floating before him, the man's skin still smoldering from the fire, fine tendrils of smoke floating lazily into the air.

Hanging around Simon's neck was a gold pendant on a thick chain. It had been under his robes before they had burned, and Sam had not been able to see it before, but Sam would swear he recognized it from his dreams. It was a pendant in the shape of a beetle, a scarab, the gold brilliant against Simon's fire-blistered chest.

"That was a mistake, boy," said the sorcerer. In an instant, gone was the alluring Jesus figure that had almost made Sam drop to his knees in religious rapture. Now, Simon's face was ugly, brutal, twisted with hate. The scarab pendant around his neck began to move, squirming as if the golden beetle were longing to be off its chain and free to attack. Its little golden legs clicked together. It began to glow.

Clara's voice broke the spell: "SAM! IT SPITS!"

(spits?)

The beetle reared back, mandibles clicking. Bright green liquid shot from its mouth. Sam jerked his head left. The arcing stream whispered past his ear. Sam's rooted feet flinched and then began to run left. Simon pivoted in the air, the acid tracking Sam as he fled. It was going to catch up to him in seconds. The stream was only a foot behind him, the liquid spattering to the ground with the sizzle of frying fat, eating the marble floor where it landed, eating great, yawning holes into it.

Terrified and desperate, Sam climbed the steps in a crouch, and with his trident held before him, dove directly at Simon. The stream of acid arced over his head as he slid on his forearms, coming to a stop just underneath the floating form of Simon. The trident clattered away from his fingertips. The acid stopped raining to the floor. Sam rolled out from under Simon's feet and dared to look up. Simon was staring down at him. So was the beetle, little red rubies for eyes. Sam clawed at the floor for the trident, but his fingers found nothing but cold marble. Panicked, he looked up again.

The pendant reared back to spit.

-9-

Jacques thrust his sword at Fley in a series of swift cuts. Fley parried, metal clanging. Jacques hopped onto the corpse of a Leech and launched another volley, this time changing the tempo, double-timing his cuts. Fley parried, teeth gritting with the effort, and was rocked back on his heels. Fley rounded a column and gained a moment to breathe.

A Leech jumped on Jacques' back and clawed three livid stripes down the knight's face with its nails. Jacques tried to shake it off, but the vampire still clung to his neck, its feet off the floor and swinging. Fley rounded the column and lunged. Jacques deflected the blade. Fley lunged again. Quickly, Jacques spun around, his back to Fley. The centurion's sword impaled the Leech on Jacques' back. The thing shrieked and released Jacques' neck. Its body, still on Fley's blade, slid to the floor.

The downward momentum of the Leech stuck on his sword forced Fley to bend at the waist. When he raised a foot to dislodge his weapon from the Leech's ribcage he heard Jacques' sword whistling in from the right. Before he had time to turn his head, the knight's blade had lodged in the centurion's neck with a thump. Amazed, Fley looked up at Jacques as the blackened knight's hilt came down on the top of his head. Fley fell over on his back. Jacques wedged a boot under the Roman and flipped him over onto his face, planting a foot on the small of his back. Fley's arms struggled weakly to push up on the floor, but Jacques' coup de main was swift. The knight's blade plunged into the back of Fley's neck, striking marble.

-10-

A loud pop rang in Sam's ear. A bolt of energy shot past him and struck Simon. The sorcerer was sent flying backwards, the crackling bolt pinning him to the back wall. Whipping his head around, Sam saw Clara standing amidst a pile of limbs, heads and torsos. At her feet, thousands of insects scurried across the floor in a moiré pattern, shifting like blowing sands across the mosaic of Hades and the underworld. Waterfalls of the bugs poured into the gaping acid holes in the marble floor. Clara's sickle was planted and wrapped in searing brilliance. The weapon had become a lightning rod in reverse; the curved blade cast a fat, sizzling continuous bolt that ended on the back wall of the immense room, ended at the pinned form of Simon Magus.

To the far left, Jacques was plunging a sword into Orace Fley amidst a pile of dispatched Leeches. Sam watched as Fley's ghost shot to the ceiling where other purple spirits writhed beneath the frescoes. Fley's form stretched and elongated. With a look of pure horror on his face, Fley's ghost was sucked from the room, through the crack in the ivory doors.

With numb fingers, his arms aching from his dive to the floor, Sam grabbed the trident and got to his feet.

Still pinned to the back wall, Simon bellowed with rage. Far to the right, one of the fluted columns began to quake, tearing itself from the ceiling and floor. It detached and rocketed towards Clara. Her sickle still arcing with light, she rose into the air, but her bolt wavered – the distraction just enough to allow Simon to free himself.

Simon flew to the center of the room. The two ancient sorcerers clashed in mid air, grappling in a ball of angry light.

Sam ran to Lucia and tugged at her straps. "They're tight."

"Oh save me, Captain Obvious!" she returned.

Sam looked stung.

"I love you," Lucia added apologetically.

"Women..." Sam muttered sotto voce while he tugged vainly at the restraints. He stopped and he backed up a step. "This might hurt a little."

"WHAT?"

Sam's eyes blazed.

Lucia squinted against the light, the smell of burning leather filling her nose. The restraints fell to the floor.

"My hero."

"I owed you one," Sam said, lifting her from the slab.

"Now, get us out of this nightmare," Lucia said, pawing away the straps. "I'm ready for Christmas."

"Quick," Sam ignored her joke and shoved her towards the mausoleum. "Get in there and don't come out."

"What? Are you kidding? I'm not going in there!"

Across the room, Clara screamed and fell from the sky, her sickle clattering to the floor.

"Okay, bye," Lucia said, disappearing into the crypt.

Simon wheeled in the air and faced Sam, eyes steely with hate. "You robbed my reliquary."

"This isn't yours," Sam shouted, stabbing the air with the trident. "It belongs to Mog Ruith. It belongs to our clan!"

"I AM your clan, boy!" Simon roared.

Something smacked into Sam's head from behind and thumped to the ground. His vision starred. He looked down. At his feet was a grinning head, a single white spider crawling out of the severed neck.

Before he fully knew what was happening, a severed arm hit him in the chest, knocking the wind out of him. Within seconds, every dead Leech in the room – or part thereof – rose into the air and came speeding towards Sam, some twirling, some barreling end over end. Sam raced to the altar and ducked just as one of the corpses hit the slab, slid across it, and tumbled over his head. Limbs, heads and entire bodies came crashing at the altar.

"CLARA!" Sam screamed. "HELP! WHERE ARE YOU? PLEASE!"

But she didn't answer. Clara was gone.

-11-

Jacques broke his cover by the colonnades and ran at Simon. The naked sorcerer, now floating just above the ground, lifted an arm and crooked his fingers. From behind Jacques the pieces of the scattered suit of armor littering the floor trembled and then flew at the knight's back. It was a breastplate that got to Jacques first, its pounded metal edge lodging into his back with a dull thump. Jacques slowed, sank to one knee and dropped his weapon. The tip of the abandoned sword lifted off the ground on its own, pointing at Jacques sternum, wavering in the air, and waiting for the wounded knight to fall forward. Jacques did, and the blade sank deep into his chest.

"Hoist with your own petard," Simon sneered.

From behind the altar, Sam watched as Jacques' spirit left his body. "No..." he groaned, wrenched by despair.

As Jacques' ghost rose, it caught Sam's eye. The face of the noble knight wore an expression that it had never worn before: fear.

Now Sam was alone with Simon.

"Clara," Sam whispered into the huge room, panic quaking through him, "where are you?"

(i'm here)

His eyes widened. It was her voice, but just like the voice of his intuition, it was coming from inside his head.

(i'm here)

"Where...?" he whispered.

(hiding)

Across the room one of the statues behind Simon – a satyr in bronze – began to move. It leapt from its pedestal, hooves clicking across the marble, and snatched up Clara's sickle. The staff flared with light and a bolt blasted from its curved blade, tearing through the air and smacking into Jacques' rising ghost. For a moment the spirit was frozen within a crackling orb. Then with a flick of its wrist and a downward chop of the sickle, the satyr slammed the dazed spirit back into Jacques' hollow corpse. The knight's body began to twitch on the marble floor.

"Not today, Monsieur," the satyr said in Clara's voice.

Flicking its arm, the satyr shot another bolt at Simon. The sorcerer dodged, flying upwards. Simon raised his arms wide. The marble floor rumbled, cracked and split open sending the colored tiles of the mosaic tumbling into the abyss. The satyr tried to leap to safety, but the chasm had widened too far too quickly. The statue plummeted into the yawning hole in the ground.

"CLARA!" Sam screamed.

Jacques got to his feet.

"STAY DEAD!" Simon roared, turning to the knight and raising his arm.

Clara rocketed upwards out of the hole in the ground in an azure streak, her sickle in hand. Simon spun around to face her.

"It's midnight, Simon," Clara said. "Time's up."

"I am finished playing with all of you," Simon snarled, "you and your French scum and your pathetic boy!"

From behind the altar, Sam rose up. "Boy? MY NAME IS SAMHAIN!"

Sam threw back his arm and launched his trident. As it flew, the bronze shaft shimmered and became the body of a snake. Its three-pronged tip became the serpent's head, two fangs gleaming from its stretched open mouth.

As Simon wheeled around in the air to face Sam, the snake struck him on the forehead, wrapping its body around the sorcerers face with the speed of a bullwhip.

Simon clawed at the coils of muscle over his eyes, roaring with anger. The beetle pendant around his neck glowed and wriggled, pissing an impotent stream of acid into the gaping hole below. The coiled snake around Simon's face hissed, reared back its head, and with a vicious lunge sank its dripping fangs into Simon's neck. He screamed. His body began to shrivel where it hung in the air until the flesh and bones slid away and tumbled into the gaping earth, leaving nothing behind but a stunned, purple spirit. The ghost was already distorting, its form stretching towards the door.

The Wraiths of The Pitch were...

(still hungry)

The spirit's purple face was a mixture of anger and utter astonishment, and it was given only seconds to meet the eye of the one who passed sentence, but Sam wasn't looking. He was at the dark mouth of the mausoleum, his arms around Lucia.

"Is it over?" she asked.

"Yes," Sam said, breathless and shaking with adrenaline, "it's over."

He kissed her beneath the ancient frescoes, in the light of the bottle flies from above.

Behind Sam, the soul of Simon Magus screamed its final silent scream before it streaked past Clara's head and was sucked out of the room.

Epitaph

My name is Tlachtga, Clara to my clan. How much longer I can control this machine that makes letters, I do not know. It is the New Year, and The Veil is growing thicker by the moment. So, I will make good use of the time I have left.

You may wonder what happened after Sam and Lucia left Black Fang, or if they left at all. If I were to tell you that Sam and Lucia woke up safely in the Cypress Lawn Cemetery back in their hometown of Colma, would you find it cheap? Disappointing? You might grit your teeth and say: "After all that, it was a dream?"

That's exactly what Sam and Lucia thought, too – at least for a moment – until they noticed a few peculiar things. They were no longer wearing the skull make-up they had gone to sleep wearing. Also, their clothes were ripped, and there was white dust on the bottom of their shoes. Suppose I added another small detail that Sam and Lucia did not know: the cemetery's night watchman – you remember, the one that almost caught them at the Laurel Hill monument – well, he found their camp beneath the spire at about 11:50 on Halloween night. Only the two were not there. He found nothing but a pair of blankets.

Of course, this may cause you to ask yourself a disturbing question: How can I ever be sure that my body is there when I am sleeping? Well, most of the time it is, but perhaps not all of the time. Maybe those dreams you are having are not dreams at all, but other worlds where you report to duty on occasion. You know where I mean, the worlds that seem familiar, the worlds you have been to more than once when your eyes close, but swear you have never visited in any of your waking moments? Those places may call you again. And, The Nowhere may call Samuel McGrath again, but hopefully not for a long, long time.

-2-

Sam and Lucia's eyes fluttered open in the cemetery on the morning of the Celtic New Year, November 1st, at 12:02 A.M. Their blankets were gone. They were cold, hungry and tired. They walked home in the dark, confused and without much to say. They remembered what had happened, but only flashes, as if their memories of the strange night were but ghosts themselves, flickering in the shadows of their minds.

But Jacques and I remember what happened, we remember very well. The four of us walked right through the front door of Simon Magus' grand tomb and into the ranks of the dead who had already begun marching towards The Fringe, their useless fetishes hanging from limp arms. Closer to The Veil, the generals, the Leeches, and even the throngs of Skinnies – ever present at the rippling horizon – stopped to watch us with guarded interest as we approached.

There was utter silence beneath that endless moonlight. The dead knew that it was over, that Simon had been beaten, that no magic would come to their aid. The Veil would only be as thin as it was ever going to be. A few of the Skinnies peeled their gaze away from us before I even addressed them, chattering their teeth and resuming their endless and mostly fruitless assault on the barrier between the worlds of the living and the dead. But I did see a fortunate soul get through, its spirit whirling into the air and disappearing into the land of the living in search of what it had once known.

I climbed onto a rock to address the gathered. The milling crowds hushed. "My name is Tlachtga," I said.

Word had traveled since our capture, and the crowd had grown large. Once ravenous with hope, their watchful eyes were now weary and bereft. We were not the great sorcerer of Black Fang, we were not Orace Fley. We were the last people they wanted to see: the sentries between order and the chaos they desired. If The Nowhere could be said to have a new day, it had come.

I continued: "My clan has destroyed Simon Magus!"

This news was met with a murmur of voices. I left the rock and Sam replaced me, his hair still spiked white with lime. He planted my father's trident and addressed the crowd: "My name is Samhain, the god of Halloween. I am returning to my world, but it is your decision whether I am done with you for good."

"He's a Thumper," cried a witch from the outskirts of the crowd, her gnarled nose sniffing the air.

"Yes," Sam confirmed, "I am alive, and I intend to stay that way. As I said, I will not stay among you. I don't care why you were sent here, and I have no idea if you will ever find peace. If you want to drop your flesh…" he cast a nod at where the ground sloped away, littered by piles of skin and clothes, where skeletons shivered and shuffled at the rippling barrier of The Veil, "then be my guest, and join the Skinnies, but know this: I will protect my world from my side of The Veil with all the heart and fury of my clan. If you strive to pollute my world with your evil, your chaos, or try and take revenge on my kind for your unfortunate plight, you will see me again, and it will be the last thing you ever see, by Mog Ruith I swear to you. The Wraiths of the Pitch are still hungry."

There was a gasp from the crowd.

Sam continued, "Leave us alone and I will leave you alone. More than anything, I want nothing to do with you. The stores of nightshade are yours. Knock yourselves out."

Sam was about to climb down from the rock when he changed his mind and turned back to the crowd: "Oh, and one more thing, just to be clear. If I ever have to come back to this shithole, I'm going to be SUPREMELY pissed off!"

With that, Sam flared his eyes at the crowd. They backed away cringing and Sam shot twin pillars of fire at a nearby clearing, igniting a pile of dead leaves.

"Long live Samhain!" came a gruff, drunken voice from deep within the crowd. It was a very old man, and he had a staff with a carved pumpkin hanging from an iron chain. The glowing ember within the gourd cast a ruddy light upon his face.

"And that's my friend, Jack," Sam said, taming a smile. He jabbed a finger at the old man in the back. "Mess with him and you answer to me!"

-3-

"Did that happen?" Lucia asked as they walked to the head of their street. It was the first words she had spoken since leaving the cemetery.

"Yep," Sam muttered. "Pretty sure."

As a black cat, I watched them from beneath the bumper of a parked car as they stared up at their own moon glowing bright between two eucalyptus trees. They breathed the menthol of the dewy leaves on the ground. The night was quiet-quiet except for a pair of teenagers at the far end of the street dressed in costumes, stumbling home, laughing softly and shushing each other before crossing a distant street and passing out of sight.

Sam and Lucia walked down the middle of the dark street until they came to their homes.

"I'm so tired," Lucia said.

"And hungry..." Sam added.

"OH, MY GOD!" Lucia cried, clamping a hand over her mouth. "Your porch! What happened?"

"Car crash," Sam said. "Father Doc is fine though. It was Simon."

"Simon..." Lucia muttered dreamily. "That's what he meant by 'I almost got the priest'." She ran her sneaker over a fat skid mark on the asphalt, lost in thought. "You're sure he's okay?"

"Yes. I'm sure." Sam replied.

Lucia deflated, blowing a sigh of relief into the night air. "I think I'm ready for Halloween to be over."

"Me too." Sam kissed her beneath the streetlight. "Good night, and, thank you. Thank you for everything."

-4-

I watched from within the mirror that hung above the McGrath's dining room table. The priest had a badly bruised knee – an angry, wine-colored blotch stretching down his calf.

Sam was in the kitchen making pancakes and could hardly take his eyes from the mild sun that washed the cloudless sky with gold. The few remaining leaves that still clung stubbornly to the trees in the backyard caught the light like rare gemstones, fluttering in a gentle breeze. Sam burned the first pancake.

"You always burn the first one," Father Doctor said from the dinette, shifting the bag of ice on his knee. "It's a rule."

Sam did better with the next batch, piling them on a plate, and bringing them to the table. Sam and Father Doctor sat in a ray of sunlight in the breakfast nook, eating rapaciously. There was so much to say, but nowhere to begin. So instead, they just ate and relished the normalcy of the morning.

Eventually Father Doctor looked up from his plate and caught Sam's eye, his voice faint: "I tried to do what I thought was best..."

"Don't," Sam said. "Really...it's okay."

The priest looked blankly at Sam, his fork suspended in the air. At that moment, I could feel Sam's thoughts. They were strong. He felt that his guardian looked more vulnerable and taxed than he had ever seen him, a man who had struggled privately with a very big problem and was far from satisfied with his decisions. Regret haunted his face.

"I'm a weird kid," Sam said. "I know all parents want their kids to be as normal as possible, to be saved from ever having to struggle or face the unknown, but you have to admit, mine was a tough call."

"You don't know how hard it was..." The priest faltered for a moment before he could continue, "...how hard it was for me to not be able to help you, or to at least have a part in it. The diocese knew...Monsignor Mullen...all of them, but they thought you could be changed, they thought it was a sickness, a defect of the soul or something. They could not accept that God had designed such a purpose for you. Even when they knew what a bright and kind kid you were, they still..." He broke off, clearly shaken, and looked down at his plate. "My boy, I should have helped you..."

"But you did help me," Sam said, "more than you know."

The priest was crying softly, his hands in his lap. Sam got up and rounded the table, stooping to one knee and hugging him. A corner of the bandage on Father Doc's forehead was coming off, and Sam smoothed it into place. "You sacrificed so much for me. I love you."

"I love you too, Sam."

They said nothing for a long time. They just held each other in the ray of sunlight streaming through the window.

Father Doctor looked at Sam, his eyes wet. "Is everything going to be okay? I mean, with..."

"Yeah...I think so."

"Will it leave you alone now?"

"It had better," Sam said and he smiled.

Sam's confidence seemed to ease his guardian for a moment, but then the priest stared through the sliding glass door at the sky and spoke, his voice barely above a whisper. He was praying aloud, "Why did you ask this of him?"

It was Sam who answered, "...because He thought I was someone special. Maybe I'm starting to believe Him."

-5-

"My mom is convinced that we were having sex all night," Lucia said into the phone, staring out of her living room window at Sam's house.

"Better late than never," said Sam. "I'll be over in a minute."

Lucia laughed. "She also wanted to know who Simon was. She's convinced it was a three-way."

Sam barked a laugh. "How did she know about Simon?"

"He left a creepy text."

Sam sighed, clicking his tongue.

"You're also a bad influence," she continued. "I had to ditch my clothes in the garbage cans in back before my parents saw them. I would have to think of an excuse for why it looked like I was sent through a blender full of mud, and my brain is not working this morning. Isn't the sun amazing?"

Across the street, Sam's garage door opened with a rumble. Lucia saw Sam, the phone to his ear, waving in the driveway.

"See you later, Senorita," Sam said. "Got a date!"

My spirit left Sam's communication device and drifted aimlessly on a chill wind. The Veil was thickening by the moment now and I knew that my ability to observe Sam was almost at an end. I would have to leave him until our season came again. But I did see him pluck his skateboard from a shelf in the garage. Undoubtedly his eyesight and his arm was bad again, and he favored one leg just like he used to. But he was smiling anyway for the sky was blue, the sun was gentle, and the day was stretching out its warm arms to him.

Hills of Eternity cemetery was deserted save for a gardener with a leaf blower far away on the crest of a hill. No one else was in sight. For an hour he soared over the freshly paved roads, the light strobing through the bare branches of the trees. On his final descent, he rounded a sharp turn, leveled out, and came to a stop.

A black cat was watching him from across the lawn, sitting motionless on the head of an angel, between its span of stone wings. Popping his board up into his waiting palm, Sam strode onto the spongy grass and approached the tombstone. He stroked the cat between its ears. The cat leaned into his touch, purring.

"Clara," Sam said. "I miss you."

-6-

I miss Sam too. The Death Realms are quiet now. Imagine that. Peace for the dead. Sure, for old time's sake, Sam will talk to me once in awhile, but he has a life, and life is insistent. It demands his full attention and Sam has certainly earned its rewards.

His senior trip to Ireland was a moving experience for him, as well as for me. I was able to see my home again with an appreciation that can only be refreshed by the eyes of a visitor. I was able to be beside him when he walked upon the Hill of Tlachtga where the first Halloween was celebrated.

The hill has now been renamed the "Hill of Ward" after a seventeenth century landowner, but there are those who visit and still speak my name. I try my best to answer them, for their faith is my fuel, as you know. The Veil is thinnest where the dead don't rest, and for all that has happened on that hill, it certainly qualifies as thin. Yet, the hill is not all about death. Love and hope have been born there too. Sam asked for Lucia's hand in marriage there, and Lucia accepted.

-7-

I still appear to my father on occasion. He is still hiding in Ireland, but he can barely get around much anymore. I know he is using sorcery to stay alive, and he knows that he would be far more spry and powerful in the Death Realms, but he still loves sitting atop Ireland's velvety, rolling hills to watch the sun rise, counting the wildflowers dotting the hills each spring.

He even gets a kick out of those who come to look for him, the modern druids who seek the wisdom of the great Mog Ruith. He hides from them, of course, but he is glad he is not forgotten. Though if someone finds this account that I have set forth and it disseminates throughout the world, my father may find it harder than ever to hide.

-8-

Sam still hears The Crackle every October, like he always has, but now it no longer frightens and confuses him. If anything, it reminds him of just how important he is. Sometimes he watches the world go by, and I know he wonders if other people have similar secrets, similar voices that require them to do great things, even when they don't believe they are possible.

Some say our clan is just a legend, but I would tell them that legends are but truths whispered. They are whispered because they are fragile truths, dependent upon the faith and willingness of those who receive them to accept them and preserve them.

So, when you are alone, when it is dark and still, and that whisper calls to you, will you listen? When it summons you, will you go? It just may be the most important thing you ever do, for that message is meant only for the extraordinary, and that's what we all are, whether we ever have the good fortune to believe it or not.

Printed in Great Britain
by Amazon.co.uk, Ltd.,
Marston Gate.